QUAK

BY

JASON BORN

COPYRIGHT

DEDICATION

To

Bernard Cornwell, for inspiring me to write.

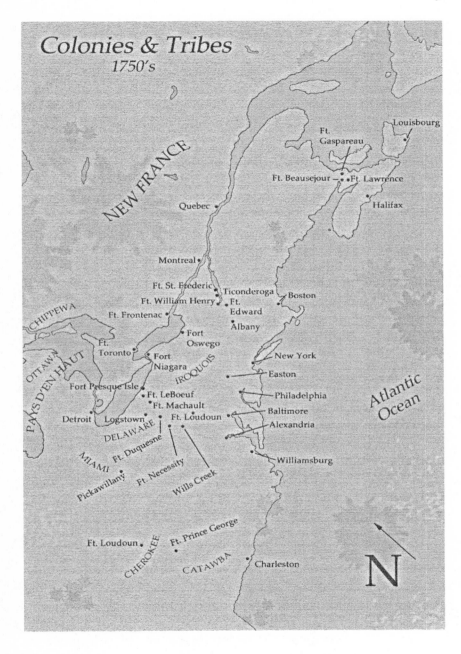

Colonies & Tribes
1750's

PROLOGUE

I'll ask you this. Who is ever more certain of the future than a sixteen-year-old Pennsylvanian lad? Unless, of course, you speak of a twenty-one-year-old Virginian planter. This man fashions himself a proud military officer – even though he's never once been engaged in battle. Or, the forty-seven-year-old Iroquois chief of a small village, he, too, may begin to think of the future and destiny and success. He might believe he has some sort of control over the events of his people. Any of these men may try to coax others to his will.

To that I say, *balderdash*! All of it is rubbish. As the teacher in Ecclesiastes often says, *it is a chasing after the wind.* A man has no more influence over his future than he does his past! And what the hell is the past worth other than as something to forget or massage until it resembles the story you want to tell? It is only Providence, in His great benevolence, who is in charge of the future, despite the woes of our collective past.

Now, I am the Pennsylvanian lad who was once so certain of the future I was destined to create. Headstrong as a mule and green as a spring peeper, I was. Though, I am a great deal older and a small bit wiser now than during the incidents that take place in my tale.

Born to Quaker parents – a German father and an English mother – I ran away from our eastern Pennsylvania farm at a young age. I understood my parents' steadfast faith and hopes for peace without violence, but after flying west to make my fortune, I quickly learned that such a philosophy, while noble, was nearly impossible in practice. Other men got in the way. On his own, anyone may willingly choose to travel the path of peace. But when another man not so inclined, levels a fully loaded, primed, and cocked pistol at your forehead, your options, if you wish to survive, become severely limited.

And that's the problem with the *certainty* of a sixteen-year-old Pennsylvanian, a twenty-one-year-old Virginian, a forty-seven-year-old Iroquois, or a fifty-two-year-old French governor-general, or a British general, or any man or woman at all. The control they have over their lives is illusory.

My experiences have taught me a little something in this regard.

The so-called independent actions of man are nothing more than reactions, wholly dependent on the previous actions of others. And those actions are merely the reactions to previous actions and so on. Man wishes to think of himself strong and defiant as he stands proud with his musket drawn, his chin jutting out. Alas, he is less an independent actor choosing his own path and quite more like a domino, delicately perched tall and simply waiting for his neighboring domino to fall and crash into him, thereby determining his reaction.

And if the reactions of men are determined with dramatic fate, the affairs of states, themselves made up of men, are no better off.

And thus was the situation so precariously set on edge in the expansive forests of the New World. In the middle of the long Eighteenth Century, when the interests, actions, and reactions of Britain, France, New France, Iroquoia, New Yorkers, Virginians, the Delaware, Austria, Spain, and a dozen other realms and tribes began inexorably careening into one another.

The decisions of the individual men involved, including my own, would determine living or dying for thousands of souls. But the fate of the world, once foreseen in the long chain of actions could not, would not, be forestalled.

This is my tale. It is intertwined with a long-burning fuse of conflict and trouble, but ultimately, with the explosion of the powder keg of liberty.

CHAPTER ONE
June 21, 1752
9:00 a.m.

Bright morning light was already streaming in through the cracks in our longhouse walls when my eyes shot open. The sound that had awakened me was a single, shrill and quite unmistakable war whoop. It was followed by a hundred others, their owners clearly surrounding us and pouring out from the dark woods.

I wasn't even supposed to be there. Instead, as a young man of my age, I should have been out hunting with the men. Two days earlier, a close-knit band of traders and Miami Indians had left our vast trading post and settlement in search of game. The place we called home was named Pickawillany and was situated in the Miami River basin. I had lingered behind in the town because my recent travels had made me too exhausted to go.

That's not exactly true.

I *was* tired, for I had just arrived at the burgeoning village the night before the hunters had entered the woods. My latest journey for the wild Irishman, George Croghan, had taken three weeks of hard travel in dense forest with no more company than a string of fifty pack animals and twelve unhygienic fellow travelers. With my arrival in Pickawillany, I wanted to sleep in a bed – even one made purely of hides – and under a roof – bark and sticks were better than nothing. Fortunately, I had found both a bed and a roof. I enjoyed sleeping in while the sun climbed ever higher at the summer solstice.

It didn't hurt that next to me slept my bride. She was clothed in no more than a single feather that was tied with a thong in her long black hair. Her people, the local Miami, didn't keep exacting records of the ages of their citizens, but as near as they could reckon, my wife, Tahki, had been born in the midst of a brutal winter during the long peace between their French fathers and their latest trading partners, the English. That meant Tahki and I were the same age, sixteen, as I've said. When I was growing up, my mother often told me that I had nearly died in the weeks following my January birth. According to my peace-loving parents the weather had been so unbelievably cold that no amount of wood piled in the roaring hearth could chase the chill from our tiny cabin.

But I had survived. I had come west to work as a trader, to get away from the towns and incessant hum of people, people, people who resided on the coast of the English colonies. And now quite perversely, when I wasn't toiling in the wilderness for Croghan, I lived in the busiest city west of the Alleghenies. Pickawillany was less than six years old. It was established by Memeskia, the Miami chief who also happened to be Tahki's father. And Chief Memeskia had a business partner in the trading venture, you guessed it, the omnipresent, George Croghan. My Irish boss was everywhere on the frontier, from Albany to the pays d'en haut. Together the two men were growing rich by offering manufactured British goods and supplies at unbelievable prices to the tribes in a wide arcing circle around the river.

Hearing the same sound as I, Tahki quickly rolled over, her eyes as wide as mine, and, I'd guess, as frightened. Her naked breasts brushed my own naked chest, but I felt none of the lust I had only hours before. The sharp whoops continued. Terrified shouts from the residents of Pickawillany were already filling in any of the brief lulls in our attackers' calls. "Ephraim," she whispered, already hoarse with worry. "It's probably the Chippewa."

"I know," I rasped as I jumped up, remembering I was as equally disrobed as Tahki. I slid into my trousers and a loose shirt while Tahki dove into her buckskin dress. Before I had finished cinching my belt, she had already begun loading my musket, a heavily used Brown Bess that I had purchased from my employer with my first set of wages.

Before we get too far afield, I know what you are thinking. A civilian owning a Brown Bess was illegal, punishable in the severest of ways. So was owning anything with the king's stamp, a crowned broad arrow. Well, Croghan knew a fella – he would never divulge his name – who worked in the Tower of London in the Ordnance Department. Apparently, this fella could get his hands on musket locks and other items assembled by subcontractors and approved by inspectors for quality, but before they received the king's mark. Croghan came by the barrels, other hardware, and even the stocks in a similar fashion. My cobbled together version of a Brown Bess had been traded and re-traded on the frontier for a good many years. The lock had the name *J. Farmer* stamped on it, along with the year of its manufacture, *1727*. Without the king's stamps, it was as legal as any other weapon and had never caused me any problems.

Musket blasts echoed throughout the settlement as Tahki handed me my loaded gun. Holding the long weapon, I nearly fell over while hopping into my boots.

She had her moccasins on in no time and produced a pistol from a pile of her personal items. The weapon appeared to be French with ornate inlays covering the wood from the curved grip and continuing along the stock. Even the ramrod was accented with swirling patterns and engravings. It was an old gun, but at one time would have been a fine specimen. Tahki began loading that as well.

"When did you get a gun?" I asked quickly.

She frantically plunged the ball into the barrel and packed it tightly against the wadding and powder. "A pregnant woman needs to be able to defend herself while her husband is away."

It was a strange time to tell me I was going to be a father. We'd been married for about three months and spent only ten nights together. But I suppose our activities during those long hours of privacy should be expected to eventually lead to children. We had not been talking.

"You're right," I said, hefting my gun, powder horn, and ammunition. "Stay here. Stay safe," I ordered, feeling like a proper husband despite the callowness of my youth.

"I'm coming," Tahki said as I stuck my head out our stick and thatch door that was hinged with leather straps. She went on, "There are only a score of men left to defend us. You'll need all the help you can get."

"Damn it!" I said, diving back inside. The door rattled closed behind me. I grabbed her hand and led her to the back of our small house. "They're coming straight for us," I explained as I used the sole of my boot to kick a hole through the thatch between the posts that formed our walls. "And it's not just the Chippewa. I saw French uniforms."

"Fort Detroit," Tahki whispered. "God save us." She and her family had been Christians for at least two generations, perhaps more. They had originally converted to Catholicism when French trappers came through. But more recently, with the arrival of so many English traders, their beliefs had swayed toward Protestantism.

"We can hope," I said, crawling out through the tiny opening.

Tahki was on all fours, ready to join me in the open space between several houses when she was suddenly pulled backward. She fell onto her belly and dropped the loaded pistol as she disappeared into the relative darkness. I heard her scream inside our home. At the same time I heard two Chippewa men cheer to one another for their good fortune at finding such a prize.

I had never been in any kind of fight, with my fists, a knife, and certainly not a gun. But when the woman you've professed to love before an entire settlement is in dire need, you do not spend a lot of time thinking. I gripped my musket, snatched up her pistol, and dove through the breach.

One of the Chippewa warriors was straddling Tahki. While half-in and half-out, I raised the pistol to his face. But his comrade used the butt of his musket to knock my hand and the gun away. The French pistol, with its fine detail, went hurtling onto the hides that had been our marital bed just moments before. Without hesitation, and with one hand, I lifted the Brown Bess. The muzzle slammed into the naked chest of the Chippewa who was astride Tahki. I squeezed the trigger and a mighty eruption occurred, sending the gun back while blowing the Indian off my wife. We were fortunate that he crashed into the side of his comrade, which delayed the second man's response with his own loaded gun.

Tahki was quick to snatch up her French pistol. She and I were then back outside in the blink of an eye. As we ran between the homes and stock houses, I felt the heat of a musket ball burn past my ear.

"Ephraim!" shouted Memeskia. "Tahki!"

We turned a corner to follow his voice without really seeing where he was. "In here!" he shouted.

The heavy oak door to the small stockade flew open and we dove in. Another set of old traders and women followed behind us. Tahki and I fell against the wall, panting.

"Are you safe?" Memeskia asked. "My grandchild?"

I glanced at Tahki. "I guess everyone knows, but me," I scoffed.

"You know," Tahki said, shrugging.

"You accidentally told me a moment ago," I protested.

Tahki shrugged again as her father helped her to her feet. "We're safe, for now, my father."

Soon, I had climbed up and, after reloading my musket, joined the other men in peering out the shooting holes. Scores of Miami women and the occasional Pennsylvanian trader were running in all directions. Whenever their pursuers could be seen, the men in the stockade opened fire, wounding or killing several. This went on for many long minutes as the chaos of the assault was just settling in.

Every few minutes a new cluster of survivors would find their way to the protection of the stockade. Groups of five or ten women, young and old, trotted in. Then came a few of the older traders who had not gone on the great hunt. A couple of Miami elders arrived, muskets in hand. But even their arrivals began to wane, so that it was clear that we were no more than twenty men and perhaps fifty women and children packed tightly behind thick log walls.

"We were in the cornfields when the French and their allies came rushing out of the woods," explained a woman. Outside, the sounds of men being scalped and women being raped was unmistakable.

"It is only a matter of time until they realize we are hidden in here," Memeskia said, his mind turning.

"We have plenty of ammunition," said one of the elders as he tapped a barrel of gunpowder. "Perhaps we can hold out until the hunting party returns to relieve us."

"We cannot eat powder," was all that Chief Memeskia said. Most of the trading post's foodstuffs were stored in a separate structure on the other end of town. None of the buildings were meant to be a fort.

"How many attackers are there?" I asked the woman who had seen them from the cornfield.

"I didn't stay around to count. But I'd guess there were over one hundred Chippewa."

"I saw at least thirty Ottawa," said another Miami woman who cowered in the corner holding her two toddlers close to her breast. "If you can't see them, you can always smell those rotten scoundrels."

"And I saw at least one French uniform," I said.

"There must have been a few dozen Frenchmen," Memeskia said. "I saw them come from the other direction with the Ottawa."

The musket fire had slowed to only the occasional crack. "They'll begin gathering captives and loot," I said. "Now is our best chance to flee if we hope to get out of here before they surround us."

"It is safest in here," protested a Miami elder. "They'll not have any cannon to blow through these walls." He used the butt of his fist to strike a log.

"Flames can penetrate the thickest forest," Memeskia said. "We mustn't be in here when they find us."

"Then we surrender," said a trader. Like me, he was young and green. He, too, had taken an Indian wife. I did not see any sign of her in the stockade. His concern was obvious. "We're civilians. The French will see that we are taken care of."

"Taken care of, you will be," Memeskia said. "This is not a European battle. A few French soldiers will not stop a couple hundred Indian fighters from making war in the manner they always have. Most of our men will be scalped. Those made captives will wish they'd been scalped, for death will surely come publicly, painfully, and slowly. Our wives and children will be taken away and forcefully adopted into the Chippewa and Ottawa tribes. They will be taught to hate the Miamis. Your wife will become the wife of an enemy soldier. The same fate awaits my daughter if we stay here. We must at least try to flee."

The young trader huffed. "I suppose you should have thought of that before you got us all holed up in here. Sounds more like a deathtrap than a fortress." As you'll see, it wasn't to be the last deathtrap in which I'd be stuck.

Memeskia's eyes flared with rage. But after just a moment he relaxed. "You are right," he admitted. "It has been many years since I've been on the warpath. I should have thought better." The chief elbowed his way to one of the peep holes and peered out.

"Croghan and the other men will come," said the young trader. "That Irishman would sooner see his mother stolen than all his merchandise. I say we wait right where we are."

"And your wife?" I asked.

I had clearly touched a nerve. "A lot of good it will do her if I go running out there and die!" the trader shouted. "Now the chief said it himself. The women will not be killed. We just have to wait for reinforcements."

"There are worse things done to women during war than being killed," Tahki said.

The young trader bit his lip and growled as he pictured those horrible things.

The chief muscled his way through the crowd to the door and placed his hand on the latch. "The chaos has died. It sounds like most of the activity from our attackers is around the storehouse stuffed with provisions. Croghan received a new shipment of rum. It would be best if we fled now while they are occupied."

"And my wife?" the young trader asked. "You want me to abandon her to these animals?"

"Unless we stumble across her as we flee," Tahki said. "You have already left her to these animals." She was not a diplomatic person.

"We might be able to mount a return or rescue once we regroup," Memeskia offered. "But we will be burned alive if we stay in here much longer."

The chief didn't need the young trader's approval to lead us out to safety. But to Memeskia's credit, he waited patiently for unanimity. With all eyes on the young man, he eventually nodded his head in agreement. "As long as we plan to come back for her," he said.

Memeskia clenched his jaw defiantly. "For your wife and the others. I have as much, if not more, to lose than George Croghan. And these are my ancestral lands, not those of the Chippewa, Ottawa, or French. I will prove victorious."

With that, Memeskia quietly opened the latch and slipped out. The rest of us jostled our way in behind him. I pulled Tahki close so that we were in the middle of the pack. "Shh!" Memeskia hissed to his noisy followers more than once. "I see a clear path to the forest."

But the path he saw would prove to be anything but clear.

CHAPTER TWO

When the head of our band of would-be refugees was but two rods from the door of the ammunition stockade I could see a course that was clear of enemy warriors. Memeskia led us on a narrow trail which snaked between a fenced paddock where the traders kept their horses and the edge of a cornfield. From behind us at the provision storehouse, the sounds of Indians and French arguing over the spoils clearly resonated. They would go for the rum first. Soldiers always went for the rum.

"We might be able to come back tonight," Tahki whispered, gripping her loaded French pistol.

"Yes," I whispered back. "Or before. They might be drunk enough in a couple hours to make their superior numbers worthless." We crouched lower as we passed a section of the paddock that would have an open line of sight from the storehouse. Once we made it into the woods and across the Miami River, our chances of escape and survival would easily double.

"Les Anglais!" shouted a French private who had the sense to keep his lips off the jugs of alcohol and his eyes on his surroundings. "Les Miamis!"

"Run!" Memeskia shouted as he stood to his full height and set himself at a jog.

A smattering of musket fire erupted from across the corral. A ball smashed into the side of the mother who had held her children so close in the stockade. She fell into the dirt, dead before she hit the ground. Her children tried to linger over her body. But Tahki slid the gun into the cord belt at her waist and snatched them both by the wrists. She jerked them after us.

Over my right shoulder I could see a large group of enemy warriors sprinting around the paddock to head us off. Even if we made it to the woods and river before them, they would easily catch our group, filled with slow-moving elders and children.

"We should form a quick defensive line!" I shouted ahead to Memeskia. "Give the others a head start to safety." By line, I did not mean the neat string of uniformed soldiers so frequently found in European warfare. I was an American by birth and at least familiar with the prevailing way of war in the colonies and on the frontier.

Chief Memeskia understood my meaning. He came to a quick halt and knelt behind a fence post. "Keep them going," he called as he leveled his loaded musket at the oncoming band and paused to pick out a target.

"Yes, father," Tahki said, tugging the children and shouting instructions to the women.

Memeskia's gun belched fire and smoke. The butt rammed his shoulder. His quarry dropped as the rest of his men fell behind trees, logs, or rocks. A few found cover behind the corner of a small house. I jumped next to my father-in-law, cracking a rib on the lowest fence rail.

"Give me that," Memeskia said as he grabbed my loaded Bess. He rammed his empty musket into my injured side. "Reload this."

The suddenly steady fire from our chief and from the others checked the enemy's advance around the corral. Like us, they dove for cover. But not before we had killed a handful. Their bloody remains lay stretched out in the rising summer sun. Soon we were exchanging random volleys and individual shots so that what had been a picturesque morning had turned into a hellish nightmare complete with choking smoke and fear. Sulphur burned my eyes and nostrils.

I loaded fast, but not as fast as Memeskia could shoot. "Hurry!" he commanded. "You make babies faster than you load a musket!"

I *was* moving slower than normal, as I believe I truly broke a rib. It was hard to breathe as each inhalation and even exhalation felt like a knife to my side. "I'm going as fast as I can!" I snapped at the proud warrior.

Splinters sprayed off the fence post. Some of them embedded in my forehead and I briefly cowered behind my arm and closed my eyes. "They're circling around the other side," Memeskia shouted. "They'll surround us if we don't move."

"We've given the women a head start!" shouted the other young trader. "It's time to run." The firefight, it seemed, had totally convinced him in the prudence of flight.

"Go!" Memeskia agreed. "Take two others and get the women to the shelter at the rapids. We will meet you there tonight."

The young trader nodded from his shelter. He then tapped the shoulders of an old, weathered trader and a white-haired Miami who would have been ancient before I was ever born. Memeskia and the other men pointed the barrels of their weapons at our attackers who were crawling and sneaking toward us from two directions. When they opened fire again, the French and their allies ducked, giving the young trader and his comrades time to jump up and run toward the woods after the women.

A ball landed in the back of the old trader's knee, exploding it like a pumpkin slammed with a smith's hammer. He crumpled and rolled to a stop, screaming in agony. The ancient Miami and the young trader did not hesitate, but continued on.

"We won't last long here," Memeskia said as he took the loaded gun from me and slapped my own Bess into my chest. "But now that they've seen us, we won't be able to outrun all of them."

"Maneuver?" I suggested, as if I had any idea how to fight a running battle as well as an Indian warrior like Memeskia. A small trail of blood dribbled through my eyebrows and dripped into my eyes.

The chief shrugged after discharging his shot. "If we split up, but still work in pairs, perhaps most of us can escape. At least we won't be easily pinned in one place." Musket balls tore through the air over our heads as our group of defenders and the enemy exchanged fire. I struggled to sit up a little taller against the fence to pound another shot into the gun's barrel.

Just as I twisted to set my musket into Memeskia's outstretched hand, I felt hot lead rip through the lean muscle of my shoulder. It was like the kick of a mule and the slice of a knife all at once. The force of the blow pushed me further around than I intended to go and my chest slammed into that of Memeskia. He went down onto his back with me on top of him.

I screamed in pain, especially when I noticed how much blood had already covered my shirt and ran all over my father-in-law's chest.

"Old Briton!" shouted a giddy Frenchman from across the way. "I've killed Old Briton!"

After rolling off Memeskia, I slapped a hand on my shoulder wound to staunch the flow and inched my way against the post. "Well," I groaned. "The French fools have shot me, but they certainly haven't killed you," I said to my father-in-law. Memeskia had become so involved with Croghan and so deft at trading goods that the wily Irishman had come to call him *Old Briton*. The name stuck and soon the entire frontier knew it. Obviously, even our erstwhile competitors, today outright enemies, the French, Chippewa, and Ottawa had labeled Memeskia as a devout ally of the English.

I reached into the dust, gathered up my Bess, and again tried to give it to Memeskia, or Old Briton. My ears rang from the constant eruptions of gunfire. And with trickles of blood from the splinters in my forehead running into my eyes, a broken rib, and now a bleeding shoulder, my aim would be as accurate as that of a drunk, blind, and deaf sailor in a dart throwing contest. "Quick, father," I said to the chief while peering over my shoulder. I saw one of the parties of French celebrating what they thought had been a lucky and mortal shot at Memeskia. "Take this. I'll carry the other musket as we run and fight."

Memeskia didn't take the weapon.

"What should we do?" shouted another old trader who was stuck with us defending the retreat of the women. Arthritic joints or not, he probably wished he had gone off hunting with the others. "Maybe we should just surrender."

I turned toward the old man. What had been tentative musket fire renewed itself with a vengeance around us. "You heard what the chief said," I scolded amidst the sound of ricochets. "A few French won't stop the Chippewa from scalping us. We need to fire and maneuver. Shoot and run."

"Well, the chief is dead you idiot!" the old man shouted back. "And with Croghan gone on the hunt, we've got no leadership now. I say we surrender. I know a little French."

"What do you mean dead?" I cried. "*I* was the one shot. That's my blood!" But when I looked at Memeskia's chest, soaked with crimson, I could at last see what the enemy had noticed right away. You had probably already guessed it. The ball that had skimmed my shoulder, had buried itself in my father-in-law's heart. Old Briton was, in fact, dead.

CHAPTER THREE

"The Quaker boy is right," called a Miami elder who exchanged fire with one of the groups of attackers that was inching perilously close to our position. It would take only a couple brave Chippewa men to make a mad dash to overrun us. Our time, and all chance for survival, was slipping away. "I'd say we have a new leader if he knows we must maneuver."

I set my bloody hand onto my father-in-law's motionless chest. I had known him but a short while. In that time I had come to understand he was intelligent, resourceful, loving, and strong. His daughter, my wife, would take the news of his death with heartrending sadness.

A staccato burst of war whoops leapt from the left side of the corral. I turned to see a trio of Chippewa warriors, hatchets raised, making a sprint over the remaining distance that separated us. The few of us who had a ball loaded quickly sent their lead flying through the hanging haze of stinking sulfur smoke. All missed. The attackers bravely advanced. Behind them their French and Ottawa allies were emboldened to follow, albeit slowly.

Two of the runners bound onto our men hidden behind the corner of the house. A vicious fight, hand-to-hand, ensued. The third Chippewa let out a fiery scream and dove at me, his razor sharp tomahawk leading his body. In that instant I saw the head of his death instrument splay the flesh of my cheek, crack my bones, and bury itself into my face. Only it had not.

He was still flying through the air when I raised my Bess and, without giving it a moment of thought, pulled the trigger. The gun jumped out of my weak hand, clattering on the ground. The Chippewa froze in midair as the ball rammed him and then he slumped heavily onto my feet. He roiled in pain while his hands blindly slapped at the flowing, gaping hole in his belly.

It was time to move. Grabbing old Bess, I jumped to my feet and ran to the men behind the house. There, the two Chippewa warriors were dead, but so was one of our traders. The rest of the defenders had descended on the corner as the suddenly courageous enemy warriors had all begun sprinting toward us. I quickly surveyed the situation and, with no authority and with no real experience, began shouting orders. During a battle, men, as I've since discovered time and again, often feel like terrified sheep surrounded by growling wolves. In the darkest moments, they long for nothing more than a confident shepherd to guide them to safety. And even though I had no idea where safety was located or how to get any of us there, I led the way.

"Work in pairs," I said, remembering what Memeskia had mentioned. The men were reloading. "Scatter. Into the village. Into the forest. Cause chaos. Meet at the shelter at the rapids tonight. Don't lead the enemy there."

Without further consultation, we split up in rough groups. Most were in twos. I was with an experienced trader and a Miami elder. The elder led us in a circuitous path back into the heart of the village with the sound of feet pounding after us. As he went, the elder screamed and yipped to draw more and more of the attackers away from the others. It was a brave gesture. But I must admit that more than once I wished he would simply be quiet and pick off the enemy when their backs were turned.

Momentarily unseen by our pursuers, he ducked into a longhouse. There a Frenchman was raping a young Miami woman. The elder used the butt of his musket to smash the man's skull. The trader finished the Frenchman by burying his knife into the man's naked back. The terrified woman crawled backward out from under her attacker, retreating into a far corner and rolling herself into a ball. She whimpered and shook. I recognized her as the wife of the young trader who had run off earlier. At least she was alive.

"We'll stay hidden for just a few moments," the elder explained. Intermittent gunfire erupted from all around and within the village as our small bands of defenders created the best defense we could.

"When a lull comes," I added. "We run again." I handed my gun to the trader so he could load it for me. My wounded shoulder had swollen to the size of a ripe apple. Below it, my arm burned and tingled. I prayed I wouldn't lose it.

Time was of the essence so we left the woman and were again on the move. The old trader shot a lone Ottawa who surprised us as we turned a corner. As soon as his gun erupted, shouts of anxious enemy sounded from all around us in the settlement. They were honing in on us. We bumped into another gang of two defenders and sprinted down a slim alley between two longhouses.

No. Allow me to correct a misstatement. The Indians and French weren't honing in on us. They were corralling us together. My first stab at command was quickly winding its way toward destruction.

CHAPTER FOUR

"The outcome, young man, was inevitable," said the French ensign in barely passable English. Despite the language difficulties, his condescension was impossible to mask. He paced back and forth with his hands clasped behind his clean white coat. I rested on my knees with a particularly sharp rock poking into my flesh through my trousers. Like the French officer, my hands were behind my back. Mine were bound with unyielding cords, however. My shoulder, stretched tightly into an uncomfortable position, screamed in pain. The experienced trader was tied next to me in a similar position. The Miami elder, beaten and scalped by a fierce Ottawa, lay bleeding next to me. His white hair, with bloody skin still dripping, dangled from a pole carried by the Ottawa warrior who lounged ten feet away. Unfortunately for the Miami elder, he had not yet died. He mumbled incoherently, his lips scooping up dirt and pebbles as he recited the Lord's Prayer to the ground.

As improbable as it may seem, we had managed to stay alive and free for a full hour while being pursued in an ever shrinking cordon. But we had kept the attackers busy, giving our women and children time to escape. I would die knowing my duty as a man and husband and future father was fulfilled. And I would die, to my pacifist parents' eternal disappointment, having killed two men in a single day.

I had been kept in this position for several hours and forced to watch as the women who had never made it to the stockade or the forest were rounded up and tied in a long line with thongs wrapped around their necks. Their frightened children were left to meander free since they would stay near the women for protection that could never be given. The whole lot of them would be marched north, adopted into the enemy tribes and never seen again. Such was the woodland way.

At least some of the women, some of the children, had escaped. I told myself this over and again while I watched the captives roughly kicked and shoved into place. Like their human spoils, the victors also took time to build a great heap of all the merchandise located in the settlement. The main path was soon filled with crates of rum, coffee, cloth, firearms, tea, traps, and much more. Wagons were commandeered, cattle and other livestock rounded up. The trading post had suddenly become a true market with everything, people included, laid out for sale, or for theft.

"You should have just given up," the ensign continued. "It would have saved so much unnecessary bloodshed."

"And end up like him?" asked the old trader, pointing his snout at the yammering Miami elder. The butt of a gun driven sharply onto the trader's temple by a looming Chippewa shut him up. The trader tipped over like a felled tree, unconscious. Without warning his attacker, angry and shouting, knelt to his victim. He rolled the trader onto his back and plunged his knife just below the man's ribs where his stomach would be. The Indian tilted the handle downward, driving the blade upward into the trader's chest. Using his wrist as a pivot point, the Chippewa's hand carved the knife in a circle. Still dripping with blood, the knife went into a sheath at his belt. His hand plunged into the trader's chest by way of the hole in his belly. The warrior looked at me while he felt around inside the trader's torso. Eventually, he tugged out the trader's heart and, after placing it just below his nose and sniffing, took a huge bite. While keeping his eyes pinned on me, he proceeded to eat every morsel of the heart. He even slurped at the crimson dripping from his fingers when he was finished.

"Especially once Old Briton fell," the ensign went on as if nothing had happened. He had watched the gruesome spectacle with a mixture of loathing and indifference. "What hope did you have?"

I couldn't take my eyes off the dead trader. Several more traders who had lately been defenders of Pickawillany were dragged to the village center. They were beaten and bruised. They stumbled as they were pushed down next to me. More than one cracked his face on the hard-packed earthen path.

The Frenchman rudely snapped his fingers within an inch from my nose. "I said, what hope did you have?" He paused, but not long enough for a real answer. "Because if it was for relief from the hunting party, you must know we have scouts watching it. The last report said it was over ten miles away. No help is coming."

"My French father is no fool," chirped the reclining Ottawa who now fiddled with his prize of the elder's scalp. He playfully batted at the moist flesh with one hand as it dangled. It swayed back and forth, slinging small flecks of blood onto his chest.

Below me, the elder himself was reaching the point of expiration. His breathing had become labored. "As we forgive those who trespass against us..."

Beyond the ensign a new batch of women were being thrust into place in the line of captives. These women must have found better hiding places than the earlier groups. Or – I shuddered just imagining it – their captors had spent a little extra time getting to know the latest bunch before bringing them to the center of the village. More children, forlorn and crying, toddled behind them.

Seeing that I intended to remain silent, the French officer grew bored. He meandered further away and watched as his men and allies continued to assemble their loot into a long train for the journey to Fort Detroit and its environs.

A few more of our dead were dragged next to us. Some were Miami. Some were colonial traders. All were scalped. One of them, I recognized as the young trader who had run off into the woods during our initial firefight. His face was bashed in. His belly bled from a gunshot wound. He obviously didn't get very far in pursuit of our women and children. I am ashamed to admit that I thought it just as well that he was dead. His wife had been raped and would be raped repeatedly on the journey until she was given to a warrior as a wife. It was best the young trader had never known.

I then began to wonder when and how I would be killed. I was in the midst of praying that the end would come quickly and with as little pain as possible when Memeskia's body was dragged by. He had already been scalped, of course, but was otherwise not mutilated. The Chippewa warriors carried him to where a fire was burning in the center of town. Sometime earlier, I had watched a group of men gather a great cooking pot from the storehouse and set it over the fire. Now, the vast amount of water they had poured into the pot bubbled vigorously. My father-in-law's body was unceremoniously dumped into the boiling vat.

It was only shock that kept me silent.

It did not keep everyone quiet. "Father!" screamed Tahki. Her voice was shrill.

I followed the sound and saw that she was among the latest group of victims, bound tightly at the end of the train. The children she had tried to save clung to her legs.

Her shout also caught the attention of the French ensign. He turned on his heel and ambled directly toward her. "You are the daughter of Old Briton?" he asked.

"Chief Memeskia was my father, a better man than any of you could ever hope to be!" she sputtered.

"Cut her loose," the ensign ordered the nearest French soldier.

A Chippewa stepped in the soldier's path and set a palm on his chest. "She is our property. She fills our need for wives. This is part of our mourning war."

The ensign stepped around his soldier and the warrior and patted my wife's cheek. "Fear not, she will be returned shortly. Her pretty face will remain unspoiled."

"It is not her face, but her womb, we require," the Chippewa answered, unmoving.

"That will be left untouched as well," said the ensign. "Now, as a gesture of friendship, I ask only that you loan her to me for a moment."

Grudgingly, the Chippewa stepped aside and the French soldier cut Tahki free. I said nothing as the ensign held her arm and slowly marched her toward the pot in which her dead father boiled. Most things are clearer in hindsight. Yet, even with forty-five years worth of hindsight, I cannot say with any certainty whether I should have spoken then or waited as I did. Perhaps, had I said something in a calm, reasoned manner, the outcome would have been different – better.

Tahki's body vibrated with anger as the French officer forced her to watch. Memeskia's bubbling skin rolled up and down in the churning water. To my wife's credit, she kept her eyes fixed on the cauldron. Her strength was one of the features that drew me to Tahki. That and, if I'm honest about my sixteen-year-old self, I was drawn to the way her naked calves fell delicately from her dress to her thin ankles the first day I saw her. She had been gutting a deer for her father back then. But I get too far afield from my story...

"I regret it," the officer said. He extended his arm over the carnage wrought on the settlement. In the distance some warriors had begun setting fully looted houses ablaze. "I regret the necessity for all of this. But I am not responsible." He pointed at the pot. "The blame lies firmly on the shoulders of your father. Old Briton knew there would be consequences to committing treason against his French father. He invited English dogs into the domain of His Most Christian Majesty, King Louis XV. It is as if your father burned this settlement, raped these women, kidnapped these children, butchered these men. I will not be blamed. My allies, the Chippewa and Ottawa, will not bear any responsibility."

It appeared as if Tahki would soon collapse from stress. Her head wobbled back and forth. "Leave her be, asshole!" I shouted. My mother and father had long forbade me from cursing in any way. To this day, I rarely use coarse language and never take the Lord's name in vain. But there are times when, to get a point across, rough talk is the only viable option. It's like defense and killing. They are unsavory options to use when necessary.

"That's my wife. She carries my child. She and her father had nothing to do with this massacre," I went on. "We bring in goods that the locals want. They freely pay us a fair amount less than what you and your French pederasts charge. It is a mutually beneficial relationship. Now, as I say, you cur, unhand my wife. Return her to my side. And leave us to mourn this attack in peace."

The smug French officer smirked. He glanced back and forth from Tahki to me. "Gone native have you?" he asked, truly intrigued. "What's it like? I've never had the pleasure of sharing a bed with a savage. Though, I must say that there have

been a few times my manhood stirred with unholy passions as the local population of half-naked women paraded themselves outside the walls of Fort Detroit." He pinched my wife's face with one hand so her lips puckered. She fought against his grasp, but succeeded only in harming herself. "And now that I really look at this one, I can see what would draw you to her. She's with child, you say? Is it like breeding a wild mare?"

"Get your hands off my wife or I'll kill you!" I declared.

My threat caused the French officer to immediately release my wife. It was not, however, fear that made him to do so. It was laughter. He doubled over laughing at my impotent warning. The Chippewa man who stirred the boiling chief laughed. Ottawa men laughed. French soldiers laughed. Apparently, I was a very humorous young man.

Tahki took the opportunity to run. Arriving at my side, she helped me up to my feet while my joke reverberated through the ranks. Her nimble fingers untied my bonds and threw the cords into the dirt. But I never had any real chance of running free with Tahki. We were surrounded by armed enemy warriors. The French officer was toying with us. He kept a sharp eye on us the whole time he roared.

Soon, his laughter sputtered to a halt. He deliberately clasped his hands behind his back and meandered over to my wife and me. Pausing, he sized me up and down. Then he did the same, but in a more lurid manner, to Tahki. The ensign pointed to the only other Pennsylvanian trappers left alive besides me. "Get these five men in the line of captives. They'll be a further gift to my Chippewa and Ottawa children from their French father."

Indians and French warriors violently jerked the five men to their feet and put them in the line of captives. The traders knew only that mature men like themselves, when taken alive by the tribes in battle, had a tortuous death waiting for them in the Great Lakes country. They struggled to no avail against the steel grips of their captors.

The booty train was assembled. Structures burned all around us. The designated cook of the Chippewa warriors had begun cutting off small hunks of Memeskia's boiled body and serving them to a string of eager native men. It was a ritualistic way to consume your enemy's fighting spirit as well as a way to put him in his rightful place – even in his death. I looked away. Tahki cried as she held my hand.

"You're a touching pair," the Frenchman said sarcastically. Then he peered around at his troop. He was sadistic, but no fool. He knew that the longer he lingered, the better the chance that Croghan and the hunting party would return. "Time to move north!" he announced.

A few of the Indian warriors jostled for a quick taste of Memeskia's flesh before joining the rest. The party began moving out at once. As more of the enemy assembled, I saw that one of the Chippewa warriors had Tahki's richly decorated French pistol stuck in his belt. The weapon was still cocked. It had probably never been fired during the confrontation.

"Will you leave us that pistol for protection?" I asked, trying my best to act confident that the ensign's sudden disinterest in Tahki and me meant that he had decided to leave us behind.

He glanced at the pistol. "Good eyes!" he exclaimed. "That's a fine piece. Old, but perhaps worth something to a trader. Put a polish on it and you might convince a foolish English merchant to pay top money for it." The officer quickly stole it from the Indian.

"Hey!" the Chippewa said.

The Frenchman pointed to the giant train of plunder. "One pistol means nothing. Now run along."

The warrior curled his lip, "Fathers give gifts. They do not take them," he scolded, but eventually obeyed.

"You said the daughter of Old Briton would be returned to me," said the other Indian, who believed he was Tahki's owner. He stood behind the ensign with his bare arms crossed in front of his naked chest. "The children that spring from her womb will become leaders of my people. They will heap shame on what is left of the Miami cowards. She is worth much to me."

The Frenchman looked at me. He rolled his eyes in disgust and waved the loaded gun around haphazardly. "A father's work is never done," he lamented. "Children, be they snotty French toddlers or savages of any age, are in constant need for direction. Always squabbling over milk."

"My French father promised she would come north," the Chippewa insisted.

The officer sighed. He met my gaze while leaning in toward my wife. He set his hand on her arm and gently pulled her toward him. "I'm sure you understand," he said to me. "We must keep the children happy."

I swatted his arm away. Like a racehorse, the Chippewa who had been behind the ensign, swept around him. Before I knew what was happening, he had pulled out his hatchet and, twisting it in midair, struck my skull with the side of the head. Blade or not, the blow hurt. I toppled over, landing on the scalped Miami elder who had finally and mercifully died. "The Englishman will not touch my French father."

Feeling as weak as at any point in my short life, I slowly climbed onto my elbows. "I'm Pennsylvanian, you turd." I lifted a weak arm to point at Tahki, who tugged against the ensign's grip. "And she is my wife. That is my child."

"The child she carries will be my son," the Chippewa said confidently. "He will be raised in our ways. He will kill the Miami. He will kill the English."

"Aw," said the Frenchman, feigning emotion. He wiped away a pretend tear. "He'll be a good little lad for his French father."

"My wife and my child are going nowhere!" I hissed, dizzy. "They're staying here with me."

The officer tired of fighting against Tahki. He let her go. She raced to me and began tending to the gaping cut on my scalp. I felt myself losing consciousness. "You are partially correct about one thing, Pennsylvania trader," said the French ensign. "You are being left behind to tell the story of what happens to English traders who invade our lands. But you'll not stay here. You and George Croghan will fly back over the Alleghenies to your little seaboard towns and farms. There you will stay until you are pushed right into the Atlantic by our French Empire."

The Chippewa who had struck me grabbed Tahki by her hair. He wildly yanked her away from me. She shrieked like a cat, clawing at his wrist. I struggled to chase after her, but collapsed back into the dirt. "But she's my wife," I moaned.

"She is my wife," countered the Chippewa.

"She goes nowhere," I said.

"She comes with me," answered the warrior.

"The child is mine!" I snapped, with as much force as a sleeping puppy.

"Mine!" shouted the Chippewa.

"Mine, mine, mine!" the ensign squealed in a mocking tone. "He did it! It's his fault! Children, children, children. I've seen nothing like this. Juvenile, that is what you both are! Well, I'm a wise and fair man. I can no longer stand this bickering among my children. Let us approach this using Solomon's method! Let's split the baby." He marched over to Tahki, pressed the muzzle of the French pistol into her tiny pregnant belly, and depressed the trigger.

I saw it all happen. In my mind's eye the episode takes as long as a half hour, though I know it played out in a fraction of a second. The jaw clamp dropped. The flint struck the frizzen. Already sparks began pouring down into the priming powder that sat waiting in the pan. By the time the sharp flint landed against the base of the pan itself, the tiny bit of powder was aglow and billowing smoke. The spark passed through the tiny vent into the rear of the barrel where the main charge had waited patiently since Tahki herself had loaded it that morning. The gunpowder burned, super-heating the air and thereby driving the heavy lead ball out the only way it could go.

And while it traveled only a short distance before stopping, along its path the projectile did terrific damage to Tahki's belly, my unborn child's body, and my life. Hell, as you'll see, even the lives of an entire continent, the entire world were destroyed, or at least altered by that flying ball of metal.

The Chippewa dragged his suddenly heavier captive another two feet before releasing her hair. Tahki dropped like a rock. My head swirled. I roared in rage, but fell face first into the dust when I tried to jump toward her. When I again lifted my face, I saw the Chippewa frowning. He crossed his arms while addressing the French officer. "At least the Miami will no longer have her womb to fill their ranks."

"And at least my Pennsylvanian friend will not have to see her march off into your bed," answered the ensign. "I'd say we've resolved a potential conflict in a most pleasing way." He stuffed the spent pistol into the pocket of his coat and turned and, for the first time all day, strode away with purpose. "To Detroit."

The Chippewa followed, the woman who was supposed to become his wife, forgotten.

I weakly crawled my way to Tahki, hoping that I'd find some life left in her. When I found the skin of her ankles still warm to the touch, I rejoiced. "I'm here," I mumbled as I drew myself toward her face. Without shame, I slid my hand under her dress and felt the warmth of her thigh. My excitement peaked.

And then it dropped precipitously. Blood and entrails poured out through a hole in her belly the size of my fist. Scarlet did not spurt. Her lovely crimson only oozed, perversely, almost pleasantly. I knew then that her heart had stopped beating.

I couldn't bear the burden of peering into her eyes. Instead, I rolled over and mustered what remained of my strength. "Ephraim Weber!" I called to the ensign. He hadn't heard my weak shout over the din of the slowly moving procession. "Ephraim Weber!" I tried again.

One of his soldiers noticed me and, shouldering his musket, jogged ahead to his commander. When the officer turned toward me, I repeated my call a third time. He furrowed his brow before fixing a perplexed look on his face and meandering toward me. Further demonstrating ease, his hands were again clasped behind his white French coat. At last he stood over me, careful to stay just out of my reach in case I still had some strength with which to lash out.

"Ephraim Weber?" he asked. "What is that?"

"My name," I muttered. "I want you to know the name of the man who will kill you."

"Good Lord!" he exclaimed in a bewildered manner. "Weber? A German? Blessed Saint Mary, don't tell me you are not only a Pennsylvanian, but also a Quaker? A pacifist? What is becoming of George II and his tiny colonies?"

"Ephraim Weber," I said again. "I'm the man who will see your brains spilt."

The Frenchman crouched to me so that the long tails of his coat swept the path behind him. He balanced on the balls of his feet while reaching into his pocket. Producing the unloaded pistol, he pointed it at my forehead. Empty or not, it was still a disconcerting sight to look down that barrel. After a few seconds of torturing me, he said, "In that case, Ephraim Weber, let me help you along." He dropped the pistol onto the trail.

We both studied it for a long while. My hand wavered as I struggled to reach for the gun. I envisioned bludgeoning him to death with the butt right then and there. But I was too weak and slow. With little effort he swept it outside my reach. "Let's at least make the game a challenge, Ephraim. I don't want you acting out in a fit of rage. No. No. When you come to kill me, I want you to do it knowing that you violate all that your people stand for. Won't it be grand to see you turn your back on your so-called Quaker faith, acting more like the savages you lived with and purported to love?"

When the officer stood, he made certain to kick dust in my face. Then, turning, he marched off to be with his troops as they filed into the forest. By the time I wiped away the muck from my eyes, he had stopped and was walking briskly toward me. To my surprise, he had left the gun behind. I reached for it a second time, but he placed the weight of his foot on it even as my index finger brushed the barrel. The ensign crouched again. I rolled onto my back feeling defeated and stared up into his face. He appeared to be mulling something over, waiting for me to ask him a question.

I'd not give him the satisfaction.

"I just thought you might want to know the name of the man you intend to murder in cold blood," he said.

I reached my left hand out and let it rest atop Tahki's palm. Her skin was beginning to cool. I felt the exertion of the brutal day catching up with me. I was fading off to sleep.

The Frenchman slapped me quite hard across the cheek. "Ephraim, mon ami, wake up." I blinked at him. "You must remember this as you hunt me down." He said it as if it were a joke. The ensign could hardly contain his spurts of laughter. "The man you expect to kill is a scion of a distinguished military family with deep roots dating back to the foundations of France. My name is Joseph Coulon de Villiers de Jumonville." He stood, placed his hands on his hips and chuckled. "I doubt we will ever cross paths, my friend. But at least you'll have a name to match to a face to hate until the day you die."

After he spun and marched away for the final time, I found myself muttering his name over and over again even as my senses faltered. "Joseph Coulon de Villiers de Jumonville." And though my emotional world had steadily grown bleaker by the hour all day, at last my physical world went totally and mercifully black.

I had passed out.

CHAPTER FIVE

"I'm not saying you forget about the bastard!" George Croghan exclaimed. He was on foot as was required of almost all traffic in the dense forests in the Ohio basin back then. He pulled a pack horse behind him that was heavily laden with gifts for the men with whom we were about to treat. I led a mare with a similar load. Croghan's associates had been in charge of securing most of the other presents. They were already in the village ahead. Our tokens were just something extra special the Irishman had procured through his extensive network of contacts.

"It's only been a month since he killed my wife!" I snapped. George was never one who cared much about decorum, unless it had to do with properly treating his Indian and white trading partners. On those occasions he was a model of frontier manners who demanded the same of his followers. But while walking in the forest along the north bank of the Ohio to Logstown, I felt safe in raising my voice to such a powerful man.

"And it's a damn shame, as I've said, Ephraim." He wasn't a cold person. Upon his initial return to Pickawillany where he found me burying Tahki, his expression of grief was adequate, but brief. Croghan was a busy man with much to accomplish in his life. "But you can either stew on it with all the effect of a gelding mounting that mare of yours. Or, you can take that anger and do something."

"I plan to do something," I said as we entered the northern edge of Logstown. It was a Mingo settlement, under the ostensible control of the Iroquois Confederacy. "I've told Jumonville and you that I'll see his brains spilt."

Croghan handed his reigns to another of his helpers who had run up when he noticed our approach. "Keep these items separate from the rest," he instructed the runner. The boy nodded his understanding as I, too, gave him control over my animal. He then led the beasts toward the rest of Croghan's great herd of pack animals that grazed in a tiny clearing nearby. A dozen or more workers unloaded and arranged the bounty that the Irish trader had managed to assemble for the conference.

Normally, I would have been toiling with them, stacking all the merchandise in a wide arc around the council fire to be given to some of the most powerful chiefs in the region. But today Croghan had informed me I'd sit with him at the fire in case I was needed to answer a few questions. Still, George had said that I was to do no talking unless first spoken to. As I watched the men and boys lugging the heavy crates and baskets around the fire, I thought I had gotten the better job that day.

"Ephraim, you shot a couple warriors at Pickawillany in self-defense. There's honor in that. It's understandable and I'd bet your mom and dad might even forgive you for it," Croghan said, continuing our conversation as we walked toward where the great council fire was being built.

"They'd not understand any of it," I countered. "My parents, like most of the Pennsylvania assembly are true believers in the Society of Friends. They believe that there's a peaceful solution to any problem. I've learned different – the hard way."

"All well and good," Croghan went on. "But killing a man in cold blood is something altogether different. You, of all people, should know better than to chase down that path."

"I'll see him dead," I insisted.

"Right," Croghan said without conviction. "I'd like to see you take that fire in your belly and turn it to help me. Take your anger out on our competitors in trading. You know, we carry goods to the tribes, but so do the French, the Canadians, the damn Virginians. I need a good, committed man."

I pointed ahead to where Croghan's main trading partner, Christopher Gist, stood talking to a middle-aged Seneca chief in the midst of an assembly of two dozen men, whites and Indians. "Gist is a Virginian now working directly for Virginia's Ohio Company, and yet here he is working with you at Logstown. You can't trust him?"

"Of course not," Croghan said, making no attempt to quiet his voice. "I've got the vipers all around me. We'll work together when we must. But you know as well as I that there's as much difference between a Pennsylvanian and a Virginian as there is between a Chippewa and an Iroquois – maybe more.

Hell, I'd say there's as much difference between men from separate colonies as there is between a white and an Indian. I need somebody I can raise up and trust."

"Half the people you have working for you are family," I countered. "Brothers, half-brothers, brothers-in-law."

"Maybe you're not the right fella after all," Croghan said with a smile. "If you think that just because two men share a parent or because one man dips his wick into another man's sister they are suddenly to trust one another, you aren't as smart as I thought." He reached out a hand. "Speak of the devil himself!"

William Trent, Croghan's brother-in-law, shook the hand. "Not a pleasant way to talk about your sister, George. She's my wife, you know."

"Aw hell," Croghan said. "Every woman is somebody's wife or sister or daughter or mother. I'd think a frontier trader like yourself would at least know where babies come from by now. Look at all the folks around you. It ain't that rare of a thing for a man to dip is wick into something wet."

"George, it's your sister," Trent pleaded again. "Don't speak in such a way."

But Croghan was working. He had moved on to join Christopher Gist in talking with the Seneca chief. Gist was a thin, lanky man, which made his feet, hands, and ears appear disproportionately large. The Seneca, a member of the Iroquois Confederation, was well proportioned. He was dressed in what I would describe as a combination of European and Indian clothes. I was left with Trent in the awkward silence of the Irishman's wake.

"Sorry for Mr. Croghan's words," I said, feeling responsible for the man who'd become my boss. "He's had to hear some unfortunate slander over the years about his own Indian wife, you know."

Trent set a hand on my shoulder and directed me toward our seats. "It's more than alright," he explained. "George only has so much diplomacy. And that he exhausts on his customers and suppliers. I'd not expect him to have much left for his employees and friends."

"Or family," I added with a chuckle.

"Or family," Trent agreed. Then he reached his finger up and brushed it across my forehead. "Is that left from the massacre at Pickawillany? I was sorry to hear about what happened."

I self consciously rubbed the spot on my flesh. Small scars now peppered my forehead where the splinters from the fence had lodged. Croghan himself had dug them out with his knife as I sat on the mound of dirt that covered Tahki's body. It's possible that the removal of the wood shards, one after painful one, was worse than their en masse entry had been.

Trent noted my melancholy. "It's tragic," he said. "And it didn't have to happen. We're traders. George wasn't there for land speculation." He pointed to Gist. "That Ohio Company man from Virginia is who the French and Ottawa had to worry about. And he and his men have no intention to run that far west. He was nowhere near Pickawillany."

"But it happened," I said, resigned. "And now we're here with Gist and it will only be a matter of time before the French want to wipe us off the map."

"Well what do you think we're doing here today?" Trent asked.

I shrugged. Croghan had not told me any of the details. He was constantly meeting with people, from tribe leaders to shamans and from royal governors to shoe makers. Everywhere and always, Croghan was forever buying and selling goods or developing new relationships to trade more merchandise with more customers. The only thing out of the ordinary for today's meeting was that I was asked to participate, albeit silently. I had figured that Croghan wanted details from my tale in order to somehow steer the proceedings to his liking.

"We're here, young Quaker, to get that man to get those men to side with that man," said Trent as he pointed from the Seneca chief, to a group of Delaware chiefs, and finally ending with Gist. "If we achieve such an outcome today," he continued. "Our efforts at commerce here in the Ohio Valley will not only be productive, but safe, much safer than what you experienced out west."

I was tired of being reminded of what happened at Pickawillany. The time would come soon enough when my hatred for Jumonville would find its just end. I meant to bide my time until that day. "Who is the Seneca chief Croghan and Gist are putting so much faith in?" I asked.

Trent's eyebrows raised in surprise as we sat on the ground cross-legged in the Indian manner. "Despite your difficult early days in the frontier, you really are green, aren't you, Ephraim?" he asked. "The man you seem not to know is the most important Indian in North America. He speaks for the Iroquois Confederacy at Onondaga in all things to King George's colonies. He speaks for all the other tribes as well, not just the Six Nations. His word is powerful."

"Have the Indians banded together and named a king?" I asked with astonishment. It was a most idiotic question. My excuse for such a waste of breath is that I was but sixteen. Of course you know that to their own detriment, tribal peoples always allow their ancient hatreds of one another to more than offset any benefits that might come from union. The same can be said of Virginians and Massachusetts men. There could never be a true union between the two.

"Heavens no!" Trent said under his breath. He giggled in a good natured manner at my ignorance. "It's nothing like that. No. That is Tanaghrisson." And Trent dropped his voice to an even quieter level. "The Half King."

CHAPTER SIX

"The Half King?" I asked without showing the same discretion as had Trent when he uttered the same phrase.

"Shh," Trent hissed, but it was too late. Croghan, Gist, and every other white and Indian halted their conversations and stared at me. Tanaghrisson, the Half King himself, paused his talk with Croghan and fixed me with a perplexed look. He appeared hurt by my words.

"Chief Tanaghrisson," Croghan said in his natural congenial manner. He quickly set an arm over the Half King's shoulders. "We are all here. Let us sit and treat with one another in the peace that comes with brotherhood. You and I are men of years and experience. We have seen many summers. And the winters, I don't have to tell you, get longer every year. As such, and in the midst of all these bountiful gifts and good tidings, sit. We have no need to listen to, much less heed, the ignorant words of a Pennsylvania boy who doesn't have the sense given to him by Providence."

That seemed to pacify the Seneca chief. The pair of men then worked their way around the fire and approached the spot where Trent and I sat. Already, the other participants had begun to forget about my obviously inappropriate outburst and find their own places.

"It's considered a title of *dis*respect," Trent whispered into my ear. He spoke it so nearly silently that I could barely hear him. The hiss of the clammy air from his lips was louder than the remark itself. "Everyone knows he is called that, but no one says it to his face."

Croghan slid down next to me, groaning slightly as his worn joints creaked. When he was settled he reached a hand up to the chief, who had halted a step away. Tanaghrisson stood over Croghan, moving his eyes from the trader to me and back, clearly ascertaining his level of trust with the current company.

"Truly, Chief Tanaghrisson," Croghan said. "We are brothers. I can think of no one in my life with whom I have exchanged as many goods and good times. Laughter, joy, and even a fair amount of profit have been the hallmarks of our relationship. I expect that trend to continue." He bobbed his head to the side, indicating me. "The words of this shit-for-brains can do nothing to change that."

Had Croghan said such a thing about me in the woods, I would have felt the freedom to respond in a most unkind manner. Elder or not, a man had no right to disparage another in such a way. But from my first day, when George had me follow behind him and pick up the shells of the walnuts he discarded on the path of an Indian village through which he walked as he discussed business, the old trader had taught me to give every potential customer more respect than he deserved. It was good business, he said. It was a good way to live, he added. As a result I accepted Croghan's insult in the midst of our business dealings without spouting a response.

The Half King gave his old friend a half smile, his angry veneer cracking under the weight of Croghan's charms. "The Iroquois, too, have youth with heads as hollow as rotten elms. Shit, as you say, George, quickly fills the void." Tanaghrisson's half smile turned into a full one. For a frontier man approaching his fiftieth year, he had many fine teeth. "If I don't take offense when my own children spout half truths about things they only half understand, how could I possibly get upset by the musings of a half man calling me a Half King. Look at him. Has he ever had to shave his whiskers once?"

Anyone who could so deftly ridicule me while disparaging himself with the title of Half King was someone who deserved respect. That was the moment when I actually began to like Chief Tanaghrisson. He watched me chuckle while I rubbed the still-smooth skin of my face. Then the chief offered me a pleasant nod before lowering himself next to Croghan. A moment later, the proceedings were turned over to the wily trader.

Croghan snapped his fingers a few times to indicate to his underlings that we had officially gotten underway. Hearing the cue, the young men and boys who worked for the trader popped open the first of the many crates that surrounded the participants. They reached into the sturdy boxes and pulled out muskets, one in each hand. The runners scattered in all directions, respectfully approaching each Indian, beginning with Tanaghrisson and working their way down by age after that. Each Indian, be they Seneca, Shawnee, Delaware, Mingo, and on and on, received a fine new musket as a token of good faith. They had been paid for by Croghan himself and the shareholders in the Ohio Company from Virginia, who were represented by Christopher Gist at the council meeting.

The chiefs, elders, and warriors were clearly pleased with the first token of respect. Almost all of them stood with their new weapon, feeling its balance in their hands by bobbing it up and down. Some aimed the guns up into the trees, appreciating the strong iron sights. Here and there, an Indian carefully ran his hands over the stock, realizing the fine craftsmanship that went into each piece.

The weapons had been imported from an excellent gunsmith in England whose name was pressed into the barrel. But Croghan wouldn't just take whatever guns came in the crate. Croghan had selected each and every musket that was to be given away. Most of the lot he had purchased was set aside to be sold to common frontiersmen as George felt that his Indian counterparts deserved to have something special. He chose the guns for beauty of the wood grain, the balance of each one. He even made sure to discard any with a metal burr or any other harmless defect.

"Beautiful, George," said Tanaghrisson as he handed his new musket to a young man from his tribe. The other recipients slowly settled back into place, their murmurs clearly indicating that Croghan had struck off on a fine foot.

"May your lives have such peace that these muskets may never be fired in anger. But, should the need for protection ever arise, I know these gifts will be most welcome." Croghan pointed over his shoulder. "And there is enough powder and shot to provide you with resources for the hunt for many winters."

"It is a fine gesture of friendship," Tanaghrisson said warmly.

The assembly was quiet as every attendee waited for the chief to continue. After glancing around at all the participants and determining that the time was right, Tanaghrisson pulled out a long leather pouch decorated with beads. From it, the chief produced his ceremonial pipe. More than one man, white and Indian alike gasped at seeing the pipe come out so soon, before anything of consequence had been agreed upon, much less discussed. But once the mumbles of their initial confusion subsided, no one spoke while he methodically cleaned out the bowl and tapped it against the side of his moccasin, scattering any leftover ashes into the dirt. The chief placed the mouthpiece between his lips and blew gently, feeling the breath come out the bowl with his thumb.

Satisfied, Tanaghrisson pulled out yet another decorated pouch, much smaller than the first, and unrolled its long flap. He began speaking while his fingers carefully packed the bowl with dried tobacco leaves that had been grown by Virginian planters, carried inland by Pennsylvanian traders, and stowed in one of Croghan's many storehouses before finding its way into the chief's pouch. "It is customary in only some of the tribes of our brothers to seal an accord by the smoking of a peace pipe. But it is universally understood among us all, including our English brothers, that an agreement made and sealed by the pipe is granite."

"Yes, Chief Tanaghrisson," interrupted a Delaware who was surrounded by a large following of his warriors. "But not a word has been uttered about the matters at hand. I'm sure you, our representative from the Iroquois at Onondaga, would agree that it is premature to utilize such powerful medicine."

Tanaghrisson had not stopped his orderly packing of his pipe during the interruption. His task complete, the chief again set the mouthpiece between his lips and lifted an empty hand. Another of his young followers understood the signal and trotted toward the great council fire. After glancing around the edge for the right match, he snatched up a thin stick with one end cool, the other white and smoking. The chief gave a nod of gratitude after receiving the match.

Soon the pipe was lit and the Seneca chief puffed to get the bowl hot. He exhaled the smoke slowly and gently waved some of it back toward his nose. "My Delaware brother Shingas speaks of powerful medicine." He breathed in the wafting smoke deeply through his nose. "I smell the pleasant aroma. My insides tingle and my mind sparks. This is powerful medicine and I thank my Delaware brother for reminding us all of this fact. But I believe we may find occasion to smoke the pipe twice during our gathering. When terms are agreed to and lasting peace established, we will seal them with another smoke."

Chief Tanaghrisson took one last, long puff from his pipe before handing it to Croghan, who bowed his head in silent thanks. While the trader proceeded to smoke the pipe, the chief went on. "I have begun calling on the pipe's medicine and George joins me. I ask that all my assembled brothers do the same. For if we cannot agree that we are all brothers and then seal the belief with the pipe now, it would be better to avoid discussion of prickly topics altogether."

Shingas and his fellow Delaware murmured among themselves for a short time. All the while they jabbered, Tanaghrisson appeared relaxed and completely unflustered. He seemed in total control over the situation even though there was clearly at least one small faction that questioned his decision. Soon Shingas straightened up on his rump, looking down his nose at his rival. "We agree to seal our brotherhood with the Iroquois and the English by a smoking of the pipe."

The Half King smiled thinly, but pleasantly, showing no teeth.

By now George was carefully flapping his hand to wave some of the smoke he had exhaled back over his face. Without warning, he then passed the pipe to me.

I, not really a part of the proceedings, began to give the pipe to Trent on my other side. He held his hands in his lap and fixed me with a most astonished glare, but said nothing. His eyes went from the pipe to my mouth several times.

I had never smoked a ceremonial pipe, or any pipe for that matter. I didn't even know if I was permitted since I was only sitting around the fire because of George's last minute invitation. But the old trader's ever-widening eyes and Trent's finger jabbing my ribs quickly confirmed that I was to do something other than hold the device. I put the mouthpiece between my lips and pretended to puff by blowing a bit of air through the shaft and billowing my cheeks.

I was actually frightened of breathing in the smoke. More than once when I was a child the wind outside our tiny cabin had blown in such a way as to shove the smoke back down the chimney. On those occasions, with my lungs burning, I had coughed uncontrollably. What if the same thing happened to me around the council fire?

I looked ridiculous and fooled no one. "George," said Tanaghrisson with a light air. "It is obvious your shit-for-brains helper tries his best, but can you instruct him in the art of breathing in?"

"What is this?" Shingas asked, growing upset. "He makes a mockery."

"Smoke the pipe, boy," George directed sternly, but measured.

He was my employer. Whatever the reason for this meeting of great chiefs, it was important beyond any of our previous gatherings. Pinching my lips and teeth tightly onto the mouthpiece, I threw caution to the wind and sucked in a giant breath all the way to the base of my lungs.

I was still hacking and puking by the time the pipe completed its circuit around the fire and returned to the Half King's firm grasp.

CHAPTER SEVEN

My green face and eruption of coughs had served as a source of great merry for the group. Apparently, the gravity of the meeting had room enough for a fool such as I. Whites and Indians alike laughed. And just when one of them would get his giggles under control, he would glance back at me, lounging on my side, gasping, and spitting into the dirt, and explode into a new fit of hilarity.

As Tanaghrisson slid his pipe back into its long, decorated pouch, I heard him lean over to Croghan and say, "I like this shit-for-brains you've brought with you. He is funny. But hopefully he serves a purpose beyond entertainment. We've much to discuss."

Croghan glared at me from the corner of his eyes. "I hope so, too."

Chief Tanaghrisson patted his old friend's shoulder. "I suppose we mustn't be too hard on him. Suffering young fools is the burden we must bear for growing to a wise old age."

My employer continued to warn me with his frustrated stare. "You're very understanding," he said to the chief. "More than I."

"Stone is heavy and sand a burden," Tanaghrisson began.

I had heard that pithy proverb many times growing up in my folks' Quaker home. My gag reflex had relaxed just enough for me to finish the chief's thought. "But provocation by a fool is heavier than both," I sputtered. Then suddenly proud of myself, I again sat up tall like the more dignified men around the fire.

Pleased with me, Tanaghrisson said, "The boy's not a total fool."

"The meeting is not yet complete," Croghan warned as he finally stopped fixing me with those eyes. The Seneca chief chuckled.

It was then Christopher Gist's turn to start out with the meat of the gathering. "I bring you tidings from Virginia's Governor Dinwiddie. He asks that I pass along his respect and well-wishes to you and your peoples. The governor and, in turn,

His Majesty King George II understand completely the importance of our relationships with the tribes of the Ohio Valley. The aspect at the top of the governor's mind today is open trade with your peoples. Such activities benefit everyone. Our people can be involved in the importation and transportation of manufactured goods to you. You, more than ever, have benefited from inexpensive goods, brought to you more cheaply by men like George Croghan and his partners than at any time before."

"It is true," the Half King said. "My English brothers have a knack for trading."

"My French fathers bring in goods, as well," countered Shingas, the Delaware chief. "And they don't multiply as quickly. You are like rabbits in spring. Your own newspapers estimate there are nearly one and a half million settlers in the English colonies. His Most Christian Majesty of France has dropped only seventy thousand onto these shores. It is worth paying a few shillings more to remain free from new white towns and farms."

It was a fair point. Gist himself was an employee of the Ohio Company. And Governor Dinwiddie, from his offices back in Williamsburg, was a shareholder. The entire aim of the Ohio Company was for Virginians to speculate on land and sell it to adventurous settlers from Virginia.

"Are the French here now?" Croghan asked. He made a show to peer around the clearing. "Point a Frenchman out to me. Are they here today with goods to give, to sell?" Croghan's trading helpers chuckled.

But Shingas had an answer. "A large contingent came through just a few years ago. Hundreds of French and Canadians. They brought with them gifts and then left."

"Oh," Croghan said, not so easily beaten. "I see. You and your people only have need to trade once every few years. No need for winter stores. Steel tools and hunting supplies last forever."

"That is not what I said," Shingas growled.

The Half King held up his hand before the meeting took an ugly turn. "Brothers, let us not be led astray by anger or the bitter tongue. Shingas, I, as a member of the Tree of Great Peace at Onondaga, have complete authority to speak for all the tribes when in council with the English. I have granted you latitude to speak today. However, if you cannot do so without causing strife, I will, with a heavy heart, revoke your license."

Sufficiently chastised, for now, Shingas pinned his lips shut and nodded for Gist to continue. I got the feeling he wasn't done protesting.

The Ohio Company man was ready. "The governor, I, and all those present today want nothing more than to secure trade for many happy years to come. We aim to bring weapons, cloth, tea, molasses, tobacco, and more to the Forks of Ohio. To do so, we must build a stockade at the Forks and then continue to fortify it in the ensuing months. This post and place of refuge will help protect our trade routes to you. It will also discourage French incursion and disruption."

"Why a stockade? Why a fort?" asked Tanaghrisson. "Why not a simple storehouse like those at Croghan's other locations?" The Half King's questions almost seemed as if they were rehearsed or planned, because instead of directing them toward Gist, he turned to Croghan.

The Irishman responded with an equally prepared answer. "Because, Chief Tanaghrisson and other noble guests, the French have already proven themselves capable of horrible acts against the English and Indians. A thick-walled storehouse with a secure iron lock is not enough. Spiked walls, swivel guns, and men armed with muskets are necessary to deter the French from destroying all *our* work and *your* goods. And don't belittle the importance of saving a shilling. We have a saying in the Mother Country, *A penny spared, is twice got.*"

"I've heard your proverb. There is wisdom. But will you be settling white families around this stockade?" Shingas asked.

"No," Gist answered fervently. If it wasn't an outright lie, it was a stretching of the truth. It was true that the Ohio Company itself was trying to accumulate mostly uninhabited land. The Delaware tribe themselves were new arrivals in the river valley as it had been unoccupied for perhaps a hundred years. But the speculators who had purchased shares in the Ohio

Company would never make a farthing if the land was not resold and developed. The white settlers would likely come later. But not too much later.

"I'm of a mind to agree to the English proposal," Tanaghrisson said. He weighed his words carefully. "My people of Iroquoia have had a steady flow of goods for many years now. And George, with his previous gifts and those today, proves he is committed to the well-being of our people."

I hadn't heard the term, *Iroquoia*, for some years. It was approaching obsolescence as half of the former Iroquoia already had been absorbed by New York and was now administered from Albany. But to a youth of my age at the time, Chief Tanaghrisson seemed very old. It made sense to me that he spoke with the occasional antiquated word. The others overlooked his faux pas as well.

Croghan snapped his fingers a few times as he had done at the beginning of our meeting. His aides scrambled to bring the crates of gifts that he and I had brought in personally on our packhorses. With pry bars and hammers, they levered off the lids. Soon the boys had scattered straw packing out of the way. Reaching inside, they proudly pulled out dark bottles of Madeira.

The crowd, even the dubious Shingas, oohed and aahed at the mere sight. Madeira, wine imported from Portugal, was a prized possession of white settlers and their Indian neighbors. It was exceptionally expensive to get on the seaboard. More so, it was exceedingly rare to be found this far inland. And, since the cost of transportation was so high, it was never, ever seen in individual bottles. Anything shipped outside of port cities made the trip in large casks that could be efficiently hauled to a single tavern.

Despite their obviously orchestrated remarks earlier, Croghan had clearly surprised even the Half King with his trading prowess. "How did you…?" Tanaghrisson began to ask. "Why, there must be over a hundred gallons here."

"Enough for each of you to share a bit with me as a toast to our years of trading to come," Croghan said. His gambit with the Madeira, as expensive as it had to have been, was a great way to demonstrate his ability to see the impossible completed where others would fail. If he could accomplish this feat, what could possibly stop him from seeing a small fort built at the Forks of Ohio?

Shingas cradled the bottle that had been handed to him. He stroked the glass like it was the soft flesh of a newborn baby. His gaze lingered on it as if it was gold. And on the frontier, and in many ways, the Madeira was more precious than either a child or treasure. It could warm a man's chest in winter. One glass could moderate an intemperate wife. It could serve as a highly divisible trade good. And on and on. Madeira was a powerful good in the wilderness.

Croghan beamed with excitement. He always grew cheerful when on the cusp of concluding a sale or treaty. He held up his hands to calm the joyfully murmuring crowd. "I know this gesture is not much." Which meant it obviously *was* much. "But if you can simply forgive us for the slight delay. The rest of your Madeira will be here within the week."

"There's more?" Tanaghrisson asked, astonished.

"I don't want to lead you on," Croghan said, which meant he was about to unveil a truly huge amount of wine that was being trekked in. "But we could only get our hands on twenty pipes of Madeira. I'm afraid all of Philadelphia will have to wait for the next shipment before anyone there can take a sip."

"How much is twenty pipes?" I heard a few men ask.

But others knew exactly. "That's over twenty-five hundred gallons!"

"Enough to keep the hearts of your people warm all winter long," Croghan said, chuckling.

"And young wives bearing children in spring!" Tanaghrisson exclaimed joyously. The older men in the crowd elbowed the younger, perhaps newly married warriors who were scattered about. "Indians will outnumber whites within a year's time!"

Everyone laughed. But I was left in shock as my mind tried to wrap itself around the princely sum that would have gone into purchasing that much Portuguese wine. Money was flowing in Logstown!

Trent saw my dumbfounded look. "Gist and the Ohio Company shareholders chipped in to buy," he whispered. "It wasn't all George. There's much at stake in the gathering. If successful, it's worth every penny."

Tanaghrisson handed his bottle back to one of Croghan's helpers, who returned it to the box. "I believe that Croghan and the Ohio Company have proven their ability to deliver goods of exceptional value. I've known George for countless years and can vouch for his uncanny abilities. I am prepared to allow them to build their stockade and fort at the Forks of Ohio in order to foster trade."

Shingas, who had been grinning at his Madeira, set the bottle on the ground next to him. "No," he said simply. He tried to resist the urge to glance back at his wine, but I saw his eyes dart more than once. Eventually, he willed himself to have strength. "No," he repeated, more firmly this time.

Tanaghrisson didn't react with any concern. He watched Shingas through the flames of the council fire. The Delaware man did the same to him. Though neither appeared angry, the short moment grew tenser by the second. But ever-so-slowly, Shingas began to melt under the stare of the Seneca chief, who had the entire weight of Onondaga behind his word.

To me and in that moment, Tanaghrisson, the Half King, took on the form of every bit of a Whole King. "Brother Shingas," he began easily, betraying no exasperation. He gestured gracefully when he spoke, making slow, sweeping motions with his hands. "The mighty council that sits beneath the Tree of Great Peace has spoken in the past. In its wisdom it gathered its children, the Delaware, and placed them here in the Ohio Valley so that you could practice the way of life you desired. But at the same time, you remain under our protection, the watchful eye of the Iroquois. It is silly to think we would suddenly allow a dangerous influence into the Forks that would be harmful to you, our children. If I say the fort at the Forks will be beneficial to all, so it shall."

One of the warriors who rested behind Shingas patted his chief's shoulder as if to encourage him. The gesture worked. Shingas, who was wilting ever-lower the longer the Half King spoke, wiggled up straight. He cleared his throat. "I cannot allow it, Tanaghrisson. There is no benefit to drawing too close to the English. Let the French and English compete with one another for our trading."

"They have competed!" Tanaghrisson snapped. "And the English have won. Every day sees them bring more diverse and cheaper goods than the French!" For the first time, I saw the stress that had been hidden inside Tanaghrisson show itself. He clenched his jaw tightly and breathed out loudly through flared nostrils. He nervously adjusted the neat cuffs of his Englishman's shirt.

Croghan saw his flash of anger, too. "Mighty Chief Tanaghrisson and my brother Chief Shingas, if Madeira is not enough to bring us to smoke the ceremonial pipe once again, I have another token to offer. This is not a product, but a tale, true and cautionary about what happens when there is not a permanent understanding between our Indian hosts and our own English traders. Though he has appeared as nothing but shit-for-brains, Ephraim Weber is more than meets the eye. You've all heard about the destruction of Pickawillany on the Miami River. Such horrific news travels fast. Ephraim was there. He is the lone survivor. Tell the story, son."

Everyone, even the powerful chiefs in attendance suddenly set their attention directly onto me. Macabre gossip of the type I had to share was universally craved by Indian and white alike. Yet, I was not prepared to talk and I didn't know what Croghan expected me to say.

As you've seen, George was no fool. Croghan got me started with a prompt. It took only one. He started with a wallop. "Describe how your wife, your *Indian* wife, was killed."

I had not expected that. It felt like a slap to the face. I was sixteen, emotional, and truly in love with my young and beautiful bride. She was horrifically torn away from the world much too early. The pictures flashing in my mind's eye made me simultaneously sad and angry. Tears welled up and my lip quivered. I raced quickly past embarrassment and into another realm altogether. "Don't make me say it."

"You've got to," George said quietly. "If you want to save the lives of others, save them from the fate met by Tahki, then you'd best talk."

"But you know what happened, sir," I pleaded, looking for an honorable means of escape from the hardened warriors.

"I do," Croghan admitted with sadness. "But they don't."

I swallowed loudly, resenting Croghan for putting me in this position, but determined to complete the task given to me. I tried and failed to contain the spring of swirling feelings that had so quickly overtaken me. I would have to jump in and start. I did, childish snot and all. No one spoke, even the usually uninterested trading assistants who sat at the outskirts of the group kept their mouths shut. Even the chirping birds and chattering creatures of the forest refrained from making noise as I told my tale in its entirety.

"A company of French regulars came to the trading post at Pickawillany?" Tanaghrisson asked at the end of my story, concerned. He had obviously overlooked or forgotten my embarrassing behavior. "It wasn't a company of Canadians?"

I shook my head, still blubbering when I remembered the images of the slaughter. "No. They were regulars. Marching in formation. White coats. From Fort Detroit."

"You said there were Indians involved. Who? How many?" Shingas asked with narrowed eyes. None of the assembly had shown any revulsion when I had described how the old trader's heart had been eaten or how my father-in-law's body had been boiled and consumed. Such things were expected in frontier warfare.

"Chippewa and Ottawa for sure," I answered. "One hundred warriors, maybe two hundred. We were sorely outnumbered," I added in order to save face.

But no one heard anything I said after I listed the tribes involved in the Pickawillany massacre. The entire assembly of men around the great council fire exploded with angry conversation.

Only Croghan himself was calm. He leaned over to me and, speaking so only I could hear over the shouting, said simply, "Good, lad. Good." He patted my knee.

I nodded and tried to regain my composure, supposing that my entire purpose for attending the council had been achieved.

Every other man around the fire was agitated – Shawnee, Delaware, Seneca, Mingo. Major tribes and minor tribes cried out, not at one another but in sudden agreement. Chief Tanaghrisson raised his hands to quiet the masses. It took many calming words before the shouts died down to sedate grumbling. "Brothers. This news is most upsetting," Tanaghrisson said, doing his best to recapture the initiative. "We had known of the destruction of the post, but not the extent of the devastation. Onondaga was unaware of the participants and the obvious amount of cooperation between the attackers."

"If the Ottawa and Chippewa can get all the way down to the Miami River with the French," a Delaware warrior shouted. "Then they can come here. We don't have enough armed warriors to withstand such an attack!"

"I don't want Pontiac and his Ottawa cowards to set foot within this valley!" shrieked a wary Shawnee.

"Yes, they can easily make it to the Forks. And if they can come, in a morning's worth of work they can wipe out a peaceful trading post built at the Forks by Croghan, just like they did at Pickawillany," Tanaghrisson said. "Defeating a warrior of the renown of Memeskia is no simple task. And the brutality with which the French and Chippewa dealt with this young man's wife is intolerable." Tanaghrisson paused, genuinely choking up.

"Making captives of women and children is something we all understand," Tanaghrisson said with a wavering voice. "Such methods have been the ways of our peoples for generations. And it is well known that my mother and I were born of the Catawba people far to the south where the sun is high. But we were taken and adopted into the Seneca tribe during a mourning war. The Catawba are now my mortal enemy. Such is to be expected. But this action at Pickawillany is despicable. I repeat, we must allow our English brothers to build a fort capable of defending itself at the Forks of Ohio. It will be for their protection and ours."

Murmuring began anew. But this time its tone said that the participants agreed with the Half King. If there was anyone the tribes of the Ohio Valley hated more than either the English or the French, it was the Chippewa or the Ottawa or the Catawba and on and on. All around the assembly, men proudly called out their approval of the private fort. At last, it came to Shingas, who had waited to the end to give voice to his feelings.

"The boy's story compels me to agree," he said. "I invite the English to build their fort."

"Good," Tanaghrisson began, breathing a sigh of relief. "It is settled…"

"On one condition," Shingas barked in interruption. "In the future *I* will speak on behalf of the Delaware. No longer will the Half King, with approval from Onondaga, negotiate with the whites for my people."

Croghan rested his hand on the forearm of Tanaghrisson in a preemptive move to calm him. It was properly timed, for the Seneca chief nearly jumped to his feet in a fit of anger. George's knuckles turned white as he gripped his friend. "Thank you, brother," the chief whispered, his voice shaking with rage. "I nearly lost control."

Shingas folded his arms across his chest, pleased at having upset the calm leader. He awaited Tanaghrisson's response while the Delaware warriors who surrounded him, yipped their agreement with their chief.

"And this is why he is the Half King," Trent told me quietly while Tanaghrisson contemplated his response. "He has only as much authority as the Onondaga council and the tribes allow him. Whenever someone like Shingas begins to think independently, his power comes crashing down in the blink of an eye."

All over Tanaghrisson's face, the thousand political calculations that his mind made were plain to see. React calmly? React in a fit of rage? Which would embolden or cow Shingas and his followers? Lecture? Negotiate? Capitulate? Or, some combination of all of them? Croghan's muskets hadn't convinced Shingas. His Madeira hadn't swayed the Delaware.

Even my horrible tale of boogey men from the Chippewa and Ottawa tribes hadn't made Shingas agree without stipulation.

In the end, Tanaghrisson's reaction proved to all present that the power that had been gained by the Iroquois over the other tribes following their victory in the late Beaver Wars had officially waned. But in an attempt to keep up the illusion of his supreme position, Tanaghrisson, the Half King, said, "Chief Shingas, it would be an honor for Onondaga and me to *grant* you the ability to speak on behalf of your people."

"Oh, no," Trent muttered. He was usually astute about these types of things. He saw no good coming from the Delaware climbing out from under the thumb of Onondaga.

Shingas smiled and raised his chin proudly. "Then, as king of the Delaware nation, *I* will allow the English to build their fort at the Forks of Ohio."

And this simple exchange, where a Half King voiced his half-hearted support for the naming of the first Delaware king in many decades, would do more to ensure the coming of a war the world over than any event before or since. It would also ensure that after much bloodshed and destruction, one sovereign power would control all of North America.

And that power would be neither the Iroquois Confederacy nor the Delaware.

CHAPTER EIGHT
October 31, 1753

Too many long months had passed since my wife had been murdered in Pickawillany. In that time, I had put countless miles on the soles of my worn shoes. I'd carried out hundreds of transactions of barter and sale in white and Indian settlements. But what else was I to do? On my own, I could not expect to take up my old Brown Bess and attack a French officer behind the walls of a French fort deep in French territory. I had no support in the endeavor, not even verbal from the likes of Croghan or Trent. Thus, I was no closer to hunting down her killer and exacting my revenge in the most painfully excessive way one could imagine. In fact, I was about as far away from the French at Fort Detroit as I could possibly be.

At Croghan's dispatch, I was sitting on a chair in an empty hallway of the governor's red brick mansion in Williamsburg. He attended a meeting of some significant importance to the colonies, traders, and His Majesty the king. So far, I had been waiting in the same spot for three hours as the adjournment of the meeting behind a nearby closed door had not yet occurred. According to George, the outcome of the gathering was also to be crucial for me. It would at least partially determine where I would next be sent. Beyond that limited information, I knew nothing of the goings-on in the hushed conference.

I could make out mere snippets of conversations. But what I was able to gather from the greatly agitated, great men on the other side of the door did nothing to help me divine my coming destination. Several of the men growled about the coming of *four French forts* time and again. I heard the name, Duquesne, uttered for the first time while resting on my chair. In a few short years, the unfamiliar name would become utterly recognizable to every single American and Englishman in the world.

As I listened to the workings of a grand clock tick away in the corner, all I could truly think about was splitting open the head of Ensign Jumonville. An angry young man can conjure all sorts of depraved methods of killing. It's sickening really, how easily such disgusting thoughts fired in my mind.

The baby Tahki had carried would already have been close to ten months old. I should have been traipsing about the Ohio Country buying and selling goods, making more babies whenever I was back home in Pickawillany. Instead, I sat in a civilized town and stewed. Impotent.

"Three letters from London," barked a man speaking English with a Scottish accent as thick as the fat on a finished hog's back. It had to be none other than Governor Dinwiddie, who hailed from Glasgow to carry out the wishes of his English monarch. He had raised his voice to reestablish his supremacy in the conference behind the door. It was something that important men did when they wanted to appear even more important. "Each letter authorizes, and I quote, *to repel force by force.* These are *royal orders to repel any hostile attempt by force of arms.* Well, tell me, gentlemen, if it is not hostile, what is it for a foreign king to build forts in the Ohio Country, the rightful dominion of King George II?"

More mumbling, more arguing proceeded from there. Apparently, Dinwiddie's bark had done nothing for his position in the council, whatever it was. Following the governor's bold question, I heard nothing more from him until the very end of the conference, which didn't happen until after another hour of burbling deliberation on topics ranging from taxation to road construction.

I had to urinate, but did not want to leave my post in case the meeting adjourned. Croghan would erupt if I failed to accomplish the one job he'd given me. *Sit here!* A servant passed by. She carried a pitcher of water that sloshed. It sounded like a waterfall, to me. I crossed my legs, fidgeting. In an effort to forget about the pressure on my bladder, I allowed my mind to wander, often thinking of Tahki or her father or my own family. As far as I knew, my parents still performed back-breaking work on their farm while raising my six younger siblings. It might even be seven siblings by now. I hadn't had any contact with them since I had left. I then briefly recalled the death of my older sister when I was five years old. It was a painful memory.

Fortunately, that is when I heard the legs of a chair scrape against the wooden floor of Dinwiddie's office. The governor announced, "Then if the Burgesses will not authorize the justified expenditures for a substantial and immediate venture, I am forced to await the cannon, shot, and powder being sent from London in order to arm the fort we will construct at the Forks. But the threat from the French and her Indian allies cannot be ignored entirely. George," the governor asked. "You've indicated in the past that you are eager for such an expedition. Will you deliver my demands to the French in the Ohio Country?"

I expected to hear George Croghan's Irish brogue wax eloquent with a long-winded answer in the affirmative. But my employer didn't respond. Instead, I only heard the mumbling reply of a much quieter, literally gentle, man. He sounded almost awkward or uncertain, though in truth I could understand nothing of what he said.

"It's settled then," Croghan said clearly when the mumbling at last stopped. "My people can get you whatever you need."

The meeting broke up quickly after that and the door swung open. Select members of the Virginia House of Burgesses streamed out first. They chatted easily while setting paces that indicated either an urgent need to find an outhouse or their displeasure with the meeting. I stood, again feeling the need to relieve myself. While wiggling to control my bladder, I wondered if any of them was the George who had mumbled his way through the meeting. I would never know, for they disappeared outside with great haste.

Next through the threshold came a solitary man in a blue uniform coat with red upturned cuffs. He was young, perhaps only five years older than I. His long, reddish brown hair was pulled back in the accepted military style. He spoke to no one. Instead, he walked directly toward the exterior door as if on a mission. All the same, his pace was not rapid, just elegant and confident. I had never seen him before, but from his endless line of pewter buttons and the smart cut of his coat, I guessed he was a major or even colonel in the Virginia militia. In those days, Virginia especially, had countless gentlemen who considered themselves officers of significant rank in the county militia.

And this man was a giant for our day, at least six foot tall. He had a tanned handsome face, with just a hint of smallpox scarring on his nose. This specimen was definitely not the mumbler, for no man who carried himself thus would allow his speech to be so humble. After gathering his cloak and hat from a peg on the wall, he efficiently exited to the outdoors. Once on the stoop he donned his hat. I watched it float away among the blowing autumn leaves as he walked southward out into the main town.

"Ephraim!" snapped Croghan, who now stood in the office door next to a well-dressed official. "Quit wiggling like a hound wagging his tail. Quit gawking at the walls and get over here and give the governor the respect he deserves." Croghan didn't have to add that the governor had probably rewarded him with a lucrative contract for supplies. Given George's many trading successes, such a win was certain. And it was also a given that any of Croghan's compatriots, myself included, needed to butter the bread of the right, honorable Dinwiddie.

I tumbled toward them and tipped my head in respect to the governor. In contrast to the energetic military officer, he was not young. I'd guess he was at least sixty, with puffy skin beneath his eyes. His girth was robust, bordering on rotund, but not obese. Dinwiddie had the face of a tax collector. He wore a permanently stern expression, even when he offered what were supposed to sound like heartfelt condolences. "It is a shame that you were forced to endure the massacre at Pickawillany, young man. The tragedy shall be righted on my watch."

His time of providing me any of his attention was already at an end. As if I had never existed in the first place, the governor quickly turned to Croghan. "George will need all the help you can muster. And don't mind the recalcitrant Burgesses. Somehow, we'll see they cover any bills you or your men encounter." Dinwiddie then set a hand on Croghan's shoulder and forcibly moved him out of the way so he could retreat inside

62

his office and close the door. He left it slightly ajar. Inside, I could hear him gather his inkwell, quill, and paper. Within moments he was scratching away feverishly.

"Things are falling in our favor, Ephraim," Croghan said with delight. He ushered us through the same exterior door everyone else had used. "But none of it will be easy. Between competition from the French, the Ohio Company, the other colonies, and the obstinate Burgesses you'll have your work cut out for you. I'll be busy organizing supplies here and there. You'll still be my chief aide, but we might not see a lot of each other for a while."

He wagged his finger in my face as we exited through the gate in the brick wall that surrounded the mansion. Croghan led us onto the main palace green of Williamsburg. Our feet rattled and crushed piles of red and orange leaves that had blown into drifts like snow. "But just because you won't have me constantly watching over you doesn't mean you are independent. You'll still work for me and my interests!"

The uniformed officer I had seen in the governor's mansion marched alone some distance ahead of us. To our left the members of the Burgesses that had been in such a rush to escape Dinwiddie laughed as they entered a nearby tavern.

"Where am I going?" I asked. "Will I be headed back toward Fort Detroit?"

Croghan stopped mid-stride, halting me in the process. "Lad, I've been kind for a year. I've listened to you go on about revenge. But revenge is as silly a thing as putting the muzzle of a pistol in your mouth and pulling the trigger. Where's the profit in that?" Croghan was a trader to the core and valued everything according to pounds, shillings, or pence. Though George Croghan wasn't a bad man, even justice could be meted out by the Guinea.

He had told me versions of this before. I had always heard him, but had chosen not to listen. "So, where am I going now, George?" I asked to avoid any more of his lecture. My revenge, it seemed, was to be permanently delayed. But at least I could hope for escape from the chattering townsfolk of the eastern seaboard. The wilderness was the place for me.

Croghan hustled us along the wide palace green, which wasn't so green this time of year. I heard the hammer of the wheelwright working its magic in the small white building to the west. The Irish trader was moving swiftly now and I trotted to keep up. He extended his neck to get a slightly better view of the crowded town, looking for something or someone.

"There he is!" Croghan exclaimed, pointing toward the shoemaker's shop. "My, he's swift. I like him and think you will, too. Some of the gentry don't think too highly of him. His formal education is lacking, they say. But he makes up for any shortcomings by being exceedingly polite and proper. He's also smart as a whip – but not always in the book sense, thank goodness. And eager! Eagerness will get you farther in this business of life than brains many times. Put that pinch of wisdom in your pipe and smoke it, lad."

"Who?" I asked craning my head around.

Croghan pointed directly at the Virginian officer just as he disappeared around the corner to the left, toward the Capitol building. "That militiaman there," the trader said. "Or maybe he's commissioned by the governor. I don't know. The only thing I know about the army is that it takes a great deal of supplies to keep them on their feet. With enough bacon and rum any run-of-the-mill army can do wonders. It takes ammunition, too. And we can supply all of it! Never mind. That officer there, he's a good man, I think, for what small amount I know of him. Now run along. He knows you're coming to help. You do whatever he says. But don't forget, you work for me, not Gist, not anybody else. Now get!"

Spurred by my employer's explosive insistence, I jogged ten paces before turning around. Croghan had already bolted toward the tavern, no doubt to ply the Burgesses in attendance with rum and ale in order to receive favor – and profitable contracts. "How should I introduce myself?" I asked, knowing that Virginian gentlemen could sometimes be prickly in their manners – especially when confronted by a backwoods rube.

Croghan crinkled his face into a sarcastic frown. "You are called Ephraim Weber. Why don't you start there?"

"No. That's not what I meant. What's the major's name?" I called.

"A nobody really," Croghan answered. "Got his job because his older brother died. You two young nobodies will get along well. He shares my given name and the king's name. He is George, uh, George Washington." He then slid into the tavern already chatting up a member of the Burgesses about importing tea from a new and cheaper source, adding something about avoiding the duties levied by royal customs officers.

And I ran off to find out just what I was to do for this nobody called George Washington.

CHAPTER NINE

I didn't get very far. My bladder was ready to explode like a keg of gunpowder set too close to a flame. There was a privy nearby, behind the courthouse, but I saw a line of well-dressed men waiting their turn. I couldn't wait that long. There were also woods a hundred yards south of the village magazine and guardhouse. But as I walked to catch the officer, I discovered that I had lost the speedy George Washington. He must have made it to the Capitol building and retreated inside. Running to the woods to do my necessary business seemed a waste of precious time.

To my left I saw a narrow alleyway between a private residence and the printing and post office. The owner of the home was something of a gardener. A clump of winding green vines with dying leaves stuck out into the street, partially obscuring my view of the alley. My bladder informed me that I had found its refuge of relief.

I darted in behind the fading greenery and had my trousers uncinched before I had even come to a complete stop. "Ahh," I released a grateful sigh just as the first of my stream splashed against the foundation of the post office.

What happened next occurred in less than a minute. It will certainly take me longer to write it. It may take you longer to read it.

A short, high-pitched scream cut through the alley, emanating just a half rod to the left of my position. Startled, I leapt and spun to face it, stepping part way back onto the street. I now faced a young woman, perhaps seventeen, who held a basket full of late-season produce under one arm. She had been gathering food from the gardens in the rear and was cutting through the alley to the street when she saw me – urinating on the post office. The hand of her other arm covered her astonished mouth. And if her mouth was held open in wide surprise, her large brown eyes were as big as those of a startled horse.

"Oh my!" I shrieked, simultaneously clenching off my stream and hiding my private areas away. I'm sure I turned to the deepest shade of red in that moment. Sufficiently terrified, every urge to urinate vanished.

Thankfully, her face went from worry and shock to surprised amusement. Her eyes remained wide, but instead of looking horrified, she began to giggle. Her laugh was a pleasant song. I think my own embarrassment helped her relax. Then gradually, as it became clear she would not call out the militia on me, I relaxed as well. It was to be short-lived.

"What could possibly be the meaning of such impropriety," said a whispering voice from just over my shoulder. For the second time in a handful of seconds, I spun. This time, looking out into the street, I now faced the tall, handsome military officer who had been my quarry. As he looked down at me, his face was rigid, displeased. And his disposition did not melt as did the woman's.

"Uh, I was looking for you, George," I stuttered.

"You may call me Major Washington, young man," he said quickly, but ever-so quietly. He spoke as if his chest was hollow with little ability to mount any type of forceful oration. His bald anger was apparent. But the great restraint he used to check his own emotions and responses proved the victor.

George Washington, confident in his right to confront wrong, did not move. He fixed himself in place. "I am certain that we have never been introduced. We are surely not familiar enough to address one another by our given names. Have you no sense of decency, man?" Then his eyes went down to my disheveled trousers. "I can see such a question is unnecessary."

He took one long stride toward me, entering my personal space, but making no move to assault my person. A glance from his towering figure was all it took to compel me to step to the side. I retreated against the wall of the house. Washington walked past me into the alley and turned to look down at where I had been doing my business. The stone of the foundation and the painted clapboard siding still bore the wet, dark traces of my work. A yellow-white pool of bubbling liquid had collected on the cobblestone walkway of the alley. Disgusted, the officer again fixed me with a disappointed glare.

From a virtuous distance away, he bowed to the young woman who had remained in her place in the center of the long, narrow alleyway. Then Washington used his whispering voice to address her. Though he was but a yard away from me, I had trouble discerning what he actually said. To the best of my knowledge, it went something like this, "My young lady, I deeply regret that I was unable to prevent this scoundrel from despoiling your sanctuary of green. But I am here now with the situation well in hand. How may I locate your husband so that he and I may deal with this to its completion?"

"To its completion?" I wondered aloud, not liking the sound of finality.

The woman and the major looked at me. She did so as if I was a welcome distraction from her daily routine. Just seeing the plump of her cheeks grow above a blossoming smile was enough to make me want to speak again. On the other hand, his look, while in no way causing his face to contort, was far from pleased. Washington's somber expression made me want to climb inside myself and never speak again. In this case, the officer's glower ruled. I would keep quiet – for now.

With me sufficiently in my place, Washington was able to renew his inquiry. "Your husband, madam?" he asked the woman again. "Please direct me. Then this criminal and I will be of no further bother to you."

"I am not married," she answered. "This is my parent's home. I live here with them and my siblings."

"Your father then? Where may I find him? He will be most displeased to hear what your delicate eyes were forced to witness from this stranger. You are fortunate I was emerging from the post office when you screamed. And while I am on a mission of some weight for His Majesty and our governor, I shall always find time to assist a member of the fairer sex. You're certain you are not injured?"

"Oh," the woman began stammering. "Uh, no. I shouted from surprise. I came around the corner and saw a shadow, uh, his shadow," she said pointing to me. "There is no need to bother yourself or my father. My mind had been wandering and he startled me, that's all. I saw nothing more *private* if that is what you are concerned about.   Besides, the sun was in my eyes."

Mr. Washington peered southward over his shoulder down the long alley as he considered her lie. Actually all three of us looked to the heavens. A giant cloud blanketed the sky in that direction, as it had for most of the day.

"It was sunny a moment ago," the women went on, digging deeper.   "The cloud must have rolled in while we talked."

The major examined his chief witness. After a short while, he again bowed. "Then I will trouble you no longer. Since this man didn't expose himself to you, I believe we do not need to involve your father.   However, there is the most reprehensible offense of urinating on the post office from your alleyway. We will, no doubt, discover upon further scrutiny that this man is found drunk, and in the middle of the day!" I placed an exclamation point here, not because Washington's tone or volume increased. It was just that the strain he pushed behind his quiet voice gathered steam near the end and I had no other way of demonstrating it.

"Major Washington," the woman said, stepping toward him.   His confidence slipped visibly and his form grew awkwardly rigid, increasing exponentially with the decrease of the distance between them.   "I apologize for being so presumptuous as to address you by name, but as my hero, I want to give you your due respect. I happened to hear your name when you said it to my cousin here." She pointed to me. "He arrived sooner than I had expected."

Washington's head tipped to the side in confusion. "This man is your cousin, you say?"

The girl fixed her bright, brown eyes upon me. I silently mouthed my name to her. *Ephraim Weber.*

"Oh, yes, of course," she said, waving her hand and laughing off the misunderstanding. She was an excellent liar – perhaps a little too experienced for her own good. But given her comely features, I would overlook it. All men would do the same just to set their eyes on her brilliant face. Confidently, she added, "His name is Abram Weber." She was a fine liar, a bad lip reader.

I rolled my eyes.

"Is this so?" Washington asked, turning to me, the accused.

"We are cousins, Major Washington," I answered, nodding my head like the arm of a water pump. "But Abram is my middle name. The last time we saw one another my parents were still calling me Abram to distinguish me from my father. My first name is Ephraim. She was probably too young to remember."

"Ephraim Weber?" Washington asked, a flicker of recollection behind his pale grayish blue eyes. Croghan had said that the major was expecting me. "And the urination?"

"I am terribly sorry and embarrassed, major," I answered, quite honestly. "I had held it for quite a while. And remember, she says she didn't see anything private."

"She?" Washington asked, seizing on my inability to name my so-called cousin. "Does *she* have a name?"

He stood in my direct line of sight so that I could not hope for the same silent communication to aid me in my lie. The position of his broad shoulders meant the woman would have to crane around him to offer help. Perhaps toying with me, or perhaps oblivious to my plight, she did no such thing, not even making an effort.

But I was not a complete fool. I had already guessed that the young woman was seventeen. I had heard a lot of teenage women with the name Betsy. With my urge to urinate suddenly surging once again, I gave it a weak try. "Betsy?"

"It's Bess now, Abram," she said to me as she now leaned around the major, fixing me with a pretty, though devious, smile.

"Oh, nice to meet you, uh, see you again, Bess. But remember, I go by Ephraim."

Washington was completely flummoxed. What had been his chance to save a damsel in distress was turning into an awkward moment between two relatives – false as we may have been. In the end, and in what I would come to understand was his default position in times of public disagreement involving a woman, he bowed politely to Bess. "Then it is clear that my presence here is superfluous. But I suggest that you have your father lecture your backwoods cousin in town manners. I bid you a good day, miss. Pardon my interruption." He spun on his heels, glanced disapprovingly at me, and as he moved back onto the street, acknowledged me simply as, "Mr. Weber." Then Washington turned right, heading back in the direction from which we'd come.

I was left alone in the alley with a pretty young woman to whom I had recently exposed myself. As much as I wanted to stay and learn everything in the world about her, I had a busy major to catch. Croghan was never a violent or overly harsh employer, but he had expectations of his workers. If you ran afoul of them, he could waste a fine afternoon in the forest cursing in whatever the hell his ancient Irish language was, Gaelic, Celtic, who knows.

With raised eyebrows, Bess awaited my thanks or at least some type of explanation for my behavior. I took the opportunity to tuck in my shirt and make sure my trousers were acceptable. Peeking onto the street, I saw that eager Major Washington was rapidly getting away. I didn't have time to chat with the pretty stranger who had inexplicably kept me from the stockade. So, not knowing what else to do, I hurried to her and planted a quick and completely inappropriate kiss on her cheek.

She was still speechless as I ran from the alley after Washington.

"I'll see you soon, cousin Bess," I shouted, giggling all the way and feeling younger and lighter than I had in over well over a year.

CHAPTER TEN

Washington, who was striding on long legs, was halfway back to the governor's mansion before I caught him. By then I was already feeling guilty for thinking another woman attractive just a year after Tahki's death – let alone planting an uninvited kiss on her soft skin. What would my mother say to such haughty actions? I remembered then that I didn't really care what my mother would say. Getting away from the clogged towns on the seaboard was just one of the reasons I had run away from my parents' farm. With every passing day since the gruesome, untimely death of my sister, my views had diverged further and further from those of my parents.

"Hmm," I chuckled to myself more than anyone else. I felt devilishly inspired by the kiss I'd stolen. "Bess."

Major Washington's ears perked up when he heard my voice. "Yes, Mr. Weber?" Washington said, cutting rightward around the brick fence that lined the governor's property. He cut a direct path for the barn that housed the horses of royal officials and their guests. The major didn't bother glancing back at me. "I suppose you miss your beloved *cousin* already."

"You know we're not cousins?"

Still marching with perfect posture, the major did not skip a beat. "The young woman's method of the lie was convincing," he admitted. "Yours, less so," he added with wit as dry as dead bones.

A slave from the stable met our approach. "My horse please, Jeremiah," Washington whispered. "It is urgent. We leave for Fredericksburg and beyond."

"Yes, sir, major. Right away," the black man said. "And your traveling friend, here?"

"Please fetch Mr. Weber's horse as well," Washington instructed.

"We don't have a horse for a Mr. Weber in the stable, major," Jeremiah said, glancing at me warily.

"I don't have one," I answered and Jeremiah promptly turned to collect the major's horse.

"Well, Mr. Weber, I am in a hurry, for we have much ground to cover before winter sets in. Run and retrieve your beast. I shall wait here for but a moment," Washington instructed.

"No, sir," I said. "I don't have a horse anywhere."

"You walked all the way from Pickawillany?"

I nodded and shrugged. "It was over a year ago I was in Pickawillany."

But Washington was no longer listening. "Jeremiah," he called with his utterly vaporous voice. It more closely resembled a gasping breath than a shout.

Nonetheless, Jeremiah heard him just before he ducked into the barn. "You called, major?"

"Please outfit a second horse for Mr. Weber. Take him from the governor's stock of extra mounts and see that the bill is sent to Mr. Croghan's trading ventures."

"Easy enough, sir," Jeremiah said and disappeared to perform his duties.

I was mildly horrified that Washington just purchased a horse from the royal governor using funds from my employer without Croghan's express permission. "Croghan is in the tavern," I muttered, turning to go. "I should go check with him about the horse."

"Halt, Mr. Weber," Washington ordered. Despite, or perhaps because of, the gentleness of his tone, I stopped after having taken only one step away. Once I again faced him, finding that I stood at something like attention expected of a soldier. He went on. "I, we rather, have been given a monumental task. It is something that the Old World would consider only proper to grant a man of great wealth, age, and experience. Yet, here we are, heading west in charge of the destiny of His Majesty's empire. Just because I do not come from the wealthiest of families, does not mean that I do not have pride in and expectations for my performance. As such, you are under my command. You will do what I say, when I say it. This is not to be some sight-seeing excursion for either of us. We do not have time for you to correspond with Mr. Croghan to verify everything we do."

Even then, when Washington was a twenty-one year old, newly minted, provincial major whose whiskers were not much coarser than mine, he commanded respect. His presence, his air, the gravity with which he held whatever task he'd been given, was heavy. Without any real detail, he had made our mission – the mission of two green men – seem to be the most important undertaking going on in the entire world at that moment.

"Uh, yes, sir," I stumbled. Unless we were in the midst of tricky trade negotiations, Croghan and I never spoke to one another with such formality.

Washington, simply assuming his command and explanation were adequate even without listening to my response, glanced to the barn. Then, showing a hint of impatience, he muttered, "What is taking Jeremiah so long."

If the slave had been gone as long as five minutes I would be surprised. Nonetheless, the efficient stable man nudged the door open and led out two beasts. It was easy to tell which was the major's and which was to be my horse. Suffice it to say, that nothing of my horse was notable enough to make a list of any length – unless one were to make an inventory of faults. Then, an experienced horseman might be able to fill two pages describing the creature's swollen hocks, uneven hips, and swayed back.

"I thank you, Jeremiah," Washington said as he took the reins and scrambled into the saddle of his sharp gelding.

"You're welcome, major," Jeremiah answered as he handed me the reins to my pathetic creature.

Out of habit, I checked the girth for tightness. Both Washington and Jeremiah rolled their eyes. "Mr. Weber," the major said. "Do not offend Jeremiah by checking his work. Mount the horse."

I was already used to unflinchingly obeying Washington's orders. I dropped the flap and stirrup and climbed into the seat. It creaked. "Good fit," I said, pleased that the stirrups were properly adjusted for my height.

"What do you expect from a man of Jeremiah's experience," Washington muttered. He then looked down at Jeremiah. "Convey to the governor that I shall most vigorously carry out his wishes and those of the king. I hope to return by spring with news of successful endeavors."

"I will, sir," Jeremiah said with a tip of his head.

Washington propelled his gelding to a trot onto the road that wound its way northward from the capital city.

"Go on, get," Jeremiah instructed me. "If you think you can catch that man once he's gotten on his way, you have another guess coming."

My heels tapped the mare's belly. She lazily moved after Washington's beast.

"Where are we going?" I called to the major. Then I thought of Bess and, despite my revulsion of town life, asked, "And when are we coming back? You said, spring?"

"That is what I said, Mr. Weber. If you will require me to repeat every phrase I utter on this journey, we shall both find much displeasure," Washington said over his shoulder.

"But what could we possibly do in Fredericksburg until spring?" I asked.

"If we tarry in Fredericksburg for longer than a half a day, I shall be disappointed," Washington answered. "We go to the Ohio Country."

I was momentarily sad that I'd not get to see Bess again. But the prospect of returning to the wilderness was a better trade-off in the long run. I prodded my beast to a brief cantor in order to catch up with the major. When I was abreast of him, I slowed the sad, panting creature. Washington glanced disapprovingly at me and I asked. "What do we aim to do in Ohio that is so important to the king and the governor? In the middle of winter, no less."

For the first time since I met George Washington, he cracked a smile. It was a handsome grin, which showed no teeth what-so-ever. His brow raised, indicating he knew much more about our mission than he would let on just yet. "Why, Mr. Weber, I am dispatched to consult with the French in the Ohio Country. There, I will explain to them they have mistakenly set up posts and forts on lands that belong to the King of Great Britain." He patted his breast pocket indicating he carried a letter.

I thought about the attack on Pickawillany where a few Frenchmen and their Indian allies dislodged an entire people. It was then that I peered around the empty road. "I hope we take with us an army, because you'll need one to send the French on their way."

Washington tutted me. "Shame on you, Mr. Weber. I carry the words of the king to a mere French officer in the wilderness. We are all gentlemen. They will vacate without hostilities." The major used his reins as a gentle switch while spurring his beast faster. "Come."

But I didn't immediately follow. I let him pull ahead. What had old Croghan gotten me into? I was stuck with an overly rigid Virginian youth who had probably been old since the time of his birth. He thought himself so important that a measly word from him and a piece of paper from the governor or king would send all of the French forces in the Ohio Country running.

George Washington was either too inexperienced to know any better or completely delusional.

I glanced over my shoulder and saw Williamsburg through the trees as the fall leaves fluttered about. Though I hated towns, I briefly toyed with the idea of returning. Bess would be fun to look at and maybe get to know. There would be other things to do, perhaps other girls to see or court. But disobeying Croghan would find me wanting work just as the most inhospitable time of year was about to begin. And I would be out of the one job that gave me the best opportunity to spend time in the west.

In the end, I did what most young men do when faced with similar decisions. I plunged ahead, not having any idea what to expect. I knew only that George Washington was leading me back to the dense trees and sparse populations of the Alleghenies and beyond. Most importantly, I would be closer to Fort Detroit and perhaps one day exacting my revenge on Jumonville, a name and face I'd never forget.

But I also had to admit something a little disconcerting. I might wind up being killed if I followed the whims of a naive man called George Washington. Believing in the inherent honor of men as he clearly did, the gullible major himself might find an early grave.

Only time would tell.

CHAPTER ELEVEN

Wills Creek was a common weigh station along the trek from eastern Virginia into the wilds of Ohio. It was not the last chance to see white settlers, but nearly so. Thereafter and the further westward a man headed, the only Englishmen to be expected included intrepid traders, trappers, or true frontiersmen. With the Delaware tribe making the Ohio Country their relatively new home, Indians would outnumber us by a considerable margin. Nonetheless, white men with constitutions like George Croghan, myself, or Christopher Gist could be found if one looked hard enough.

And Gist led our small party westward out of Wills Creek in the middle of a sleet storm. Washington had come across him in the small trading center and hired him as a guide to take us where there existed no roads whatsoever. Gist remained an eager Ohio Company man, ready to scoop up lands for its shareholders. He jumped at the chance to drive out the French.

Fat droplets of sopping wet snow splattered against my leather cloak as we ascended into the Alleghenies. Some of the drops were so large they reminded me of when my younger brothers would pack up a bundle of snowballs back home. They'd wait to spring on me when I left the barn after chores. Thud. Thunk. Splat. Heaps collected on the brim of my hat. Ice cold, yet melting, water ran down my neck and shoulders.

Major Washington had diligently driven us this far at an efficient, but not breakneck, pace. The two of us had stopped in Fredericksburg for no more than three hours. It was just enough time to re-provision our saddle bags for the next leg of our trip to Wills Creek. While in Fredericksburg, we had also picked up another traveler. This man would have a part to play in this leg of my story as well as one that takes place several years in the future. But let us stay on track.

He was an old friend of Washington who had taught the major how to fence. After reminiscing of glory days and fencing matches past for just a few moments in the man's finely appointed parlor, Washington asked him to come along with us.

"Van Braam," the major whispered with formality. "I need you to act as my interpreter."

"George, we have been friends for fifteen years. You know you may call me Jacob," said the Dutchman.

"Jacob," Washington conceded with an almost pained expression. "But I shall refer to you as Mr. Van Braam while on the trail. A professional force needs discipline, not familiarity. Please pack. We must retain your language skills."

Van Braam laughed. "My skills, as you call them, are weak. Other than the king's English, I speak only a smattering of French and a bit of the Indian tongues."

"That's what I remember," Washington said confidently. "We require your proficiency with French."

"George," said Van Braam, who was a handful of years older than the man he dared to call, George. "I can get you the names of more than a dozen men in Fredericksburg alone who speak better French than I."

"I require *you*," the major answered simply.

The Dutchman fixed his old friend with a curious gaze. "You intrigue me, George. What is it we are to do?"

Washington, who had said something less than a score of words to me since we'd left Williamsburg, suddenly looked at me as if he expected me to give an answer. Van Braam took the hint. "George seems to think you'll tell me what I'm getting into should I agree to go."

I knew very little of what was to come. "We're going to the Ohio Country to ask the French to leave."

Van Braam burst into uproarious laughter. "Oh, if that's all!" He rested a hand on Washington's shoulder. The major did not recoil, but made no reciprocating move of friendship. A moment later, Van Braam's amusement came to a slow stop as he realized that neither the major nor I joined in his mirth. "You're not serious."

"The governor has received word from the king," Washington said in explanation, tapping his breast pocket. "He has seen fit to send me. I require you to come and provide service to the crown."

"Let me understand something. Dinwiddie is sending a newly promoted, untested major of the provincial militia to politely *ask* the French to leave lands claimed by their own king?" Van Braam asked, incredulous. Then he frowned. "George, by the way, I am sorry about your brother Lawrence's passing last year. He was like a father to you. It's a hell of a way to earn your rank through the death of such a fine man."

Croghan had briefly mentioned it on the palace green in Williamsburg, but Washington had revealed nothing further of his brother's death. He'd certainly said nothing about stepping into Lawrence's vacated soldiering shoes. During the trip to Fredericksburg, I had talked incessantly about how much I'd miss my wife and her family – and I had only known them for a short while. I yammered about my righteous hatred for the French, the Chippewa, the Ottawa. Washington hadn't so much as offered an appropriately timed, *uh-huh,* to encourage me to continue. And even though it was clear that the major still mourned the death of someone so close to him as his favorite brother, he had made sure to keep his emotions bottled.

"He is sorely missed," Washington said with just a crack in his strong façade. But he quickly regrouped. "I am instructed to convey the message, yes. I am empowered to assemble a troop of my choosing, gather Indian allies, and present a united front to the commander of the French forces in the area."

Van Braam again looked to me, considering that he must be the butt of an un-funny joke. "It's true," I said. At least it was the same story Washington had told me all along. It was still hard to believe the governor had actually designed such a poor strategy.

"Well, George," the Dutchman said as he laughed skeptically through his nostrils. "If that is all we're doing, then count me in. When do we leave?"

"I'd like to leave yet today," Washington had answered, earnestly gathering his cloak and hat. Van Braam's brow wrinkled as he saw just how serious his young friend was. "I have dispatches to send to Governor Dinwiddie. Mr. Weber and I shall return momentarily to gather you. And Mr. Van Braam, from here on out please address me as Major Washington. Military decorum, you see?"

Which brings me to our climb through the sleet of the Alleghenies as we trailed behind Gist.

"It won't take the French or any Delaware to kill us," Van Braam said as he rode his horse next to me up a steep mountain. His head was tucked low as he unsuccessfully attempted to use his shoulders as shelter from the elements. There was no path so we spent much of our time ducking beneath ice-laden branches. "George will do that all on his own by getting us the chills. Soon our voices will be as hollowed out as his." Van Braam had quickly gotten used to referring to his young friend as the major. He only slipped and mentioned Washington's first name when he was frustrated with the sober officer. The pace Gist had set was slow and Washington had ridden ahead to spur him on so now was a safe time to speak with such informality.

A particularly frigid river of melting ice raced down the middle of my back and sent me shivering – more than I already was. "Do you regret coming?" I asked.

"Hell, yes," he answered. "Oh, hell, no," he then said. "There's no telling George, I mean Major Washington, no. Once he gets an idea in his head he can't be stopped. Providence guides him, he always says. I'll just have to sleep extra close to the fire each night to dry out. If I survive."

"Good luck," I muttered. "Looks like this storm means to settle in."

"What about you?" Van Braam asked. "Why are you here? I'm the interpreter, and a poor one at that. Gist is our guide. Those fellows are our muscle." He pointed to a grand total of three men whom Washington had hired at Wills Creek. The trio trudged on foot behind us. They slipped with each step in the slushy mud of the slope. "It's clear Dinwiddie is funding this *most important* mission on the cheap, so why have an extra body along?"

Van Braam clearly didn't put much faith in a positive outcome for our assignment. In truth, neither did I. "I work for Croghan. And in my short time out west, I've been all over these parts. I know some of the customs of the people. I know a little of the language. Maybe that's why I'm here. Croghan has an interest to see Ohio open to trading."

"Gist can do all those things you said," Van Braam answered, doing anything to make the conversation last a little longer. Anything to forget the miserable conditions.

I bristled as a gust of wind howled, slapping pellets of ice needles into my cheeks. "Gist works for the Ohio Company! You can't trust them." I sounded more like Croghan than myself. I had heard him say it enough. "A bunch of land speculators! Croghan has to have somebody he trusts out here. Besides, I know the Half King." I said it as if Chief Tanaghrisson and I were longtime friends.

"Who is the Half King?" Van Braam asked.

"Only the most important Indian from Ohio to New York and down to Virginia!" I snapped, acting as if the Dutchman was a complete idiot for not having heard of him. I would never tell him I had no idea who the Half King was until a year ago. "He's a Seneca member of Onondaga – that's the ruling council for the Iroquois League. He's their king!" And then I went on, spouting all I knew and making up some things I didn't. All of it was meant to make it sound like I held the keys to a ship load of information. But if Van Braam had had just an extra moment to probe my story, he, and everyone else would have known I was full of nonsense. Maybe they would have shut me up. Maybe lives, thousands of lives, would have been saved.

"King, you say?" said Washington falling back with his horse next to us. "Of the Iroquois? Near the Forks of Ohio?"

He was a Half King, but I didn't correct the major. "Yes, sir. Chief Tanaghrisson," I said. "Not only does he speak for the Iroquois, but all the other tribes as well." I never mentioned that Shingas, the Delaware chief, had peaceably won his independence at last year's Logstown Conference. "He's a king and I know him," I proclaimed, pushing my chest out against my clinging coat.

What would my father think of me stretching the truth for no good reason other than to make myself feel important? Oh, that's right. I didn't care what he would think. We didn't see eye-to-eye on a good many things.

"Well, then, Mr. Weber," Washington breathed, icicles forming on his eyebrows. "This is the first time I've found a legitimate reason for Mr. Croghan to have burdened me with your presence. Ride ahead to Mr. Gist and see that he takes us to this king's village."

"His name is Chief Tanaghrisson," I said, again hunching against the cold. But the major hadn't heard me. He had already curbed his horse back to chat with the tough men travelling on foot.

"Congratulations, Weber," Van Braam said as a particularly brutal gust of wind whipped over the mountain above and belted us in the face, bringing slivers of ice with it. "Now all we have to do is survive the journey."

CHAPTER TWELVE

Our days were spent under constant toil, continually ascending and descending hills made sloppy with mud. At night, it would snow or rain or sleet or some dismal combination of all three. By midday, the sun would melt the newest accumulation except what was in the lowest, shaded valleys.

Never once did I feel warm.

My nighttime hours were consumed with shivering beneath damp blankets, cowering under trees. We all silently warred over the precious real estate that was within an arm's length of the fire. During the short and infrequent hours that I actually slumbered, I dreamt of a real bed with warm, dry blankets. I dreamt of Tahki, the sweat on her brow as we made love, the way her breasts slowly rocked as I pressed my body against hers. At times these pleasant, yet bitter, memories left me disconcerted. As the days passed since her death, I found that the details of her face faded. Oftentimes, I'd awaken while it was still dark. Not only was I still freezing, but whenever my dreams lacked Tahki's face, I was left angry.

Twice during our outbound trip the face of the woman sharing my marital bed was that of Bess. My mind had to conjure up what her naked body would look like. I found the task pleasurable. But then when I awoke feeling momentarily chipper, I was soon rewarded with guilt.

When my eyes snapped open to the smell of tea this morning, I needed no mirror to know that my face wore a broad grin. The imagery with Bess had been particularly vivid. I rolled over and tried to return to my dream.

"She must be quite something," John Fraser said from over my shoulder. I heard him rattling a pot and pouring boiling water into cups for all of us. "If those moans of yours were anything but the yips of love, I don't what are."

I groaned and rolled to face him. It was obvious I wasn't going to get back to sleep. I stared up at him, standing in just his trousers. His chest and feet were bare. My dreams had put my bare chest against that of Bess. I smiled.

"See there," Fraser said, stooping to hand me a cup. "To be young again and have a young man's dreams."

I remembered then that last night had been the first night since we'd left Wills Creek that we'd slept with a roof over our heads. It was a crude roof, to be sure. The quarters were cramped as all seven of us joined the owner in sleeping on his floor of packed dirt. But it was mostly dry inside John Fraser's isolated cabin.

I sat up and sipped at the hot liquid. It burnt my tongue, a welcome change to the frigid temperatures we had endured for weeks. The warmth of the cup seeped into my hands and I closed my eyes to relish the moment.

"See there," Fraser said as the other men began to stir from beneath their blankets. "I'd want to go back to my dreams, too, if I was you. Look at that tent you've got pitched in your lap. What's her name?"

"Bess," I said without thinking. I bunched the covers up at my waist to mask my erection. "Tahki," I added.

"Bess Tahki," he repeated. "Indian girl, huh? They make as good a companion as any, sometimes better."

"Just Tahki," I corrected him.

Fraser stepped over Van Braam as he rolled himself awake. The trader then squatted in his corner and took a sip of his tea. There was not a lick of furniture in his tiny cabin. "You know Chief Memeskia, Old Briton, God rest his soul, had a daughter called Tahki. Saw her on one of my trips out west. Stunning thing. She was going to make some Miami husband a happy man for many years. Now, after the massacre, I suppose she's hauled away making babies for an Ottawa or Chippewa dog. Poor thing."

Gist crawled out of his covers. "That same Tahki was Weber's wife," he warned our host. His eyes dropped at the same time as his voice. "She died in the massacre." At this point in our trip, Gist still seemed a reasonable man to me.

"Oh, no," Fraser said, genuinely saddened. "Sorry to hear it. But, Ephraim, you'll not soon forget the face of that angel."

As you know I had actually begun forgetting her face. "What do you know?" I barked, angrier with myself for dreaming of Bess and not my wife last night.

Fraser chuckled. "A whole lot," he answered. "Live on the frontier long enough and you'll see your fair share of tragedy. I've had a couple of my own wives die out here. A couple women who weren't really my wives died carrying my children, as well." He patted the wall of his home. "But my small trading post provides me with a living. It will provide me with another wife soon enough. There's always some Indian willing to trade a young woman for a bottle of rum."

I threw the steaming cup of tea at him. None of the water splashed against him, but the cup itself bounced harmlessly off his arm that he'd raised to block it. "What's your problem?" he growled.

"You're my problem!" I snapped. "My wife died carrying my child, too! But she died when a Frenchman shot her in the belly with her own pistol!" I reached into my pack and tugged out the gun, waving it all around. "And here it is. She didn't have a chance to give birth. Didn't have a chance to get away. And I'll not take another wife so soon as you. They aren't just some trade good that shows up at a post to be taken or given for the price of liquor!"

Fraser settled back onto his haunches and shrugged as he inhaled the aroma of his tea. "That's what you say."

I stood and leveled the pistol at him, bringing the hammer back. "*This* is what I say!" It is strange how my own sin of lusting after Bess, made me so angry with Fraser. I believe I would have killed him that morning.

Had Washington not burst in from the cold. He slammed the door behind him and was speaking as he brushed a lake's worth of water from his cloak. "Mr. Gist, you say that Mr. Fraser's cabin is not far from the Forks of Ohio. I should think you are eager to take me there and yet here you sit nestled inside." The major stopped dead in his tracks when he finally looked up and saw me pointing the ornate pistol at our host.

When he fixed me with his pale gray-blue eyes I was left convicted and speechless. "Mr. Weber," he began slowly and quietly. "Your utility to me and this mission began in a most limited fashion. It has only grown slightly since I've come to discover your acquaintance with Chief Tanaghrisson. But I warn you that the worth I place on your attendance is far from unlimited. Lay down the weapon."

Embarrassed, I carefully released the hammer and set the gun onto my blankets. Washington stood tall with his long limbs held straight while he examined the half-thawed, half-awake men scattered throughout the room. "What provoked this incident?" he asked.

I wasn't going to say anything. In truth Fraser had done little beyond uncouth talk to invite the near assault. Gist intervened. "They got to talking about their wives, major. Fraser said something that upset young Ephraim here."

"Is this true?" Washington asked me.

I nodded, ashamed. And knowing that he was a proper gentleman, I wondered just what type of military justice the major would devise for my punishment.

Instead Washington bent down and slung his pack over his shoulders before resting his hand on the latch. "Mr. Fraser, the bond between a man and his wife is sacred. I do not need to know what was said. But you will give this man an apology for the insult. And you shall not join in our party as we travel onward."

I do not think Fraser cared at all that he was required to apologize for something he didn't really do. But I do believe he was upset that he'd not come with our group to march among the French and Indians. He had spoken of grand plans to make further trading contacts, of the legal and illegal variety.

"Mr. Fraser," Major Washington repeated in encouragement. His pace was slow and deliberate.

"Best do it, John," Gist told his longtime acquaintance. The other men, including Van Braam had decided it best to say nothing and move little.

Fraser stood and scattered his tea into the roaring fireplace. He dropped the cup into the dirt at his feet. "Oh, dear little Ephraim Weber, I am sorry your savage wife died in such a manner. And I am sorry that I ever said anything to hurt your dainty feelings."

I bolted toward him, but Van Braam reached out from his blanket and tripped me. By the time I landed with a thump, he had already wrapped his arms around my legs, fixing me in place. I rolled and struggled for a moment, but when I glanced up, I saw Washington bending over me. He studied me with a grim face. I had to stop my thrashing just to hear him.

"Mr. Weber," he said. "We men of America, being so far removed from Mother England, have had to learn to govern ourselves, our towns, our provinces. It is most difficult to restrain our own emotions, yet it is not impossible." He pointed toward Fraser. "There is nothing that man or any other can do that ought to cause you to lose control of yourself." The major dropped his pack next to me and began fishing through it. In time he produced a book, dropping it from a height down to my chest. Thud. "*Dialogues of Seneca the Younger*," he said as if I would have any idea what that meant. Then Washington pulled out a second book. I braced to receive it, but this one he held. "And Addison's *Cato*. You'll read this one after you've read the other."

Washington stuffed the second book into his pack and lifted the whole thing onto his back. "Gentlemen, we leave in five minutes. His majesty thanks you for your hospitality, Mr. Fraser. Good day." He darted through the door.

And, as the others hustled about trying to shove food down their gullets and get dressed, Fraser and I stared at one another with a newly planted hatred sown in a bed of very little reasoning.

CHAPTER THIRTEEN

"Yes!" Washington exclaimed, unable to hide his bubbling excitement. We had made it to the swollen banks of the Monongahela where it and the Allegheny came together to form the mighty Ohio River. Across the icy river sat the very place where the Half King had allowed Croghan and his men to place a fort. Not a stick had been cut or hammered into place since the Logstown Conference. Things moved slowly on the frontier if Croghan wasn't around to spur action. And he had been tied up with his vast set of responsibilities for over a year. But I was certain that the wily Irishman would see the fort built soon enough. He always followed through on his promises. "The Forks of Ohio."

The major's gelding stomped aggressively along the shoreline. The creature was not quite as beautiful as it had been when we'd left Williamsburg nearly a month earlier. It had lost weight. Every horse had lost muscle and fat. So had every man.

Chunks of ice floated to the edge, bounced off rocks, and careened back toward the center of the frigid water. "Remarkable," Washington said. "Let's cross."

Van Braam, who had not once been forced to use his limited linguistic skills, cleared his throat. "The river is swollen, Major Washington. Wading through a babbling brook is one thing. But a man could die in that mess."

Washington would not argue. "Suit yourselves," he muttered, before directing his beast into the strong current. Whether on purpose or accident, he cut a heroic figure as he stood tall in the stirrups. The obstacles of frosty water and tumbling ice the size of a hogs gave him no pause.

Those of us on the shore were frozen in place as we watched the water rise above the horse's fetlock and cannon then the knee and forearm. A chunk of ice bounced off Washington's shin when the water was up to his calves and swirling into the tops of his boots. Still the major kept his gaze ahead, only murmuring to calm his beast. I cannot say what the others thought of our young, inexperienced leader at that point. I still believed he was gullible, but something about his bravery – or was it bald ambition – made me admire him.

Soon enough, the water level dropped as he and his mount crossed over halfway and began to climb out from the icy waters. He emerged, dripping wet, on the other side which was nearly a quarter mile away. He reined his beast to face us. We could see that he shouted, but could not hear him above the rushing waters.

"I suppose he wants us to make canoes or rafts to take us and the animals across," said Gist. The dense forest that surrounded us would provide ample raw materials for our boats.

While Washington padded his horse around to survey the land across the river, we spent the next five hours carrying out his wishes. And not one of us felt embarrassed from taking the safer and dryer route across. We would leave the heroics to the major.

When we were through, I held a coat over my pathetic horse's eyes as we crossed the river on a raft. It would do no good to have a spooked animal jump into the icy water and get itself or one of us killed. One of the strong trappers who had come along as our protection used a pole to shove against the bottom and propel us across.

Gist was on another raft that floated nearby. "Sorry about Fraser this morning," he said. "Awful way to talk about your wife after what happened. Once you get to know him, he's a fair man."

"I'd rather not get to know him," I said.

"In either case, you did well," Gist said. "Fraser's proven useful to us, but in the end he still competes with Croghan. And he'd compete with the Ohio Company if given the chance. It's best he's not with us as we move north from here."

I looked at Gist in profile as he patted his horse's shoulder in a soothing manner. As he had spoken to me his tone had been friendly, but it was clear he cared little for what had happened to my wife and her father at Pickawillany. He was just happy that Fraser wasn't along on this trip to muscle in on his future profits.

"This site is extremely well situated for a fort," said Washington as the rafts bumped into the opposite bank. He indicated the ever-so slight rise of land behind him. "High ground, well above the high-water line." The major then pointed to where the two rivers collided together into a single body heading northwest. "With absolute command of both rivers feeding the Ohio." The outside of Washington's boots were covered in ice from his crossing of the Monongahela. I was afraid to imagine what was happening to his cold feet inside the rigid leather.

Gist and I filed off our rafts, leading our beasts. The Ohio Company man uncovered his creature's eyes and tied it to a sapling some distance from the shore. Soon the temporary ferrymen were shoving back to the south bank to gather up Van Braam and what was left of supplies.

"Mr. Weber," Washington ordered. "While we wait, march two hundred fifty broad paces in along this line." His long arm acted like a sign post pointing into the woods. "You'll find a natural clearing. I want you to begin to widen it so that Croghan's men will know exactly where I intend their fort to be constructed for maximum effect."

While I obediently fished out an ax, Gist raised his eyebrows. "Where did you learn the craft of military engineering, Major Washington?" he asked.

Washington hopped from his horse. "I have spent a half dozen years surveying the wilderness for Lord Fairfax. What I did not learn about the attributes of land from firsthand experience, I acquired from the written works of the masters. And, Mr. Gist, run along with Mr. Weber. See that several trees are felled."

Gist sighed, but complied, knowing that to argue with someone with the bearing of George Washington, no matter his youthful inexperience, was futile. He and I marched inland while the major waited for the others at the shore.

It was drizzling again by the time we found the clearing and set our axes to singing. "You know," Gist said between swings. "We could use a good man working for the Ohio Company."

"They've got you," I said, noticing that I landed three strikes to his one.

"And I'm their chief man in the Ohio Country. You seem handy in the wilderness. You know a thing or two about the Indians. Ever think about leaving Croghan and working for us?" he asked, setting the head of his ax in the muck at his feet. He leaned on the handle.

I went right on chopping. "What do you need me for?"

Gist set his ax between two fallen logs, parallel to the ground. He used it as a dry place to sit. "Croghan doesn't just pull in anybody as his helper, especially someone so young. Then he sends you on this important trip without supervision. He must see something in you. I'd like you to use whatever that talent is for us."

So Gist wasn't even sure what I could do for him. He only knew that he wanted to deprive Croghan of my skills, such as they were. "Nah," I said.

"You'll make a fortune," he coaxed. "Maybe you can even get paid in Ohio Company shares. When the settlers come streaming into these parts from Virginia, selling the land will make us all rich."

"You mean selling the land that you told Shingas and the Half King wouldn't be sold to settlers," I accused, now setting the head of my ax into the mud. Slowly, the tree on which I'd been working creaked. It began to tip, groaning and whining all the way down until it landed with a whoosh amidst cracking branches. I peered around into the woods surrounding us that had been left quiet in the fallen tree's wake. Something seemed amiss, but I could see or hear nothing.

"The Half King knows exactly what is going on," Gist said, smugly defending his actions. "Do you actually think he cares what happens to the Delaware that have settled here? Does he have any love for Shingas? They are enemies as ancient as the waters of the Monongahela. He'd sell the Delaware tribe out for a few pounds of sterling silver or some of Croghan's Madeira. It's his adopted tribe, the Seneca, he loves. And his beloved Iroquoia." There was that antiquated term, Iroquoia, again. Gist raised his finger to make a further point. "And, by the way, Shingas would do the same to your friend the Half King."

He was right that the various tribes of North America had perpetually been at one another's throats. The coming of the French and English had done nothing to unify them. But my impression of Chief Tanaghrisson was that he was, or at least attempted to be, above the pettiness of lesser men.

I hefted my ax and moved to another tree, a tall straight beech. Soon I had carved out a wedge-shaped crease. "You think you're better than me?" Gist asked, clearly interpreting my silence. "I come to find land for settlers. But what are you doing out here?"

"Trading," I answered as large chips of green wood spilled onto my feet.

"Ha, trading will bring profits and men to the Forks of Ohio just as sure as my plans. The paths lead to the same end," Gist said. "The Half King knows it. At least he is smart enough to earn what he can for his family along the way. To the extent Shingas fights against it, he will be less wealthy, or dead."

I paused my cutting, again studying the forest over his shoulder. "Maybe you'd better talk less and chop more," I suggested. "You know as well as I that the woods have ears."

Gist smiled. "Wise beyond your years," he conceded while rising with ax in hand. "The Delaware could be watching us even now, ready to report back to Shingas that no matter which empire rules here, English or French, his way of life is at an end." Gist held out his hands wide and faced his chest toward the north woods. "But even if those Delaware spies kill me, within a decade there will be a thousand others in my place. It is inevitable."

Through the drizzle I saw the flicker of an eye. It was the raw, angry eye of a man bent on murder. "Down!" I shouted as I dove onto Gist from behind. We slammed into the semi-frozen mud just as a solitary musket shot rang out. Chunks of wood belched from the tree I had dropped earlier as the flying ball just missed our heads.

A frustrated Indian war whoop cried out and I saw the underbrush scurry and shake as the lone spy I had sensed earlier ran away. "I knew you'd be of value to me," Gist said as we climbed up to our feet covered in mud. He grinned victoriously while extending his hand. "Be smart, lad. Be like the Half King and choose expediency and riches over some high-minded notion of virtue."

Washington, Van Braam, and the others burst into the clearing, guns drawn and ready for action. "What's the trouble, Mr. Weber," the major asked.

"No trouble," I said, ignoring the outstretched hand of Christopher Gist. I took up my ax once again. Soon, chips from the pale-barked beech were again pouring into the muck. "Just tell Mr. Gist that next time he wants to try to kill himself, to make sure he's nowhere near me."

"Then drop a few more trees, gentlemen," Washington ordered as he and the rest retreated toward the shore. "And try to be more careful with your firearms."

Gist looked at his empty hand. I had signified as clearly as I could that I would not accept his offer of a job. He awkwardly rolled his fingers through his palm and brought it to his side. "I can't decide what's worse," he muttered, clearly wanting me, and no one else, to hear him. "Is it an inexperienced, but earnest, Virginia major who is much too willing to tempt fate and invite death. Or, is it a high-minded Quaker fool who doesn't use the sense his peaceful God gave him." He took up his ax and lazily began working on a tree at the opposite end of the clearing.

I had probably made another enemy. Two in one day. Fraser in the morning. Gist in the evening.

But what Gist did not understand about my personality is something that Croghan had immediately understood in our first meeting at a frontier trading post a few years earlier. It is what Tahki and Chief Memeskia had quickly gathered. And why the Miami chief had allowed me to marry his favorite daughter in the first place. Soon Washington and Van Braam would come to appreciate its value. It was a trait that was more important to men and women of knowledge than anything else I could offer. It was more significant than map reading, hand-to-hand combat, negotiating prowess, wealth, and any of a hundred other things.

Once I had promised to do something, I did it. Money wasn't going to change that. Whether the task involved taking care of Croghan's frontier interests in his stead or carrying out my threat to kill Ensign Jumonville, the chore – any chore – would be completed.

Once I made a pledge or oath to a man or a cause, I stuck with it to the end.

You see, I was, and still am, loyal.

CHAPTER FOURTEEN

The next day we stood in the very same clearing in which I had first met the Half King. It was wetter, colder, all around less hospitable, and much less populated. All of the lesser chiefs I had met at the prior Logstown Conference were sensibly in their home villages, staying warm for the winter. Only Shingas, who had been unfortunate enough to be traveling through, was standing with his bodyguard of warriors spread out behind him. I recognized one of the warriors as having been the man who had shot at Gist the night before at the Forks of Ohio. That particular warrior watched me closely, not caring that I knew. Perhaps he even reveled in my knowledge and fear. Shingas listened to the major with bored incredulity.

"As I've said," Washington went on earnestly. His voice was quieter than usual, which forced the seemingly indifferent Delaware chief to lean forward if he hoped to gather anything of meaning. "I shall not discuss topics of worth until Chief Tanaghrisson arrives. I am told he is a king among the Iroquois."

"He is a Half King," Shingas corrected, but Washington thought nothing of it. My modest overstatement of the facts about Tanaghrisson's leadership status – a lie in common parlance – was safe for the moment. "I, however, am King of the Delaware, recognized in this very spot. You may say to me whatever your distant king wishes."

"I speak only when Tanaghrisson is present," Washington insisted with soft firmness. "It is commonly understood that the Iroquois, having won the Beaver Wars, now speak for the various tribes under their jurisdiction. It will do me no good to waste time discussing things with a member of the Delaware, whether or not he calls himself a king. I'll only talk to a real king."

"Tanaghrisson's a Half King," Shingas said again.

Washington ignored the man he'd already decided was not in a true position to discuss political affairs. "And I've summoned Tanaghrisson from his hunting trip. I'm told he'll be here shortly."

"*You* summoned *him*?" Shingas said, smiling as he sized up the tall major with the perfect posture. He also eyed our thinning horses that were tied up to a line behind us. They had continued to lose weight. More than one of them would soon be lame. "A boy of not twenty summers *summons* this Iroquois he thinks a king? He who may be controlled by a whelp is not much of a ruler."

"My twenty-second birthday fast approaches," Washington corrected the Delaware king in a manner which was supposed to refute the assertion of the major's callowness. "I sent Tanaghrisson a wampum belt as a sign of friendship. I'm certain he will heed its call."

"He comes to every command from the English," Shingas said derisively. "Or the French. In that way, he is like the rest of his Iroquois members of Onondaga. They are ever careful to curry favor with whomever will give them the most riches. Or is it table scraps fit for the dogs they are?"

Washington refused to take the bait. He remained composed. His face suddenly struck a curious pose. "Speaking of the French, Chief Shingas, have you come across any Frenchmen of late? More than usual?"

"Of course I've seen more French than usual. Our French fathers build a string of new forts near here," he grumbled in a manner that plainly indicated his intense displeasure at the interlopers. My ears perked up. Shingas and perhaps his people were not overflowing in their support of the French – a positive sign.

"Very good," Washington said, nodding. "I'll invite you to speak at the coming conference when the time is right. You may relay what you know about the French." He rubbed his chin, thinking. "So our information is correct. The French are making significant inroads on His Majesty's Ohio Country."

It was probably not the best stroke of diplomacy to claim the ground on which we stood belonged to King George II, a man sitting thousands of miles away. Shingas, if he'd been angry about the French a moment before, bristled at the group of Englishmen standing in front of him. With frustrated sarcasm, the Delaware king said, "I thank you for your kindness in allowing me the chance to speak at your gathering of friends."

The major was not completely tone deaf. He sensed the hostility, but decided to continue his earnest course. "You are welcome, Chief Shingas," he said with a slight bow.

"But I can help you more than simply speaking at the conference," Shingas went on. "Won't it be better to have a Frenchman or two in attendance? Why not three?"

Washington and I were taken aback. "Frenchmen? Here?" I asked. The last Frenchmen I had seen were dragging away captives from Pickawillany.

"Why, yes," Shingas said with a satisfied grin. "My company of men includes three of them. Why have one father when you can have three? I'll make certain they come to the assembly, Major Washington, my brother."

"Washington?" said a voice emerging from the wooded path to our side. We turned to see the Half King emerging. He was on foot, carrying a musket and the wampum belt Washington had sent him requesting a meeting. Behind him two men carried a deer carcass that hung from a pole strung between them. "I knew I was coming to meet an officer of my brother's army. But Washington? I know this name. It is the name of the Conotocarius."

Shingas' eyes involuntarily shot wide in surprise. He studied the major with a newfound respect. There was no love behind the gaze, only fearful admiration.

"What is Conotocarius?" I asked, seeing that the major was just as confused as me.

"Washington is the Conotocarius," the Half King answered, gesturing with the wampum belt.

"The Destroyer of Villages," Shingas interpreted.

CHAPTER FIFTEEN

Gist and I had obediently seen to starting the next Logstown council fire. It began with fits as a single plump snowflake was enough to extinguish the nascent flame. And many snowflakes were falling. Thankfully, there was no wind to speak of and the damp snow was actually quite beautiful as it silently dropped and stuck to everything in sight. But a quarter of an hour later we had the kindling roaring well enough to add a fat log or two.

"You burn a campfire much better than you burn a pipe, my brother, Shit-for-brains," the Half King said to me. He reclined comfortably on a chair which had obviously been built by a Quaker in Eastern Pennsylvania and then lugged over the Alleghenies to his small village. It had been dragged out from the Half King's home by one of his grandchildren. It, along with some simple logs, had been arranged beneath a tarpaulin stretched overhead. Washington and the others sat on the damp logs, occasionally wiggling when the dampness soaking through their breeches became unbearable.

Croghan's training had worn off on me so I didn't react to the Half King's insult. Besides, the sparkle in his eye told me he was joking in a good-natured way. "Thank you for noticing, Chief Tanaghrisson," I said as I settled beneath the canopy. I was situated near the edge and so the falling snow soon blanketed one shoulder.

The Half King turned to Washington. "It is difficult to miss a young man vomiting around the fire of peace," the chief chuckled, playfully remembering our last encounter.

The major had not seemed to enjoy the nickname given me by the Half King. Nor did he find any humor in the picture of me throwing up in this clearing. "I see," he said, clearly wishing that his mind had not conjured any image whatsoever. "And so how do you and Mr. Weber know one another?" he asked, testing the validity of my story. Of course, I had proven myself a liar in my first meeting with the major.

The Half King examined his earnest young counterpart. At length when it became clear that Washington was skipping directly to business, he shrugged and answered. "Mr. Weber, as you call my brother Shit-for-brains, was in attendance here at last year's conference. I dare say that without his testimony, I could never have agreed to your Ohio Company constructing a fort at the Forks of Ohio."

Pleased with the response, Washington gave me a polite nod. "Your moniker notwithstanding, it appears your mind and presence are of value to me and His Majesty, Mr. Weber."

"Yes, Shit-for-brains," Shingas said, interrupting and giving the Half King an icy glare. His tone carried none of the good-natured charm of Tanaghrisson. "Nor could I have agreed to the fort's construction. As King of the Delaware, do not forget that I, too, must be placated."

"Of course," Washington said as a throw away courtesy. He focused all his energy on the man whom he believed to be the true king in the region, Tanaghrisson. "What is this Conotocarius you mentioned?" the major asked. "I have never destroyed any village."

"Not yet," Shingas muttered.

"Brother Shingas!" the Half King barked in rebuke, sitting up tall in his chair. He said no more, but faced the major. "My tribal fathers told me of a man named John Washington who was the first Conotocarius. His reputation casts a long shadow from the late wars when the Iroquois and the English madly killed one another. Are you related to such a man?"

"My great-grandfather was named John," Washington answered. "He fought in several wars against the Susquehanna. But he has been dead for nearly eighty years."

The Half King offered a sad smile. "He was a worthy adversary who is still mentioned around the winter fires of my people, for we now look after the remnants of the Susquehanna. It is the great task of the Iroquois to take care of our little tribes."

"Yes. I understand the place of the Six Nations and your place in it. And yet clearly, I am not John Washington," Washington said. "I have not earned such a nickname."

The Half King stretched his back against the thin spindles of his chair. "Nonetheless, it is a name you shall have to un-earn. Already a soldier of considerable rank at your age means you are well on your way." When the major opened his mouth to protest, the Half King shushed him with a wave of his fingers. "Do not take offense. Conotocarius is a name I bestow with profound respect."

Washington glanced at me with a puzzled expression. I could tell he wanted to mount a vocal complaint. I was fast learning that Major Washington was eternally focused on propriety and correctness. Being called a name that was not properly given was far from appropriate. "And what do you say, Mr. Weber?" he asked.

"Uh," I stuttered, thinking about all the negotiations I'd endured with recalcitrant traders, woodsmen, and Indians in the presence of Croghan. "I believe it is a strong name and one that is obviously well known in these parts. My brother, Chief Tanaghrisson, uses it for you as a sign of affection despite the negative connotation."

Still perplexed, the ever-sober major relented. "So be it, Chief Tanaghrisson. I shall be honored to answer to such a name. But in the cause of decency, I request that you address me by my rank in our provincial forces."

"Certainly, Major Conotocarius," the Half King said without the least bit of sarcasm. I believe he was truly warming up to our sincere major.

"And why is this fort that the master of Shit-for-brains promised us a year ago not yet built?" Shingas asked. He eyed our rather sad and cold group. "You men will not get much done."

Gist fielded this question. "Planning such an excursion takes time, even for Croghan. I should think the coming summer will see the initial stockade built. In time, more structures, earthen walls, and palisades will be constructed. But trading will commence immediately."

Shingas eyed Gist. His warrior-spy had clearly reported what Gist had said about the future of the Delaware and their king at the Forks. "Well, I should think that my French fathers will soon lounge in their beds in these very woods if you wait much longer," Shingas ridiculed. He raised his hand and waved to one of his warriors who was stationed just outside the flapping door of an Indian lodge. The warrior acknowledged the silent command and ducked inside.

Washington proudly patted his breast where beneath his layers of clothing he still carried Dinwiddie's letter. "Chief Shingas, your English brothers take the unlawful invasion by the French very seriously. There is no reason to think that it will continue."

"You speak of war?" Shingas asked, not the least bit concerned. "Our English brothers wish to fight our French fathers?"

"Only if necessary," Washington said with a surety that comes either with true foreknowledge or, on the other hand, with extreme inexperience.

"Let us pray it doesn't come to that," the Half King said with a despondent shake of his head. "Even with the great Conotocarius on our side, much suffering would occur."

"A wise sentiment," Washington said.

"So what do you want from us?" Shingas asked. He had involuntarily shivered from the damp cold. His warrior who had been perched at the distant house door now approached with three men in tow. Each of the followers was clearly of European extract. All wore the breeches of regular French military men, though the pants were soiled and worn to such a degree as to indicate they had not been in sight of a strict French officer for many weeks. The length of their beards demonstrated a similar amount of time had passed since razors had been scraped against their faces. Shingas grinned as if he had something hidden up his buckskin sleeve.

Washington saw them, too. They began to squeeze beneath the tarpaulin as the major answered. "Virginia's governor requests Indian escorts for our party for the remainder of our journey. We know that there are new French forts nearby. And though we know exactly where they are located, Governor Dinwiddie asks that I bring along as many of our brothers, our Indian allies, as are willing to make the trip." We actually had no idea where the newest French forts were located. Williamsburg had been informed of their general placements by the rumors spread by traders, smugglers, and frontiersmen.

Honest Washington was proving that even he could adapt his principles for wilderness living.

"I presume a simple Virginian provincial soldier does not speak French," Shingas said in a condescending tone to Washington.

"I do not," Washington conceded, disappointment in his lack of formal education dripping in his tone.

"Then I shall gladly translate what my French fathers have to say," Shingas offered, undoubtedly all-too happy to act as a gatekeeper of the information.

"Oh," Van Braam interrupted the Delaware chief. "Ce n'est pas nécessaire." He then turned to the party of Frenchmen and asked, "Quel est le nom du fort le plus proche?"

Shingas, defeated in his small gambit, angrily folded his arms in front of his chest and buttoned his mouth beneath a curled lip.

"Fort Machault est le plus proche," said one of the French newcomers.

"Fort Machault is the closest," Van Braam translated, giving Washington an amicable grin at being able to effectively utilize his translation skills for the very first time.

Another Frenchman then argued with the first. The third joined in after that. I understood a little French. A trader had to speak a few words of the language if he wanted to survive on the road with Croghan. Half the tribesmen we had come across since I ran away from home spoke at least some French. But the pace these men set was too much for me.

Van Braam concentrated, watching their rapid-fire mouths. "One of them is saying that the others should shut up and not say anything to the tall English officer. The first man is telling the second man to mind his own business. The third is saying that we should not go to Fort Machault, but rather to Fort LeBoeuf. The most senior officer can be found at LeBoeuf."

Washington smiled at all the valuable intelligence he was gathering with little effort. Already, he had learned more about the French military plans in the Ohio Country of America than every royal officer here or in Britain.

The argument slowly settled with the two who had elected to share information winning over the cantankerous one. For his part, the loser angrily strutted back to the relative warmth of the house at which they'd been staying.

"All three are deserters from the French post at Venango – they call it Machault," Van Braam explained as the excitement died down. "They were set to be placed on trial for some minor crime but, rather than face punishment, they left about a month ago. They fell in with Chief Shingas, who is guiding them southward to safety."

Major Washington examined the men with disappointed contempt. They could hardly help being born to French parents. Washington understood that there were men of noble character represented in all nationalities. But these three could have certainly avoided whatever crime they had committed, let alone compounding the dishonor by proving themselves deserters. The major drew the corners of his mouth back as he considered his next move. At length he said, "Then we will merely pass through Venango on the way to this Fort LeBoeuf. Ask them the name of the commanding officer at LeBoeuf."

Van Braam translated the major's question. There was some minor yapping between the remaining two French deserters before our Dutchman translator said, "They say it is Captain Jacque Legardeur de St. Pierre. He is an experienced soldier who was not given his rank via simple patronage."

"Thank them for the information, Mr. Van Braam," Washington said.

"And ask them if they know of a French officer by the name of Jumonville," I interrupted, quite out of place. Even so, I held out little hope that these deserters, stationed where they were, would know anyone from distant Fort Detroit.

"Jumonville?" the Half King asked, surprised.

Van Braam looked to Washington for confirmation of my misplaced order. The major, recently pleased with me, gently waved for him to proceed. To my surprise the conversation took longer than I had anticipated. When Van Braam was done, he said, "They say they know two officers by that name. They are brothers. One is a captain, the other an ensign."

I shoved my way past several men toward the center of the canopy, unintentionally dropping snow from my shoulder onto Gist's head. He elbowed me, holding none of his force back. I ignored the assault. "The ensign," I breathed while all eyes had fallen on me and my sudden excitement. "What is the ensign's name?" Though I was sure there could be only one.

The two Frenchmen argued a moment before agreeing. Van Braam then translated. "The older brother is the captain. His name is Louis. The younger brother, the ensign, is Joseph."

I had found the murderer of my family. I pictured the ornate French pistol in its place among my tiny amount of baggage. It would soon find itself put to good use. But before that action, I would polish the piece until it shined brightly. What better way to snuff out a murderer's life than with a finely kept weapon? "And where are they, these brothers?"

"Mr. Weber," Washington said. "Is there anything beyond a personal nature for your interrogation?" The major made no pause to permit my answer. "I let you begin, which I am now coming to regret. We shall cease this line of inquiry."

"Where is Jumonville?" I asked Van Braam forcefully, ignoring the major. When our translator wouldn't convey my question out of his sense of duty to Washington, I looked directly at the French deserters and repeated the question in my own bastardized version of French.

Major Washington slowly stood up to his full height, facing me. His long reddish brown hair brushed the canopy. He was an imposing figure without making any attempt to enhance it. And though I had yet to see him lift a finger in anger or violence toward anyone, I swallowed nervously and retreated a step. The deserters held their tongue as they watched the spectacle. "Mr. Weber, you may remove yourself from these proceedings at once. We will discuss your behavior and its consequences presently," said the major.

My teeth ground involuntarily against one another as a surge of vitriolic anger flashed in my gut. My emotions raced from fear of Washington's authority to rage at his audacity. This gentleman major was going to deprive me of learning the whereabouts of the man who had butchered my wife, unborn son, and father-in-law. My right fist balled at my side.

"Shit-for-brains," said the Half King, who had quietly reached a hand and snatched my wrist before I could get myself into real trouble. The muscles beneath my damp clothes flexed in order to tear myself from the chief's grasp and punch Washington. For his part, the major watched the proceedings with unflinching curiosity. "Ephraim," continued the Half King. "Ensign Jumonville is the man who led the attack at Pickawillany, no?"

"He is," I seethed, slowly relaxing my arm. "And he executed an unarmed woman and unborn child." I stared again at the Frenchmen and this time shrieked, "Where is he?"

Not comprehending, or wishing they did not, they blinked at me, hoping to be hastily dismissed by Shingas.

"Mr. Weber," Washington began in his ever-quiet tone.

"Major Conotocarius," the Half King interrupted. "I approve of your desire for formality and manners. But in this case, I do not think it will do any harm to allow the young Quaker to find out the location of the man who has massacred his family. It pays to know the location of one's enemy. Is that not why you are here, to locate the French?"

Washington was baby-faced when compared to the near-regal Half King. But he did not let his youth stop him from asserting his authority. "Chief Tanaghrisson, I am on a mission of immense importance for the crown, for Virginia, for the Ohio Company, for the Iroquois and her subordinate tribes…"

"The Delaware are subordinate to no one," Shingas hissed.

Major Washington would not stop. "And I will not tolerate the inclusion of this man, Mr. Weber, no matter how justified he may be in his anger toward this Jumonville. Ephraim may just lash out for revenge and destroy our peaceful goals."

"You ask for Indian escorts to the French?" the Half King asked.

"The governor does," Washington admitted. "I merely act in his stead."

"Then I will come along with some of my representatives. If it pleases you, I will take it as my sole responsibility to make certain that young Shit-for-brains does nothing to provoke the French by attacking Ensign Jumonville."

Washington considered this suggestion from Tanaghrisson for a few moments. He did not want to upset the man whom he believed to be the key to English rule at the Forks of Ohio. "Very well," the major said.

The Half King faced Van Braam. "Then please ask the location of Ensign Jumonville so that we may conclude this portion of our talk."

After getting approval from Washington, Van Braam asked the deserters. They traded information with one another to verify what they knew. Eventually, our interpreter gave their best answer. "The Ensign was recently reassigned from Detroit to join his brother's command. The elder Jumonville, Louis, is stationed at Fort Niagara. But for some months the pair has been traveling back-and-forth between Niagara and LeBoeuf. The French command has plans for the coming year and it obviously involves the Ohio Country."

"Yes, but where is the ensign?" I pleaded, not caring a bit about the broader plans of the French. Washington, for his part, took note of the extra French activity in the Ohio watershed.

There was more speaking between Van Braam and the deserters. "The deserters have been gone long enough that they cannot be sure," our interpreter answered. "The weather may have stranded either or both of the brothers at Niagara or LeBoeuf."

"If he is not at LeBoeuf," I said to Washington. "Then we'll continue on to Fort Niagara. Besides there will be an even more senior French officer there than the one stationed at LeBoeuf. We should see them all evacuated."

The major slowly shook his head in disagreement. "Our mission is to request that the French honor King George II's rightful claims to the Ohio. Niagara is not in the Ohio Country. We go no further than LeBoeuf."

"And I will not risk a decline in weather to traipse up to the falls at my age," said the Half King, pleasantly agreeing with the major. "I will take your party to Fort LeBoeuf and not a step beyond."

And it was decided. I was angry, hungry for revenge. But I was not a complete fool. If I ran off by myself in the middle of winter looking for a French officer, I'd be dead from exposure or unfriendly Indians within a week. And my enemy would live out his days in bliss. Jumonville, if he wasn't at Fort LeBoeuf, would have to wait for his day of reckoning. Tahki's pistol would remain silent a while longer.

"And you, Chief Shingas," Washington said, glad to move on from my personal matters. "Will you and your party accompany us to bid the French goodbye?"

Shingas stood to examine the earnest major. "Will you acknowledge that I am King of the Delaware and that I alone speak for the well-being of my people?"

Washington was out of his element, though his inexperience did not allow him to see that fact. He bowed and pointed to the Half King. "I cannot single-handedly undo the hierarchy created in the many decades before this day. The Iroquois rightfully claim suzerainty over all of the region's tribes. Unless, Chief Tanaghrisson speaks something different, I cannot recognize you as such."

Shingas smiled and I knew why. The Half King had been forced to recognize him as King of the Delaware a year earlier. Gist and I were the only whites in attendance both times, but most of the Indian men under the canopy had been in the clearing to hear Tanaghrisson's proclamation. The Delaware chieftain awaited the words he longed to hear affirmed.

But the Half King was shrewd. He looked from Gist to me, affixing us both with a look that said *keep your mouths shut*. When he actually spoke, he said, "Chief Shingas, I believe that a king must be recognized as such by his merits, his peers, his neighbors. A man cannot claim with his lips to be king and it is miraculously so. If the English understand that the Iroquois speak for the Delaware and the Iroquois have been widely recognized as such, I will do nothing to jeopardize that longtime understanding."

Shingas physically shook with rage. His face, though it was below freezing outside, bubbled to a bright red as if it was the hottest day of the year. I am sure he briefly toyed with the idea of unleashing the product of his rage under the canopy, but a quick look around reminded him that he was in one of Tanaghrisson's towns of power and he and his warriors were badly outnumbered. The Half King, essentially having successfully revoked his recognition of Shingas as king, stared silently at his rival.

Washington did not want a full-blown fight on his hands. "Chief Shingas," the young negotiator began. "I understand your disappointment. But you must admit that the Iroquois have only the best intentions when they negotiate on your behalf. Now, in this case His Majesty, the governor, I, and, I'm sure, Chief Tanaghrisson would be honored to have you and your representatives join us as we complete our journey to expel the French."

"It is so," the Half King said, diplomatically resuming a posture that showed him to be a Whole King. "Come, my child."

"Mon pére Iroquois," Shingas said in perfect French. He had better control over the forms and structure of the language than did the deserters themselves. And the frustrated Delaware Indian went on and on, continuing in French, frequently gesturing and, no doubt, cursing along the way. When he was finished with his soliloquy, he turned and marched into the mud, not stopping as he snatched up his musket and trudged into the wilderness. His warriors followed in silence, the one who'd shot at Gist giving the Ohio man a snarl. The two French deserters called to their comrade who had hidden away in the home. When he reappeared, all three chased after their Indian guides, heading south.

"What did he say?" Washington asked when the party was well away.

"No?" I guessed sarcastically.

Washington fixed me with a disapproving glare.

"It's a little more than that," Van Braam said as snow flurries swarmed around and under the canopy. "Shingas says that if he cannot trust his Iroquois fathers or his English brothers, then he is forced to turn his back on them. He added that he is a man of honor. If the English build their fort at the Forks of Ohio, he will do nothing to stop it since he agreed to it in principle. However, should the French get there first, or dislodge us, he will support their effort with more than his words. Chief Shingas will take up the hatchet for his French fathers, the only ones who seem to understand a father's role. He gives his children gifts, he does not steal from them."

The news was weighty, but not devastating – at least to us then. In a few short years thousands of Pennsylvanian and Virginian frontier families would come to feel just how profound this moment had been. I even ventured another attempt at levity. "So, I was right. He's not coming with us?"

Washington glared at me with his quiet determination. He showed no hate. I don't think he ever had hate in him for any man. But I shrank from his sight. When he fastened me with those pale gray-blue eyes which conveyed nothing short of supreme disappointment, I was a convicted man. It is admittedly sacrilegious to say, but I looked on the countenance of God that day. As sure as if I had killed a man in cold blood in front of twenty impartial witnesses, I was guilty. Without a word from the major, I said, quite sheepishly, "I am sorry, Major Washington."

"I'm sure you are," he answered before stepping briskly into the pelting snow. "Make your preparations with haste, Chief Tanaghrisson. We leave for LeBoeuf tomorrow before dawn."

The Half King smirked at the intense young major who felt at ease ordering him and everyone else about. "Certainly," said Chief Tanaghrisson. "But may I make water first?"

Washington did not pick up on his humorous tone. He peered up into the gray, snowy sky. "Of course, but I'd not waste time." The major then resumed his march toward the lodge in which he had stowed his gear.

The meeting broke up at that point, with Indian men retreating to their warm houses. Members of our party followed after some of them, having been invited to stay inside for the night. After a time it was just the Half King sitting in his Quaker chair curiously examining me.

"Thank you," I told him. "But you take on a lot of responsibility for my behavior. Because if I see Ensign Jumonville, I will kill him in a most bloody way."

He nodded. "I am old enough to recognize hate in a boy's eyes." Tanaghrisson then rubbed his weathered cheeks as he pondered all that had transpired. He said nothing more, but tipped his chair up onto the back two legs. They squished into the wet, snowy mud. Whatever his mind considered must have included me because now and again he would glance in my direction. I had somehow been transformed from a bit player on the wilderness stage to someone he deemed important.

The silence was awkward. I felt inclined to confess. "I lied and told Washington that you and I were very good friends. I also told him you were a king."

"That was no lie," he said at last, slapping his knees and standing up in the mud. "We *are* friends. We've smoked the peace pipe together." He got a twinkle in his eye. "Well, I smoked it. I'm not sure what you did with it."

I smiled at the older man. I liked him. "But based on what I told him, Washington may think you are king of all these peoples," I confessed. "And Shingas *is* the King of the Delaware."

"Shingas *was* the king. No longer," Tanaghrisson said simply as he turned to brave the snowfall and walk to his lodge. "He needed to be put back in his place and you and Washington allowed that to happen. Onondaga rules the tribes. I am the local representative sent from that noble body, from the Tree of the Great Peace. I was adopted into the Iroquois League when stolen from my people as a child. It would do Shingas good to accept his fate and voluntarily join us, Iroquoia, now."

I watched him go. I realized then that the politics of the towns were not just the politics of the towns. They were the politics of men. And whether those men lived among the cobbled streets of port cities or among the never-ending canopy of oaks and maples, they brought their political positions with them. They would fight and cajole to achieve victory, no matter how minute.

The Half King had hesitated at the door to his home. "Clean the legs of my chair, Shit-for-brains," he called. "Bring it to me when you are finished. You will stay in my home with my family tonight. There we will discuss just what revenge on Ensign Jumonville must look like."

CHAPTER SIXTEEN

We were five days traveling to what the French called Fort Machault and what we called Venango. As we moved further north and the calendar pages dwindled closer to the year's end, the weather deteriorated. It alternated between snow, ice, and rain every single day. The trip was one of the most miserable in my long memory – and I've had many such adventures, as you'll see. Nonetheless, Washington was resilient and anxious to keep moving. He would not allow anything or anyone to impede our progress. The young man ordered us and our new Indian guides about in constantly polite, but firm, terms.

Our party tarried for only three days at Venango, enjoying the wine and conversation of the small cadre of French officers stationed there. Washington placated our hosts by telling them he had an urgent message for Captain Legardeur at Fort LeBoeuf. And just like he did with us, he tapped the folded papers in his breast pocket. Furthermore, mentioning the French captain by name, I think, gave our mission an air of legitimacy in the eyes of the strangers. The French officers didn't know if we were spies for the French monarch sent among the English or newly minted traitors to our own king.

If our sober major had gleaned a bushel's worth of information from the deserters we'd met at Logstown, he learned a storehouse worth during our three dinners with the French at Venango. Looking for any excuse to forget the dreadful temperatures, the French and their guests swilled many glasses of wine, to well-past the point of drunkenness. Our Indian guides succumbed to the blight of intoxication as well. The Half King and the three Mingo he'd brought with him fell into a stupor each night, snoring in corners or slumped over tables. But not Major Washington. He tentatively sipped at his glass, nursing the same one all night while probing the French soldiers for intelligence. Curious, I followed the major's temperate lead, while they unwittingly gave up supply schedules and troop placement in the Ohio Country. Washington would then diligently record everything in his journal when his fellow revelers fell asleep or unconscious.

It was now ten days after our departure from Venango. Through swamps and unending precipitation of the most monstrous varieties, we slogged. Our horses weakened with every passing day. I spent most of my time leading my sad creature. For the last half of a day, I'd taken more pity on the beast and lugged much of my supplies on my own back. Our pace was disgraceful. Exhausted, my shoulders slumped and I stooped like my spine belonged to a frail nonagenarian who'd been thrown from his horse one too many times.

But the Half King, teeth chattering and sneezing from illness, assured us we were close. So when darkness fell and we normally would have stopped to make camp in the mud, we pressed on. After what had happened at Pickawillany, I had never imagined that I would see a French outpost and have any warm or positive thoughts. And yet, that is exactly what I felt when we emerged from the thick, saturated wilderness to see a group of crude structures patched together with bark and planks. But it was the roaring bonfires behind the feeble walls that gave me profound hope. My heart leapt with excitement. For a few moments, I had forgotten that my adversary Jumonville might lurk within and that, with the Half King's promised assistance, I might soon be a murderer. I thought only of thawing out my tingling fingers and numb toes.

"We are here to treat with Captain Legardeur," Major Washington hummed after introducing himself with grave seriousness, his voice wavering from the cold. All of us, whites and Indians alike, pressed forward around the major and toward the gate that remained closed. We saw only the face of a Frenchman through a peephole bored in the heavy timber gate. "His Majesty, King George II of Great Britain sends his regards and his wishes."

Our spokesman, Van Braam, quickly communicated Washington's greetings and requests that we may be permitted to enter. The door to the peephole slammed shut and we heard squishing footsteps retreat on the other side. "He says we should wait," Van Braam chattered. He crossed his arms and rubbed his shoulders vigorously. Like me, he had walked on foot for the past several days. Except his horse had come up fully lame.

With no better options, we had abandoned his bay in the woods. Ravenous wolves or Indians had likely devoured it by now.

The Half King tugged a thick hide tightly over the European style coat he wore. "When he comes back, tell him that we'd prefer to walk home rather than wait."

Even Washington smiled. His chuckling matched the pace set by his shivering, however, so it was hard to tell when his mirth began and when it stopped. After what seemed to our freezing party like hours, the sentry returned and tore open the tiny peephole door, squawking to us in a formal, displeased manner. Then he slammed the small door closed.

"Captain Legardeur will receive you when he is ready," Van Braam told us as the large gate creaked open. Washington adjusted his uniform and posture, even though both were always the epitome of perfection. He would not allow us to pass through the gate until it yawned wide and the smattering of French troops who had come to inspect our strange band had seen him. The major appeared to have emerged like a specter from the bleak forest – like an impeccably dressed ghost, that is.

"We represent our country, men," he whispered, barely audible over the crackling of a welcoming bonfire that burned bright just twenty paces ahead. "Conduct yourselves accordingly."

Gist salivated at the sight of the blaze. The Half King and his warriors couldn't take their eyes off it. And in truth its undulating form was more alluring, more beautiful than the shapeliest woman I'd ever seen in the eastern towns. I wanted to break into a run and strip off my soaking clothes. I briefly toyed with the notion of diving straight into the flames. Anything would be preferable to the way my limbs slowly died with pins, needles, and icicles constantly poking them. But Washington's behavior, not his words, held me in check. He was as frozen as the rest of us. And yet there he stood, tall and proud, conveying more with saying nothing than if he had spouted off a thousand word treatise on the superiority of the Englishman over the French.

The major lifted off his hat and swung it down to his waist, bowing at the same time. The French corporal who had opened the gate gaped at us, for it wasn't every day that a mismatched band of men materialized from the darkness. "Eh, bienvenue," he said, taken off guard and managing only a curt nod.

"Thank you, sir," Washington said, replacing his hat and stepping inside. We pressed behind him, drooling over the sight of the fire. "Now we require food and warmth. Our horses, too, are in dire need of a respite. See to it that these men of yours that loiter about take good care of them. Meanwhile, you may lead us to a place of refuge so that we may be prepared to meet your commanding officer in a fashion expected of gentlemen in a civilized world."

The sheer audacity of the request, as Van Braam translated it, set the bewildered Frenchmen to action. The reins of our horses were taken and the creatures led to a tiny stable. The corporal splattered off ahead of us across the courtyard. We followed, walking directly past the fire. I ever-so-briefly felt its warmth brush across my left cheek. Then it was gone. I craned my head as the flames retreated in our wake and I wistfully longed to curl up next to it.

But the corporal led us to an even better place. It was tiny, dark, and cramped. In the dim light it resembled a jail cell. I had become a true frontiersman over the years and was therefore accustomed to shoddy structures. This rat trap of a building was among the worst I had encountered with a sagging wall and many drafts blowing in through cracks. But inside it was dry and, compared to the conditions we'd experienced over the previous month, exceedingly warm. It had a large fireplace where a low fire burned over glowing orange embers. A brick oven was situated at one side of the chimney. We wasted no time in stripping down to nearly complete nakedness once the Frenchman left us unattended in the bake house. Formal Washington was just as quick as the rest of us to shed his clothes and huddle next to the burning coals.

Slowly the feeling returned to my hands. I found the bakery's supply of wood and piled it high on top of the embers. Soon a roaring blaze swirled its way up the brick, sending tongues of flames right up the chimney. We were so cold that no one even considered warning me of the potential danger should the walls of the chimney catch fire. So maniacally and single-mindedly focused on finding warmth were we that a roaring chimney fire may have actually been preferable. Before long the soaking wet hair on top of our heads steamed as the temperature of the tiny shed climbed higher and higher. One-by-one we stopped shivering.

"Bread," said Gist when he found a few loaves leftover from the French fort's daily rations.

"Distribute it evenly, Mr. Gist," Washington ordered, certain that his French hosts had placed us in the kitchen for this very hospitable and nourishing reason. That bread – I received two chunks – was the tastiest bread I had ever eaten in my life until that point. Since then I've been hungrier and leaner and have eaten terrible things that to me tasted wonderful at the time. But that bland bread, on that cold December night, was most delicious.

As the minutes wore on, Washington's sense of propriety returned. He was the first to shake out his clothes and hang them near the blaze. Minutes later, the major was the first to rotate them and eventually climb back into them.

Hours later as the rest of us had all fallen asleep on the floor, he was the only one awake when the door to our bake house burst open. His anxious pacing had helped lull me to sleep in the first place. And it was his firm grasp that shook me from a pleasant dream involving Bess, the lovely girl I'd met for mere moments in Williamsburg. "Mr. Weber, as you represent the interests of Mr. Croghan, you will accompany Mr. Van Braam, Chief Tanaghrisson, and I to Captain Legardeur."

"Uh, huh," I mumbled and then rolled over to restart my dream. "See you in the morning." The tie that held Bess' bosom in place was perilously loose and ready to unveil her chest when he'd shaken me awake. I tried with all my might to begin the tale right where I left off.

"Mr. Weber," Washington said jerking me to face him as he crouched. "Clothe yourself. We are due to meet with the captain right now."

The thought of marching back into the weather outside, even if just across the courtyard, was unbearable. Washington saw my hesitation and the minor horror cross my countenance. I dropped back onto the ground with a heavy sigh. "Have you read the book I gave you?" asked the major.

"What?" I asked rubbing the gobs of welcome sleep from my eyes.

"*Dialogues of Seneca the Younger*," he said as if I should forever have the tome on my mind.

"Yes," I lied, quite perturbed by the question. I hadn't read a lick of the book. *When was I to read it*, I silently wondered. Should I have read it while the major had me gathering firewood for our night camps? Should I have perused its pages while marching through rain and snow and wilderness? Maybe he expected me to read it while I was sent out on a scouting trip to make sure the French or Indians weren't sneaking up on us.

"You have not," Washington quietly accused, not the least upset. "You harm only yourself by not taking advantage of what wisdom you can gather on your own. A lack of formal education has been most distressing to me in my life so I am determined to make up for it." He spoke as if he were many decades my senior. I had to remind myself that the serious individual was just a handful of years older.

He stood, reaching out a hand to pull me upright. I took it. "There," he whispered as he tugged with the French corporal standing over his shoulder. "Now quickly make yourself presentable. We proceed as a united corps."

I hurriedly dressed myself in my dry and warm clothes. They were still filthy from the trail, but the skin of my arms and thighs received the warm fabric as if they were newly made from a tailor of renown. Soon, I was again plodding through mud.

"You have a book about the Seneca, my adopted people?" the Half King asked as we crossed the yard.

"Yes," I said. Of course I didn't have anything of the sort. Washington's book was about some ancient Roman stoic. But I was sleepy and again felt the cold quickly creeping into my bones. My answer was better than explaining details.

The Half King looked ahead to where Washington marched almost in front of the corporal who was supposed to lead us to the French captain's office. "Major Conotocarius is a more informed man than I initially thought," said the chief. "It is wise to read about one's allies as well as enemies. If he has told you to read about the Seneca, then you should obey."

"I will," I said as we passed into another building. This one was a barracks. A narrow hallway ran straight in from the exterior door. A door on the left side was propped open. Inside was a long room with rows of bunks. Several soldiers lounged. Some played cards in dim, flickering lamplight. Others snored on straw-stuffed mattresses. The corporal knocked at the closed door on the right and announced our presence.

"You must read it," the Half King reiterated. He could tell I was only half-listening.

"I said, I will," I hissed. And at that moment, there was no lie hidden in my words, for I fully intended on doing so – someday. But the events of my life and my interests continually conspired to make reading the musings of a two thousand year old stoic seem pointless. Even now in my advanced and infirm years, I have yet to crack open that book, though I still carry it with me wherever I go. I proudly pull it from my pack and tell folks that it was given to me by the most famous man in the country, in the world!

The corporal opened the door after the deep baritone voice beyond gave him permission. He led us into the room and closed the door behind us. We found ourselves oriented in a semi-circle around the desk of a silver-haired soldier with thick shoulders and a square head. One of his eyes was missing, its remnants covered with a leather patch. Scars shaped like jagged spider legs extended out from the hollowed orb, indicating that a gruesome injury had stolen his sight. He trained his one good eye on the young major, ignoring the rest of us. He silently stared.

The corporal announced us to his captain, who listened to our names with indifference. Until, that is, Chief Tanaghrisson's name was announced. The captain's one eye opened a little wider in recognition and he smiled. "Ah," he said. "Le Demi-Roi!"

The Half King bristled.

"What is it?" Washington asked quietly.

Van Braam translated that and the other things that the French captain went on to say. "Ah, the Iroquois Half King, the impotent savage who wishes himself influential among the various tribes or, God forbid, even at Onondaga. Alas, he holds sway nowhere, perhaps not even in his home. No doubt his wife looks down on him. His plight has grown so dire that he now travels in the middle of a winter storm like a simpleton. The Seneca *chief* serves as a babysitter to a half-grown Quaker pup and an overgrown Virginian bull."

The major and the Half King exchanged frustrated glances. Washington, for his part, clearly wondered how a French captain could get away talking to Tanaghrisson, a king, in such a manner. The Half King bit his lip, fearing that Washington and I and therefore all of the English might find out that the Iroquois influence, especially that of Tanaghrisson, had waned.

And so began the critical conference that had been the entire reason for our perilous journey.

CHAPTER SEVENTEEN

After several more formalities and niceties on the part of our French host that were decidedly unpleasant, Washington reached into his coat pocket and, for the first time on our adventure, unveiled the papers he'd been carrying since Williamsburg. The packet looked to consist of two or three pages folded and sealed with wax. Embedded in the wax was the official mark of Virginia's Governor Dinwiddie.

The one-eyed captain received the letter and broke the seal, hardly paying it any attention. He took one look at the script that littered the page and realized it was written in English. Legardeur tossed it to the side. It was offensive to think of all we'd gone through during our journey only to have him so casually disregard the message.

The captain's baritone rumbled a few words before Van Braam translated. "He says they will have it translated tomorrow and, if it warrants a response, will give it to us thereafter. We may return to our accommodations for the night."

"Partir!" the captain snapped from behind the desk. I knew that it was his command for us to go.

Washington was not about to be so easily dismissed. In defiance of the French officer's order, he raised his chin and, as if he had memorized the correspondence before the governor had sealed it, began reciting its contents. He was several lines in before Van Braam, still rusty, realized he was to translate Washington's entire speech into French on the fly. The elderly captain looked on the major, the letter, and us with both amusement and concern.

The lands upon the River Ohio are so notoriously known to be the property of the Crown of Great Britain that it is a matter of equal concern and surprise to me, to hear that a body of French forces are erecting fortresses and making settlements upon that river, within his Majesty's dominions…

I must desire you to acquaint me by whose authority and instructions you have lately marched from

Canada with an armed force, and invaded the King of Great Britain's territories...

In obedience with my instructions from the King, my master, it becomes my duty to require your peaceable departure; and that you would forebear prosecuting a purpose so interruptive of the harmony and good understanding, which his Majesty is desirous to continue and cultivate with the Most Christian King of France.

Wow, I thought. In other words, I'm George Washington, a young fella you've never heard of, and I'm here in a snowstorm because the Scottish governor of Virginia says that the King of Great Britain is angry – so get the hell out of the Ohio Country, you French pig. Oh, and by the way, no hard feelings. We still really like your king.

As Van Braam finished with his stumbling translation he let out a breath as if he'd just run a full mile. "I think I got most of it right," he whispered to Washington.

"They understand well enough," I said, pointing with my eyes at the captain whose face was turning a few shades of darker red by the moment. "And I don't think he's happy."

I later learned that Legardeur had served the Most Christian King of France in forts and conflicts all over North America. This wasn't his first prickly discussion with a few neophyte warriors or an aging Half King of the Iroquois. The captain quickly regained his composure. He cleared his throat behind an obviously forced smile and spoke.

Van Braam gave us his words as best he could. "Major Washington and other English and Iroquois representatives," he said with stiff formality in an effort to appear hospitable. "As servant of my Most Christian King, I extend to you gratitude at so diligently delivering this urgent message in such inclement weather. It is clear that your dedication to your King who rests in Great Britain is something to admire. I, too, have a duty to my own king." He plucked up the pages and waved them in the air. "My translators and I will pour over this letter and pen a complete response back to your governor so that he may, in turn, inform your king. In the meantime, replenish your supplies and strength. You are free to move about as you please."

The major bowed with a stiffness that equaled that of the captain. "Thank you, Captain Legardeur. I shall happily give you several days to consider your reply, which will also grant you, and your officers, ample time to begin the arduous task of packing in preparation of vacating these premises."

The captain smirked as Van Braam finished. "How very gracious of you," Legardeur said.

CHAPTER EIGHTEEN

Several Canadian women entered our sleeping quarters, the bakery, long before the sun came up. None of Van Braam's tardy translations of their snarling French were necessary to tell us that our presence was most unwelcome. The bread bakers clattered about cleaning, measuring, and mixing. They stepped over, around, and quite frequently on us as we lay curled up on the floor. We were more efficiently driven from our bunks than had Legardeur sent in his infantry against us.

With no other sustenance to begin the day, we descended to the small stable that now housed our horses and tack. Among the gear were several salted pieces of meat that we split among ourselves. "Van Braam and Mr. Gist," said Washington after he'd consumed his meager meal. "Locate the corporal from last evening and begin assembling the supplies Captain Legardeur promised for our return trip home." He pointed to the trappers that had come with us. "You men," the major had not bothered to learn their names, a trait of command that he would learn to remedy only through trial and error, success and failure. "Assist them in stowing the gear next to the horses so that we may leave as soon as the captain has penned his response, an agreement, I suppose."

Gist rolled his eyes, possibly regretting he'd ever come all this way with the earnest major. He was used to running his own schedule as the Ohio Company man on the frontier and did not appreciate being subordinate to one so young and so seemingly sincere. Van Braam and the trappers merely nodded their assent as they finished gnawing on their salty breakfast.

"Major Washington, sir," I said, crouching while I rubbed the leg of one of our sad beasts. "After what we put these creatures through, they require much more rest than just a few days. I doubt they'll make it a week before keeling over."

Washington studied the horses, patting the nearest on her shoulder. "I see that," he agreed. "But I have no funds with which to purchase us new mounts from the French garrison. Our horses will have to take us as far as they can. We'll travel the rest of the way on foot."

Such a prospect sounded horrible to every man in our band.

"Why can't we just stay here over the winter?" Van Braam asked. The trappers, never before shying from harsh conditions, actually piped up with grunts in agreement this time. Van Braam added, "We're not at war. It's simple hospitality for Legardeur to allow it."

"Because, Mr. Van Braam," Washington answered evenly. "We must convey the French answer and any intelligence we've gathered while on our expedition as rapidly as possible. Whether they acquiesce to leaving or not, the governor and the king must know in order to prepare with due haste."

"Then we will have to make canoes. The rivers can take us some of the way back," I said. "That is, until they freeze over. Then we'll be on foot until we can get at least to Wills Creek, maybe farther."

"And then that is what we will do," Washington said, as if marching hundreds of miles on foot in the snow through the mountains without a road or shelter along the way was as simple as falling out of bed. "Chief Tanaghrisson, Mr. Weber, come with me. The rest of you secure those supplies." The major marched out into the mud of the fort's yard, passed a group of gawking sentries, and then tramped outside the walls.

"I suppose we should go, too," the Half King sighed, glancing through the barn door and up at the gray sky. At least the maddening precipitation had altogether ceased. In no hurry, he merely ambled after Washington. I followed, setting a similar unenthusiastic pace.

It took us several minutes to locate Major Washington. A woods encircled the fort on the side opposite the nearby river. Some distance into those trees is where we found him dashing about. He held his journal in one hand and a writing instrument in the other. Careful to avoid being seen by the French sentinels guarding its walls, he sketched out the shape of the fort, its dimensions, its materials, how it was defended, and its elevations and approaches. In daylight, it was clear that the fort was only partially finished. Marking stakes, driven into the ground and sticking out from the snow, indicated that the French obviously had plans to expand it in the coming season.

"Chief Tanaghrisson," said Washington, not taking his eyes off his feverish scribbling. "Run to the river and get a precise count of any canoes, bateaux, or other sea craft docked or beached. It will assist in getting an accurate picture of not only the population of Fort LeBoeuf, but of their intentions for the coming spring." It was an order that sounded like it had come straight from a military manual.

The Half King crossed his arms in mild disgust at his callow English comrade. But Washington's sincerity was frequently disarming. Still facing his page, he glanced up through his brows and past the brim of his hat. "I beg of you, Chief Tanaghrisson, not to delay in performing your duty. Such intelligence may mean the difference between success and failure, life and death, of not only French and English, but perhaps countless Indian peoples."

"I shall bring you the information," the chief said, compelled by the major's intensity. He slowly walked off toward the sound of the rushing river. "Enjoy yourself, Shit-for-brains," he said, bidding me a friendly adieu.

When he was gone, Washington led me around the other end of the fort, sketching the entire way. "How fortunate for His Majesty that Mr. Croghan placed you in my care," said the major. "Do not think it has passed my observation that you and Tanaghrisson are true friends. Your work with the native peoples is of great service to our cause."

"Thank you," I said, though I hadn't really worked at becoming friends with the Half King. He was likable. And when at Logstown for the second time, I had discovered that he and I had a similar ax to grind against the French – to be exact, one Frenchman in particular, but that complete part of my tale is coming soon enough.

"What do you think of Chief Tanaghrisson?" Washington asked, stepping through shin-deep snow. The drift had a crust of ice on the top that was strong enough to bear our weight for only a moment before collapsing, sending our feet whooshing down. "I was disappointed that he could only produce a handful of

Mingo followers for our journey north. How much more powerful it would have been if we had a score or more Indians with us. He is supposed to be a king, after all."

You know he wasn't really a king, hence his frontier nickname. Washington merely suspected the truth, but was in no position to alter his course. "It is winter," I said in excuse. "Any warrior with a brain stays home in weather like this."

The major considered my argument, which had been made-up on the spot. "I suppose," he said, warily. "But I fear that your friend has been lying to you about his influence among the tribes. Captain Legardeur certainly seems to think so."

You may believe it would have been simpler for me to just concede and tell a version of the truth. I could have just told Washington that perhaps I had been misled by Chief Tanaghrisson. But to do so would have accused the chief of lying. And the Half King had never lied to me. "Oh, he's a king alright," I said, piling on. "I've seen him in many powwows, many councils." And then to turn the conversation, I added. "Major Washington, you remain a very young man. How do you find you are able to order about Indian kings and French officers many years your senior?"

One side of Washington's mouth curled into a thin, prideful smile, which was the most of his intense ego he would ever permit to be seen. His eyes sparkled. "Because, Mr. Weber, the first and most formidable general I ever had the pleasure of encountering was that most honored madam, my mother. An hour at her knee, if survived, would make even the most timid creature, courageous."

I grinned along with him. It sounded as if we had grown up with similar mothers of admittedly different means.

"Two hundred twenty canoes ready to go in the water," Chief Tanaghrisson said. I jumped when he spoke, as his approach had been silent. Washington, if he was surprised at all, would not show it. "Each with enough space for eight men – fewer with supplies. Many more canoes are under construction."

"And how many men would you estimate in the garrison?" Washington asked.

The Half King chewed on the side of his cheek as he thought. "One hundred soldiers and quite a few officers."

"Mr. Weber, tell me what you think one hundred men at an isolated fort intend to do with more than two hundred canoes," Washington quizzed.

Many traders I had met paddled a small canoe and dragged one or more others behind them as they transported goods from village to village. "I suppose it is how they supply this fort and the one we passed through at Venango."

"Another possible theory, Chief Tanaghrisson?" Washington asked, giving no indication, good or ill, of what he thought of my suggestion.

"With so many well-dressed officers scurrying about, the French fathers mean to invest the Forks of Ohio in the coming season," the Half King said as if it was obvious. When Washington nodded in agreement, I felt like a dolt. "More Canadians will, no doubt, arrive from the north. Today, these men construct canoes to transport soldiers and supplies to the Forks in spring. Unless my English brothers have a similar expedition already planned, His Most Christian King of France has already beaten them. Croghan's fort won't be built."

"I concur with you about the French plans," the major said, slapping his notebook closed and tucking it into his coat. "Regardless of what the captain tells us in his letter to the governor, we must assume he means to seize the Ohio."

Croghan wouldn't like that one bit. His vast trading network would evaporate if he couldn't pass through the Ohio Country. Likewise, Gist and his investors wouldn't care for that outcome. The land speculators in his Ohio Company from Virginia would find their shares worthless.

"Gentlemen," Washington said, dropping his already hollow voice to an even quieter whisper. It was a wise decision. The leaves were long gone from the trees and anyone who has spent more than a minute outdoors in the winter knows that sound travels exceptionally well. "Van Braam and I will make ourselves somewhat of a nuisance to Legardeur in order to hasten his reply. We must return to Williamsburg with this information as swiftly as possible. In the meantime, you two will lead the

128

rest of our party in constructing our own canoes here and now. We abandon the horses to the French and will waste no time in beating our way home."

"Yes, sir," I said to the confident major, but he was already marching to the fort to gather his interpreter.

"It sounds like we have only a little time if we still wish to achieve our own portion of this mission," the Half King whispered at a volume lower than Washington had employed.

"Jumonville," I muttered.

"You have your French pistol? To make it look like a suicide?"

"In the baggage," I assured him. Then I added, "I don't care what happens to Williamsburg, the governor, or the king as long as Jumonville is alive."

The Half King squeezed my shoulder. He suddenly turned grave, almost cautious sounding. "I, too, wish to wash my hands in the drippings from his skull. But consequences cannot be avoided. Life begets life. Death begets death. You must remember that our actions, when we take them against Jumonville, may affect many thousands, including some of those you love."

I thought I loved very few people in those days. My youth allowed me to be so certain and self-righteous. Memeskia and Tahki were dead and so I had only memories of them to love. However, if Tanaghrisson had really pressed me, I would have admitted that I loved my siblings. Even my parents who, in my version of events, had veritably driven me from my home, held onto a somewhat sizable and fond portion of my feelings. And the Half King, though he had as many, if not more, reasons to see Jumonville dead, seemed to hesitate when it came to murdering the ensign. More experienced in the ways of the world, he considered what would happen to his loved ones, his family, his tribe. His sudden burst of caution was warranted. Perhaps I should have listened to the quiet warning carried in his words.

I did not.

"We still do it," I said with determination.

"Then before we build any canoes for Washington," the Half King said, again eager to move forward with our plan. "Let's go find out if our prey is even here."

But first I ran to gather up Tahki's loaded French pistol from my gear.

CHAPTER NINETEEN

Unfortunately, at this point in my tale there is not much to tell regarding my ongoing, one-sided feud with Jumonville.

Between the two of us, the Half King and I could speak only meager French. But after gathering Tahki's pistol and refreshing its load, we discovered that he knew some words I did not and vice versa. It took us only ten minutes to politely request the whereabouts of the fort's youngest officers, the ensigns.

According to the garrison, there were eight ensigns, far too many for an out-of-the-way fort with only one hundred rank-and-file men on duty. This information, by itself, was enough to confirm that many more French soldiers and officers would soon descend to LeBoeuf and perhaps be dispersed elsewhere. His Most Christian Majesty in Paris did indeed mean to invest the Forks of Ohio. Sooner than later.

My heart beat with excitement of the vilest type as we traipsed around the fort from one cannon embrasure to another, from one storehouse to the next, and from bastion to bastion. Whenever we came across one or two ensigns diligently performing their duties I would casually reach beneath my coat and grip the pistol. It had come to feel warm in my grasp, like a security blanket for a child. Also each time, however, I was disappointed and the gun left stowed. Not one of the eight ensigns on staff at LeBoeuf was Jumonville. For me, the five-hundred-mile journey had become a wild-goose chase, a babysitting mission under miserable conditions.

"It is for the best," the Half King had said when it was clear we needed to go to work building Washington's canoes rather than murdering a Frenchman.

According to the tale told to me by Tanaghrisson, he had nursed his hatred of the ensign for much longer than I. That is when I suddenly feared that the cause for his loathing had occurred too long ago. Complacency may have set in. Perhaps the Half King had never really intended to carry out the bold words he'd so bravely spoken on the evening I'd spent with his family in his home at Logstown. Perhaps the rum he'd been sipping that night had given him courage he'd not otherwise have.

"It will be best when he is dead and no more!" I snapped.

"So it will," the Half King said evenly. "But timing is everything."

That had been two days ago. Since then, we had toiled at the riverbank building the canoes that would transport us back home. We were in full view of the Frenchmen who performed a similar task, albeit multiplied by many dozens. They had no concern that we watched what they did. More than once a group of them had the gall to ask us for the temporary use of our hands as they bent a limb to form a canoe's gunwale. While knowing that the canoes would be employed to attack British and Iroquois interests in the coming months, we yet complied. What else was a motley band of travelers to do when faced with two score of artificers armed with tools enough to bludgeon us to death several times over?

Gist, whom I had come to view with extreme distrust, sat on a large boulder near the river. He had set down his tools a full hour before we'd finished the last canoe. He'd spent those many minutes excoriating the French and even the Pennsylvanians for the audacity they had in believing they had a rightful claim to the Forks of Ohio. According to Gist, the land of the Ohio would always be a part of the Old Dominion.

From his stone pulpit, he lectured us like he was a Massachusetts preacher, or and much worse, a lawyer. He said that it was the Second Virginia Charter of 1609 granted by James I that took precedent over the much later Pennsylvania Charter given by Charles II to William Penn. According to Gist, Penn's bogus charter and all his Quaker disciples could be damned to hell.

"Why don't you shut your mouth," I told him when we had finished our job.

"Why don't you make me shut my mouth, you pacifist turd," he answered with a smirk. He had not yet forgiven me for turning down his offer to work for the Ohio Company. At the same time, Gist conveniently forgot that I had saved his life when one of Shingas' warriors had fired at him.

Wishing I had let the lead shot hit its mark, I grabbed a hammer and strutted toward him. "I guess I'll have to show you what an angry pacifist can do." My rage raced at a full gallop, unsated by my failure to locate Jumonville.

The Half king did not make a move to stop me, even though I had expected him to. Relaxing against a tree, he used a long knife to whittle a stick to a useless point. The trappers who'd worked with us certainly made no move to come between Gist and me. They, too, had found his company annoying. In the rough and tumble world of the frontier, a good brawl was often the best way to settle things once and for all. And the onlookers hunkered down to watch one.

Gist had held his spot, not wanting to cower before a Quaker boy. He glared up at me defiantly from his rock. "As I was saying, the Indian-lovers in Pennsylvania have no more rightful claim on the Ohio Country as the dirty Canadians."

"Hit him, Ephraim," scoffed one of the trappers. "Needs to learn his manners."

"Hit me, Ephraim," Gist goaded.

His tone alone was enough to invite the assault. I gripped the hammer handle and raised it over my head. In a wink it was hurtling down toward Gist's face. But my momentum was instantly checked as a firm hand gripped my wrist.

"Slow down, Ephraim," said Van Braam, holding my arm. We hadn't seen him for two days as he and Washington had dined with and prodded the senior French officers for their prompt answer to Dinwiddie's letter.

"Damn it, Jacob," cursed a trapper, who'd been spoiling to see a fight.

"Damn it is right," whispered Gist.

I glanced down at him. Instead of sitting with his hands in his lap as he'd been when I approached, one of his arms was extended toward me. I felt a sharp poke in my belly. He was pressing the tip of his knife in through my coat, just barely pricking the skin. "I was looking forward to having one less mouth to feed on the trip back."

"Put down the weapons," Van Braam ordered, taking a page from Washington's confidence. "We are ordered to the fort. Captain Legardeur has his official response to Dinwiddie and has called for a small ceremony among such warm *friends*. The major wants us all there to show unity." Van Braam looked around at the canoes we'd constructed. "Then we fly home." He released my wrist.

Neither Gist nor I moved a muscle. We stared at one another's eyes. "I should have let you die at the Forks," I muttered. "You are a liar, especially to the Indians."

He was a liar. He knew it. And he didn't care. That is, he didn't care until he was accused of lying publicly. Gist's eyes flashed with anger. His knuckles whitened around the knife and he began leaning his weight toward me. Van Braam saw it, too. He cracked Gist's arm with his fist. A second set of arms tugged me back from the attack before I had a chance to react.

"Spilt innards will make it difficult for you to fulfill your obligation to your wife and father-in-law," the Half King whispered into my ear. His grip was firm, almost painful. I fought against it for only a moment before I realized the struggle was useless. For a man of his years, pushing five decades old, he was strong.

"But Gist lies to the Indians," I accused. "Doesn't that make you angry?"

"Everyone lies to the Indians," the Half King said. "And the Indians lie to everyone else. If you are to operate in the frontier, you'd best not reason like a child, Mr. Weber." He picked my feet off the ground and used his hip like a fulcrum. My knees were soon crashing down onto the shingle.

By the time I got back to my feet, Gist, while rubbing his sore wrist from Van Braam's assault, was laughing at me. "See there, Quaker?" he asked, slipping his knife into its sheath. "What good do all your Indian friends do you now?"

"Don't answer that!" Van Braam ordered. He swatted the hammer from my grasp. "The major requires our presence at the fort." Without tarrying any longer, he tramped his way toward the patchwork fort. The trappers and the Half King followed lazily, leaving Gist and I behind.

We stared at each other for what felt like ten minutes. "After you," he said sarcastically. "Unless you are afraid to turn your back to me," he added with a wicked smile.

In truth, I was a little frightened. But to admit such a thing would invite contempt. I tossed my chin up high and slowly walked after the rest, who by now had disappeared into the fort. The pace I set gave Gist ample opportunity, should he wish, to renew our feud.

He did not. For now, he did not. Any fear I had was quickly replaced with boiling anger. Gist had insulted my heritage and my Indian friends and family. He was a lie and a cheat and even Tanaghrisson didn't seem to care. The Half King's maddening indifference served only to enrage me further.

Thus livid, I entered the fort.

And I came face-to-face with Jumonville.

CHAPTER TWENTY

Angry at Gist. Enraged at Jumonville, I knew only one thing. The intervening year had been most unkind to Jumonville. As I stared directly into his face, he appeared to have aged almost ten years, with the start of crows' feet and laugh lines lightly etching his skin. A confused ball of vile emotions at so unexpectedly facing him, I blinked and stuttered for a moment before finding my wits. He must have made the perilous winter trip southward and just arrived. I then set about patting my coat in search of the French pistol.

Damn, I remembered. I had not carried it around for the past two days out of fear of arousing suspicions among the French. Besides, it wasn't like shooting him in the middle of the fort could in any way be construed as a suicide. This was going to be a murder, plain and simple. If I wanted him dead, I needed a weapon, any weapon, and fast. My eyes darted everywhere for something within reach. A rock. A knife. A bayonet.

Yes! A French private stood at attention two foot away. I could snag his musket and run Jumonville through with the fixed bayonet before anyone knew what happened.

Gist intentionally brushed his shoulder into mine as he passed. "Oops," he muttered with sarcasm dripping.

I fell forward into Jumonville's chest. He gently caught me and helped me stand upright. His touch sickened me. "Monsieur Gist and Monsieur Weber, I presume" he said, nodding to me when he had said Gist and to Gist when he had uttered my name. "Your Major Washington has asked me to escort you to your places."

"I presume?" I asked incredulously. "You know exactly who I am."

Gist paused, smirking. He set his hands upon his hips preparing to watch whatever show I had in store.

Jumonville manufactured a confused countenance. It was quite believable. "Oh, I am sorry, Monsieur Gist. I have forgotten that we've met."

"Don't give me that Mr. Gist business," I growled. "You know I'm Ephraim Weber, husband of Tahki, son-in-law of Memeskia." I waited for him to recognize me and my name.

His brow furrowed. "You mean Old Briton, the Miami chief?" he asked.

"You know exactly who I mean since you watched him being eaten!" I snapped, reaching for the nearby musket. The private had not expected this and I was able to easily tear it free. I lunged with the bayonet toward Jumonville's undefended belly. It wasn't as elegant of a weapon as Tahki's pistol, but it would do the trick.

Washington's sword crashed down on the bayonet. Instead of impaling the murdering Frenchman, I stabbed the mud at his feet. "Mr. Weber!" Washington gasped. "I send men looking for you! And now I must come and find this! Seize him, Mr. Gist!"

Gist needed no further encouragement. With the tip of the bayonet buried harmlessly in the muck, he pounced on me. Between Gist and the embarrassed French private, I was soon pounded into the ground by balled fists and boots. I had no choice but to submit. Soon, they painfully wrenched my arms behind my back and lifted me up to face Jumonville and Washington. Both officers were in utter shock.

"Captain Jumonville," Washington said, searching for words. "I cannot adequately express to you how horribly I view this event. I can only guess at what has come over a very confused Mr. Weber. But please rest assured that any danger from him has now passed."

"He's no captain," I slurred, blood pouring from my mouth.

"Not that it is worth my time, Mr. Weber," breathed Washington. "But I assure you Mr. Jumonville is a captain."

"Then he was just promoted," I grunted, squirming. "The French must be desperate to raise a cur like him."

Jumonville scrunched his forehead. "I've been a captain for nearly two years," he said.

"Liar!" I snapped, sending flecks of my blood onto Jumonville's white coat.

"Do you know this man?" Washington asked.

"Of course I do," I began.

"I wasn't asking you, Mr. Weber."

"Before he attacked me, he said I should know him as the son-in-law of Old Briton," Jumonville answered.

Then the facts of the situation clicked for Major Washington. "Oh, Mr. Weber has somehow mistaken you for your brother. Perhaps I should have remembered that when I asked you to gather my stragglers. I could have warned you of the history."

Jumonville slowly nodded. "It is not your duty to recall every name ever given to you. But yes, I had received news from Fort Detroit last year that my brother, *Ensign* Jumonville, was involved in a defensive raid on Miami warriors. Old Briton was among the casualties."

My all-encompassing hatred for Jumonville slowly cleared and I could see that this man was not Joseph Coulon de Villiers de Jumonville. Still, I seethed. "A raid on Miami warriors!" I declared. "Pickawillany was filled with women, children, and old men."

"Let me guess," said Captain Louis Coulon de Villiers de Jumonville. "You, a young man of fighting age, were there, too."

"Well, yes," I said.

"As I say, Major Washington, the letters I received indicated a violent threat from Pickawillany with certain trespassing traders in league with the upstart Miami. This young man's presence in the village confirms that. My brother, *Ensign* Jumonville, responded to the armed menace accordingly."

"As one would expect of a soldier," Washington said deferentially. "As to this incident today, I offer my humblest apologies. Furthermore, since this assault occurred within the bounds of this fort at a time of peace between our two kingdoms, I must insist that you take Mr. Weber into your custody and try him as you see fit."

"Captain Jumonville!" shouted Captain Legardeur in his deep baritone. He stood across the sloppy parade ground. Van Braam repeated his words as best he could. "How many officers must we send to gather a few English traders? I mean to get this over with and show Washington on his way!"

"Right away!" Captain Jumonville answered his elder. He glanced at me and then at Washington. "And this Mr. Weber is merely doing what is expected of a son-in-law when he believes his family has been wrongfully killed. But now that we have the misunderstanding remedied, I believe there is no need to hold him. We all recognize now that the raid was within the bounds of His Most Christian Majesty's rights – no one was murdered. I was hundreds of miles away." He leaned in and whispered to the major. "Besides, in these tense times, it might be best to avoid such entanglements as a French garrison holding an Englishman prisoner – no matter the grounds."

Captain Jumonville's gracious attitude violated Washington's sense of justice, but it appealed in spades to his appreciation of a polite and gentlemanly society. "How kind," the major admitted with a tip of his head.

"It is best for all present," the elder Jumonville countered magnanimously.

"Can you control yourself, Mr. Weber?" Washington asked skeptically, fixing me with a narrow-eyed stare. "Will you?"

Having no reason to hate Captain Jumonville other than his last name, I still managed to silently watch him for a long while. After what I'd witnessed at Pickawillany, I had vowed to never trust a Frenchman. My face contorted with an unrighteous variety of hate.

"Mr. Weber?" Washington asked as the fort's captain resumed his frustrated calls for us to quit dawdling.

"Yes, sir," I managed with modest conviction.

The major turned to Captain Jumonville. The pair then began walking toward Legardeur. "Very kind of you to understand the emotions of a young man," Washington was saying. Then over his shoulder he said, "Release him, Mr. Gist."

The private tossed away my arm like it was disgusting to the touch. Gist held on a second longer. When he did let go, he shoved me forward, extending his leg just enough to trip me. I again crashed into the mud.

"And, Mr. Gist," Washington said, turning to face us. He disappointedly looked at me wallowing in the muck. "Keep an eye on him, will you? See that he gets into no further trouble."

"With pleasure, sir," Gist crowed.

CHAPTER TWENTY-ONE

The life of the fort continued on despite our tiny ceremony. While perhaps twenty men gathered in a tight circle around Captain Legardeur and Major Washington, the rest of the garrison went about their business, from drills to construction.

Legardeur was viewing Washington with a distrusting eye as I found my place in the group of onlookers. The one-eyed captain saw me and noted my filthy, blood-soaked clothes. I appeared like a hunchback, leaning to one side and guarding my ribs with one arm. Gist and the French private had broken several of my ribs. It hurt to breathe, but I was smart enough to know I'd get no medical attention or sympathy from either the French or my English comrades. From across the circle, the Half King and his Mingo followers shook their heads at me in disgust.

"Le problème?" Legardeur asked the major.

Washington needed no help from Van Braam to understand what was said. "No," he said, embarrassed.

The fort's captain gave a curt nod, for he did not really care if his English interlopers had suffered from any issues at all. Seeing the nod as a signal, a lone French drummer beat a startling fanfare that reminded me more of the time just before a man was about to drop from the gallows than when a mere message was to be conveyed between gentlemen. Knowing the events that transpired over the ensuing years, I suppose the executioner's clatter was fitting enough.

With all of us as witnesses, Legardeur reached into his coat pocket and produced a sealed letter. When his arm extended toward Washington, the fanfare stopped abruptly, leaving its last beat echoing through the fort. It was suddenly very quiet. The French soldiers who had heretofore been busy bees, ceased their activities and gaped at us from the walls and through windows.

The major accepted the correspondence and inspected the name written on the exterior as well as its seal. Satisfied, he opened his coat and slid it into his breast pocket, tapping it twice when the coat was again fastened. "You have been an elegant host, Captain Legardeur," said Major Washington. "I shall have nothing but kind words to express to Governor Dinwiddie regarding your assistance."

Legardeur glanced at my disheveled person. "And your men have been exemplary guests," he stated in a stilted tone.

"I understand that our enfeebled horses will be something of a drain upon your provisions over this harsh winter," Washington said. "However, I truly hope that after they've recovered from the ordeal we've put them through, they are able to relieve at least a portion of your burdens while serving your masters."

"Your sentiments are appreciated," Legardeur answered flatly. "However, our provisions are aplenty." This was a lie, for we had seen his storehouses. "And the beasts you leave in our care shall indeed be of assistance when we are again blessed by milder weather." In truth, I thought it more likely that the garrison would eat our horses before we put the first mile between ourselves and LeBoeuf. When the snows piled high around the thinning soldiers in an out-of-the-way fort, meat was meat, be it bovine, equine, or canine. Growling bellies transformed any of it into a delicacy. "I bid you safe travels."

"Indeed," Washington said quietly. He hesitated a moment, still looking at the older man and hoping for a continuation of their talk. When Legardeur held his tongue, the major slowly understood that the limited pomp was already over. He turned and took several steps toward us. It was a bittersweet moment for me. I desired to escape from the French fort and all of the past it reminded me. But I had no desire to return to the wet and cold wilderness for what would amount to at least of month of perilous travel. I valued my fingers and toes greatly and did not want to sacrifice them to the elements.

Washington would delay our departure for a few more moments, though. He stopped directly in front of me. He gave me a *funny* glance. It was in no way funny as you and I might think of the word. Washington was old even then. He was not without joy, but I do think he was forever without humor. His glance was just strange.

He turned to face Captain Legardeur and began retracing his steps. For his part, the captain was visibly irritated that the major prolonged our stay even for another minute. But he pasted on the smile of diplomacy and through Van Braam asked. "Is there something else, Major Washington?"

"Yes," the major said, even quieter than usual. "As I will most certainly respect the dignity of my charge and refrain from looking on the correspondence I carry, I wonder if you would be willing to provide me with just an indication of its contents."

I chuckled inappropriately. For once, the major was allowing his youthful side to shine through. He was curious. But, as you know, curiosity killed the cat. I stopped giggling when Van Braam hissed at me.

Legardeur considered the request for but a moment before smiling with all the pleasantness of a prison guard locking up a thief. "Of course, I can whet your curiosity." He faced his square head directly at the tall, young American and said, "First, I would like you to be assured that I will forward Governor Dinwiddie's letter on to the Marquis Duquesne in Quebec with haste so that he and other proper authorities can decide what to make of the pretensions of the King of Great Britain. Secondly, and in broad terms, the letter you carry states that the rights of the king, my master, to the lands along the Ohio are incontestable. It is not my duty to argue the point. Whatever may be your instructions, my general's order brings me here. Governor-general Duquesne was explicit. And I entreat you, sir, to be assured that I shall attempt to follow his commands with all the exactness and determination which can be expected from a fine officer."

Van Braam muddled his way through the interpretation, but the meaning couldn't have been clearer.

Yet, it wasn't so apparent to Washington, who was still charmingly naïve. "So you mean to ignore the petition from my governor and my king?"

Legardeur found it mildly amusing that Washington had actually considered it possible that he would take his men and vacate his post based upon a message carried by one so young from one so far. With only a modicum of pity, the French officer said, "As to the summons you send me to retire, I do not think myself obliged to obey."

Washington swallowed rather loudly and offered a brisk nod to Legardeur. The young major had just suffered a sizable defeat and it took all of his reputed self-control to muster his composure. He again turned to face the rest of us. This time, however, he marched swiftly through us toward the gate. Our gear had already been piled at the river's edge. "Let us depart, gentlemen."

Legardeur and his gathering of officers snickered at Washington's plight.

One-by-one we began ambling after our major. Even I, who had never believed it possible that our mission could be successful, felt a tinge of disappointment. Through the swelling around my eye, I dejectedly watched my feet plod through the mud as the others, including the Half King and his Mingo warriors, chased after Washington. I felt only the presence of Gist over my shoulder as he was pleased to act as my babysitter for the time being.

A pair of boots blocked my path and I stopped, looking up. Captain Jumonville faced me. Wearing a smile like an honest badge of friendship, he offered his hand. "Your attempt on my life has been happily forgotten," he said. "I pray you do not suffer any punishment from Major Washington after his public embarrassment."

Had his brother not killed many of the people I loved, I might have thought this particular Jumonville a decent man. Alas… I took his hand and shook it, gently tugging him closer.

"Weber," Gist warned from behind.

"It is alright," Jumonville said.

"Thank you for your well wishes," I said, brightly. "But since this trip has been all about delivering messages, I wonder if you would carry one to your brother, the ensign."

Captain Jumonville pulled back an inch or two, wary. But my tone had been so friendly that I believe he thought I was about to offer my forgiveness to the younger Jumonville in the deaths of Tahki and Memeskia. He leaned back in. I whispered into his ear. "Please tell Joseph I will never forget that he butchered a peace-loving people. My wife was pregnant when he shot her in cold blood." Jumonville tried to pull away, but I clutched his hand and wrapped my other around his back, giving him something like a hug. My lips wiped blood on his earlobe as I spoke. "Someday, I will split his skull and wash my hands in his brains. After that, it will be up to you whether or not you wish to make me your enemy as well." I released him and he stumbled back, staring at me.

"Come on, Weber," Gist said, shoving me in the direction of the gate. "Don't give me any reason to beat you down again." Though I know he really wanted one.

I spun, waving a finger in Gist's face. "I'll give you reason to do whatever you will. Let's just see if you're able to get the job done without help from a French private."

"When the time is right, dear boy, when the time is right," Gist said, playfully patting my cheek. He stepped around me and headed out the gate. "I suppose you can stay here if you wish. It seems you get along very well with the French." He disappeared around the corner.

I snarled at Captain Jumonville. "Remember what I said."

The muscles of his jaw flared in anger, but he was a true gentleman. There was protocol to be followed when a man of superior breeding, such as Jumonville, found himself in a dispute with someone of lesser breeding, like me. "I should like to settle this with a duel, but I know that the honor of killing you must go to my brother. If I see him, I shall tell him to expect such an event."

"Washington was correct, indeed," I said brightly. I gave Jumonville a silly bow as chunks of dried grime sloughed from my coat. "You are too kind." With that, I left the speechless officer standing in the center of the muddy fort.

And the next leg of our adventure began. It would be more of the same for all of us – wet and cold. But for one of us, at least, it would be deadly.

CHAPTER TWENTY-TWO

By the time several days had passed, we had already lost our escort of Indians. The weather, turning exceedingly poor as if Providence had intentionally waited until we were away from the shelter of the French fort, had convinced the Half King to go no further. The younger Mingo warriors who accompanied him had been fortunate enough to take down a deer on a brief hunting expedition. They had begun butchering the creature right on the spot a short distance from the creek on which we'd been canoeing. The four Indians refused to move an inch until they had filled their bellies, a sentiment with which I agreed, but was reluctant to support vocally. My standing with the major, to this point, had not improved.

Washington did not wish to proceed without them. They could provide us additional protection while we were so distant from English settlements. Yet, our major was unwilling to wait. He spent a half hour cajoling them in the loudest manner he was capable. An isolated doornail made more racket. In the end, as the Half King's followers built a fire over which to cook their feast, the effort proved fruitless. In fact, the wasted time may have been harmful to our cause. Because as the spitted carcass was set over the flames and the outermost flesh and fat began to sizzle and hiss, an aroma most pleasant reached our nostrils.

The trappers, our solitary muscle before the arrival of the Indians, needed no more encouragement. They promptly sat down and announced they, too, would go no further until they had their fill.

Washington could hardly understand such short-sighted behavior. "Haste is in the interest of the king," he had said at one point. The argument sounded silly to a group of men who were cold, hungry, and had hundreds of more miles to travel in canoe and on foot before they could hope to lay eyes on a kinsman, let alone a king. Washington had lost all of his authority. The weather and his failure at Fort LeBoeuf had seen to that. No amount of his confidence and grace could overcome it now.

Well, he hadn't lost all of his ability to rule. "Come, Mr. Weber," he said when he saw me inching next to one of the trappers who had abandoned us. The major held the elbow of Van Braam and tugged him along. Gist, shoulders sagging, slowly trailed after them. Remembering Croghan's instructions that I was to stay with Washington while minding the Irishman's business, I sighed and padded along. Though not in the military, I was already acting the part of the good soldier.

Thereafter, I remember looking back at that roasting venison with something approaching lust as I followed after Washington. Chief Tanaghrisson caught my backward glance. "Shit-for-brains," he called happily as he warmed his hands by the fire. "I'm sure the French captain's refusal to listen will serve your interests in the long run. You will have cause to come to these parts again. And again, you will have a chance to fulfill your mission with young Jumonville." Then he laughed at me as he touched the burning deer flesh nearest the flame with his fingertips. "Stay warm out there. This looks tasty. I'll save you some."

"I hope you choke on it," I called. I had meant it at the time.

But the Half King took it as a joke. He roared in laughter while chewing on the half-done meat. His comrades, the trappers and Indians both, joined in. "Wouldn't that be a cruel ending! Choking out here." Tanaghrisson exclaimed. "I'd rather pass to the next life while spending quality time in bed with my wife!"

I had seen his wife. She was of his age. And my young mind did not care to picture the two them performing any amorous activities whatsoever. The Half King saw my expression as I retreated. "Just because I'm away up here, doesn't mean you can cuddle up to the old girl when you pass through Logstown. Don't get any bright ideas, Shit-for-brains."

Nearly to our beached canoes, Washington could take no more of our banter. "Bring Mr. Weber forward, Mr. Gist," he ordered from the front. "If I am forced to listen to his so-called nickname one more time, I may find reason to tie him to a tree and forget he ever existed."

I skipped up to the major before Gist could fall back to lay a hand on me. "Safe travels, Shit-for-brains," the Half King called as we dropped out of sight at the water's edge. The snickers from his party could be heard echoing over the creek. Even I was getting tired of hearing my new name, but when I saw the intense frown carved into Washington's face, I couldn't help but chuckle, too.

It was another several days of water travel until the ice chunks in the river began growing in size and melding together. The temperature was dropping. "We won't make it to Logstown on the river," Gist announced, now being the member of our band who was most familiar with this part of the wilderness. From his post in the rear, he turned the canoe he and I shared into a tributary. "We'll freeze out here if we don't find a shorter route. I think we can get to Murthering Town faster."

Though we all thought it, no one questioned his use of that most equivocal phrase, *I think*.

At any rate, less than a day later the bottoms of our canoes scratched the shingle adjacent to Murthering Town, a Delaware village about fifteen miles northeast of the Half King's dominion. Despite the harsh conditions, I began to feel more at ease now that we had moved so far, so fast from LeBoeuf and Machault. But I should have realized that Murthering was also about fifteen miles from Shingas' town, only in the opposite direction. I should have wondered to which chief these Indians pledged their allegiance – Tanaghrisson or Shingas. Nonetheless, catching sight of the tiny settlement for the first time, each of us breathed a sigh of relief. The smoke chugging from holes in the roofs of the Indian dwellings was welcoming, indeed.

"If we are welcome," Washington warned before we could elevate our hopes too high. "We stay only overnight."

"But the river," Gist said, using his thumb to point at the giant chunks of ice that even now bumped against our beached water crafts.

"If we cannot employ the waterways, we go on foot tomorrow," Washington announced.

I could feel the collective energy sucked from our group. Only the major remained unperturbed. "We have a duty to perform," he reminded us as an excuse for his mad, single-minded focus.

"But I cannot say I am familiar with the trails in this particular area," Gist protested rather loudly. "We were fortunate to make it this far in these conditions." It was one of the first things he'd said that I did not think idiotic. But I would not ever voice agreement with him.

"We should ask to stay at least until there's a break in the weather, George," Van Braam pleaded softly. "I understand your urgency, but even the French must abide by the demands set upon them by winter. They'll not be able to get to the Forks from their forts any faster than we can move."

Washington bristled slightly at the use of his first name. "Mr. Van Braam, I'll take your suggestion under advisement."

"Advisement?" I pressed, still young enough to think living a long life was something worth striving toward. "I know some of these woods, but not all. Gist says he can't be our guide on land. What choice do we possibly have?"

"Is all order falling away just because of a modicum of hardship?" Washington asked in an accusatory tone. "What choice do we have, *major*?" he added. Several of the residents from the nearest houses had heard our discussion. Four Delaware men emerged, unsure as to our intentions, brandishing muskets. I watched their cautious approach.

"Well, Mr. Weber?" Washington asked, completely at ease as the unfamiliar warriors drew closer.

I could see that he wasn't going to forget that I'd not followed his ideas of military protocol. The esteem I had held for him was hastily retreating. "What choice do we have, major?" I asked, relenting.

"I'm glad you've asked, young man," the major said cheerily enough to remove the obvious condescension. He stepped toward the Delaware men and extended his hand in friendship. "I'm willing to wager that one of these fine Indians will agree to guide us tomorrow morning."

CHAPTER TWENTY-THREE

The Delaware Indians of Murthering Town had little provisions to spare. But what they did have, they gladly shared as we stayed up late into the evening eating and drinking with the men of the village. We ate corn that was chalky, dry, and tough. It was more fitting for a horse than man. They also shared several slabs of dried meat which was also desiccated and hard, but at least retained the taste and pleasant aroma of hickory. All of it was quite delicious, considering our alternative was to shiver under a tree in the woods and eat the last of the food given to us by the French. Our warm accommodations made all the difference in the world.

The only common language we could use to converse with our hosts was French. Van Braam did all the talking for us, while about half of their men spoke French with passable ease. After exchanging news, both sides began to trade in the diversionary currency of stories. Some were sad tales. Some caused uproarious laughter. But one thing was certain. As the long night grew longer and the rum jugs became lighter, the yarns thus spun escalated to the height of folly. In short, the evening was a wonderful respite from our miserable adventure. We even got the blessing of the village elder to allow one of his young men to guide us on foot the next morning.

I do not have to tell you that Washington drank only one mug of rum during our revelry. I followed his lead, but not exactly. While Gist and Van Braam and the Indians each consumed perhaps ten drinks apiece, I believe I had less than five.

I later questioned the accuracy of my count. Sometime just before dawn, I awoke with a great headache, something that normally didn't happen unless I drank excessively. The bark home in which we had slept was dim and silent. But something had stirred and startled me.

Rolling over to relieve the sudden bout of pain stabbing my temples, I saw a young Delaware warrior leaning over and talking to the eldest of our hosts. Buried beneath his covers, the old man looked as disheveled and unhappy as I felt. The young man, on the other hand, was alert. He wore thick leggings and warm moccasins that dripped with snow melting due to the nearby embers. His back was covered with warm hides. He panted as he spoke, indicating recent exertion, in a version of the Algonquian tongue. They hadn't noticed that I was awake.

The old man groaned like all men who have drank too much the night before. He rubbed his eyes with the fleshy part of his palms. "Répéte ça," he mumbled.

His visitor quickly hushed him and looked around the room full of sleeping men. I kept my eyes open, betting that he would not be able to see them in the low light. My bet paid off, for the young man resumed his talk. "Pas en français!" he hissed before quickly returning to his use of the native language.

"Quelle?" the old Delaware asked, fully confused, after listening to a low, rumbling report. He slowly crawled up onto his elbows, muttering curses the whole way.

Simmering with impatience now, the young warrior again repeated what must have been an urgent message to the local chief. He faced away from me whispering softly. This time he spoke slowly, pausing often so that his listener could nod his understanding. It also gave me a better chance to understand snippets of the conversation. Their language wasn't so different from that of my wife's people.

I heard words that you would expect from a messenger. *Carry. Sent. Convey. Order.* But I also heard things like *Half King, Conotocarius, Shingas, traitor, French, attack.*

Since the chief faced me, I could make out his response with ease. He shook his head in disagreement with whatever had been said by the young man. Then the chief said, "No. In fact, Hunter will leave with them in the morning as a guide." The old man added, "Go find someplace to sleep," before he rolled over and tugged his hides up around his shoulders.

The young man jostled the chief and growled at him for several minutes. The effort produced no results as the chief soon snored. Our visitor stood quickly, peered down at the forms of Washington, Gist, Van Braam, then me before racing back out into the snow.

150

It was then I began to wonder if I had actually consumed quite a lot more than five mugs of rum. My brain, weakened by drink and tortured by a headache, feebly turned on the conversation I had just heard. It would be something I should tell the major about when we awoke. Not right now, I reasoned. I was too tired. Later.

Just as soon as I had decided on my course of action, I faded back to sleep.

Or, it is more likely I passed out.

CHAPTER TWENTY-FOUR

Sun poured in at an angle through the smoke hole. It had finally risen enough to cast its beam directly onto my face. The additional warmth felt satisfying. However, the light torched my eyes, hidden as they were behind my eyelids, and reignited my headache.

I had obviously drunk more than I was willing to admit at the time.

"We're leaving, Ephraim," Van Braam said, leaning over me.

I peeked at him with one squinting eye. "Two steps to your left," I ordered hoarsely. It felt like a whole sheep had been jammed down my throat.

He complied. "There," he said, his body now shading me from the sunlight. "Time to go. Washington is beside himself. He allowed himself to sleep until morning was half over. You're the last one I need to gather."

Van Braam wasn't exaggerating. When I glanced around the one room home, he and I were the only ones inside. Even the hung-over chief was long gone.

The Dutchman threw my shoes and gear into my lap. He waited while I moved ever-so slowly to climb back into my pathetic winter clothing. My glacial pace was not the result of apprehension of returning to the cold – though I was not looking forward to it – it was because I had to concentrate on every move I made. My limbs felt like they were apart from my body. I briefly recalled my activities from the night before. Had they involved a drinking contest with one of the youngest Delaware warriors? I couldn't be sure. But if they had, I certainly swilled much too much rum.

"I'd think Gist would not want to miss a chance to drag me from bed," I suggested as we ducked out the door flap.

"He had a certain look in his eye," Van Braam said. "After last night, I knew you'd not be able to defend yourself if he came in to knock you on the head. I volunteered to drag you out."

"Thanks," I said, tasting regurgitated corn and hickory with a hint of sour molasses in the back of my throat. "What happened last night?"

Van Braam chuckled, but said nothing. That was enough of an answer to confirm that I had many drinks. It was best to say no more on the subject, to leave any of the actions I'd performed while under the influence in the past where they belonged.

"Mr. Weber," Washington chided as we came to the edge of the clearing in which the village sat. "You are fortunate that I value Mr. Croghan's worth so highly. Otherwise, I would happily abandon you to the wolves or hostile Indians here in the wilderness. Your antics of last evening cause me to question your upbringing."

I felt queasy. My stomach lurched, doing back-flips. "It won't happen again," was all I managed to say. Though what *it* was, I had no idea.

"I should say not!" Washington said. Gist grinned over the major's shoulder.

The old chief then emerged from a path in the forest. He carried a small rabbit carcass. When he saw me, he dropped his quarry into the snow and stood so we were nose-to-nose. His hands slapped against my cheeks and he squeezed them like some men do to their dog's face. He giggled joyously and, through Van Braam, stated, "Never has anyone beaten my son when it comes to drinking. But you did!" He stepped back and sized me up from head to toe. "You're so tiny. It's a miracle you can still stand. My boy lies sleeping next to his mother like a baby!" He broke into a fit of laughter, shaking his head while he scooped up his rabbit.

"We really must be leaving," Washington prodded.

"Yes, yes," the chuckling chief said. He was recovering from the previous night much more quickly than I. The benefits of experience, I supposed. "Follow the path. My tracks will take you directly to Hunter. He waits for you and knows the quickest way overland to Croghan's trading post at Wills Creek. It will be several days, perhaps a week of walking, but he'll get you there. And from his name, you should be able to tell, you won't have trouble eating."

"I humbly thank you," Washington said with a precise bow.

"Why isn't Hunter meeting us here?" I asked.

"Because he was busy getting me this," the chief said happily as he raised the rabbit. It swung and a little droplet of blood flecked my face. "Hunter may be younger and more nimble than I, but he shares my wisdom. He didn't want to walk the same path more times than he had to." The chief was already plodding through the clearing toward his home. "Don't be afraid, Rum-guzzler. You can't miss him. He'll be the only Indian sitting alone on a rock next to the path. Ha, ha. Rum-guzzler," he muttered at the end before ducking into the warmth of his abode.

"You forever surprise me, Mr. Weber," Washington breathed. "You make friends with the natives with nary an effort. Now come along, Rum-guzzler." He gave a wry smile as he led us into the woods, a bulging backpack strapped over his shoulders.

Buoyed by the prospect of walking in the rare sunshiny day, we chased after the major. He diligently followed the path and the footprints in the snow that would take us to Hunter. Sometime in the first half-mile or so, we heard the crack of a musket from far ahead. Hunter was obviously living up to his name.

Twenty minutes later, just like the chief had said, we found an Indian casually sitting on a rock next to the path. He wore thick hides on his back. He had on warm leggings and moccasins. A musket was cradled in his arms as if it were a child. "Bienvenue!" he called, waving as if we were long lost friends and he'd been expecting us.

We paused at the rock to exchange greetings. He looked familiar to me. I decided he must have been one of the participants in our night of drinking.

"You have blood on your hands," I said to the Indian.

"His name is Hunter, Weber," Gist reprimanded. "He just field-dressed the little rabbit that your chum the chief held."

Hunter glanced down at his hands, noticed the blotch of blood, and bent down to the snow. He dug out a handful and used it to wash. "Yes," he said. "I just missed some of the rabbit's blood." He tossed the red snow away and stood, hiking his weapon. "I'm told we are in a hurry." He reached for Washington's backpack. "I'll carry that for you, sir. Let us not waste any time."

"Now here's a fellow that understands urgency," Washington said as he handed over his pack. In seconds, Hunter was leading the way down the path, followed by the major, Gist, then Van Braam.

I was late in catching up. For, just as Hunter understood the need for urgency, so did I. The rum was finally demanding to be released. I set my gear down on the rock and raced off the path for privacy. My hands fumbled with my trousers below all my layers. I found a cliff that led down into a shallow ravine and let loose over the edge.

The cold made my privates shrivel. Steam raced up into the mid-morning sky as I urinated. "Ahh," I sighed, giggling when I thought about how I had met Washington and Bess in a similar pose. Thankfully, there would be no one to catch me this time.

I glanced down at my feet and saw a splotch of red on the snow. Moccasin footprints surrounded it and I decided it was where Hunter had shot his morning rabbit.

The bright sun had started to feel good. My mood was improving as my headache receded. I even thought the march to English civilization might be an enjoyable experience if this type of weather held.

That was a lot of blood for a rabbit, I then thought. Glancing back down, I confirmed that it seemed like too much for one rodent. But perhaps Hunter had killed a few and dressed them all right here.

But there were no entrails. There was no steam rising. There was no turned earth indicating that Hunter had recently buried rabbit guts to help keep the wolves at bay. There were, however, skid marks in the snow leading to the cliff.

That answered my question. Hunter had been careless. He'd dressed a few rabbits and swept their innards over the cliff into the ravine.

"Ahh," I breathed again while my stream sputtered to a satisfying conclusion. After I cinched my trousers and adjusted all my wraps, I stepped to the edge of the precipice. I had given this action no thought whatsoever. I had seen entrails before. They were as common on the frontier as they were in any woman's kitchen back in the colonies. But my mind wanted to solve the unremarkable mystery of the blood splotch and the missing innards.

And I quickly solved the mystery. Only it was replaced by another – this one remarkable, indeed. For there was no pile of guts laying in the ravine.

There was, however, the body of an Indian, cold and dead. He wore a gaping gunshot wound on his forehead. A brace of dead rabbits lay on his chest.

CHAPTER TWENTY-FIVE

Everyone in our time, of course, has come to know the exploits of George Washington. In two hundred years more, I imagine people will still talk about the man. They'll make up larger legends to supersede his already illustrious life. He will become myth with monoliths erected in his honor. And rightly so.

Likewise, but in the complete opposite manner, no one knows a thing about me or what I've done in my many days. They never will. But I like to think that without my twin, intense urges to urinate, at Williamsburg in Bess' alley and in the wilderness outside Murthering Town, that Washington, for all his devotion to Providence, would have been killed without me.

You see, had Bess not shrieked when she saw me, the major may never have found me. I undoubtedly would not have caught up with him as he bolted around the city. He certainly was in no mood to wait around for me that fall day a few months earlier. And if I was not along on the journey with him, I would have never had too much to drink with a band of Delaware the night before. And I never would have had to piss so suddenly. Therefore, I never would have seen the recently murdered Delaware hunter in the ravine.

And Washington, there is no doubt in my mind, would have been killed that very day.

My headache completely forgotten now, I was sprinting through the snow to catch up. The group had rounded another short cliff on the top of the trail and I couldn't see them. I had briefly toyed with the idea of snatching the handsome French pistol which I diligently reloaded every day. But that shot was saved for someone special. In any case, I left my heavy pack behind and proceeded to load my old Brown Bess on the fly. I should have loaded it for the day before leaving the town, but, well, you know I wasn't in the best of condition for making wise decisions. The act of plunging through snow and loading a fifty-eight and a half inch musket was cumbersome to say the least.

"Hey!" I panted when I saw the back of Van Braam.

He paused and then slowly turned to see what I was excited about. Ahead of him, I could see Gist still rounding the cliff side. The forest briefly ended thereafter. The major and the guide were halfway across the small clearing.

"Is your gun loaded?" I asked as I came to the Dutchman.

"Of course," he answered. Afterward, he probably thought, *why carry a musket in the wilderness if it's not loaded?*

I rammed my half-loaded piece into his chest and stole his gun. "I need it!" I shouted and continued on.

"What are you doing?" Van Braam shouted.

"Saving the major's life!"

I couldn't resist slamming into the shoulder of Gist as I ran by. He cursed up a storm, but could do nothing to hinder my progress.

Washington heard the commotion and turned. "Mr. Gist, what is the meaning of such an outburst of heathen language?" He was startled to see me rushing headlong toward him. "Mr. Weber, what do you think you are doing?" Behind me, I heard the feet of Gist and Van Braam rushing through the snow in order to catch up.

The Indian guide, who was nearly in the woods opposite, had spun to see what was happening. His eyes met mine and he knew that I knew. "Duck!" I shouted to the major. "He's not the real Hunter!"

The false guide was already leveling his weapon at Washington's back. I slammed to a halt and raised Van Braam's gun, pointing at the Indian through Washington. The hammer clicked into place when I gave it a tug with my thumb. "I said, duck!"

Suddenly realizing what was going on, Washington whirled to face his would-be attacker. The major was obviously disobeying my order to drop. Now I had no way to shoot without risking his life.

Crack-boom! The Delaware man had fired at the dumbfounded major. Washington jerked to the side as his cloak billowed and a hole was bored through it. The Indian was already fleeing ahead into the woods.

"Damn!" I cursed, again setting myself at a run.

I curbed myself next to the major and aimed the weapon I carried. The Dutchman's musket was newer, better weighted, and an all around finer piece than my tarnished Bess. But his felt odd in my hands. Like a new wife in an old widower's bed, I suppose. She's welcome and fresh, but not as comfortable as the old. She bucked, discharging with a roar. I knew before I saw the bark of a tree scatter that I had missed.

"How'd you know?" Van Braam breathed as he came to the other side of Washington.

"I had to piss!" I screamed, shoving the spent musket into the major's chest. I tore off in pursuit after the unknown Delaware. "Come on Van Braam!" We left Washington and Gist in the clearing.

Our chase didn't last as long as it could have. The Indian was weighted down by Washington's heavy pack. He should have abandoned it for the sake of speed, but he likely wanted to have at least something to show for his failed assassination attempt.

Like a hawk swooping onto a field mouse, I pounced onto him from behind. The musket he carried cracked against a tree. We both toppled forward into the snow with a series of puffs and thuds as we bounced down a gentle hill, careening off a sapling here, a root there. We came to rest on the bottom of a swale. The Indian was up first. He reached in his belt for a war hatchet. I struggled in a snow bank to right myself. The tomahawk was halfway out and I was a moment from death when Van Braam slammed into him from the side.

From there it was a long series of punches and kicks as the two of us subdued him. He was strong and swift. It took every ounce of our collective effort to tame him. When I found that I held the hatchet at the end of the tussle, I raised it. I had one and only one intention. The Delaware's eyes widened in fright.

"No!" Van Braam shouted. "Washington will want to question him."

I hesitated, panting. All three of us were bloodied. I wanted only to take out the last of my aggression, especially when the Indian's terrified grimace morphed into a crafty, crimson smile. "This isn't some backyard brawl!" Van Braam insisted. "We are on a diplomatic mission from the governor."

"Fine!" I barked. Of course Van Braam was right to remind me that there were other forces at work in this remote wilderness which were much bigger than he or I or the beaten Delaware. Wherever man went, I remembered, he brought his politics. I stuffed the hatchet in my belt. "Fine!" I repeated, though I didn't feel fine. I still wanted to crack our captive's skull in two.

I'd rather you not think of me as an angry youth with bloodlust in his heart and killing on his mind. I don't believe I was. But I will admit that some deep-seated rage was awakened during the fight at Pickawillany. Maybe the seed had been originally planted when I had witnessed my older sister killed years before. Regardless of the impetus, and with more and more frequency, I found myself trying to right every wrong that crossed my path. This man had wronged Major Washington.

We used a short amount of cord from the major's pack to bind our captive and then dragged him back toward the clearing. It took many long minutes because he was brawny and constantly fighting against us. He nudged and kicked. We returned the favor twice over. Eventually we straggled out of the shadowed woods and into the sunlit mountain field.

It was peaceful and, except for our footprints running in a line through its center, was pristine. Even Washington was still. He knelt on one knee, facing away from us. His head was bowed. His hat was held in one hand. His great cloak was spread wide like a tent over his back. I could see the sun reflecting off the snow and shining through the cloak's newly acquired bullet hole.

"Praying," I muttered. He was no doubt thanking God for preserving his life. Such was his way. Had he ever had occasion to meet my mother, she would have instantly fallen love with the dear boy's piety, probably wishing he, and not me, had been her son. Maybe even hoping that he might court one of my penniless sisters.

"We caught the bandit," Van Braam called proudly as we approached. "He's here for questioning, major."

"In time," Washington whispered.

I peered around the clearing. "Where'd Gist get off to?"

"He's here," the major answered.

This surprised me. Washington had somehow gotten Gist to hunker down in the snow and pray with him. I snickered at the image of him cuddling beneath the major's broad coat.

"Some men call it destiny," Washington was saying as we came next to him. Gist's body was sprawled out in the snow. He lay on his back, his own pack pressed beneath him. His arm was outstretched toward his musket which was buried in the white powder. His face was now permanently etched with the tortuous pain he had felt as he expired. A gaping hole was ripped into his clothes and continued into his belly. Scarlet painted him and his surroundings.

Washington lifted his hands and studied them. They were covered in Gist's blood. "But I shall forever consider it Providence that guides my path and sees me through each day. It shall be Providence that keeps me safe. It is Providence that has created me for deeds beyond those which I myself am capable. It shall be Providence that provides me the means."

He slowly washed the blood from his hands using the ice-cold snow. "What our imposter guide meant for evil against me, Providence in His wisdom, has set upon another. Mr. Gist has paid the price and I shall not forget that. His name shall find reward, even in death." The major stood to face us. He reached a hand and set it on my shoulder. "And it was Providence that gave you the discernment that saved my life today. This Indian's aim was rushed because of you. I am unable to adequately express my gratitude. Thank you, Mr. Weber." And in one of his rare moments of allowing his guard to drop, he added. "Thank you, Ephraim."

Washington was the type of man who fostered respect much more than love. He cultivated this detached personality with cool efficiency. And, I believe, he and those who followed him were completely at ease with the situation. However, for that brief moment after he uttered my given name in heartfelt appreciation, I loved him like an older brother. He became something of a real commander to me, not a young man pretending to be one. Were I a real soldier then, I would have considered following him.

He released his grasp of me and surveyed our prisoner. "We haven't much time to waste. Though tragic, the loss of Mr. Gist or even my own life matters little. We must resolve matters here and continue on."

And that is just what we did. With all the haste allowed by our gentleman officer's etiquette, we hammered through the snow and frozen ground to bury Gist. We then surveyed the dead man in the ravine, which could have only been the real man called Hunter.

Via Van Braam, Washington also questioned the captive, whose Delaware name translated to Fox. As you probably expect, he had been the runner whom I had seen – and forgotten to mention – in the chief's home that morning. Sent from Shingas to get rid of the problem of the earnest Virginian and possibly the Half King, the assassin had taken matters into his own hands when the drunken chief proved unwilling.

I lobbied heavily to execute Fox on the spot and return to Murthering Town for another guide. It would also do us good to explain to the chief what had happened to Hunter. We needed the chief to understand we had no hand in his death. There was no sense in creating enemies where they weren't necessary.

"No," Washington had said. "It will be well over an hour, perhaps two or more, before we can return to the village and explain all this, let alone gather a new guide. We must keep going. We did not end Hunter's life. This man did."

"But the Delaware warriors in Murthering Town and beyond don't know that," I argued, knowing the inherent distrust on both sides. "When they find his body, what are they going to think?"

"Which is why we will let Fox go free," Washington said. "Such an act will prove to him we are honorable Englishmen and mean no harm. He will feel compelled to explain the truth."

As you are aware, this supposition was complete horse shit. But Washington was back in his callow leadership mode and his ability to listen had vanished – so had my desire to ever follow him.

With two guns drawn on the captive, Washington cut Fox free. Van Braam translated Washington's words into French. "Now go, explain what has happened here to the chief in Murthering Town. He may understand your devotion to the orders given you by Shingas and even forgive the slaying of Hunter. I am certain a remedy can be negotiated. Then, I beg of you, send word to Shingas that we are on the side of his people. We are Englishmen, allies of Onondaga and all her children."

Unarmed, Fox walked toward the path leading back to the village. When he was twenty yards away and no longer a direct threat to us, Van Braam and I lowered our guns. Fox had sensed he was far enough away as to be mostly out of danger from us, as well. He stopped and spoke calmly in his Algonquian tongue, obviously unaware that I knew a fair amount of his language. When he was finished, he smiled and went on his way.

"See there, gentlemen," Washington said, hefting up his pack. "We may find honor in men of all stripes. He thanks us for compassion and no doubt wishes us well. What could have become an enormous misunderstanding has been averted. We may have just deprived the French of any Indian allies."

Then, without a guide, the major turned and began leading us in the general direction of Williamsburg by way of Wills Creek. When he had plunged back into the woods from the clearing, Van Braam turned to me. "You work for Croghan, right? You know some of the native tongues. Is that what Fox said? He wishes us well?"

"No," I said simply.

"Huh," he muttered. "Do I want to know what he really said?"

"No," I said. For Van Braam would not have wanted to know. I wish I had not understood the Delaware's threats. They sounded all too real.

CHAPTER TWENTY-SIX

We headed southeastward for four days. To my surprise I came to recognize some of the scenery and realized that our leader had actually brought us to within a one day march of Wills Creek, the trading post. While our initial departure from Murthering Town had begun in bright sunshine, each subsequent day was darker and colder than the last. Thankfully the precipitation stayed put in the clouds and did not fall on us. Even so, we awoke every morning on the trail shivering and hungry. But our spirits remained buoyant. We knew that from Wills Creek on out, our return to Williamsburg would be frigid, but our route would transition from trackless forest, to path, to road, and finally to the wide avenues of the capital. I had never wanted to walk among the towns so much in all my life.

We had but a single obstacle in our way before we could – rather improbably – trot into Wills Creek in the dead of winter. Given the bitter cold we expected the last river of any size to be frozen from shore to shore. It was not. The edges had ice that was thick enough for us to brave walking on for a least six feet. The icy water in the center, however, coursed along at a breakneck pace. And we had no horse with which to ford the river. We carried no canoes. And there were no bridges or ferries for hundreds of miles. Our choices ranged from following the course of the river and delaying our arrival in any settlement for several more days or constructing a crude raft.

Gone was all the bravado that had compelled Washington to ride across the cold Monongahela at the Forks, getting soaked to his knees just a couple months earlier. Unanimously, our numb, pale fingers made the decision for us. All three of us would happily build a raft.

As we'd elected to travel light on the return trip from Fort LeBoeuf, some of our tools now resided in that garrison's shed or even in the old chief's home in Murthering Town. We had only our muskets, a smattering of shot, and gunpowder. The only thing approaching a real tool of any kind was the war hatchet I had commandeered from Fox.

With this one poor hatchet we spent every bit of one full day making the saddest looking raft you'd ever seen. Our hands hardly followed the instructions given them by our heads. The shivering, which had heretofore confined itself to the morning hours, now lasted all day. During construction every knock or scrape felt like a spear plunging into our ice cold flesh. Our knuckles were bare by the end. Van Braam, I think, looked on the verge of tears at one point.

Nonetheless, with barely enough room for two, let alone three, men, we shoved the tiny raft over the ice along the bank. It scraped loudly, marking its path with etchings in the ice. Ahead, the current was swift and tried desperately to snatch our craft out of our frozen hands. We managed to cling to its slippery timbers, just barely. And one-by-one we hauled ourselves aboard the bouncing raft.

"Less than five minutes," Washington encouraged us as he shoved his setting pole against the shore. His hands were white, his lips blue. His teeth clattered more loudly than the water rushing beneath us.

We were off. The wild ride began immediately. It was all we could do to keep from capsizing in the bouncing stream.

Van Braam used his pole to catch the bottom and attempt to propel us across, rather than down, the stream. Our raft began to spin slowly. One moment we faced forward, the next we found ourselves staring upstream. Desperate to prevent us from tumbling over, Van Braam again rammed his pole into the muddy bottom and pushed. His action had the desired effect – sort of. We now were in the middle of the river where the current was strongest. Ahead, the river split in two around an island that was coming closer with every passing moment.

Giant, bouncing chunks of ice raced around us. During one twirling stint when we dizzily gazed upstream, Washington saw a particularly menacing mass of ice heading right toward us. If it struck us, our cobbled raft would disintegrate and our important mission would come to an abrupt and deadly conclusion.

Like an ancient hunter thrusting a spear at wounded prey with two hands, Washington lifted the setting pole and used every bit of his tall frame to hammer the end into the approaching hunk of ice. He even raised his voice to its maximum level (still quiet by most standards) and shrieked a war cry.

His attack was a resounding success. The iceberg careened off to the side, leaving our raft unmolested and fully intact. However, the ice had likely outweighed the major by one hundred pounds or more. He was no match for its considerable momentum. The force of the blow sent him reeling. His abandoned pole rattled onto the raft. The major splashed down into the frigid waters and was enveloped by the murky, swirling deep.

Washington's head reappeared five feet away, further downstream. He immediately went down again after bouncing off a log that was partially submerged.

I actually gave a smattering of thought to my next set of actions. I wasn't about to report back to George Croghan that I'd lost the one man I was supposed to accompany on this mission. So, snatching up the major's pole, I leapt toward the island that we had come near. My foot hit the ice and punched through, soaking me to my knee. But I was able to scramble onto the island and race along the bank. The major resurfaced for what might have been the last time and I dove back onto the ice shelf from the bank, sticking the pole over the rushing water. It clubbed his head, but he was able to loop an arm over. His weight and the force behind it nearly hauled me in with him. Fortunately, my foot caught a root in the bank and we held fast.

Van Braam guided the raft to the same island and jumped off to help. He was thinking only of saving the major. Perhaps he should have considered our only way of escape from that island. The current stole the raft and the pathetic remains of our supplies a second later.

Nonetheless, this minor, last incident on our journey has, as you might expect, a happy ending. Washington crawled out of the water, ice crystals in his hair, his skin a grotesque shade of blue. Van Braam quickly kindled a fire in the center of the island. None of us cared whether or not we caught all of North America on fire at that moment. The Dutchman and I heaped as much wood as we could on what became a massive bonfire. We spent the rest of the evening and all night drying, thawing, and warming ourselves. Despite its beginning, I do believe that after several hours, that night became one of the most comfortable of the entire expedition. I felt my fingers for the first time in many hours. Next to the conflagration, Washington slept like a baby.

We awoke the next morning, feeling blessed to have survived. "It is Providence, gentlemen," Washington said when we crossed to the other side of the island to find that the river there was frozen enough to walk atop.

And I suppose it was Providence. Though God's Providence had placed me among Washington's traveling companions so that I could save him from harm – twice – to me as a young man at the time it felt an awful lot like it had been Ephraim Weber that did all the work.

But I smiled as we hiked, for our great toil was near its end. Wills Creek and its food and shelter were just a few hours away.

I was also certain that important men like Croghan, maybe even the portly governor himself, would congratulate me when word of my heroics spread.

CHAPTER TWENTY-SEVEN

Imagine my surprise at the end of January 1754 after we'd been back in Williamsburg for several days when I opened the *Virginia Gazette*. Just beneath the newspaper's motto, which stated, *Containing all the Advices, Foreign and Domestick*, was an account of Major Washington's perilous journey of diplomacy among the Indians and to the French. Supposedly, the report came from Washington's own journal, in which I had witnessed him write at the end of most days. However, there were many flaws or inaccuracies to the story in the paper.

I'll not get into all of them, for a journalist's license with the facts is known far and wide. Anyone who would believe a newspaper's account at face value ought to consider admitting themselves into a lunatic asylum. However, I will note one particular inaccuracy that raises my ire to this day – more than forty years later! My name was not among the many mentions of Christopher Gist, Jacob Van Braam, the Half King or any of our other, even transitory, traveling companions. To make matters worse, in the tale that I quickly understood was spreading more rapidly than a fire in a dusty flour mill was that it was Gist, and not I, who had saved Washington from Fox, the Delaware Indian, and from the icy river. The names Washington and Gist were reprinted in couriers, gazettes, and newsletters in all the colonies from Georgia to New England. It was as if I had never been there at all. Yet my skin still bore the bruising left behind from my fist fight with Fox. My toes still tingled from what could only have been frostbite earned while crossing that last river.

"You mustn't let it get you down, Ephraim," Bess said as I accompanied her toward her father's home. The sun had melted all of Williamsburg's snow the previous day. Fortunately it had grown cold enough over night to refreeze the muddy sludge so we walked on top, rather than within, the muck. "You'll get your due. From what you've told me, Major Washington is a fair man. He'll see the error corrected."

I grinned at her. Despite the chill in the air, my skin felt flush when she spoke. She'd matured in the months since I had first seen her, growing lovelier. The fact that Bess allowed me, a backwoods trader's assistant, to amble next to her in plain sight made me all the more smitten with her. "You're probably right," I admitted, not believing it. But who could be contrary to such a divine angel?

"You'll see," she said happily as we breezed past the post office on which I'd urinated a few months prior. Bess then climbed up one of the steps to her father's home and turned, holding the yarn she'd bought in one arm. "Soon all of Virginia will be abuzz with your exploits. I can tell by the way you talk that you will amount to much more than even you think at the moment."

Hearing her give me such compliments was numbingly pleasant. I felt a little drunk.

The front door swung open. A smartly dressed gentleman stepped out. "Inside, Elizabeth," he said rather sternly.

"Of course, father," she said as she skipped up and out of sight. I had hoped she would have protested at least a little.

Bess' father closed the door and faced me. He crossed his arms and lowered his voice to a whisper. "I've seen you skulking about with my daughter these past days. I should think that even if Elizabeth is prone to flights of frivolity that someone who wishes to act as a suitor would have the decency to introduce himself. Well? Do you consider yourself a suitor of my daughter?" He sized me up from my hat to my buckskin gaiters.

Suitor? I had not considered myself a suitor to Bess. I still considered myself Tahki's widower.

"Your grin, young man, whatever your name is," said her father. "Your smile tells me that you do have some type of plans that involve Elizabeth – none of them holy."

"My name is Ephraim Weber, sir," I said.

"A backwoodsman?" he asked, showing little in the way of approval as he flicked with his finger a part of my coat that was torn. He again gandered at my dirty boots and worn leggings. "A frontiersman?"

"I do work on the frontier and even beyond. I've even been to the pays d'en haut," I admitted proudly. "I'm a trader."

"With the Indians?" he asked, incredulously.

"There's not much else out there," I said. "Unless you mean the few French goons we come across."

"There's not much of an American future in either case, I'm afraid. The days of the Indians and French are numbered." He didn't know just how prescient his words were to become.

Seeing that Bess' father was a difficult nut to crack, I carefully wiped my hand on the breast of my coat and offered it up to him. "I'm sorry that I am only just now introducing myself, sir. Bess and I met briefly last fall before I went away on the expedition with Washington."

The name Washington piqued his interest. The major had become something of a celebrity in Williamsburg, invited to all manner of parties since our return. "You were with young Major Washington, you say?"

"Yes," I said, sticking my chest out an extra inch. I wiggled my hand so that he could see it was still offered. "Had a chance to save his life twice on the return trip alone."

"I see," he said dubiously, his momentary interest in me now completed faded. "Well, Mr. Weber, I'll be direct. My understanding in working with men from the frontiers is that bluntness is the only thing they understand. But my firm words today will save you a crack across the cheek later. You are not to speak to my daughter ever again. There will be no courting for you. She is to marry a proper gentleman. One with a future. Is that clear?"

I sheepishly withdrew my hand and stuffed it into a pocket. "Yes, it's very clear," I stammered. "But if it is a matter of money, sir," I said, thinking of his possible objections. "I work directly for George Croghan, sir. Our enterprises stretch from the seaboard and nearly to the Mississippi. I would be able to provide for Bess." Here I was defending my right to court a girl I had never really considered courting. Not yet, anyway. Well, maybe I had considered it. But I still felt guilty.

"Income and wealth are important," her father admitted, nodding with his eyebrows raised. "You may not be a complete fool to realize that fact at such a tender age. However, I have no idea who this Croghan is, nor do I care. The frontier life is not for any daughter of mine. Indian raiding parties. Scalping. Weather. Disease. What kind of father would I be if I allowed such a thing?"

"I'm sure you're a kind father," I said. "Bess could stay in Williamsburg."

"Bess *will* stay in Williamsburg," her father countered. "And you should know I am not necessarily a kind father. Nor am I a cruel one. No. I am a loving father; one who knows what is best for my daughter and is willing to do what needs to be done. Say what needs to be said." He reached for the knob and twisted it. "That is what I have done. That is what I will do. Now, it is cold out here. I retire inside where sensible people reside. Stay away from my daughter, Mr. Weber." He slipped inside, closing the door halfway. He stopped and stuck his face out. "And next time you hope to tell a lie about saving a man's life, make sure you make the claim about someone who is not written about in every newspaper in the English-speaking world. I know. My wife knows. Even the lowliest farmer knows that it was Christopher Gist who saved Major Washington's life." He tucked his head back inside and slammed the door.

"You old capon!" I shouted through the oak.

If he heard me, Bess' father didn't react. The street remained quiet except for the several slaves, housewives, and merchants who made their way among the shops on that cold January day. I heard one or two snickers at my expense.

Dejected, I slowly retreated from the steps and grumbled. "He's nothing but a fat barrow." In truth, Bess' father wasn't plump at all. But it did make me feel better to say such things about him. And I can be fairly certain he was neither a capon nor a barrow. But the idea of him losing his manhood in the manner of an unfortunate rooster or boar made me smirk with satisfaction.

I heard a light, though incessant, tapping from above. Glancing over my shoulder I saw Bess in the sole upstairs window that faced the street. Through the speckled and pitted glass she smiled. Her brown hair had tumbled down around her shoulders after she had removed her cap. My heart pattered a little faster when she waved and then gently pressed her palm against the window.

"Elizabeth!" I heard her father scream from inside. Through another window, I could see him pacing in the parlor on the first floor with his hands on his hips.

Bess' head jerked to look over her shoulder toward the stairs. When she looked back toward me she wore the most mischievous grin. It was clear that she was no stranger to reprimand from her parents. Bess then leaned forward. And I'll not forget what she did for a hundred years. She slowly closed her eyes and pressed her lips against the cold greenish-blue glass, passionately kissing it in my stead. Vapor soon spread over the glass from the warm breath from her nostrils. When she straightened back up I could no longer see her face due to the fog. I did, however, see the tip of her index finger. It traced a heart in the mist she'd left behind.

And then in the blink of an eye, Bess turned and raced to heed her father's call.

I, in turn, stared at the heart in the window for many long moments until it had totally faded away. By the time I resumed my course down the street, I had forgotten about my lack of notoriety or Bess' father's public rejection. Instead, I was focused on just how I would go about courting Bess out from under the watchful eye of her father.

CHAPTER TWENTY-EIGHT

"Good work, lad!" Croghan exclaimed as I sat with him in the corner of one of his many *offices* spread over the land. This particular office, as with most of them, was a tavern. This one went by the name of *Maude's Rooster*. Across the room a pocket fiddle sang a lively melody. Twenty or more conversations ebbed and flowed to their own tune, paying the wandering fiddler no mind. Pipe smoke as thick as sour milk, though sweeter in the nostrils, hung from the ceiling to the floor. "Strike that! *Great* work, lad!" The Irishman then slapped my back for the third time. He had been giddy since hearing my report of the adventure.

"But Gist is getting all the credit for saving Washington," I protested.

Croghan burst into an uproarious laugh. Then he pretended to peer around the room. He even bent to look under the table. "Where is this hero called Gist?" he chuckled, lighting the Virginia tobacco he'd just pressed into the bowl of his pipe.

"I told you, he's dead."

Croghan slapped my back in the same spot. It had begun to sting, but what was I to do? I owed the old trader my very existence, my livelihood. "And I've told you, good job!" ol' George bellowed merrily. "Gist is deader than a Jacobite's prick! And what your mission did was put some fire under the hefty Dinwiddie! Why, the Scot suddenly wants to fund my little fort at the Forks with Virginia's money – not mine, not even the Ohio Company's. Maybe he'll use a little from Mother England! Looks like those tight-fisted Burgesses will even agree to the endeavor. We'll outfox those Franks faster than you can say, *Sacrebleu!*" He laughed even more.

"You're finally getting the fort that Tanaghrisson and Shingas promised you? It's going on two years ago we had that conference," I said.

"Yep," Croghan said, waving off the delay. "And I'm not out a penny. But that journal of Washington's is causing a stir. Sounds like the French at Fort LeBoeuf mean to send a force down to the Forks of Ohio themselves and make a permanent claim."

"It'll take them only a week or two to get there once the winter ice breaks from the streams out west," I said. "From here, the trip will be well over a month. We'll never get to the Forks in time."

"Don't be so sure!" he snapped, happily puffing his pipe. "Thing about these royal governors is that they're old, fat, and lazy. But once you get that big ball of blubber rolling, it's hard to get them to stop. That's just what you and young Washington did with your report."

"The report that is all wrong! I told you, I saved Washington. Gist was already dead by the second time!"

Croghan made no attempt to hide his eye rolling before he set a hand on my arm. "Boy, now listen. What have I told you about business? Don't answer." He went on, sounding like a mother exhausted from repeating herself for the hundredth time. "I'll tell you because you clearly forgot. There comes a time when you must let the competition think they are winning."

"Competition?" I asked.

"Gist, the Ohio Company, Washington," he said as if it was the most obvious fact in the world.

He saw the confusion spread across my face. "Lad, Washington inherited more than just a military post from his dead brother, Lawrence. He also received shares in the Ohio Company. That's why Washington made the Ohio Company man, Gist, look like a hero in his journal. And so you see, the good soldier had two reasons to be so hasty this winter, honor – which he clearly has by the bushel – but also money. If the French get to the Forks first, young Washington's shares will be worthless. In a way, such a thing would be a slap in the face to his dear deceased brother. Washington's pride would never allow that to happen. And Dinwiddie, too, owns shares. Now that they are both convinced that the Froggies are coming, they'll move to the Forks lickety-split."

"But if it's an Ohio Company fort, won't the Ohio Company have the advantage?" I asked. "If they are competitors, how is that good for us?"

Croghan leaned back in his chair and propped his boots on the table. "It's not, lad," he said solemnly.

"Then why are you so excited?"

A thin smile curled beneath his great snout. A wisp of smoke crept from one corner of his mouth and swirled along his cheek and temple before it parked itself beneath the brim of his hat. "Because the Ohio Company man, Gist, is dead. That's one man out of the way, God rest his soul. I do wish it didn't happen in that way. Dinwiddie has sent Washington to Alexandria to recruit a couple hundred men for a small army that will march toward the Forks. He'll be busy for months. That's a second Ohio Company man out of the way."

"And?" I asked.

"And you and I, lad, are heading to Wills Creek. You'll have to again fight some weather, but without a whole huge train of men, you won't be delayed. You'll be at the Forks in just a couple weeks – long before the French wake up from their winter slumber." Croghan waved some papers with Dinwiddie's seal affixed at the bottom. "And we'll have men I know, if not trust, as commissioned officers working for us. The fort will be finished, the Indians happy, and trade begun before Washington can even get the first man under his command to understand the difference between salute and salut."

I had begun to see why Croghan was so happy. He had much to teach. I had much to learn. From a hastily established base at the Forks, he'd use his profoundly deep network of contacts throughout the interior to build up another empire of trading and land speculation before the Virginians even knew what hit them. His in-laws, nearly all of them Indians, and his friendship with the Half King would secure for him fast riches. "So give Gist and Major Washington the glory in the papers while we reap the benefits in sterling?" I asked.

"Exactly, lad," Croghan said, wagging a finger. "I knew I had seen a spark in you when you showed up on my doorstep some years ago. All of ninety pounds dripping wet, you were. Oh," he added. "No more Major Washington. The strapping chap is now a lieutenant colonel. Seems Dinwiddie was chomping at the bit to get his new celebrity a promotion. Makes them both able to bask in the glow." He rattled the commission papers again. "But we've got promotions of our own to hand out. They and early possession of the Forks will be all that we need." He slapped the documents onto the table and turned to the nearest tavern maid. "Rum here! And keep it coming. We're celebrating."

"Certainly, Mr. Croghan," she said courteously.

"Mr. Croghan!" he shouted. "Nobody would ever call me mister anything had I been stuck in Ireland, boy! This truly is a New World. It's a land that is ripe for harvest."

The maid came and left several times in quick succession, for we drank aplenty. The pocket fiddle began playing a melancholy tune even as Croghan's spirits rose higher. Some of the patrons slowed their conversations in order to listen to the sad song. With only its haunting notes and no words, it told of the heroes lost in battles past. I saw a tear or two shed as men recalled the late Indian wars and the last war against the French when fathers, sons, and brothers had died.

When George went on about how we'd be leaving Williamsburg in the morning, I realized that my ever-so brief and wholly unsuccessful courtship of Bess had already reached an unfortunate pause. It wouldn't take long for another man to weasel his way into her heart. But in looking at the bright side of things in the manner of my employer, I also grasped that seizing the Forks would make Croghan and I something of celebrities ourselves. That, coupled with the riches that were doubtless to fall into our pockets, would do everything to soften up Bess' father that my genial demeanor could not.

"Rum!" Croghan hummed to the maid. Our cups had been dry for less than a minute.

While he fiddled with his empty mug, I spread out the governor's commissions that George had shown me earlier, wondering just who *our* officers would be. The first commission was for a captaincy to be bestowed upon William Trent. He was, of course, Croghan's brother-in-law. Trent was a fellow trader who was diligent and actually quite caring for a man who lived on the harsh frontier. He'd see that we got the fort built in a hurry.

The second piece of paper granted the rank of ensign to Edward Ward, a young man not much older than I, who also happened to be Croghan's half-brother. He was another good choice as someone the wily Irish trader could trust. It was obvious that George Croghan had whispered these names into Governor Dinwiddie's perked ear.

Finally, I set those two sheets aside and looked at the third and final commission.

"You'll be operating with all three of those men and their workers!" Croghan said joyfully. "I'll stay at Wills Creek to organize the first pack train of goods to arrive at the Forks in the spring, while you run ahead with them to build the fort."

And though I didn't look forward to the weather, working with George's relatives would not be the worst task I'd ever done. Or, would it? I had just noticed the third name. To me, the gloomy music of the fiddle became truly miserable at that moment.

Croghan raised his mug for a toast. "To a little peace and a whole lot of prosperity!"

"Prosperity," I mumbled and downed my drink along with Croghan. I didn't have it in me to proclaim peace, for I doubted there'd be any. Because the man whose name was written on the third page and who had been awarded the rank of lieutenant in the Virginia militia was none other than John Fraser.

But perhaps it wasn't to be such a miserable experience. It was possible that he had forgotten that I had threatened to kill him in his own cabin.

Or, and more likely, even now he contemplated just how he would retaliate against me.

CHAPTER TWENTY-NINE

By late February our crew of about forty men had been at the Forks for nearly two weeks. We had suffered through foul weather, but were somewhat better prepared compared with when Washington had dragged us out there. Once there, I was able to keep warm during the day due to my rigorous exertions as a laborer felling trees in the exact spot selected by then Major Washington at the start of winter. By night we huddled together in tents and heated our chests and thawed our limbs with ample ale. Croghan had supplied us with plenty of alcohol because he understood what kept the average laborer working. He also knew that ale was popular among the Indians and could be traded for any necessary provisions even easier than a stack of the king's money.

I found Trent to be a capable commanding officer. He understood the backwoodsmen he had working for him, for he was one of them. He knew just the right amount of pressure to apply to keep us going while not making us bitter. Trent set the tone of the work camp and despite the difficulties inherent in carving out a settlement from the ice cold wilderness, those early days passed by with each of us in fair spirits.

When the clearing was large enough to begin actual construction of the tiny fort, word was sent to Chief Tanaghrisson at Logstown. He was invited to set the first log – a brilliant stroke of diplomacy suggested by young Ensign Ward. By the time the chief arrived some days later, an official letter had also come to camp from Croghan, who hustled about at Wills Creek setting everything in place for a triumphant arrival at the Forks in spring. Trent read the message aloud to the assembly of momentarily idle workers and Indian witnesses as the Half King dropped the end of a great oak log – our foundation – into the mud. The light drizzle did nothing to dampen the Iroquois chief's obvious attitude of relief. His gambit to support Croghan's and our English colonies' move into the Ohio – two years in the making – had at last been realized.

"And so, in honor of our promises to the Iroquois League and their Indian wards at the Logstown Conference of 1752, I, George Croghan, am proud to have my friend, Chief Tanaghrisson, set the foundation in place. This site will grow to house great trade among our peoples. It will be a source of wealth and peace for every man, regardless of his race. It shall be a fort of the English, a fort of the Indian." Trent finished reading and rolled up the letter. "We are ahead of schedule," he called proudly. "Thus, we can afford to rest our tools for the remainder of the day and be adequate hosts to our Indian guests."

A cheer from the workers echoed through the forest.

"George has also indicated we ought to double every man's ale rations this afternoon and share a healthy portion with our Indian friends." This exclamation brought a chorus of joy from the Delaware and Shawnee representatives. And though Shingas and his most loyal of followers were conspicuously absent, the tone of the celebration began and continued in a most positive manner.

"Shit-for-brains," said the Half King sometime later. He had just pulled himself away from visiting with Captain Trent. The pair were as good of friends as were the chief and Croghan. I, decidedly less congenial than our commander and Tanaghrisson, had been competing in an intense card match beneath a tarp while nursing my ale.

I had already won several of the other men's afternoon rations of dark malt in a highly contentious game of loo. Since I was in the midst of a round that appeared to be heading in my favor, I tried to dismiss the chief. "Not now," I muttered while nervously chewing on a thick piece of bark I'd picked off a tree. I felt it made me look tough. "Ensign Ward is about to be looed."

Croghan's half-brother protested, "Not if I show a flush plus Pam!" He tried to put on a threateningly grave expression, but his pleasant demeanor would not allow it. Several of us smirked at the earnest young man.

"You've got no flush," barked Fraser. At first, I hadn't wanted him to play. But when he insisted, I realized his money would fall into my purse as easily as anyone else's. "You've got no Pam." By the way, Pam was the erotic name given to the Jack of clubs. I have no idea why poor Jack was treated that way, but we all knew the slang.

"Both of you shut up," I mumbled, laying my cards down on a log for all to see. "Because I've just looed the board."

"Damn you!" Ward exclaimed, throwing his hand at me. The cards fluttered onto our boots. He had no face cards, let alone Pam. He had just lost his last remaining cup of ale.

"You cheat!" Fraser accused. He was at least as drunk as I. But while I had won my drink by gambling, Fraser had drunk from a stash that he'd brought from his home. Until that afternoon, we'd successfully steered clear of one another during the project. It hadn't been difficult. It was obvious that Fraser wished to be at his own little trading post rather than act as a commissioned military man building a fort for another trader. Instead of toiling, he spent most of his time trying to undermine Croghan by secretly meeting with small congregations of Indians. A lot of good it would do him. Once trade with Croghan got underway at the Forks, Fraser's tiny outpost eight miles up the Monongahela would be put to shame and out of business.

Fraser and I each jumped to our feet, our fists balled, our chests within an inch of one another. "I don't need to cheat when I compete against a horse's ass!" I said. The other participants in the card game gathered what small amounts of wealth and ale they had left and scattered.

Perhaps I was drunker than Fraser. My reaction time was certainly slower. He swung at me with all his might and I would have been laid out in the muck had it not been for the Half King. The old chief's palm stopped Fraser's blow in midair. "You may have my share of the ale, Mr. Fraser," he said as their hands wavered just below my chin. "Do not waste your time on little Shit-for-brains."

There was a moment when Fraser was open to attack as he laughed at my nickname. I ought to have slammed my forehead into his, but I could never help but see Chief Tanaghrisson as anything but a friend and customer of Croghan. To go against his wishes would seem an unnecessary affront. I slowly stepped back out of the way. "I'll take no more from you today," I announced, thinking myself magnanimous for giving up the rations I had just won fair and square.

"Come now, Shit-for-brains," Tanaghrisson said. He tossed away Fraser's fist.

"You run on along with your Half King," Fraser slurred.

Tanaghrisson bristled. His jaw flared and he moved his nose to that of Fraser. I believe his fingers twitched toward the hatchet in his belt, but his age and experience quickly got the better of his rage. Before Fraser could bring his arms up in defense, the Half King was back next to me. He steered us both along a track into the wilderness.

"An Indian and an Indian-lover!" Fraser snapped after us. "Cowards."

"You should have rammed your tomahawk into his manhood," I told the Half King after we'd moved a safe distance away.

"I'd have had to find his tiny manhood first," Tanaghrisson said with a smile. Then he patted my shoulder in a fatherly manner. At least I assumed it was the way a caring father would have done such a thing. I was fairly certain my own father had never done the like. "My blade is reserved for the same man who is to receive the shot from your loaded French pistol," he reminded me. "If you somehow fail in your revenge, I will be there to back you up. Besides, I cannot strike at even a cur like Fraser. I cannot risk alienating myself from the English. I need strong allies right now."

"What do you mean?" I asked. "You're a sachem of the Seneca, one of the Iroquois tribes that rules over the lesser tribes."

"Humph," he muttered with a forlorn smile. We walked along an animal path that had been widened by us, the workers at the Forks, in order to drag logs to the worksite. A robin fluttered to land on a branch nearby. We both took note of the sure sign of spring and continued on. The Half King watched his feet step as we walked, frequently glancing at me as if he was unhappy about something.

"Seems like something is wrong," I prompted him. "But how could there be. You've got your fort, your alliance. Shingas will have to back down now."

"Uh, huh," he said absentmindedly. "You seem like a good boy. It's a shame you are wrapped up in the middle of all this."

"The middle of what?" I asked. "It's all going in our favor."

"So it does. Do you know Deganawidah?" he asked.

I was normally fairly proficient with Indian words. But I butchered it to incomprehensibility when my drunken tongue repeated it.

"Close enough, Shit-for-brains," Tanaghrisson said, gradually emerging from his moment of melancholy. "The Great League of Peace and Power, that which we call the Iroquois today, was formed out of chaos. Mourning wars, honorable when limited, had exploded into a series of constant blood feuds between the tribes. We could no longer control the hatred and bloodlust for one another that resided in our hearts. The spirit, Deganawidah, appeared to each of the heads of all the clans in the original five nations. He called them to a meeting beneath a tree at Onondaga."

"The Tree of Great Peace," I whispered. Tribes as far away as the Miami often spoke in wonder about the tree beneath which the Grand Council of the Iroquois met. Though in reality, more often than not, they now met in a longhouse at the end of the meadow that held the tree. Even noble chiefs like to retreat inside from the harshest weather now and again.

"Yes," Tanaghrisson said. "We have met at Onondaga ever since. We became a force for power and peace. Tribes who were not members were sucked under our wing because of our sudden sheer size."

"Exactly," I said. "It is the English who need you. Not the other way around."

"And that is partially true. But you know what I am called by the whites and some Indians."

"Chief Tanaghrisson," I answered quickly, unwilling to look him in the eye.

"You forget, Shit-for-brains, that you called me Half King at our first meeting. Don't worry about it," he added when he saw how ashamed I became. "It bothers me when lesser men like Fraser or Shingas say it. Not you. My power in this region is just like that of the Iroquois on the whole. It is waning. Those lesser tribes you speak of want to claim independence from Onondaga. As such, it becomes more important than ever for the Iroquois to select which, between the French and English, will become masters of the continent."

"Masters of an entire continent?" I asked, incredulous.

"Don't be so surprised," he said in reprimand. "You are many. Indians are few. Your natural ways are to look forward and chase dreams. Our ways tie us to the immovable land. They cause us to peer back to our ancestors. Two hundred years from now, your children's children will be instructing their children. What small amount left of my people will still be praying to Deganawidah and their ancestors to bring about a past that never was. Not unless I act decisively today."

"So, you believe the English will come to rule all of America?" I asked. It seemed utterly implausible. Our settlements were trapped up against the Atlantic seaboard, with Indians and the French surrounding us in a great arc from the St. Lawrence to the mouth of the Mississippi. The maps were clear.

"I do," he admitted. "Like the French, your people come for profit. But unlike most of the French, you also come to settle and build families. The English invite other Protestants, like Germans, to join them. Together, you build cities and schools. You outnumber the French by twenty times! I shudder when I try to estimate by how much you outnumber the Indians. If every Indian from here to the Pacific banded together – something that will never happen because we hate each other too much – the English probably still outnumber us." He studied the soggy ground, lost in thought, perhaps about a time that had never existed. "Nonetheless, until you showed up here at the Forks to actually build this fort, I was beginning to think I had backed the wrong horse. If the French got here first, the inevitable English victory would have to spill buckets of blood when it all could have been accomplished with nary a drop spilt."

Relieved, he added, "Thank you for coming so quickly. I believe the fort's presence will save many lives – Delaware, Mingo, Shawnee, English, French. The sooner we all come to understand that, the better. Iroquoia can only benefit."

Tanaghrisson appeared exhausted. Being a king, whole or half, was taking its toll on him. "You think Shingas will come to support us?" I asked. "He was clearly on the other side when we last met."

He rubbed his tired eyes. "In time, I think he will. The fort will bring trade, wealth, and stability." The Half King pointed an accusing finger in my direction. "But you and Conotocarius have done nothing to help the situation with Shingas."

"I thought you just thanked me," I said.

"For bringing these men and trade here, yes," Tanaghrisson said. "But killing that Delaware Indian, called Hunter, over the winter may have just alienated all of the Western Delaware, not just *King* Shingas."

"We didn't kill anybody!" I protested. "It was that other Delaware, Fox. And he killed Gist!"

"I suppose you were very disappointed at that?" he said sarcastically.

"That's not the point."

"It's not," Tanaghrisson agreed. "But Fox has spread rumors among all the Delaware that Conotocarius has resumed the ways of his name. He killed Hunter. And it is he who will come back to finish the rest of them off by burning villages and carrying off women. You should have returned to the old Delaware chief you so happily drank with and explained what happened rather than flee."

"Which did you want?" I asked, growing frustrated as I became sober. "Did you want Washington to run home with his message and encourage this fort to be built. Or, did you want him to turn around and negotiate while the French descended on the Forks?"

"Both. I wanted both," he admitted.

"Well, I wanted a peaceful life and a pregnant wife. I got neither!"

The Half King quietly considered my outburst. He, too, had lost at the younger Jumonville's hand. He again patted my shoulder. "I suppose we got the right one, then. The fort is more important. I ought to be thankful that it will be Croghan coming in the spring and not Conotocarius. If we can keep Major Washington away a little longer, Shingas and the others might well fall in line by midsummer."

Of course, the Half King was wrong. It was up to me to correct him. "Washington's a Lieutenant Colonel now."

"Oh. Whatever the rank, it is good that he is not here for the time being."

I didn't have the heart to tell him that within a month's time Washington would probably be cutting a road toward us, leading his grand army.

CHAPTER THIRTY

A lot can happen in the hills surrounding the Forks of Ohio in two months. Patches of early flowers can replace what eight weeks earlier had been tufts of snow. Stark, naked branches backlit by sunlight and made to look dark in winter, suddenly come alive with blossoms and budding leaves. And supplies, especially foodstuffs, can steadily become exhausted.

This should not have been a formidable problem when we were not officially at war with anyone. There were plenty of idle Delaware men living nearby who were capable of bringing in ample game to keep our workers fed and the fort on schedule. After the Half King returned to his home at Logstown, Trent frequently consulted with representatives from the nearest Delaware, offering them hard specie and alcohol in exchange for providing meat to the Forks. To a man, those representatives declined.

Eventually, after slowly cutting our rations and expecting resupply from Wills Creek to arrive not for another month, Captain Trent requested Chief Shingas come to the Forks in order to consult and iron out any differences. After several terse exchanges via runners in which Shingas insisted Trent refer to him as king, a meeting was set.

"It was your plea at Logstown that originally brought Shingas around to support the building of this fort," Trent reminded me.

"That and the fact that he got Tanaghrisson to agree that Shingas' people could operate without direct Onondaga control," I said.

"Nonetheless, you shall join me in talking with the Delaware king and his followers."

Trent led me into the tiny building inside the partially finished fort that had become his temporary office. It consisted of a single room with a dirt floor. The log walls were over a foot thick. The windows more closely resembled tiny sniper holes and therefore the interior was dark. The light given by the only two candles we had was dwarfed by sunlight whenever the door was opened. He used a log for a chair and sat behind a desk that

186

consisted of a single plank ripped from a local tree that was set between two upright logs. The furnishings were crude indeed.

Since we had left the door ajar for light, we could see when one of our carpenters led Shingas and his clingers toward us. The Delaware king studied the inside of the fort as they crossed the miniscule yard. I was surprised to see him genuinely impressed, an emotion which he quickly stowed away as he ducked under the door.

"I'm not sure what you wish for me to do," Shingas uttered before we'd even begun exchanging pleasantries.

"You are king?" Trent asked, unruffled.

Shingas nodded with a careless air and began looking for a place to rest. I saw his displeasure at the accommodations and remembered that Croghan had always told me a comfortable man will be more apt to do business. I lifted the desktop plank from the logs and set it against the back wall. Then, I kicked over the heavy logs and rolled them toward the Delaware men. Surprised, Shingas said, "Thank you." He and his men sat.

"I am King of the Delaware," Shingas agreed. "But I am not a tyrant. If my hunters refuse to work for you for wages of any kind, that is their business."

"Certainly, King Shingas," Trent said, also well-versed in Croghan's legendary salesmanship. "A word of encouragement may go a long way, however. Those same men might be willing to hunt for us if they discover their king wishes it."

"Perhaps," Shingas allowed.

"And such an effort on your part would be compensated as well," Trent offered, knowing full well that gifts among Indian leaders of all the tribes brought prestige. Gift-giving was a time-tested way to show honor among the Indians. The more gifts a chief received, the more his power was recognized by others, the more he could in turn share gifts with others, appearing generous. "It is in all our interests to see this fort properly completed and trade begun promptly. Such an outcome is our best chance at keeping the French away and preserving the peace."

Shingas glanced at his young warriors who, to a man, shook their heads to indicate *no*. He then peered out the open door at where workers continued to build the palisade. Their pounding, laughing, and cursing echoed through the door. Shingas gnawed on the inside of his mouth when he again faced us. "The fort is of the right size," the chief admitted. He sounded surprised. "When fully garrisoned it should protect the area and trade. But it is not so large as to pose a threat to my Delaware and our way of life."

I smiled. "It is what George Croghan promised. It will keep the Delaware as well as the English safe from invasion by the French and their Ottawa or Chippewa allies. But the fort is not so large as to dominate the local inhabitants."

The Delaware hated the Ottawa and Chippewa, perhaps more than they hated the English. Even the young warriors growled at their mention. Shingas sighed. "I did give my word that I would support Croghan's fort. Since my English brothers have shown their willingness to work even in winter and they've beaten the French fathers in the race to the Forks, I ought to see that none of you starves." Perhaps the Half King had been correct. Shingas would only need time to fully support our mission. "Forward what gifts you deem appropriate to my village. I will then see how serious of a partner you intend to be. My support will be in proportion to the gifts I receive."

Captain Trent clapped his hands. "Oh, thank you, King Shingas. We won't let you down. We will get the walls finished and hang this gate in no time. That way, when Lieutenant Colonel Washington arrives with his army, there will be no way a Frenchman or any power dares make an attempt to take the Forks."

Shingas' temporary smiled faded. "Washington?" he asked. "The same man who intentionally got a senior member of our tribe drunk, only to murder a young brave in broad daylight?"

Trent looked at me in confusion, properly sensing that his diplomatic coup was about to explode. "Washington did no such thing!" I answered.

"You'll pardon me if I don't believe you, Shit-for-brains," replied Shingas. "I'd sooner believe Conotocarius himself as to believe a Pennsylvanian Quaker."

"Conotocarius?" Trent asked. "I'm sure there is a mistake."

Shingas stood quickly, all of the subtle hints at conciliation now vanished. His braves followed him as he stormed out the door. Trent chased after them and only cut them off at the bare patch of ground where the gate would eventually hang. "Please reconsider. We need those supplies and you need this fort."

Shingas peered around at the workers who had halted to watch the spectacle. "I will do nothing to slow your progress for I have given my word. My English brothers are welcome at the Forks *if* they can hold them. However, I will do nothing to help you hold them either. We refuse to feed the belly of the Destroyer of Villages."

That was the second time I watched Shingas and his warriors march off in anger. His back was becoming a common sight.

Trent watched him go, too. "I guess he changed his mind," he said.

"He's got a problem with Washington's ancestors," I answered.

"And now I've got a problem," Trent said. Determined, he turned toward the stables, which consisted of a set of tarps strung together and stretched between a group of posts. "I've got to run east and organize supplies sooner than later. Things will get sparse around here quickly if we don't get a pack train on the way."

"What about work on the fort?" I asked. "Who'll manage it?" Trent had been good for morale and had fostered brisk work.

"Tell Lieutenant Fraser and Ensign Ward to keep up the pace. I'll be back as quickly as I can."

"What if the French come?"

He chuckled. "My presence alone would help very little if the French descend aboard all those canoes you and Washington saw up north in the winter. Let's just hope those supplies and Washington's army get here before any Frenchmen. Or else our stay at the Forks will be short indeed." He mounted his horse that was already saddled and provisioned for an extended ride. Trent saw my curious glance. "I didn't really expect Shingas to agree," he explained.

As Trent's beast walked out past the partially built wall, he called out to Fraser, who was just returning from one of his many wilderness disappearances. "Fraser, cut the rations by another half until you hear differently. And talk to Weber if you have any questions." Captain Trent then spurred his horse to a trot, bouncing off into the woods.

Fraser, not sure exactly what was going on, but very certain he'd just been left in charge, gave me a devilish grin.

It was to be a long and, I feared, bloody four months.

CHAPTER THIRTY-ONE

But not for the reasons I had thought. I had expected Fraser to lead with a heavy hand, commanding me and the others for his sole benefit. And to some extent he did exact control. Only instead of lording over us while at the Forks, he disappeared altogether.

With no superior officer to reprimand him, just one hour after Trent had run after supplies, Fraser had packed up his gear – and a fair amount of the company's untended provisions – and trotted off to his home up the Monongahela. It was almost as if he knew that something awful was coming, something of which he wanted no part.

We were left under the command of young Ensign Ward. He was about Washington's age, but with none of the gravitas. Sure, Ward was liked well enough, but he commanded no respect. And with rations cut, Ward had almost no hope of achieving the task that had fallen into his lap. Older men took advantage of his youth. Young men acted as if Ward was merely their friend, not their commanding officer.

Work on the fort slowed to a crawl as men refused to work on empty stomachs. Ensign Ward did his inexperienced best and sent out hunting parties once a day. This was successful in that it prevented us from more quickly depleting our food or worse, starving. But it also pulled more men away from construction. Between hunters, foragers, and the inevitable injured or sick men occupying the open-air infirmary, our workforce was halved. After two weeks went by with Captain Trent absent, the ends of our walls had just barely grown closer together. Likewise, the great gate still lay sprawled out in the dirt, half-assembled.

In hindsight, things could have slowly progressed in that manner with little difficulty. However, life is rarely without impediments. While many such obstacles are erected by each man himself, others come from outsiders. And that is just what happened on April thirteenth in the year seventeen fifty-four.

I remember it so clearly because I was standing behind Ensign Ward in the cramped office as he had just set his pen to his journal and scratched out the date. By default, I had become his aide-de-camp and was giving him the names of the men we had sent out for that morning's hunting party. Not knowing what else to do, Ward had decided to record all of his actions so that Croghan and Trent would know he had always acted sensibly. And, in truth, he had.

Shouts and pounding footfalls drew our attention to the doorway. Outside, I saw Tommy Stewart sprinting across the clearing toward us.

Ward returned his focus to the page. "Didn't you say ol' Stew was one of our hunters this morning."

"I did, but that was yesterday."

Ward scraped the name on his page. "They must have had good luck to have taken so long," he said. "And the other names?"

"Eddie!" called Stewart as he skidded to a halt in the threshold, his form casting a dark shadow throughout the interior of our office. I could just barely see the rest of the hunting party running through the gaping hole where the gate was to eventually be. Their faces matched that of Stewart – worried.

"What did you find for us, Tommy?" Ward asked. "Will we dine on venison tonight?"

"The French, Eddie!" Stewart panted. "We found ass loads of French!"

CHAPTER THIRTY-TWO

Though green by any sense of the word, Ensign Ward quickly came to grips with the requirements of his command. In moments after learning from Tommy Stewart that hundreds of Frenchmen and Indian allies were slowly canoeing their way toward us, he set men in orderly action. Because according to Stewart, we had no more than four days before the Forks were fully infested with our uninvited guests.

"Retrieve Chief Tanaghrisson!" young Ward barked to a swift, long-legged carpenter. "We'll need him here to talk sense into the French! Tell him not to delay." That man snatched up his musket and raced off toward Logstown.

"Trent is too far away," Ward muttered to himself. "But I'll still send word later." Then he pointed to another lanky carpenter who was known to be friends with John Fraser. "Run up to the Lieutenant's place on the Monongahela. Tell him what is going on. Bring extra supplies from his cabin via the river. Remind him that the coming of the French is as much a danger to him as it is to us. You should be able to have him here by tonight or tomorrow morning!" This second runner tore off.

By now all work had ceased. Rumors travel fast in any environment and it was no different among the artificers toiling at the Forks. Ward was soon surrounded by every able-bodied man. And it seemed every able-bodied man shouted questions at the young officer about what would happen when the large force of French arrived. *Would we fight? Could we have any hope? Where was Trent? Was the captain coming? Was he bringing artillery? Where was Washington and his army of Virginians?*

"Gentlemen, please!" Ward shrieked when he had had enough. The young officer marched out through the small throng and stood looking down at the gate. He placed his hands on his hips and peered up at the walls that required another ten feet be added if they were ever to be the right size to receive the gate. "Five of you will spend the next three days gathering whatever food, meat, roots, or berries you can find. Bring it all into the fort." He then counted off three groups of twos, including Tommy Stewart. "You six set up patrols to keep us apprised of the French movement and exact whereabouts. 'Round the clock!"

Stewart led those men away, each making sure to carry extra shot and powder. "And the rest of you," Ward went on. "Unless you want to end up as part of a Frenchman's glorious war story to his grandkids, you had better get your asses to work and set this gate. Move!"

His bark was only a tiny squeak, but the men, thinking of their own skins, jumped to action. It was nothing like the previous two weeks had been. Timbers were raised and lashed together. Holes were bored. Pegs were driven at a frenetic pace.

For men not involved in any official war, I will tell you that I saw a lot of worry etched across faces over the coming three and a half days. Over that time, a few things worked out in our favor. Some things did not.

CHAPTER THIRTY-THREE

Our foragers brought in enough filling, though not tasty, supplies to extend our light food rations out another five days. We used the last of our salt to preserve what small amount of meat they carried – a few squirrels and a rabbit. Most of the big game had been scared away from the area by the racket we created while building. We also took inventory of our flour, which amounted to two measly sacks that would run out quickly. And since we didn't yet have a well, water was hauled up from the rivers and stored in leaky barrels. We could have used the services of a cooper. The rest of the provisions consisted of edible leaves and roots. Our meals wouldn't be the most bountiful or finest, but if Trent or Fraser could arrive soon enough with aid, at least we'd not starve.

On the second day, with no sign or word from Lieutenant Fraser, we received the Half King and his handful of Mingo followers with relief. They certainly didn't constitute a strong military addition. And I didn't know what the others thought, but I was sure that Tanaghrisson's long experience in these types of diplomatic affairs would soon see a peaceful resolution. The Frenchmen would vacate the Forks. Croghan would have his fort and lucrative trade with the Indians. The Ohio Company would begin to speculate on the surrounding lands. I could again *peaceably* go about finding Jumonville and exacting *violent* revenge. I'd then return to Williamsburg to court Bess. Marriage and a family, trading and wealth would follow. In short, my plan for life would return to normal.

As the workers finished the gate and walls, all we could do was wait. The Half King relaxed, smoking a pipe that was nowhere near as ornate as his ceremonial peace pipe. This one had probably been purchased in one of the shops in the eastern towns. He whiled away his time by sharing stories with his Mingo friends. They patiently watched the river as if expecting to see many squadrons of old acquaintances arrive at any moment. Fortunately, those *friends* did not appear so quickly.

Until the fourth day.

Stewart raced into the clearing as our carpenters hoisted the gate into its upright position.

"I hope you can make that a hundred feet high!" he shouted to them. "And just as thick!"

"They're here?" Ensign Ward asked, tramping from the fort while clutching a wrinkled ball of paper. He snagged me and guided Tommy back toward the river bank to speak with greater privacy. "A little quieter," he instructed our scout. "I don't want to worry the men."

"Each day we watch the French and Indians, they look like a lot more than the day before," Stewart replied at a whisper. "They've taken their time to arrive because their numbers swell with reinforcements."

"How many now?" the Half King asked, still smoking as we approached. A cloud of smoke hovered around his head. He slowly stood, his body passing through the haze.

"Five hundred?" Stewart answered as a question. "The lead elements will be here in a half hour."

"To our forty artificers," Ward mumbled. "Not a single proper soldier, including me!" He took his hat off and angrily slapped it against his knee.

"But you sent word to Fraser and even Trent," Stewart said. "Surely they're coming."

"Trent might not even know about the French yet," Ward answered. "Tommy, pull all the patrols into the fort. No sense in getting anybody accidentally killed."

"Sure, Eddie," Stewart said, adding a lazy salute and sprinting back into the woods.

"You, too, should retreat into the fort for now," the Half King said to Ensign Ward and me. "Seeing you may only provoke the French fathers to hasty action."

"And leave you men out here to meet them alone?" Ward asked, wondering as did I, what a few Mingo and a Half King could do to stop a determined army.

"I see no reason for a confrontation. Now is not the time," the Half King said placidly. He took a few more moments to puff on his pipe. "The French fathers cannot hastily disregard the wishes of Onondaga and her children tribes. We've asked our English brothers to build here and you have. You were *invited* by the League of Six Nations *and* the local Delaware *king*. At worst, I see whatever Frenchman who arrives here today quickly storming off back to Quebec. There, Governor-general Duquesne will send envoys to Onondaga to whine, I mean, plead their case. They will find the men beneath the Tree of Great Peace have grown deaf to their cries."

Ward examined the older, confident leader. "I hope you are right."

Tanaghrisson again sat down next to his comrades. They rejoined their easy conversation which I took as a good sign. At least they were not in the least bit agitated.

"Weber!" Ensign Ward yipped. "Follow me."

I trotted after him. By the time we entered the palisade, Tommy and his scouts had returned. The gate, at last finished, swung closed behind us and was tightly latched. Though I should have felt protected by its timbers, I suddenly felt alone and exposed when it had crashed shut. We were rats cornered in a flour mill with the miller and his entire family surrounding us, armed and angry.

Ward had said nothing while he led me directly to his office. He shoved the door open and held it. I ducked inside and he followed, this time slapping the oaken door shut. "Read that!" he said, ramming the balled page he had held into my chest.

I uncrinkled the page on the rough tabletop as he lit our last remaining, ridiculously short candle. "It's from Fraser," I said while scanning the script.

"It's his latest letter," Ward said. "Arrived this morning. I've been going back and forth with him for three days."

I didn't need to finish reading the bullshit. "He refuses to come and take command," I guessed.

"The ungrateful son of a bitch says that he can make more money working from his tiny outpost if we're not here than if we are. His tiny military salary from Old Dominion isn't worth the risk, he says. Thanks, Croghan, but no thanks."

"Does Fraser think he can work with the French breathing down his neck?" I asked.

"I don't know what he thinks," Ward said hastily. "Maybe the lying bastard made a deal with the Frogs." He then found a small scrap of paper and set it within the minute circle of light on the desk. In moments, he was finished writing a very short letter that was addressed to Trent. I watched him write every word. None of them were heartening.

He folded the sheet twice and stuffed it into my breast pocket. "Take a horse and go to Wills Creek. Get Trent. Washington's army should be there by now. At least, I pray it is. Bring them all here with haste."

It was easier said than done, for there was not a single passable road between Wills Creek and the Forks. Certainly nothing an army could efficiently traverse. None of us had given much thought to what would happen if we had won the race to the Forks – as we had – but then found ourselves unable to hold them – as we may.

But I saw the grimness in the ensign's face. "I won't sleep," I said in uninformed, youthful audacity.

"Neither will we," Ward answered, shoving me on my way. "Get out before the French land."

Five minutes later I was riding a horse through the Monongahela in the same place Washington had used to ford it over the winter. Thankfully, there was no ice with which to contend this time. The Half King paused his pipe smoking long enough to ask me, "Just in case I'm unable to get the ensign out of his jam?"

"Just in case," I answered as my boots got wet.

"Ward is a smart boy," the Half King observed. "You best make yourself scarce. I hear the canoes."

And he was right. Even above the sound of the river, I could hear the gentle lap of water slipping past paddles and slapping against bark canoes. Voices echoed to our ears – voices speaking French.

My heels tapped the beast's belly and she plunged through the remainder of the river to the south side. She loped up the bank and into the forest through the thorns that grew thick at the river's edge. Sufficiently sheltered, I paused, turning the creature so we both faced the Half King.

It took only ten minutes of waiting for the first of hundreds of Frenchmen, Canadians, and their Indian allies to unload. Behind, hundreds more paddled their way toward the far bank. Some of those in the rear grabbed ahold of branches overhanging the river and waited for further orders.

"Ah, one of my favorite French fathers," the Half King said loudly to the group of newcomers who had marched directly to him. He spoke in English. "It is good of you to visit and wish us well as we peaceably deepen the bonds of commerce with our English brothers. But you need only to send a small band of representatives to the council at Onondaga to convey your whole-hearted approval of such actions. Such a large convoy as this, while appreciated, is wholly unwarranted. Shall I call our mutual friends from the fort so that we all may sup by the river? Surely you've brought gifts."

The French officer at the head of the inland armada removed his hat from his silver head and stiffly bowed thick shoulders. The back of his white coat was remarkably clean after such a long and dirty journey. When he was again upright, his deep baritone gave away his identity.

Captain Legardeur, whom we'd met at Fort LeBoeuf, spoke in formal French. His interpreter wasted no time in repeating the words and emotions of his commander. "Chief Tanaghrisson of the Iroquois, it is beneath even you to align yourself with such riff-raff as these Virginian interlopers. Your French fathers have always been supportive of their Indian children, giving gifts and resolving disputes among the little ones. As these lands belong to His Most Christian Majesty, King of France, the Englishmen cowering behind you, in the shadows of those illegal walls, are trespassing."

"These lands are held by some of Onondaga's favorite children, the Delaware, the Mingo, the Shawnee," the Half King answered evenly. "They are like my very own children, a joy to spoil. They have asked, and the Iroquois council has agreed, that our English brothers build a fort for trade at the Forks of Ohio. This is all a part of Iroquoia. No one, captain, has done anything illegal. Should you wish to take it up further, I suggest you ask the governor-general of Canada to consult with my fellow elders beneath the Tree of Great Peace. And if you'd rather not break bread with us, I further ask that you leave the gifts you've obviously brought with you and return northward behind your own peaceful walls."

A canoe of Indians slid into the bank behind the French captain. Shingas and his closest advisors climbed out, standing behind, and clearly in support of, Legardeur. Tanaghrisson's face noted the obvious betrayal without so much as a twitch.

Legardeur spun. I could see his one eye squint in anger as he cranked his arm to direct his men. "Entourez le fort!"

Hundreds of Frenchmen more quickly disembarked and ran to surround the fort. The immense size of their force made our weeks-long project seem utterly small and inadequate. I could just barely see the heads of Ensign Ward and Tommy Stewart silently peeking over the palisade.

"Chief Shingas," the Half King began. None of the Delaware king's followers or any of the other Indians who had accompanied the French to the Forks had made any move to surround the fort. They were keeping their cards close to the breast, awaiting the outcome.

"*King* Shingas," the Delaware corrected. "My French fathers are more than willing to acknowledgement my rights as royal."

The Half King bit his lip, but marshaled the inner strength to continue. "King Shingas, you have sworn an oath on several occasions to support our English brothers in their endeavors at the Forks. A ceremonial pipe was smoked. Will you now not only break those vows but also go to war?"

The Delaware king smiled. "I break no pledge. I take up no hatchet today. We observe events at the Forks as they unfold. My English brothers, should they prove able to hold the fort against this overwhelming force, are welcome to keep it. Otherwise, I will have no other choice than to cooperate with the new stewards of the Forks. Their powder will protect trade as easily as that of the English."

"The French will post an even larger garrison here than what was proposed by Croghan and our Virginian friends," Tanaghrisson countered. "It would be best to stop the incursion before it begins." It sounded like he was now prodding Shingas to fight today, not the English, but the French.

"Captain Legardeur has brought these men to dislodge you. A smaller force is all that shall be required to hold it once it is in their hands," Shingas answered. "What you see is temporary."

"Enough!" barked Legardeur through his interpreter. "The Half King has no reason to know of our plans."

Chief Tanaghrisson remained composed even while an increasing number of gun-toting men raced about. "This is a mistake, captain," he said calmly to the French officer. "Nothing good can come of this, especially for your people, the French, and your allies. Blood has a way of spilling when no one wants it to."

Legardeur laughed as the interpreter finished. "Iroquoia! Demi-Roi!" he scoffed and walked away from the Half King like he was discarded trash. Shingas and the others followed. Tanaghrisson could only watch in stunned, rather impotent, silence. The Half King's fellow Mingo travelers were equally dazed, babbling among themselves at what they'd just witnessed.

I, too, was mesmerized by what I saw next. An endless stream of canoes carrying even more men came around the bend in the river. Bateaux were pushed and guided by long poles. From these, at least eighteen cannon were unloaded. Methodically, Captain Legardeur went about organizing his soldiers into ranks and marching them within musket range of the fort's palisade. A half hour later, when one thousand men surrounded the fort, Legardeur stood at the fore. He raised his hand aloft and held up one finger. After he'd shouted to the English inhabitants briefly, he extended a second finger and shouted again.

"You have two choices. One!" barked the interpreter. "Immediately surrender this illegal fort! Two. Have your post taken by force."

Then the clearing grew eerily quiet.

The Half King consulted with his followers and they quickly decided it was time to flee. After giving me a dejected wave, they raced off. I was sure that Tanaghrisson would have to ride to Onondaga to convey the setback in events. Whether his Mingo friends intended to hide at Logstown, to flee the area altogether, or to fight back, I could not guess.

Shingas and his fellow Delaware then took over the Half King's post, sitting near the river, patiently waiting for the outcome of the siege. They kindled a fire, clearly expecting the process to take some time. Some waded ankle deep into the water to fish.

And though I knew exactly what Ensign Ward had written in the letter to Trent, I reached into my pocket and retrieved it. Unfolding the message, I read his bold words, "We hold out hope that Chief Tanaghrisson can help relieve us from our current situation. However, as we are to be besieged by hundreds of French soldiers, we intend to hold out to the last extremity lest it ever be said that the English retreated like cowards."

I quickly folded the note and spurred my horse for the long ride to Wills Creek. I prayed for almost any small miracle so that there was no need for Ensign Ward, Tommy Stewart, and the rest to give the last extremity.

CHAPTER THIRTY-FOUR

Three days and one hundred grueling miles later, my tired horse and I lumbered into Wills Creek. For as long as I could remember, it had been a fair-sized trading hub with perhaps one hundred permanent residents. But by the numbers of additional men and tents stuck in every available nook, it was clear that at least a part of Washington's army had gotten this far.

After bumping into a lowly provincial private, I was swiftly passed up the command food chain until I stood in a dimly lit storeroom with Trent, Croghan, Van Braam, and Lieutenant Colonel Washington.

"One thousand Frenchmen, you say?" Washington asked, betraying neither concern nor confidence.

I on the other hand was worried enough for all of us. "Heck, ya!" I answered in something more frenetic than my normal pace. "And Lieutenant Fraser skedaddled. Ensign Ward is doing a great job, but he's just a kid."

A young soldier wearing no shoes padded softly into the room. "Your pack, Colonel Washington."

"Thank you, son," Washington said, extending an arm to take it. He wasn't really older than the provincial enlisted man, but after our experience over the winter and his time recruiting and training his army, Washington had indeed matured. The young man saluted and left.

Washington wasted no time. He pulled out a sheaf of pages from his pack and spread them on a nearby shelf. We gathered behind him, peering around his strong shoulders. His papers consisted of maps of the entire region drawn in his own hand during our travels to and from Fort LeBoeuf. "There is not a single, passable road fit for a brace of oxen, let alone an army, between here and the Forks," he said, tracing his finger on a curving line from Wills Creek to the scrap of land that held our besieged outpost.

"Indeed," said Trent. "We are safe from the French for now. They cannot easily drive toward us. We have time to call for reinforcements."

"You and Washington *are* the reinforcements!" I said, worried more with every second of delay. "Ward won't be able to hold out very long at all. Maybe they've already been stormed."

"Lad," Croghan said with a pained expression. "You've said it yourself. They have at least a thousand men. I'd like to do nothing but drive straight toward those French turds and scare them away. It's my living we're talking about, after all. Those Indians in the area are my friends, my wife's family. I don't want the Frog-lovers skulking around there any more than you. But a thousand of them!"

"If Washington is here, then so is his army!" I exclaimed, thinking that the military men were missing an obvious fact.

It was a curious thing how I had become so deeply attached to the men with whom I had toiled for such a short time at the nascent fort. But such was the nature of service, even at the mere fringes, in the military. It felt like everything – their very lives – depended on me getting help to them as quickly as possible. I had seen men and women killed and captured at Pickawillany. I had watched men whimper while slowly dying, their scalps sliced away. I'd not allow any of Legardeur's Indian allies do that to Ward, Stewart, and the rest. And the thought of what those cannon would do to the souls behind our temporary palisade made me exceedingly fearful.

"We've arrived at Will Creek with one hundred sixty men," Van Braam said flatly, facing me. He was now a captain in the Virginia militia.

"And the others?" I asked. "They are following?"

"That is all we could raise," Washington answered solemnly. "They are as green as a spring sapling. Some have inadequate clothing. You saw the young man's lack of shoes. He is not the only one, I'm afraid. Our arms are equally sparse."

"That's not an army," I said.

"It is the size and type of army you are able to recruit when the House of Burgesses only authorizes a payment of eight pence per soldier per day," Washington quietly lamented. And he was absolutely correct. Offering to pay soldiers one third of the wages of the average laborer would draw into the ranks only the most desperate.

"So, the only choice, really, is to dig in, fortify our position here where supplies can easily reach us. In the meantime, we send urgent word to the governor for reinforcements," Trent said in summary.

"Mr. Trent, when you received the initial news from Ensign Ward that the French were drawing near, I immediately requested additional men and supplies from Governor Dinwiddie, as well as from the governors of Pennsylvania, Maryland, and the Carolinas," Washington said, still peering down at his maps and absentmindedly tapping the pages with the tips of his fingers.

"Very thorough!" Croghan said, clapping Washington on the back. The Colonel stiffened at the familiarity. Meanwhile, I could see the Irishman's wheels spinning behind his bright eyes. By the time Wills Creek was bolstered and roads were constructed, the current setback in his trading empire could possibly be righted in a year's time. Not ideal, but not a disaster either.

"Do we just sacrifice those men at the Forks?" I asked, incredulous.

"Hopefully, this Captain Legardeur you mentioned is an honorable man," Trent said. "There is reason to think that after a spirited resistance, Ward and the others will be allowed to surrender and march away with the honors of war."

"By resistance you mean that many of them will die?" I asked.

Trent dropped his chin to his chest. "I'm afraid so. We just have no way to get there in time." The room grew silent for a short period while the knowledge that even as we had spoken some of our comrades, mostly carpenters and other artisans, were being killed in an undeclared war.

Captain Trent cleared his throat, finding the courage to marshal on. "Shall I inform the men to improve defenses and increase patrols of the surrounding area, Colonel Washington?"

Washington sighed and turned to face us, leaning back against the shelves. He crossed his arms and appeared heavily weighted by the decisions inherent in his command. "How was the fort progressing when you were forced to come east for provisions?" he asked Trent.

Taken aback, Trent said, "Well, I think. It was not going to be the largest fortification on this continent, but once completed and armed, it would hold its own."

"Ensign Ward saw that the gate was hung just minutes before the French arrived," I said. "Oh, and he gave me this," I said, producing the missive.

Washington took it, unfolding it as he brought it into the light from a window in order to read. He must have read through several times, for even though it was no more than a few lines, the process took a long while. When he was done, he passed it from man to man so the others could see what the young ensign had written.

"That, gentlemen," said Washington, pointing to the letter that had been returned to my hand. "That is why we cannot sit idly by, waiting for governors and legislatures to send us aid. We, like Ensign Ward, are Englishmen. And we will always be Englishmen. Our brothers have been threatened by a foreign force and we are the closest army that can possibly offer relief."

I grinned.

"There is no road," Trent warned.

"We shall cut one," Washington answered simply.

"One hundred sixty volunteers against a thousand or so French regulars won't be much of a contest," Croghan advised.

"A summer of toil and discipline will do much in the way of preparing the men for fending off the enemy," Washington said, filled with just the sort of headstrong confidence I had witnessed on our earlier trek.

"George," Van Braam stammered. "I am only recently made a military man, but what Captain Trent says, makes sense to me. Maybe we should trust his and Croghan's wilderness experience."

"Mr. Van Braam," Washington said coolly. "You may have forgotten the orders given to me when we left Alexandria with this army, but I have not. Governor Dinwiddie, speaking as representative of the king himself has instructed me, and I quote, *to restrain all such offenders and in case of resistance to make prisoners of or kill and destroy them.* We cannot carry out those directives while cowering a hundred miles from the offenders!"

"Yes, George," Van Braam answered.

Washington stared tranquilly at the Dutchman until Van Braam added, "Yes, Colonel Washington."

And so, on the same day I had arrived at Wills Creek, we began making preparations to slash a road through harsh, virgin country. With hope that the dawdling governors would send additional help and that those properly armed men would soon catch up; our best estimate was that we could bring our feeble fighting force to bear on the enemy at the Forks by autumn.

Unfortunately, our isolated and besieged fort had but a week's worth of provisions.

CHAPTER THIRTY-FIVE

When I had been sent away from the Forks with Ensign Ward's message, one hundred miles had passed by in three days' time. The hills and thick foliage had been a blur. But in the three weeks since pulling out of Wills Creek with Washington's scruffy army for the return trip to our new fort, we had traveled just fifty miles. Each one of those miles was more exhausting than the last. Trees had to be felled. Swamps circumvented. Slopes smoothed. Creeks forded. All of it to construct the most rudimentary of single-lane wagon roads.

And the road we made was indeed primitive. Those ancient Romans would have mocked our sorry attempt at linking the civilized world with the wilderness. I'm told the broad, majestic roads of the Caesars had crowns in the center to aid in drainage. Theirs were built along the best routes, chosen for efficiency of travel as well as the durability of the site itself. Washington's road was none of those things. Ours was narrow. If anything, it was shaped more like a bowl so that when it rained, water pooled. Even before rainfall, however, our road was made rough from the millions of snaking tree roots we could not hope to excavate within such a short time table. Then when the rains did fall, we added to the road's miserable condition by slicing ruts in the mud. Hooves – single-cloven and double – as well as the feet of men and the wheels of supply wagons wreaked havoc on the landscape, churning the earth into a mangled quagmire. Then, after a day of drying out, the road had become a teeth-shattering, rock-hard nightmare for everything and everyone that passed by toward the rear of our great train. Axles snapped. Wheels broke. Ankles sprained. Horses and other beasts became lame.

And so, it was with grand relief that we stumbled into what was called, by whites and Indians alike, Great Meadows. It was a sweeping valley between Chestnut Ridge and Laurel Hill, two formidable mountains. To his credit, Washington immediately saw the secluded spot as a useful weigh station, a place of respite for his tired soldiers. Great Meadows was well-known among frontiersmen. Extending about a mile in length and about a quarter mile in width, it was slightly boggy, but had ample grassland for our herds of horses and cattle. The little creek that gurgled its way through the center provided abundant fresh water for man and beast alike.

For several days, we rested. Bones, joints, and equipment mended.

But we were not idle. No army on the march can ever lean toward sloth. To do so invites disaster and our young colonel would not allow such a thing. The most active among us were scouts and messengers. They came and went with great frequency, dozens each day. And mostly over that week of recuperation nothing but good news poured in.

Chief among the favorable developments was that Ensign Ward and every artisan under his command walked into camp. They were hungry and dusty but otherwise completely unharmed. Neither Washington nor Trent had anything critical to say when it was discovered that after several harrowing hours of negotiations with the French, Ward had surrendered the fort without a fight. Britain and France were not officially at war, after all. Ward had believed he did not have the authority to set his king and an entire people on such a track. Besides, the long odds of the defense were obvious to all.

No one had the heart or indecency to remind young Ward of his overly bold letter, which Washington now carried among his papers.

Ward had further told us that Captain Legardeur laughed when he toured the small fort after the surrender. It would be replaced, Legardeur bragged, by something befitting the name *Fort Duquesne*. I have already told you the name Duquesne would come to carry mighty consequence in the world. Now you see why. The very French Fort Duquesne would now sit in the place of our very British fort, that had never even been given the dignity of receiving a name. The new structure would be a fish larger than Jonah's, a leviathan bigger than Job's. It would have proper bastions, ravelins, a dry moat, log and earthen walls, guardhouses, bunkhouses, bakeries, magazines, a hospital, and a smithy. I could still see the sadness in Ward's eyes when he said that the French had set our tiny structure ablaze before he and his troop had even crossed the Monongahela.

"What did Chief Shingas think of the plans for the new fort?" I had asked Ward.

"If he wasn't too pleased with our sad little post, the mention of this giant Fort Duquesne made him quite angry," Ward had said. "I don't think we ought to count him out as a potential ally."

"The French mean to stay!" Washington had exclaimed, forgetting all about how the Delaware king fit into the situation. "All the more reason to press on. They must be evacuated before they can take root with their beastly garrison. A sapling can be jerked from the ground with but one hand. A hundred-year oak takes considerable toil as our laborers on this road will attest."

But still, a total of perhaps two hundred inexperienced colonial volunteers against one thousand superbly drilled French regulars and well-supplied Canadian militia was quite a lot more than a long shot.

Fortunately, good news continued to arrive. Letters came from Dinwiddie saying that an inter-colonial effort was underway. They would comply with Washington's repeated calls for help. Bits of assistance would soon arrive from Pennsylvania, Virginia, and the Carolinas. Strangely, the destitute colony of South Carolina had heeded the summons with uncharacteristic speed and zeal, better than all the others combined. A full company of one hundred British regulars plus forty beef cattle was already en route! For such a positive response from so many, we could only assume that the colonel was still riding high on his celebrity status from our wintertime exploits that had by then been published in newspapers as far away as London. The colonial politicians suddenly found it difficult to withhold assistance from the favored man of the moment, especially when faced with a threat from the most-hated French.

And more good reports. Chief Tanaghrisson had fled Logstown with his entire village, becoming refugees due to the French. While that, in and of itself, was not pleasant news, he and his warriors, a total of two dozen, were camped not far from

Great Meadows. And though it was not an awe-inspiring force that the Half King was capable of bringing, having such a renowned figure on our side would go a long way in securing future Indian partnerships. And the French, by overplaying their hand at the Forks with such a massive presence, were driving Shingas and his Delaware into our fold. I was sure of it and frequently conveyed those thoughts to the officers. They came to feel the same way. The Indians, from the Six Nations down to the most insignificant tributary tribe, would fall in line behind King George II.

Or so we all believed.

On our fourth day at Great Meadows, just when Washington was getting excited about renewing our push westward, John Fraser flew into camp on a chestnut horse lathered white with sweat. He appeared just as exhausted as his beast. And, as something of an unofficial aide-de-camp to everyone from Ward, to Croghan, to Washington, I was privy to almost all meetings. This one was no exception.

"The French bastards came in and torched my entire post!" Fraser said excitedly just as the sun began to set. Clouds, which had been swiftly rolling in all afternoon, had begun to coalesce and blacken. "They even killed my cow! My cow! What gives them the right?"

I smirked at the man's misfortune, but a glare from Washington made me clamp my mouth shut.

"Which way did they head when they left?" Captain Trent asked, wasting no time berating Fraser for his absence from his post during those crucial moments.

"I don't know, they rode off in this general direction," Fraser answered, perturbed. He threw up his hands. "I'm a lieutenant in the governor's army. Who's going to compensate me for my loss?"

"How many men were in the party?" Washington asked. "Describe what you saw."

"Not until somebody tells me who is going to pay me and how much it is going to be," Fraser said defiantly.

"Now wait a damn minute!" Croghan shouted. "You aren't owed a farthing you weak-kneed skunk!" The first peal of thunder shook the poles of Washington's command tent. What little breeze there had been settled, allowing the heavy canvas of the tent to sag heavily. It resembled the skin of a formerly fat man after he'd just lost weight. The canvas hung and clung. "I stuck my neck out and convinced Dinwiddie to give you that commission, not because I trusted you, man! But at least you weren't another Ohio Company stooge to get in the way of my Indian trade! Now I see no one should trust you! You're a coward. You're a turncoat who thought you'd benefit at my expense. Thought you could make a deal with the Froggies. Well look now, you imbecile!"

"Mr. Croghan!" Washington snapped quietly. "I'll not have this discussion descend into the depths of name-calling." The colonel turned and ambled to a small desk that had been set up at the rear of his tent. We silently watched as he rummaged through a drawer, setting out the stacks of correspondence that came into our small camp every day. One-by-one he began looking for a specific memorandum. "Ah, here it is. I have a resolution to the problem of Mr. Fraser's compensation."

"We can't pay this man! He left his post! He defied his governor and king!" Croghan growled. "This ass has made me a fool in Williamsburg, Logstown, Onondaga, and beyond!"

"Exactly," Washington said with a thin grin. "Mr. Fraser left his post." One of the colonel's eyes sparkled. "Captain Legardeur allowed Ensign Ward to bring with him paperwork required of his small force. As a result, Mr. Ward brought this to me when he arrived after the surrender of the Forks." He held out a page and pointed to the writing. "It says here that Governor Dinwiddie has commissioned you as a lieutenant in the Virginia provincial army for a term that does not end for some months, Mr. Fraser. As such you will be paid the full amount due your rank from the time you began your service through its end. Today, I will instruct the paymaster to compensate you for the time you've already served. And if you rejoin us now, I am willing to overlook your recent neglect to your duties, your absence. I don't think a stockade is the right setting for you at this point, do you? A military tribunal is likely something you want to avoid," he added.

"But my compensation for my losses," Fraser tried again.

"Lieutenant Fraser," Washington said quietly. "As an officer under my command, you will answer my questions." Outside, rounds of thunder seemed to string together endlessly. Lightning flashed, casting bursts of shadows across the tent's door.

Eventually, Fraser saw that to defy the colonel and to continue to demand a payment for his destroyed property would only lead to his imprisonment, or worse, under military law. I silently celebrated his comeuppance.

"Thirty-five French regulars," Fraser said, grumbling. "White coats, red collars, red cuffs. Brass buttons. Hat lace was gold. The whole deal, if you must know. They were under the command of some pompous ensign. He laughed while he shot my cow."

"Perhaps just a patrol," Washington speculated.

"We know the French have been keeping eyes on our progress the whole time," Trent agreed. "Our scouts watch them, watching us."

"What was the ensign's name?" I asked Fraser before anyone else could speak.

He shrugged as the wind renewed, smashing into the tent and sending its sailcloth canvas yawning in and out. "Some impertinent little shit. His men called him Jumonville."

CHAPTER THIRTY-SIX

"It's definitely not a patrol," I blurted as the first drops of rain splattered loudly onto the fabric above us.

"Now don't go yammering about revenge. Just because that's the name of the turd who attacked Pickawillany doesn't mean this is not anything other than a patrol," Croghan warned. "How can you know otherwise, boy?"

You know that I had no idea whether or not it was a normal French patrol, sent to watch our movements, or if it was an advance force, portending the entire army that had descended on the Forks. Yet, you also know I had waited rather impatiently for two years since Tahki's death. It was time for me to spin some selfish lies. Because the eighteen miles that separated Great Meadows from Fraser's post was as close as I'd been to Ensign Jumonville since that fateful day.

"Speak if you have something pertinent to add, Mr. Weber," the colonel said. "Otherwise, let us work with the information we have, free from rampant speculation."

"The information we have is enough to make sound judgement," I proclaimed, disingenuously but with supreme confidence. "The French forcibly dislodged us from the Forks. Though no life was lost, nor any blood shed, it was done with a direct threat of unassailable force. And now our small army cuts through the wilderness in an area that has never been touched by so many armed Englishmen at one time. They have to know our objective is to dislodge them. They must believe we are the advance elements of a larger force because only a fool could hope to attack so many with so few. Well, colonel, I ask you. If you were Legardeur and you had numerical superiority to a coming attacker, but you thought they might soon even the odds with reinforcements, what would you do?"

Colonel Washington didn't bother with an answer. He glanced at Trent. "The boy makes a valid point, colonel," said the captain. "I'd want to cut up the enemy piecemeal before they could assemble and face me on even terms. Legardeur has to know that a European-style siege, once begun, usually triumphs.

He wants to avoid such a thing coming against his half-finished fort."

"Yet you saw no other signs of a larger force?" Washington asked Fraser while fixing him with his pale gray-blue eyes.

"Just Jumonville." Fraser shook his head in grief then muttered under his breath, "He killed my cow and giggled while she died."

"We need to be vigilant. The French may want to overwhelm us in the open, away from their new fort," Washington said, thinking aloud. "We'll send out a screen, in force, under Captain Hogg of, say, seventy-five men. They will locate the French army if it is coming to meet us."

"Prudent, sir," agreed Trent.

That was close to the outcome I desired. But not exactly. "In the meantime, should we not find Ensign Jumonville and just *ask* him what are his and Legardeur's intentions?"

"Lad," Croghan warned. "I had a fondness for Chief Memeskia and his daughter, too. But this isn't a personal mission." Even though, for Croghan's trading empire and all the shareholders of the Ohio Company, it most certainly was personal.

"That's not what I meant," I said before they could move on to other matters. "We don't look to attack Jumonville at all! But, thanks to the return of Lieutenant Fraser, we know generally where the ensign's band is located. We are technically not at war with France. No Frenchman has killed an Englishman. No Englishman has killed a Frenchman. We, ourselves, were just guests of Legardeur over the winter. Why not send a small body of men, of diplomats, to meet the ensign? We can even stop by and add some of Tanaghrisson's warriors to our ranks, not for force, but for greater diplomacy. It will be clear to the young ensign that we have powerful Indian allies on our side. He'll convey that information to Legardeur whether or not the captain is marching toward us or still sitting at the Forks."

Washington's face showed genuine surprise. "That's a surprisingly good idea, Mr. Weber." It was one of the few compliments I have ever received from him over the years. Had he known that it was all a ploy to get my desired results, the colonel would have sent me away and barred me from any more of his meetings.

"Shall I organize the mission to Jumonville?" Trent asked.

"No," Washington answered, pondering the idea further as the rain pounded above our heads. Small rivers were already curling beneath the walls and winding their way among our scattered feet. "I'll do it. In fact, I'll go along. We leave immediately for Chief Tanaghrisson's camp. The sooner we find out the intentions of the French, the sooner we can make plans of our own."

And that was how I was able to set in motion the final stages of my revenge with Jumonville – at least I hoped. It was also, unbeknownst to me at the time, how I ensured that our little party in the woods of North America would initiate the first battle in what would become a bloody, world-wide struggle.

We were the spark that would ignite the long fuse.

CHAPTER THIRTY-SEVEN

It was ten o'clock that night before we had assembled the forty-seven men who would trek with Washington, first to the Half King's camp, and then on to find Jumonville. By then, Captain Hogg had already taken his force out to search for the main French army – if such a thing did, in fact, linger nearby. Trent was left behind in charge at Great Meadows, while Croghan and his workers continued to organize supplies between Wills Creek and the valley.

As you've come to expect, there were no permanent roads or even tracks in this part of the country so we elected to travel on foot. The night was black as pitch. If there was a moon of any size, the thick, ink-like clouds acted as deep shrouds. Even the sudden bursts of lightning during the storm did not help us in finding our way. With every flash, we were blinded with bursts of whiteness. The following rapid return of the stygian darkness only made it more difficult to see. On at least ten occasions, my forehead smacked into low-hanging limbs, leaving a few throbbing lumps behind.

Given the conditions, we moved about in a long, single-file line. That way, as long as every traveler followed the man immediately in front of him, none of us would get lost.

I suppose the formation saved some. We only lost track of seven men that night. The sheets of rain and the mountainous terrain itself made even our single-file line break cohesion. Washington had to pause every quarter-mile or so that the rest of us could catch up. Every step was perilous. Men slipped and fell into mud, rocks, and trees. Thuds, grunts, and curses were more common during that march than any pleasant conversation. One man tumbled down a ravine, his shadowy figure disappearing before my eyes in a whoosh. In order to keep the line together, I marched on after saying a prayer and counting him as dead. But an hour later, during one of our frequent breaks, there he stood. His face was bruised and he had fitted himself with a makeshift splint on his forearm, but he was most certainly alive.

Thus soaked and surly, we walked into Chief Tanaghrisson's refugee camp just before sun-up the next morning. It took ten minutes to find and rouse the Half King from his slumber, a time period during which our men rested and extricated fouled powder from their guns.

"And so," Washington said after describing what he hoped to accomplish by finding the local French detachment. "We ask that you and some of your warriors come with us to make our inquiry."

The Half King was still rubbing the sleep from his eyes as he sat at the colonel's feet. "You don't want me, Conotocarius. I'm of no use to you. You see what good I did in keeping the French away from the Forks." He appeared to be hung-over from a night of commiserative drinking with the last of his followers. I'd not come to expect such self-loathsome behavior from one so proud.

Washington peered around the camp that was just beginning to come to life as the rain slowed to a maddening drizzle. It was a sad, desperate-looking place, half-assembled, shoddily built. The few women who walked about doing chores, did so with shoulders sagging as lowly as snowy pine boughs at Christmastime. It was a far cry from the Half King's orderly settlement at Logstown. "Chief Tanaghrisson," the colonel said. "Separately neither of us wields much power. I hope that together, with Onondaga and Williamsburg united, we can put a scare into the French and once again bring the region under control."

The Half King found his interest piqued. He raised his eyebrows. "Spoken like a true diplomat, Conotocarius. Perhaps there is hope for you yet in this world of men." But then his chest sunk inward, his shoulders drooped like those of his women. "But I doubt very much that I will ever be welcomed back beneath the Tree of Great Peace. My days at Onondaga and my time as sachem are over. I am lucky to be chief over this rabble. Why they follow me this far is beyond my ability to comprehend. I am left in a most desperate state."

Frustrated, Washington looked at me, the toe of his boot tapping in a murky brown puddle. He clearly blamed me for proposing the idea of uniting with Tanaghrisson and then having the offer thrown back in his face. But I smiled. For I knew with certainty that the Half King was about to change his mind. He had to be told just one more bit of information.

"Chief Tanaghrisson," I said after clearing my throat.

"I'm not in the mood for you, Shit-for-brains," said the chief. He massaged his temples. "You'll not convince me to go on such a pointless errand. The French have peacefully taken the Forks. There will be no war. Iroquoia is doomed."

I thought that he should be happy that war might yet be averted. It is what he had hoped for all along. But he sounded almost despondent at the possibility of peace between France and Great Britain. No matter. "I would never try to convince you to do anything," I said. "I just wondered if you or any of your warriors knew the exact whereabouts of *Ensign Jumonville's* camp. Even if you do not come along, Lieutenant Colonel Washington and I could use directions."

The Half King eyed me. Colonel Washington had neglected to indicate the name of the French officer leading the patrol. I knew the mere mention would get us the assistance we needed.

Tanaghrisson sighed heavily. His mind was already made up, but he had to act like he suddenly gave the matter much consideration. "I suppose I can't just send a bunch of English babies into the teeth of those Frenchmen," he groaned. "Conotocarius, if you are so bent on going, you'll have my warriors and me as guides and diplomats."

"Thank you, Chief Tanaghrisson," Washington exclaimed. "Now, may my men and I tarry here for a few hours to dry off and eat? We've had a long night."

"You may," the Half King said, rising from his seat, suddenly sober. "But if you want to retain the element of surprise and perhaps catch the French literally with their pants down, we can be to their camp in fifteen minutes. Some of them will still be sleeping. My scouts have kept their eyes on them."

"A quarter of an hour?" Washington breathed excitedly. "Good work, Mr. Weber. Mr. Van Braam, be prepared to parlay with Ensign Jumonville. See the men organized. We follow Tanaghrisson shortly."

A grand total of twenty minutes later, I was sprawled out in the mud next to the chief and the colonel. We peered down into a small glen where the French had set up their tents to weather the storm. By now the rain had stopped and the sunrise indicated a pleasant day stretched out ahead.

"Look at them down there," Washington whispered. He curled his lip like an angry dog. "Hiding in a hollow. Skulking around. It's hard to think they are anything but a reconnaissance force for the main army."

One of the Frenchmen had climbed out of his tent and wandered off to relieve himself. We patiently watched for his eventual return. When he finally splashed his way back through the clearing and climbed back into his tent, the man's tent-mates grumbled loudly. One of his muddy boots was even tossed out by an angry comrade. Eventually though, the noise from that particular tent died and the snores of its occupants joined with those of the other tents.

"Their arms," I rasped, pointing to where a single sentry sleepily watched over muskets and ammunition supplies.

"We want to surprise them," the colonel said. "But not too much. We don't need to kill anyone on either side."

The Half King and I looked at one another, each sensing that the other was happy with at least one Frenchman in particular dying that day. Just then, another tent flapped open and Ensign Jumonville himself emerged, stretching away the kinks in his back. He wore his white trousers and a shirt with the tails untucked and dangling nearly to his knees, but no coat. After rubbing his stubbled face, he slowly padded off to where the other man had gone to complete his morning business.

"Come," Tanaghrisson whispered, swiftly sliding back down the hill on his belly. He jerked roughly on my foot and gave Washington's boot a tug. When we were all at the base of the hill, he said, "I'll take my Indians and Shit-for-brains with me. We can circle around the other side of their camp before they know it. You may then enter under a flag of truce, but we can swoop in to help if you need us."

"You'll do nothing to provoke them unnecessarily?" Washington asked, though it sounded more like a stern warning.

The Half King was already yanking my arm out of the socket. "No," he said as we disappeared into the trees. A moment later his braves were on our tails. To me he whispered, "I hope you brought your wife's pistol with you."

I patted a small satchel. "Cleaned, dried, and reloaded this morning before we left your camp."

"Then let's hope the antique still works. It's time for our revenge."

CHAPTER THIRTY-EIGHT

The dozen or so Indian warriors who had accompanied us were dispatched to the other side of the French camp just as Tanaghrisson had promised the colonel. There they would wait. He and I, however, moved rapidly toward where we hoped to find Jumonville alone, exposed, and quite unarmed.

You may think it strange but, for the first time in two years as I rushed through the underbrush, I was having second thoughts. It was easy to dream of murdering someone for revenge. I had envisioned the act a thousand times, each more gruesome than the last. But I was not a murderer – not yet anyway. I had killed in self-defense. In moments, I knew that I would walk up to another human being and, with the flick of a finger, send a ball of lead hurtling into him, ripping flesh and crushing bones. In short, I would end a life.

"Washington will hear the shot," I warned, feeling cold feet. "No one will believe it was suicide, French pistol or not."

"Shh!" the Half King hissed.

"Qui est là?" came a voice. I would never forget its condescending tone. It was Jumonville. He was close.

Tanaghrisson growled at me for making our enemy aware of our presence. He grabbed hold of my wet shirt and shoved me toward the sound of the ensign. We plunged through a thicket that tore at my clothes and skin. A moment later I, with the Half King at my side, was an arm's length away from Jumonville. We stared at one other. I'm certain that I looked as confused as he.

But seeing that I made no abrupt move toward him, he slowly finished fastening his trousers. "Are you and your Indian friend lost, frontiersman?" Jumonville asked in broken English.

He hadn't recognized me. And why would he? But I was suddenly offended that such a tragic event in my life had seemingly slipped his mind completely. My hand fumbled into my satchel and quickly produced the gun. I cocked and leveled it at Jumonville, who stepped back a pace, lifting both hands out to his side to show they were empty.

222

"A hero to your governor and king, I'm sure," Jumonville said, surprisingly relaxed. "But I must warn you that killing me will only bring about your own deaths." His chin craned over his shoulder. "In case you are unaware, there are a hundred French regulars in a camp not fifty feet from here."

There were about thirty-five. He was a liar.

"Do it," the Half King encouraged, boring a hole of hatred through the ensign with his frosty glare. "It must be done. This is the only way."

I hesitated. "But he's right. The sound of the gun."

"Smart boy," Jumonville said patronizingly.

"It's a French pistol," Tanaghrisson said through gritted teeth, his patience clearly ebbing. "Shoot him in the head and drop the spent weapon onto his body. We'll go back to my Indians and it will look like a suicide. The setting is as perfect as it could ever be."

Jumonville's icy cool slipped a little. "French pistol?" he asked. He tipped to the side to get a look at it.

"It is," I said. "And everyone knows that it is mine. Well, it was Tahki's. No one will be fooled." It was a shame I had never thought of that before. But, I had been blinded by rage.

"Men will believe whatever is most convenient," the Half King assured me. "Now kill him before you lose the chance. I want to see him suffer."

"Tahki?" Jumonville asked, searching his memory. I was strangely hopeful and so I waited a moment for him to find an image of the day he had murdered my pregnant wife. If I was so inclined, I would have to wait an awfully long time. No such memory came.

Still confused, Jumonville raised his hands higher in surrender. "You have me at a disadvantage. Perhaps if you tell me your names and I tell you mine, we can clear up this misunderstanding. I have no quarrel with civilians."

"You are Joseph Coulon de Villiers de Jumonville, ensign in His Most Christian King's army, scion of a distinguished military family with roots dating back to the very foundation of France," I said bitterly, the well-rehearsed words rolling naturally off my tongue.

He was now fully intrigued. "Oh, now I am at a complete disadvantage. You know all there is to know about me, but I know nothing of you. Surely, you wish to explain yourselves." He pointed to our filthy clothes. "You've come a long way on a stormy night for some reason beyond *anonymous* revenge."

"Tahki," I growled, stabbing the air with the pistol. "You murdered my wife. She was with child."

He thought about what I had said for a moment. "You'll have to be more specific. Tahki sounds like a name of the Miami people. I've killed many of them over the years. Enemies of our allies the Ottawa and Chippewa, you see."

"Two years ago, at Pickawillany," I began.

He snapped his fingers. "The Quaker!" he exclaimed with a chuckle. I gathered that he had known all along, but had felt the need to torture me. "The pacifist Pennsylvanian! My! You are persistent." He put his hands on his waist and shook his head in disbelief. "I never thought I'd see you again."

"Didn't your brother tell you to expect me?" I asked.

"Of course, he did. But really! Here you are!" He grinned in wonder. "And who is your old friend? A mix of English and Seneca fashions. Iroquois, yes?"

Without ever really taking my eye off Jumonville, I glanced toward the Half King. His face was stern, gripped with anger and hatred. "You may tell him, Ephraim. And then you will stop talking, stop yapping. You will kill him. A Frenchman must die today."

It was surprisingly pleasant to hear Tanaghrisson use my given name rather than my nickname.

"Yes, do tell me, Ephraim," Jumonville said mockingly. His use of my name was decidedly less pleasant.

"This is the great Seneca sachem, Chief Tanaghrisson," I rumbled.

When Jumonville's eyes widened in confusion, I felt a rush of confidence. At that moment, I knew I could, and would, murder him. Because even the wretched Jumonville knew that what he had done to Tanaghrisson and his family deserved death, or even much worse.

The flesh of my finger was just pressing against the trigger when Ensign Jumonville shrieked, "Oh, mon Dieu. Le Demi-Roi!" Then he bent over, laughing and mocking me. "Do you think I care about a washed-up Half King? Have you not heard what happened at the Forks?"

Stupidly, I hesitated. As he straightened up to his full height, Jumonville reached beneath his shirt tails at the small of his back. The pistol he produced was cocked and discharged before he had even aimed it. I heard the ball whistle between the Half King and me.

Jumonville then used the thick smoke from his blast as a screen. I watched as his shadow spun and bolted away through the brush. I saw my quarry of two years slipping away. I squeezed the trigger again, firmly this time. The hammer released, scratching its flint against the frizzen, and slammed into the pan. I had reshaped the flint so that it was as perfect as could be. It sent sparks like a downpour into the waiting dry powder. With a crack, the pan erupted in a blinding poof of smoke that shot upward. Less than a second later the powder packed tightly at the back of the barrel exploded, creating such heat in such a small space that the ball had but one place to go. It bounced its way down the barrel and out the muzzle.

I could see nothing but smoke. I heard Jumonville yell out in pain.

And that is when things got interesting.

CHAPTER THIRTY-NINE

From his vantage point, the Half King had had a slightly different view through the smoke. "You just grazed him, Shit-for-brains! Can you do nothing right?"

By the time each of us were running after Jumonville, agitated shouts from the French camp echoed through the forest. Equally worried calls came from Washington above.

"L'anglais!" Jumonville screamed. "Le Demi-Roi!" Through the brush, I could see half-dressed Frenchmen tearing from tents, running to arms.

"They've fired at us!" I could hear Washington shouting from above. "Form your ranks!"

On the ridge to my left I saw a long line of men jump from the trees and level their muskets without the slightest hesitation. Just as Jumonville burst into the clearing ahead, the colonel shouted, "Remember that you're on a hill! Aim low! Fire!"

A great cacophony erupted. A roar of crackling guns. Washington's soldiers were not His Majesty's regulars. As such, the timing of their blasts was not precise, so the entire line did not fire as one. Nonetheless, it was a deafening and frightening sound, the initial staccato burst lasting just over three dreadful seconds. Clumps of dirt exploded in the camp. Holes were ripped through tents. Frenchmen shrieked and fell. Shot pelted the trees in front of the Half King and I. We dropped to our knees as the echoes of that morning's shots rang around and again in that glen.

"Reload!" barked Washington, straining his hollow voice.

The Frenchmen, most of whom hadn't yet touched a weapon, abandoned the camp. In helter-skelter fashion, they raced in the direction opposite Washington's soldiers.

And right into the Half King's band of warriors who had begun to advance when they heard the fight erupt. Hiding behind trees and rocks, the Indians pelted the retreating Frenchmen with sporadic, but deadly shot. After discharging their muskets, the Mingo warriors snatched hatchets from their belts and leapt out, making a mad dash toward the oncoming French.

For their part, the disoriented and frightened French soldiers skidded to a halt and, after quickly deciding that the English might be more apt to give quarter, turned again and raced back toward the camp. This time, their hands were held high above their heads. They peered up to the smoky hill where Washington and his soldiers stood. The bewildered Frenchmen cried out, "Nous abandonnons!"

They'd given up. Without his enemy firing a shot, Washington had won his first ever battle in a lopsided fashion.

And quite unwittingly, the volley fired by the tall Virginian in those backwoods of America had just set the world on fire. Or, maybe it was I, in my quest for revenge, who had lit the fuse.

CHAPTER FORTY

"Diplomatie!" Jumonville repeated sternly. Other than a few words uttered here and there, he had retreated from his broken English in the face of Washington in favor of his native French. Yet, though Van Braam scrupulously translated to his best ability, even without the Dutchman's services, it was clear that Jumonville was insisting he had been sent from Fort Duquesne on a mission of diplomacy. He had merely sought a conference with Washington.

Around us, we had piled the dead bodies of the French. A third of them had perished in the hail of shot from the ridge and the Indians behind. The survivors were huddled in a rough circle, guarded by several of our men, more for their protection from Tanaghrisson's Indians than any fear Washington had of their escape. One of the commonalities among most of the tribes was that what their warriors craved above all else was a prize or totem to take away from battle. That could be a scalp in the case of a dead or dying enemy. Or, in the case of those yet living, it could be a captive.

Jumonville was smart enough to seek protection from the Half King or me. He stayed as close to Washington as possible while one of our men tended to his wounds. My shot had ripped away a chunk of the muscle at the back of his arm. It gave me pleasure to see a tear bubble over and run down his cheek as a bandage was affixed in place. He'd also been wounded from a ball during Washington's volley. It must have ricocheted off of a tree, for it, along with bark, was discovered floating rather superficially in the lean muscle of his calf. Excruciatingly painful, yes. But neither injury was fatal.

And that made Tanaghrisson more agitated than I had ever seen him. "You were supposed to shoot him with your damn pistol!" he grumbled quietly to me. While Washington and Van Braam tried to have a conversation with the stubborn French ensign, the Half King paced back and forth outside the circle of Englishmen. He never let his gaze slip from Jumonville. "I needed a dead French officer!"

228

"I thought we wanted *him* dead," I whispered, referring to Jumonville. "Not just any officer."

"That's what I meant!" the Half King growled.

"I gather you are trying to tell me that you are a diplomat of sorts," Washington said to the prisoner. The colonel wore impatience stretched across his face. "But what diplomat attacks the homestead of a peaceful man? Lieutenant John Fraser tells me he has been burnt out. And what diplomat, if he was sent to intercept me, prowls around for several days instead of coming directly to my camp at Great Meadows? My whereabouts could not have escaped your knowledge. We are encamped in the middle of a well-known valley. We make a tremendous racket felling trees."

Ensign Jumonville crossed his arms and hobbled next to the ambling colonel. "Diplomate," he mumbled. "Diplomate, diplomate, diplomate!"

"Of course, you are," Washington said, cutting off Van Braam before he could offer a repeated translation. The colonel removed his hat in frustration. He pointed down to the dead. "And what are we to do with these poor men? It was not my intention for such a thing to happen."

"La faute va au commandant," Jumonville said accusingly.

"Excuse me, ensign?" Washington asked.

Jumonville smirked. He then rediscovered his ability to speak English. "The fault lies with the commander, colonel." He said the rank with a fair amount of mockery. French regulars, like their English counterparts, held provincial soldiers, be they American or Canadian of any rank, in low esteem.

If Jumonville had hoped to stir the colonel's ire, he was unsuccessful. "It is a burden of command, that is true," Washington said thoughtfully.

Still pacing, the Half King said, "You have your victory, Conotocarius. My warriors will need some proof of their valor in this battle. They require captives and scalps. The living and dead belong to me."

The few Frenchmen who understood English became worried. Their eyes darted around, on the lookout for the assault they expected at any moment. Those men then quickly interpreted the Half King's remarks to their comrades so that every one of our captives began fidgeting nervously. The prisoners were set to burst from fear.

"Chief Tanaghrisson," Washington said. "This skirmish was between your former French fathers and your English brothers. I'm afraid I cannot turn any of them over to you."

"You cannot possibly think that you will let them go!" the Half King shouted.

"What else can I do? Jumonville insists he is a diplomat. Once I actually get him to convey his message, I must let them go. We are not at war with France. These men are not prisoners of war."

"My English brother may kill for territory. But I'll remind Conotocarius that his Seneca and Mingo brothers go to battle for revenge, for honor, for plunder, and captives. We did not risk our lives here today to go home empty-handed!" The Half King's warriors barked their agreement, pumping their muskets in the air a time or two for emphasis. Unfortunately, theirs was a sentiment which neither the French nor the English would ever fully understand about their on-again, off-again allies, the Indians.

Washington stood assessing the situation. He looked at the angry chief, who had never before lost his control in matters. The colonel also noted the growing ire in the Mingo braves as they grumbled. Still, the young colonel remained calm. "Chief Tanaghrisson, I cannot allow you to take a single soul or any of their effects. We are not common thieves. And so, if I set these men free to return to their commander at the Forks, will you and your men pledge to refrain from attack?"

The Half King seethed, nostrils flaring like a winded pony. His chest expanded and contracted forcefully as he sucked in large, rapid swaths of air. After a long while, he sighed, seemingly forcing himself to relax. When his breathing slowed, he calmly stepped between the shoulders of the Virginians who guarded the prisoners and approached Washington. Jumonville retreated so that the colonel blocked the chief's potential line of attack. "Colonel Conotocarius, will you at least allow us to take the ensign as our prize? It has been the way of warfare on this continent for centuries. Should he wish it, he may be adopted into our tribe. Otherwise, he will be ransomed to the French fathers. The rest may go unmolested."

"None will go into Iroquois or Mingo captivity, regardless of the terms," Washington insisted. He drew himself taller.

Tanaghrisson's face hardened. He shook his head in irritation and fixed me with an accusing glare. "You had one thing to do, Shit-for-brains."

"What is your decision, Chief Tanaghrisson?" Washington asked, not wishing to draw me into his disagreement. "Are we to agree and part as friends?"

"It will be as you say," the Half King said grudgingly. "And though you have much to learn about frontier warfare, we will honor your wishes. None of these men will be attacked if you set them free."

"Thank you," Washington said earnestly. Now victorious for a second time that day, the colonel stepped toward Van Braam. "Allow the French to pack their gear – without their weapons. Once Ensign Jumonville actually speaks with me about his so-called diplomatic mission, see them fed and on their way."

"Yes, colonel."

Washington turned to see that the Half King still stared at Jumonville. The chief's muscled jaw bulged. The ensign appeared small.

"I look forward to a long alliance, Chief Tanaghrisson," Washington said. As a balm for sore feelings, he added, "In time, I hope you will come to agree that releasing these soldiers was necessary for peace."

"Yes. I believe I will," the Half King said in resignation. "And I hope that one day you will understand that this, too, was necessary for war. For all our brothers. For Iroquoia."

"This, too?" Washington asked.

The chief ignored the question. He pointed to Jumonville's wounds. "Thou art not yet dead, my father."

The colonel sensed something was amiss, but it was too late. The Half King had already jerked the war hatchet free from his belt. All the while he raised and then lowered it in a blinding flash, he gave a chilling Indian war whoop that turned my blood to ice. And he went on whooping and whooping as he brought the sharpened iron head down onto Jumonville's skull time and again. The chief pounded and pounded while Jumonville crumpled, instantly dead. Debris from the ensign's head splattered the Half King. Blood flecked the horrified and frozen colonel's boots.

And all around us our Mingo allies swooped onto the French, starting with the wounded, carrying out deeds that mimicked those of the Half King. Like water in the mighty Ohio River, crimson ran in that small glen.

CHAPTER FORTY-ONE

Over the years since that damp morning, I have heard at least four different versions of the events from start to finish. There was that of Washington's official journal. His account was measured and decidedly brief. There were those details carried back to Duquesne by one of the French survivors who managed to escape at just the right time – amidst chaos. The story told by the French was nothing if not salacious. There was also a third tale told by a man named Private Straw. He was at Great Meadows at the time of our encounter with Jumonville, but said a member of Washington's force had come back and given him a blow-by-blow account. I think Private Straw just wanted to be famous for something in his otherwise unremarkable life. And finally, there was a fourth version propagated by an Iroquois Catholic who had a relative fighting along with our Indian allies.

I won't bore you with the all these fanciful tales from would-be storytellers. Suffice it to say that the four versions coalesce into two main camps. Those siding with Washington refer to the entirety of the action that day as the *Battle* of Jumonville's Glen. And during the short period of Washington's volley, the French retreat, and the Indian envelopment, it was rightly a battle. On the other hand, those siding with Governor Duquesne and his Frenchmen call the encounter the *Massacre* of Jumonville's Glen or, more generally, la guerre sauvage. As you will see, the events that followed the murder of Jumonville could accurately be termed a massacre.

"Chief Tanaghrisson!" Washington breathed. He was as successful in getting the furious warrior to halt his beating as is a steer in impregnating a heifer.

All the Englishmen guarding the French could do was scatter out of the way as the Half King's warriors descended. Not one of my fellow Protestant soldiers wanted to lay down his life to protect a Catholic Frenchman from harm.

The Iroquois used knives, tomahawks, and the butts of their muskets to unleash a stream of fury on their helpless prey. None dared to touch Washington, Conotocarius, who was trapped inside the circle of death. But as a mark of the colonel's bravery, something which he has conspicuously demonstrated time and again over the years, he didn't try to flee that belly of hell. He stood his ground, accomplishing little as he demanded the murderous activity cease. A dozen previously wounded French soldiers died in an area not greater than a rod in diameter. Washington, the Half King, and Jumonville's bloody corpse were at the center.

And as quickly as it began, it ended. The Indian warriors had sated their bloodlust by seeing the earth stained red. They then quickly morphed from a murderous band to one of thieves. They strung scalps on poles. They picked over the trinkets carried by the dead.

Not knowing what else to do, Washington's soldiers successfully re-herded the surviving Frenchmen into another, more distant circle. A few of the younger prisoners even clung to the coats of the English. They looked like fearful toddlers cowering behind their mothers when on the clamorous streets of Boston for the first time.

The Half King bent to one knee over Jumonville's remains. He tossed his bloody hatchet to one side and scooped both hands into the mess of brains that oozed from the many craters in the ensign's skull. Then, as if he washed them in a basin of water, the Half King scrubbed his hands using the gray matter as something of a lubricant. When he was done, he flicked his fingers and brushed his palms across one another. He snatched up his hatchet and stood. "Shit-for-brains has said he would wash his hands in Jumonville's brains. That is at last finished. And a new day has begun."

"The ravings of a boy bent on revenge is one thing!" Washington breathed. "What have you just done? You've murdered an unarmed French officer."

"We are now allied, Conotocarius," the Half King said, his shirt and face covered in slimy remains. "By the blood of these dead men, especially this officer, you are at war with the French. Through you, Onondaga is allied with your army, with your king. I am the lynch pin, no longer half of anything. Iroquoia is suddenly important again."

"But why him?" Washington asked. "I understand Mr. Weber's anger, but what did you have against Ensign Jumonville?"

The Half King ignored the colonel. He bent and scooped up Jumonville's scalp. It lay in three sections separate from one another and from his skull. He tied two at his waist so the fresh blood dripped down his thigh. Then striding toward me, he offered the third bit of hair and flesh. "Your prize. Proof of retribution so that your agitated soul may rest easy. Look on it during the cold winter's nights. When you are old, with children and grandchildren, you will know that your youth was not wasted. You were not tread upon by lesser men."

I doubt I would have taken it. As hate-filled and obsessed as I'd been, Jumonville's death was enough of a trophy. The grisly scene will never leave my mind's eye. Today, I can still see the spot of earth that received the ensign's body. Macabre. "You'll not be a part of this, Mr. Weber," Washington warned. "My army cannot be involved in this slaughter."

"But you already are," the Half King said with a devilish smile.

"Keep the scalp," I told the Half King, using ever bit of diplomacy taught to me by Croghan. "You deserve the prize. You did the killing. I merely watched."

Satisfied with that answer, Tanaghrisson affixed the third section of the scalp next to the others. He then ordered his followers to depart with him. "We are allies in your great war against the French," he repeated to Washington. It was as if he was trying to build a case in a court of law. He thought that if he made the claim often enough to the jury, no one could question its veracity. "Should you require my assistance do not hesitate to ask." Chuckling, he and his band of chattering warriors crept off into the woods.

"We shall have to make the Frenchmen prisoners," Washington sighed, his mind vigorously turning to make sense of the situation. "For their protection and ours."

"What do you mean, ours?" Van Braam asked.

"For their protection is obvious," Washington admitted. "We cannot have the local inhabitants ambush these defenseless survivors. But if we let these men run off to tell Fort Duquesne what happened here today, we will invite our own destruction. We will not be permitted to fight in the manner to which Europeans and colonists are accustomed. I fear it will descend into the blood feuds of old."

About that fact, Washington was correct. But our keeping of the prisoners would do nothing to alter it. Very quickly the war we'd just started would indeed descend to la guerre sauvage. It was inexorable.

"Did you know the Half King sought some type of revenge against the same man as you?" Washington asked me. It was the first time he'd ever used the phrase Half King in a derisive manner.

"Yes, colonel," I said, hoping that would be answer enough.

It wasn't. "Then what was his reason? Why did you not think to tell me?"

"I work for George Croghan, colonel. And George has always told me not to reveal the secrets of our compatriots in the trade game, especially devoted ones like Chief Tanaghrisson."

"You carry a firearm in my presence, Mr. Weber. You accompany my army. You are under my command whether or not you are in the employ of Mr. Croghan." His words were stern, breathy. He was angry and this was the most he'd ever show it.

"Yes, sir," I said meekly.

"What's done is done, I suppose," Washington said while examining the carnage surrounding him. "But you will tell me what caused Tanaghrisson to so hate Jumonville."

And I did.

CHAPTER FORTY-TWO

"The rape and murder of his daughters is an evil that cannot be comprehended," Washington had said after I told him the reasons Tanaghrisson wanted revenge against Jumonville. "But someone as experienced in diplomacy as the Half King should know not to rattle the tree of peace at such a fragile time as this. He may have just started a full-blown war."

That's just the way it seemed to all of us at Great Meadows over the weeks following the *Incident* at Jumonville's Glen. A war was brewing between France and Great Britain, even if everyone in Paris and London remained happily unaware.

Governor Dinwiddie had come through with his promises. Two hundred more volunteers from Virginia arrived at our camp during June. They brought with them nine swivel guns, not as powerful as cannon, but many multiples of our prior firepower. Croghan, through his own network of traders and contacts, informed Washington that the House of Burgesses and the governor had forwarded on a pack train containing fifty thousand pounds of flour in order to extend the campaign. It arrived shortly after the new recruits.

Washington immediately sent his thanks to the governor in Williamsburg. He also forwarded the surviving French prisoners toward the coast. His note to Dinwiddie stipulated that he was certain Jumonville's band had been spies sent to watch our movements. It said nothing of the Half King's actions or the brutal executions at the end of our confrontation. However, the headstrong colonel did go on to boldly request the raising of even more colonial militiamen in order to permanently extricate the French from the Forks of Ohio. In light of everything he had seen, Washington was certain that Dinwiddie would grant his entreaty.

And more positive developments unfolded, confirming in our commander's mind that a true inter-colonial effort to defeat the French was underway. Just three days after the arrival of his fellow Virginians, the expected independent company from South Carolina came to Great Meadows. It consisted of one hundred British regulars and, perhaps more importantly, those forty head of cattle.

The commander of these men was a true fart in the wind named Captain James Mackay. A gasbag like few I've ever seen. Upon his arrival, the blustery turd made it plain that his commission was from the king and not merely from some royal governor like Washington's. Turns out, Mackay believed his shit did not stink. And though he was useless, he would find that his men would die just as easily as would ours.

Finally, Hogg's reconnaissance found that no skulking enemy was found anywhere. The French who had taken the Forks did not descend on us. Not yet anyway.

Washington processed all these mostly encouraging signs. As a result, he decided to aggressively renew our advance on the Forks. But before we could leave he had one, and only one, defensive operation in mind. We built a circular stockade of split logs with walls only seven feet high. The diameter of what was to be our last refuge should we need to retreat back to Great Meadows, was a mere fifty feet. It could hold only sixty out of our hundreds of men. He had a small shelter built inside the walls to store ammunition. Outside the walls we dug trenches all around the perimeter. These ditches, should they become necessary, would house the rest of us if the French decided to attack.

The colonel said a prayer of dedication on the day of its completion, christening the crude palisade as Fort Necessity. While we bowed our heads along with Washington, I remember peaking up from within the fort's walls. Necessity sat on the bottom of the valley floor. All around, I could see hills and trees and mountains giving an endless selection of perfect sites on which to rest sharpshooters and cannon – French cannon. After Washington said *amen*, I added my own prayer that the use of Fort Necessity would never, ever become necessary.

"Conotocarius, you sent for me," the Half King said as he walked in through the gate of the fort. We had not had any contact with the chief since the incident in the glen.

Eager, Washington stood from where he had knelt in the dirt of the fort for his prayer. He called to his officers and advisors to join him. Those men, in turn, each one thinking I served him in some capacity, bade me to follow as well. Croghan, Trent, Ward, and perhaps more still thought of me as their own personal assistant. A group of about twenty of us, whites and Indians, followed the colonel and Tanaghrisson back out of the fort and into the meadow. We casually strolled through the swaying summer grasses that grew lush and green in the clearing. Cattle, oxen, horses, and mules, the staples of military vittles or transportation grazed all around us. It was a peaceful day, the kind where nothing could go wrong.

"I have valued your friendship," the colonel said with uncharacteristic timidity, unwilling to bring up the confrontation with Jumonville.

"And I, yours," answered the Half King. He seemed somehow distant, as if he pondered great questions. He hadn't even given me a wink or wave as he normally did upon greeting me. I felt a little discarded.

"I require your assistance once again," said the colonel.

"We are allies," Tanaghrisson said easily. "Coordinated in this great war against the French fathers. They shall be punished, I'm sure. It is what good Englishmen do."

The colonel stopped about one hundred yards from the fort, just where the land began to swoop upwards into the surrounding hills. We fanned out around them as if we watched a stage production. "Will you and your warriors accompany my men and I as we again strike off toward the Forks? Not as diplomats, but true fighters. Perhaps even gathering other Indians."

Tanaghrisson looked to his young Mingo warriors who, remembering the recent effortless victory, grinned in support. "Your Captain Hogg did not find the French army coming to you?" the chief asked.

"We believe they are still at the Forks," Washington said. "That gives us time to drive the fight to them."

"What do you hope to do once you are there?" the chief asked. "I saw what was happening at the forks. Shit-for-brains was there, too. He'll tell you that they began with a thousand men. It could be more now." I noted that the Half King had entirely given up calling me Ephraim. Such was his prerogative.

"We've received reinforcements. I expect more to come before the weather turns in the fall." Washington was all confidence. "I'll take my men, leaving a small force here. The rest of us will hold onto the banks of the Ohio and Monongahela by Thanksgiving."

"Some of these are not your men!" Captain Mackay interrupted. Several of us moaned in disgust. I told you he was a turd. "We will not be ordered about the country by a backwoods gentry bumpkin on a fool's errand."

"Then why have you come at all?" asked the Half King.

"Because a soldier follows orders," said the captain, pompous even for a British regular.

"And won't you then follow the orders of your colonel?" said the Half King.

"Not if he is a provincial colonel so wet behind the ears he makes a river jealous," came the abrupt reply.

"Ah, bickering," Tanaghrisson said, not as a lament, but almost fondly. He then returned his focus to Washington. "It sounds like you do not have the reinforcements you thought."

Washington was unfazed. "Then I will happily leave Captain Mackay and his men here to mind the fort and our supply train. I'll take my Virginians and cut a swath to the Forks. In the meantime, reinforcements, *willing* reinforcements, will arrive to bolster our numbers."

"I see," the Half King said circumspectly. He pointed over the pastoral scene through which we had just walked. "And tell me, what is that little thing upon the meadow?"

"What little thing?" the colonel asked.

"The structure in which I found you praying. Is it some type of open air church?"

"Fort Necessity," Washington answered earnestly. "We shall utilize it only if all else goes wrong. I thought it best to prepare for every possible contingency."

"And you are sure about this *fort*?"

"If it comes to the point where we must defend her, I'm certain she could withstand the attack of five hundred men," Washington answered.

"If it comes to that," Tanaghrisson huffed. "Your little fort will become a deathtrap."

"I disagree," Washington said, somewhat ruffled. Mackay, whether he agreed with the Half King or with Washington or neither, chuckled at the public rebuke of the young colonel.

"Remind me of how many battles you've fought," the Half King asked Washington. Gone was Tanaghrisson's normally easy-going manner. It was replaced by an almost threatening air. I had never seen him act in such a way. To call out the colonel's inexperience in front of so many, I could only assume he was bent on instructing the young Washington in something important.

"Sir," Washington stuttered. "I am well studied in command. I have read every important treatise ever written in English on military matters. I know the wilderness. I know men and terrain."

"And battles?" the Half King pressed.

"One, Chief Tanaghrisson," Washington answered more quietly than usual. "A victory, sir."

"That skirmish against Jumonville was hardly a battle," the Half King said.

"Yet you claimed that your warriors deserved great prizes for such a fight!" Washington said in retort.

"And we *took* them, didn't we?" the Half King answered.

"You did," Washington said evenly. He remained silent a moment, collecting his thoughts. "Chief Tanaghrisson, I was sorry to hear what happened to your daughters at the hands of Ensign Jumonville. But now that you've had your revenge in the ancient ways of your people, you cannot just retire to the council fire. You've said we are allies and I believe we are. The goals of Onondaga and the English are the same."

"They *may* be the same," Tanaghrisson allowed. "But I cannot commit Onondaga to war just because you and I are friends. I must do what is in the best long run interests of Iroquoia."

It took a full twenty seconds for the gravity of these words to sink in. "But are you not the local representative of the Tree of Great Peace, of Onondaga, of the Six Nations of the Iroquois?" Washington asked.

"I am," Tanaghrisson answered.

"Then you *can* make such a commitment." Warriors and soldiers, Indians and whites watched this discussion with ever greater interest. Croghan elbowed his way to the front.

"I'm afraid I cannot," the chief said. "I have a nickname among the English. I believe we all know what it is."

His warriors chuckled. One of them said it aloud. "Half King."

Tanaghrisson laughed, too. "A Half King has no more power than a quarter king or a tenth king. I must go see what Onondaga has to say. They may choose to support their English brothers as they have in recent generations. They might decide to support the French as in previous generations. The French do hold the Forks, you see? Now that war has come to the two great powers, Onondaga will do what is best for Iroquoia and may support neither. Who knows?"

"But." That was all Washington could say.

"You're not serious! We've worked together for years," Croghan barked. "You can't just act like you've no power. Like you may support the Froggies in all this! The damn Frogs!"

"George," said the Half King patiently. "My local Delaware and Shawnee children have decided they want to be more independent from Onondaga. Shingas even thinks of himself as a king. But my power, the power of the Iroquois, is greatest when these subordinate tribes know their place. As such, whether they decide to cozy up to the French or the English makes no difference to me. What matters is that the French fathers and the English brothers begin to wear themselves down with war. That, I believe, will leave the Six Nations in an even stronger position than at the end of the Beaver Wars."

Croghan blinked in disbelief. "Why you…"

"So, you intentionally started a war between France and Britain so that your people could wind up in a stronger position?" Washington asked, aghast. A rider from the fort tore through the peaceful valley, cutting a line directly toward us. The grazing livestock scattered as he came. The rider and the Half King were ruining everything about that peaceful morning.

"You are a reader of books, Conotocarius," the Half King said. "It is said you read the Stoics, a man named Seneca, among other Roman authors."

The Half King was a bastard, I thought. He'd known all along that Washington's Seneca book had nothing to do with his own people.

He continued. "I, too, am a reader. You should have read your Julius Caesar, Colonel Washington. You could learn from such a military man rather than mere philosophers."

"I have read about his conquest of Gaul in his own words," Washington answered, defending his rigorous self-procured education. "Translated, of course."

"Then you've read his lesson before. But perhaps it has slipped your mind. What did he do to the Gallic tribes? I'll tell you. *Divide et Impera.* Divide and Conquer. He let them fight one another. It is what the English and the French will do here and now."

"This is insane," I cried in disbelief. "You didn't just start a war to start a war. Why are you lying? You've told me again and again that you know the English will prevail in North America. You've said you wanted to avoid bloodshed for all peoples."

"I'm afraid you'll have to understand that not everything a man says should be considered as true as the gospel," Tanaghrisson said, feigning sheepishness. "People have thought I use the word Iroquoia just because I am old and feeble. They think that I cannot recall that there is not much of an Iroquoia remaining. But, to me, it never left. It shall rise among the ruins of your war, even as both powers come to Onondaga pleading for our assistance."

"But if that was all a lie," I began, scrunching my brow.

"Then most of what I've said was perhaps not the truth," the Half King allowed. "Come now, Shit-for-brains, you must know something. My family at Logstown, with whom you resided for that night in the winter, was the entirety of my family. I have never lost any daughters to anyone." He laughed at his own successful charade. "I had never heard of Jumonville until you mentioned his name. You, with your hatred, seemed like a good candidate to begin the war. And I'm glad I began down that path. I had hoped Legardeur would start the killing at the Forks. But Ensign Ward made it out alive."

For me, the killing of Jumonville had suddenly lost much of its power. I was glad he was gone, but the manner of his death left me sickened. He and I had become pawns sacrificed by a Half King who desired to control the board.

"So now that you have what you wanted, a war between France and Great Britain," Washington summarized. "You will abandon us."

"Colonel you are an honest man," said Tanaghrisson, setting a fatherly hand on Washington's shoulder. The colonel was too stunned to pull away. "But even if I was a strident supporter of my brothers, the English, you would not ever catch me cowering in that so-called fort. I do not wish for death to come so quickly – even to these old bones."

"And you, sir, are *not* an honest man," came Washington's reply. "Furthermore, you will not ever catch me cowering in Fort Necessity. Because with or without you, my Virginians and I." He glanced angrily at Mackay, who for all his bluster was shocked silent by these revelations. "My *Americans* and I will march out to the Forks and clear away the enemy."

The rider from the fort sent clumps of sod up as he curbed his beast to a rapid stop. "Colonel Washington, sir," breathed the man as he dismounted. "The French are coming. They've finally left the Forks. The whole damn army is coming this way!"

With a genuine, sad face, Tanaghrisson said, "It would be best if you took your men and returned to Williamsburg, colonel. At least go back to Wills Creek. I truly wish you no personal harm. You have no hope in this valley against Captain

Legardeur. His hair is silver. Yours is dark with youth. He's donated one of his eyes to battle, but gained wisdom. You have fine eyesight, but little experience, little ability to see."

When he then saw the steadfast determination forming in Washington's pale eyes, the Half King broadened his audience. He called out to the officers and staff standing on the gentle slope. "Colonel Washington is a good-natured man. But he has no proficiency in war. Who would follow such a man to his death? This war will stretch on long enough, years perhaps. There will be many chances to fight for victory, for glory. Save yourselves this day."

There was a series of incomprehensible mumbles from the men. All were non-committal. Except MacKay, that is. There was no mistaking where his loyalties lay.

I had trusted the Half King as a confidant, as someone who cared for the plight of my family. He had sworn to help me find the revenge I so desired. Instead, he had used me as a trick card held in reserve. My anger flared. If Washington had proved unwilling to start an all-out war, the Half King himself would start it – by blaming me and my French pistol! It hadn't worked out that way. We had all witnessed him murder Jumonville. Nonetheless, with our two armies drawing nearer to one another, the Half King still had his war.

"I will follow Washington to the death!" I shouted.

Colonel Washington fixed me with an appreciative glance. He looked like a proud father.

One-by-one, the other officers slowly discovered their backbones. Trent, Ward, Hogg, and more repeated my call. MacKay, cowed from the overwhelming support for a lowly provincial officer, kept his mouth shut. Croghan, too, said nothing. He was a trader, not a soldier. I had expected to hear no such bold talk from him. His mind, I'm sure, went to calculating all the provisions Washington's army would need if it survived the coming assault. And if we survived, the wily Irishman's profits would climb higher than ever. Perhaps getting kicked out of the Forks was not the worst thing for him.

Tanaghrisson had no plans to be around when the wave of Frenchmen rolled in. He also knew that Washington would not risk apprehending a respected member of Onondaga. The colonel didn't need to create any more enemies. And so, the Half King easily walked off with his warriors to gather their horses. "Well, then, Shit-for-brains," he said as he passed by. "Down in that little fort, you'll do just that. You will follow the fool Washington to your death."

CHAPTER FORTY-THREE

Three days later we were holed up in and around Fort Necessity. I had never thought I would be glad to call the slapdash structure home. But I, like my compatriots, decided that it was better than nothing. The French would do their best to prove us wrong.

What food we could fit inside the fort was packed in the single, small building along with the ammunition. A few animals and fodder were brought inside as well in case some had to be butchered during the siege. Even so, a few shitting cows, casks of rum, and some sacks of flour were not going to keep four hundred men fed if the siege went on very long at all. The rest of our baggage remained outside the trenches, abandoned in the remnants of our train.

Washington had hoped that his further pleas to Dinwiddie would be swiftly answered. He had even sent more letters imploring for immediate relief once the size and make-up of the French force was known. Six hundred French regulars, their white coats and blue waistcoats looking smart, and one hundred Indian allies bore down on us from Fort Duquesne. Their commander was clearly determined, as if on a personal mission. He drove them hard. They ate up as many as a dozen previously unhewn miles every day.

The extra time we had to prepare was only helpful at the margins. We were able to mount several of the swivel guns on the rickety walls of Fort Necessity or out front behind our trenches. The guns wouldn't halt a proper siege, but they might slow down an infantry charge if loaded with grapeshot. Nothing sapped an advancing army's determination like watching a dozen comrades sliced to shreds.

On the negative side of the ledger, a sickness had begun racing through camp, making nearly a hundred men unfit for duty. Diarrhea and war go together like hand and glove, I'm afraid. As such, we didn't have the time or manpower to rebuild or extend the walls to protect more of us. The only thing those of us who were healthy enough to work could do was dig. We made our trenches wider and deeper before settling into them and waiting.

It didn't take long for the first of our enemies to arrive.

Rain.

We should have expected him.

I cannot begin to explain the reasons but, without fail, rain comes so often to battles it is as if its only purpose is to make a miserable situation more dismal. It saps the will. It makes the skin of a man's feet rot. It makes sewage ditches flow into drinking water. It makes men sick, sick, sick. This was one of those times.

Great Meadows was picturesque with its swaying greenery and surrounding mountains. At first glance, it seemed a miracle that no one had ever decided to build a town there. It held bountiful fodder for beast. Water for man and animal bubbled in the creek through its midsection. But what made Great Meadows such an ideal spot for pasturing creatures or pausing an army for a respite, made it a hellhole to defend in a downpour.

The land was naturally boggy, its soil thick and silty. Drainage of excess standing water after a long storm, we quickly learned, would take many days of sunshine to accomplish. And those were days that the good Lord did not see fit to grant us. He and I had a different understanding of his Providence.

It rained. And it rained. Off, but mostly on. Steady and drizzling, it rained for two days straight – day and night.

No one slept. Not one person. Even the officers, who huddled under a single tent that was stretched inside the fort, could not sleep. Water percolated through, and raced over, the ground at their feet. Men grumbled, dripping wet. The makeshift roof of the ammunition and food depot began leaking. Most of the gunpowder was fouled before the leaks were discovered and crews began hustling what was left beneath the officers' canopy. The barrels were stacked on their cots, meaning even fewer men could hope to find rest. With one stormy act of God, half of our ability to fight was washed away.

By the middle of the night, our trenches were filled with water so that Fort Necessity was surrounded by a moat that would have made a Medieval lord proud. The problem was that most of us were still in the moat! We had nowhere else to go. And to make matters worse, our personal powder stores were ruined as we treaded water or waded to what had become the outer banks of the circular river.

Normally, when morning breaks to men on campaign, I've discovered that there is generally some sense of relief. It is as if their hearts are light simply because they lived through a night that they may not have expected to survive. The morning following our most recent hellish night was not one of those mornings. Dawn came, I'm sure. But with it the rain continued falling so-much-so that it was impossible to tell whether or not the sun ever rose.

By midday our situation only grew worse.

Our second set of enemies, the deadliest, arrived. The French came with their new allies. But it was Shingas who was the first to appear on the scene.

He rode a sturdy pony through the swamping bottom land. His face was covered in red paint and adorned with white blotches that had begun to run downward due to the rain. As a result, he was given a permanently menacing frown and scowl that would prove to give me nightmares for months after. His pony had a rope snugged about its neck that dragged a heavy load about ten feet behind. Quite fearlessly, Shingas whooped and rode up directly to our trench. He curbed his pony so its hooves were within arm's reach. They pranced heavily in the thick mud.

I looked up into the stern eyes of the Delaware king. He returned the gaze showing neither fear nor worry. Courage and rage had ramped up within him. Shingas gave me a derisive smirk as he pulled a knife from his belt and cut the rope from his pony. The frayed end slumped into the muck. "You and Conotocarius have begun war against my masters at the Forks, my French fathers. I now give a present to you and your English friends, Shit-for-brains. The first of many more to come."

He caused his pony to pad back and forth a few times in front of us, daring someone to fire. A few men tried. Impotent scratches and clicks could be heard as flints struck slick frizzens.

Only one of them was successful enough to have the fresh powder in his pan burst with a flash that momentarily lit up the dismal sky. But the gunpowder buried deep within his barrel was already too damp. Nothing of consequence, not even a groan belched from his muzzle. Shingas laughed and galloped back toward the woods just as the rest of his Delaware and the French could be seen dispersing in a wide arc about five feet from the forest's edge. They were surrounding us and we could do nothing about it. So much for Washington's great and defensible fort.

"Where are you going?" Tommy Stewart called. He'd been stuck in the mud next to me most of the night. With Shingas gone, I had crawled out of the moat on my belly.

"Get back here, Shit-for-brains!" Lieutenant Fraser barked from his spot in the moat. He'd become slightly more reliable after the burning of his trading post.

But he was still an ass. And Fraser was one man to whom I would not listen. If anything, hearing his voice helped set my determination to continue. "Shut up!" I said. Then to Tommy, I answered, "I'm going to see my present from Shingas."

"It ain't going to be good, no matter what it is," Tommy warned.

"I know," I said, continuing my crawl as the first musket ball from the French splashed nearby. A muddy waterspout from its impact slapped my cheek. I reached the cut end of the rope and used it as a guide toward the heavy gift.

More musket fire peppered us from the surrounding ridges.

"Then get yourself killed, you Indian-loving Shit-for-brains!" called Fraser. I heard him and many others dive against the outer bank for protection.

The intensity of the fire increased. The French had obviously not spent the night with their gunpowder literally underwater. Behind me, I heard Washington's calm voice giving orders. The much louder voices of his officers then carried his commands to the men. Mackay's bombastic shouts were audible, too. His directives were no different from

Washington's, but he preferred to order his South Carolina regulars himself. Soon thereafter, a small amount of those in and around the fort began issuing return fire to the French. What exactly my comrades shot at was difficult, if not impossible, to identify given the low hanging clouds and enemy cover. And compared to the immense racket from our enemies in the hills above, our defensive efforts could only be called middling at best.

Scooting lower into the mud, I finally reached my gift from Shingas. It had no special wrapping. In fact, it was clearly a man. He was stripped naked and very dead. He lay face down in the muddy grass, his hands bound above his head. Swarming wounds blanketed his body. The mottled skin of his back was scraped raw from tumbling while being dragged behind Shingas' pony. He had been scalped, but even those normally bloody remains had been grated away from the dirt and grass.

The manner of this man's death made it clear that it was done by the Delaware. The French may have watched and even condoned the killing, but this was Indian work, plain and simple. And it was painfully obvious that this man had died at the hands of those who viewed killing him as some form of retribution or as an answer to a blood feud.

Lead sung as it zipped overhead. The air burned. Keeping my head low, I crouched in the grass and stuck my hands between his chest and the ground to roll him over. My knees skidded out from underneath me and my face flopped onto the peeling flesh of his back. A piece of shot struck and shattered my powder horn, knocking me to the side.

"You alright?" Tommy called, sticking his head up from the bank only long enough to shout.

"Ya," I said, gathering myself again to roll the body over. It took two more tries until I was successful.

Identifying the man was difficult. But it was not impossible. Like his rear, most of the skin covering his front half had been shaved off, either deliberately beforehand or incidental to his dragging. His face was a pulp of oozing tissue.

I patted the man's bare shoulder on the one place where any reasonable amount of his flesh survived. After heaving a great sigh of conflicting emotions, I crawled my way back to the flooded trench.

"What was it?" Tommy asked when I flopped back into the water. Lead ricocheted off of pebbles on the bank.

"Who was it," I corrected.

"Ew," he said. "Anybody we know?"

"Used to," I said, not able to identify exactly how I felt at the moment. "The Half King is dead."

CHAPTER FORTY-FOUR

The news of the Half King's tortuous death traveled quickly through our soggy domain. Most of the men greeted the news with emotions bordering on excitement, for he'd been branded a traitor after our last little meeting. He had received his just desserts. Tommy had said, "Frontier justice," and most agreed. Or so the conventional thinking went.

As I've said, I was initially more conflicted. But in the end, the musket balls that slapped into the walls and bodies around me, forced me to consider his death with indifference, if at all. In fact, none of us could think of anything other than survival. As the day wore on and the gunfire from above intensified, the only thing that fell with more ferocity than lead continued to be the rain. For every fifty shots taken by the enemy, we successfully sent one in reply. The French and their Delaware were concealed. We were laid naked and bare for even the poorest of marksmen to kill at will.

Even our dumb animals were not left unmolested. We had abandoned most of them to the pastures of Great Meadows when we retreated into the fort and moat. Now the French entertained themselves by slaughtering them one-by-one. Accustomed to the sound of gunfire from our own army and its practice, the herd stood grazing as their number dwindled. The horses of the officers and the pack and wagon animals were killed. A few of the men had brought dogs from home. These were shot dead. The strays, too – every army on the march accumulates stray dogs – weren't left alive.

Dead and wounded Englishmen piled up as well. Whenever there was a brief lull, the wounded were dragged inside and jammed into a tight corner between the palisade and storage building. There being no more room inside the walls, the dead were shoved up and out of the moat, their bodies providing only slightly more protection to us from the raining musket balls.

You could always tell when a heretofore living man was hit. A ball striking the walls of Fort Necessity made a sort-of clack sound. Its echo rang a rather long time like the peal of a bell. On the other hand, when shot hit the water of our moat, it sounded like a sharp kiss that was over as soon as it started. There was no hovering or lingering like a set of lovers' lips during an embrace. Likewise, the muddy ground was so saturated, when it was pierced I could only just barely tell the difference between it and the water. But a man's body being struck, that made a sound that was unique.

Most would describe it with one word – *thud*. And it is a thud, to be sure. A thud is the way I described it afterwards when telling lies about my heroism to Bess in Williamsburg. But writing a memoir affords one a little more space and time for reflection, some would say embellishment. And after you've heard a full one hundred men struck by gunshot over the course of an eight-hour battle, you come to grasp the fullness, the richness of the diabolical thump.

Most often the strike starts as a compressed tearing sound through the fibers of a man's cloak or shirt. Immediately thereafter, the ball begins its rapid descent through the layers of its victim's body. Skin is flayed in something resembling a knock or bump. Soft fat squishes. Firm, living muscle fights back against the bullet, the two interacting to create a pulsating throb. Usually, at this point the man begins to grunt if he is able, his sharp cry adding a layer of complexity to the already complicated sound.

Next, bones are broken. Some pop. Others shatter, sounding like a plate of glass being hurled to the floor. Finally, the shot reaches a man's innards. These sounds are muffled due to the depth of coverage by all the rest of the tissue. I do believe I've heard them though. To me they resemble a wet rag being tightly wrung. Finally, if the man might live, he falls to the ground shrieking. If the wound was instantly fatal, you just hear a faint slump.

But on we fought. With Washington's firm encouragement and Mackay's dimwitted defiance, we stayed put, shooting back on the rare occasions we could. More men died – Virginians, Pennsylvanians, South Carolinians.

Between the two of us, Tommy and I managed to find a horn full of dry powder sitting uselessly on the belly of a dead man. We set about filling each of our muskets and packing it and a ball tight. When I was loaded, I kissed the stock for luck, pretending my illegal Brown Bess was the real Bess from Williamsburg. I raised my gun and pointed it toward the woods. I could see no discernable figures. Our opponents were wisely keeping themselves hidden. They had to take no great risks to steadily slaughter us.

A flash of white, a Frenchman's coat, jumped from behind one bush to another. I fired blindly into the second set of thorns. A moment later I was rewarded with an enemy body rolling down the distant slope toward us.

"Great shot, Ephraim!" Tommy exclaimed. In reality, it was dumb luck.

"Wait until you see the next one," I bragged.

I then heard one of those tell-tale thuds that announced a man had been hit. It was nearby and I suddenly feared it was Tommy. But he was very much alive when I glanced his way. He had just fired his own gun into the murky forest, not knowing if he'd ever hit anyone.

Someone bumped into me from behind.

"Careful," I warned. But now the man was repeatedly nudging me.

"It's Fraser," Tommy said, glancing behind me as we both went about reloading our weapons.

I knew I'd kiss my musket again – for luck, of course. It had worked last time. But I would also kiss the Brown Bess in order to think of Bess, Bess and not the fact that I stood chest deep in a murky, urine-filled, shitty, bloody, rainwater moat.

"Tell Fraser to go to hell," I snapped as I withdrew my wooden ramrod from the muzzle and slid it through the series of brass pipes beneath the stock.

"Looks like he already has," Tommy quipped. No one liked a coward. Fraser was a proven coward.

When I turned to see, Fraser was floating face down in the moat. He had a gaping red hole in his back. The current created by all of our men struggling in the water caused his head to bump into me like a boat at the dock. "Hold this," I said, giving Tommy my gun. He held his and mine up out of the water as a sudden increase in musket fire from the ridges slapped all around us. I clutched Fraser's body and rolled him up onto the bank. My feet slipped in the mud beneath the water. He fell back onto me. Though not obese by any measure, at that moment Fraser weighed a ton. Finally, exhausted, I shoved him in place. At least in death he'd be good for something. He might even have kept me alive when three balls, meant for me, slammed into his corpse.

"Now give me back the Bess," I said, turning to Tommy. "Let's kill some more of these bastards."

Tommy's face snapped forward, his chin clunking his chest. The back half of his head was sheared off. Bits of his hair, flesh, and skull sprayed the water. He dropped straight down like a rock. His body, both our muskets, and our formerly dry powder went down with him. "Tommy!" I shouted, reaching down into the brackish water where he had disappeared. My hands came up holding only my dripping Bess.

A moment later he resurfaced a foot or so away. Gone was his life.

"Damn you Frogs!" I heard Croghan shout from within the fort's walls.

Seemingly in answer, the French replied with a huge burst of musket fire, leaving me wondering how they kept their gunpowder stores so full and dry.

"Come on, Tommy," I muttered, pulling him closer to me. I'd not shove his body up on the bank to absorb musket balls. It seemed a rude thing to do to him, a friend. Instead, having no dry weapon to speak of, I waded toward the palisade, towing Tommy behind. We reached the inner bank and I waited. After a minute or two, the enemy fire dwindled enough for me to feel safe dragging myself and my friend's body up and into the fort.

Without a hitch, we entered the fort.

It was difficult to comprehend, but inside the fort may have been more woeful than outside. These men, with Washington marching around in the very center completely unharmed, were like caged rats. A hail of bullets from the enemy had taken a toll, killing many of our officers, gentlemen, and common volunteers. There was hardly a place to move between the stacks of dying and dead. Before we had built Fort Necessity, the site had been covered in lush green grass. After building it, the grass was quickly pressed down into the earth so we had marched on gray-brown dirt. The rain had turned the fort floor into mud, with our feet churning it to an ankle-deep black pudding. Now, after hours of killing, we walked in a slurry that was as crimson as the finest red wine, though decidedly less elegant.

But it wasn't wine that had begun to consume the minds of the men inside the fort.

"If I'm going to die like the rest of these men," shouted a surly volunteer. His shirt was gone, used as a bandage for a superficial wound on his arm. "Then you can bet, colonel, that I'm not going to do it sober!" Van Braam, Washington, and Mackay suddenly gathered together in a tight circle as a score of other volunteers joined the angry man and formed a mob. Croghan, who had parked himself next to the colonel for the fight, wisely stepped out of the way.

Preferring to avoid any more confrontation that day, I skulked along the palisade. Soon, I deposited Tommy, face-up, on the top of a pile of the dead. It seemed disrespectful to place him face-down and show the gaping hole in the back of his head. I then snuck behind the leaky storage building to where my little pack of gear had been stuffed. In a moment, I had found Tahki's pistol and set my Bess aside. The pistol wouldn't do much good at any distance, but it was the only weapon I had that was not waterlogged. Now I had to find dry powder.

I returned to the dead and dying and began looking them over for supplies.

"There's not a lick of ammunition left anywhere," the angry crowd was shouting at Washington. "We've stripped it all bear. There's no more fighting to be done. Now give us the rum!"

"You'll do yourself no good, private," said Washington. "If you insist on dulling your mind, you might as well invite the French in among us now."

"Better to see their faces than to be killed from a distance!" said the mob leader in retort.

"They'll not listen to you, Washington. And, why would they? You're but a callow farmer!" Mackay bellowed. Then he proceeded to chastise his South Carolina regulars as well as any Virginians in earshot. "Disobeying my orders, the orders of an officer commissioned by the king, just may mean trial and death! Return to your posts and defend this fort."

"Hell with you all," shouted the mob leader. "Our posts in this fort mean death as sure as hell will come to you!" He shoved roughly past Mackay, but I noted he steered wide of Washington – something of a sign of respect even while he disobeyed orders.

"Men," Washington tried to warn them again as the horde followed after the gang leader. In the blink of an eye, the casks of rum were dragged out from the shoddy building and tapped. Direct from the tap or from mugs, the men drank greedily. Croghan, who had obviously decided that the most immediate threat to his life was not from the French outside but from the mob inside the walls, helped dole out the rations as evenly as the mass of men would allow.

For ten minutes, the officers and I watched as the men laughed and carried on. They sang as if they were drunk long before the rum could have possibly dimmed their senses. But so stressful had been the previous twenty-four hours that the men felt it their right to become drunk on nothing more than hopes. They'd become pre-emptively inebriated.

Outside, I could only hear one thing, the smattering of musket shot coming from our trench. "Colonel!" I shouted, running up to the flabbergasted Washington.

"What is it, Shit-for-brains?" he asked. His use of my nickname could only indicate that he'd reached his last nerve.

"The French! They haven't fired on us for over ten minutes! Maybe they've left."

Washington's countenance went pale. He faced me, but actually looked through me, before he himself ran to the palisade and scaled a crude set of steps to one of the swivel gun firing platforms. Van Braam and I scampered up after him. Mackay stayed put, preferring to keep his head at least somewhat better protected than ours.

The three of us dumbly peered into what had become the black night soup. A few sputtering torches lit the area so we could see clearly for no more than two rods. We, on the other hand, were likely well-lit for those looking in. If any of the Frenchmen or Indians could see us, we'd be excellent targets. But, except for our men below in the moat, who nervously expelled the last bit of our dry ammunition, it was silent. Nothing out in Great Meadows moved.

"Ahh!" shrieked a man behind us.

The three of us bolted around to see that the gang leader had now stripped off his trousers so that he stood stark naked in the fort's center. Under one arm he held a rum cask that drained its contents onto the reddened earth below. He didn't seem to care that he wasted the drink that had been so precious to him a few minutes earlier. His other hand extended out to his side, like he offered himself as a sacrifice to any able French shooter.

"Ahh!" he shrieked again. "Come on you French bastards! Now I'm ready for ya to put a musket ball between my eyes. Come on."

Washington and Van Braam were mesmerized by the sight of the men so flagrantly disobedient at such an inopportune time. The ever-confident colonel even let his chin sink down to his chest in shame. His great chance at command, his one shot to live up to the looming shadow cast by his brother, was slipping through his fingers. Fort Necessity had become a bloody debacle.

I couldn't bear to look at the drunkards as they danced with embarrassing glee. I'd decided it was better to turn around and face my enemy in case any of them were lucky enough to shoot me dead. And that's the moment when I realized that Washington's bloody debacle at Fort Necessity would only get worse.

"Colonel Washington," I said quietly.

Relieved to have something call his attention from his blatant failures at command, he slowly turned to look out into the night. He followed the direction my arm was pointing. Coming out of the rainy, dark fog was white – a row of smart, white uniforms marching against a black horizon.

"The French have not left us," Van Braam muttered.

Washington finished the thought. "On the contrary, they come to finish us."

CHAPTER FORTY-FIVE

But we had already done the work of finishing ourselves. The French army was hardly necessary at that point.

The white we had seen waving in the rainy night had actually been a flag of truce carried by a Canadian soldier no older than fourteen. He had been accompanied by a young lieutenant who looked terrified as he picked his way through the dead livestock and drew to the edge of our trench. These two green and unarmed soldiers, in turn, were guarded by a handful of experienced regulars with enough discipline to hide the worry they themselves might bear. Each of them wore the white coats – surprisingly and impeccably clean – you would expect of French soldiers. Their boots, gaiters, and breeches, however, were splattered with thick mud that might have added ten pounds to each of them as they trudged.

The young lieutenant managed to squeak out a surprising number of words even as he stared at the heaps of our dead that littered the moat's bank. A few of our defenders who still stood in the trench pointed their soggy and quite useless muskets at the officer's head. "Quit your yapping. None of us can understand you, anyway. But I'll be happy to remove those lips of yours if you mean to keep on talking." The defender's soaked and tired friends chuckled.

"Pipe down," Washington commanded quietly. "Let the man speak." He glanced to Van Braam. "What did he say?" It was nearly impossible to hear the lieutenant with the rum drinkers behind us still, their grand celebration in full swing.

Van Braam shouted down, asking the young French officer to repeat himself. More confident this time, the lieutenant found his voice.

"He says something about guaranteeing safe passage and terms," Van Braam interpreted while our revelers used some of the officers' furniture to kindle a bonfire.

"A ruse?" Washington asked. Trent and Croghan joined us on the platform while Mackay had made himself scarce. I cannot prove it, but I believe that when he heard the French were coming, he hastily found a hiding place among the sodden powder stores in the block house.

"Maybe," said Trent.

We all squinted, trying beyond hope to peer into the darkness behind the Frenchmen to see if there was an ambush lying in wait. We knew if there was, they'd hit us at the edge of the woods. Unfortunately, the meadow and the woods all appeared to us as the same bleak blur. We could see nothing.

"Whether or not they legitimately offer terms or it is a ploy doesn't matter. Either way, they know they cannot take our fortress without severe loss of life," Washington said. "The Half King was wrong. This is no deathtrap."

Croghan and Trent exchanged wary glances. Washington noticed them. He dropped his voice. "It is a deathtrap, yes," he admitted sheepishly. "But perhaps the French don't know that yet."

"Maybe they hear our drunken celebration and believe we've got more fight left in us," Croghan offered. "Lord knows they haven't ventured close enough to get a good look."

"In which case, the offer to discuss terms might be a hoax, indeed," Trent added.

"Yes," Washington allowed. "We cannot risk sending anything or anyone of consequence to our command and fighting abilities with the Frenchmen below."

"So, who do you think you'd send?" I asked. "Who would be fool enough to go out there?"

My question was promptly answered. Ten minutes later, Van Braam and I were following the French lieutenant and his small entourage up into the trees on the ridge. We had stumbled over the bodies of dogs and cows mostly. "Mr. Van Braam," I said, mocking the colonel with my best imitation of his hollow-chested, southern gentleman voice. "Kindly take Mr. Weber with you and see what the young French lieutenant has to say."

"That's enough, Ephraim," Captain Van Braam chastised as we entered the main French encampment. If the Frogs had hoped to lure out a large body of us, they'd clearly been disappointed. No ambush came for just the two of us.

I looked for any signs of the enemy's distress within the camp. We passed by the bodies of two French soldiers that had been covered with clean blankets. They were set neatly beneath a peaceful tree on a patch of soft grass. Compared to the grotesque heaps of our dead and wounded, the casualty rate of the Battle of Fort Necessity had certainly been lopsided.

All around us, French, Canadian, and Delaware warriors relaxed around great fires. Shingas and his men were there, lounging with the rest. Their faces wore the satisfied looks of soldiers with full bellies. The scattered remains of several of our own cattle lay about. They'd been butchered, roasted, and eaten while we'd been left with little more than nothing for well over a day. The sights and scents caused my stomach to turn on itself. I even heard Van Braam's belly growling.

King Shingas came alongside us as we walked. He sucked out the marrow of a steaming bone that he'd already licked clean. "Did you enjoy my present, Shit-for-brains?"

I shrugged. "You did the world a favor."

"But the mighty Half King was your friend," Shingas said, disappointed by my calm reaction. "He was a grand ally of the English."

"About as much of an ally of the English as he was of the Delaware," I muttered as we marched through rows and rows of lounging soldiers.

"He was no friend to those of us he called his children," Shingas grumbled.

"No," I agreed. "No friend to the Delaware. No friend to the English. And no friend to the French. He set this whole confrontation in motion. From encouraging Croghan to build the fort in the first place to killing the French officer. He started all this."

Shingas was quiet for a moment as he thought. His brow furrowed as he puzzled over what I had meant. Then he snapped his fingers. "Iroquoia! He thought this war would benefit the leaders at Onondaga."

"That's it," I said.

Shingas grabbed my arm and pulled me to a stop. Van Braam and our French escorts halted as well. The young lieutenant squeaked an order to the Delaware king. But one scowl from Shingas forced the lad to button his lips. The more experienced of our guides rolled their eyes and struck up a conversation amongst themselves.

The Delaware chief dropped his voice. "I don't know which of these Frenchmen can understand English, so I'll be quiet and brief." His eyes darted while he spoke. "Now that I see the scale of what the French have begun to build at the Forks and now that I know you English are not on the side of the Iroquois." He hesitated and peered around, verifying no one approached. He noted that the lieutenant and his guards still waited impatiently, caring little for what an Indian chief had to say. Shingas finished his thought. "My people may be willing to aid their English brothers should your king ever want to take back the Forks. Tell that to Conotocarius." He stared into my eyes intensely so that I could tell just how serious he was. Then he squeezed my arm a little too hard before walking away. "It was a fine day for a battle, Shit-for-brains! Too bad you decided to side against my French fathers," he added loudly.

"Le sauvage," the lieutenant mumbled so that Shingas couldn't hear him.

Stunned, I stared as the Delaware king walked away. Had I sided with the wrong Indian ally all along?

"Viens!" the lieutenant ordered. He promptly resumed his course with Van Braam and I chasing after him. He led us past a wagon. The corner of a tarpaulin that covered its load was folded back to reveal kegs of powder. Only two remained under the tarp. Empty kegs were scattered all about the camp. I peered out past the soldiers cooking fires and saw no other powder stores.

We followed our guide into a large tent at the center of the camp. After ducking inside, I expected to find the silver locks and stern eye of Captain Legardeur. But instead, I was greeted by the unemotional gaze of Captain Louis Coulon de Villiers de Jumonville, who was of course the elder brother of the man murdered by the Half King. The last time I had seen Captain Jumonville I had attempted to kill him and then threatened to murder his brother. I doubted he had forgotten the incident. My head darted quickly to the left and to the right, expecting soldiers to pounce on me.

But other than the three of us, after the lieutenant withdrew, the tent was empty.

"Sit," Captain Jumonville said graciously. "S'il vous plait."

"Merci," Van Braam said, taking a seat across from the table between us and the French officer. Then seeing that I stood with my eyes darting around the tent, still waiting for someone to run me through with a razor-sharp bayonet, the Dutchman ordered, "Sit down, Mr. Weber."

"Oui, Monsieur Weber, do sit," Captain Jumonville said with professional courtesy.

I did so, warily.

Jumonville stared at us in motionless silence for a long while. If he held any hatred toward us, me in particular, he was gifted at hiding it. After those long minutes, the Captain looked down at two pages filled with French script that rested in the center of his table. He made a satisfied mumble before turning them so they faced us.

At this point in my tale it is important you understand that my reading of my own English tongue was only at a most basic level. It has since improved. My ability to read French back then was non-existent. But even I could see that the first word at the top of the page was *Capitulation*. Jumonville was indeed offering us terms of surrender.

Van Braam pulled the documents closer and began studying them while Jumonville again examined me. His stare told me that if we'd met outside of that highly stylized ritual of parlay, he would have gutted me like wolf's prey. But he kept his mouth shut.

"We are guaranteed the honors of war?" Van Braam asked after just a short while.

"You have put up a brave defense against overwhelming odds," the captain allowed. "It is the least I can do as a gentleman."

Van Braam nodded his understanding and returned to the pages while I withered under the determined glare of Jumonville.

"What is this section here?" asked Van Braam, pointing to a paragraph.

Jumonville leaned forward, looking down his nose at the verbiage in question. "The French prisoners that your colonel illegally sent off to your capital will be returned immediately," he said.

"Illegally?" I asked.

The captain shook his head in disbelief. "Virginians," he huffed. "Your inexperience in the policies of war astounds me."

"I'm a Pennsylvanian," I retorted.

"Well, then, I stand corrected," the captain said, holding his palm to his mouth in feigned horror. "The inexperience of *all* the English colonists is something to behold."

"Just answer the question," I said.

"Your colonel had no right to seize those men. Our countries are not in a state of war."

"You could have fooled me," I said.

"Ephraim," Van Braam scolded me. Then he turned to the captain. "Those men were taken as prisoners more for their own protection from Tanaghrisson's Mingo warriors than anything."

"Regardless of your reasoning, they must be returned," the captain insisted.

"I'll convey that to the colonel," Van Braam assured him.

And they went back and forth, going over one term after another. One stipulated that none who had taken part in Washington's expedition would return to the region for the period of one year. If we were allowed to walk away from Fort Necessity, I was sure that George Croghan and I would violate that term within the month. We belonged in the frontier. A second term stated that two officers would have to retire to the Forks with the French as prisoners to guarantee that we complied with their demands. I breathed a sigh of relief that I was not an officer. Unless, of course, Washington saw fit to promote me in the field just so that I could become a captive. I didn't put it past him.

The entire negotiation process was all very professional, very antiseptic, impersonal. There was discussion of the wounded and the dead in very general terms, but no mention of the bloody carnage wrought by the engagement. Not once did Jumonville bring up the murder of his brother, let alone the method of his killing with his head split into several pieces and his brain splattered about.

"What does this mean?" Van Braam asked, his brow furrowed. He pointed to a short paragraph that I had seen him struggling to read several times over. Apparently, his ability to read French was even more limited than his ability to speak it. Still, he was more proficient at both than was I.

"It merely says that the undersigned English officers are responsible for the death of Ensign Joseph Coulon de Villiers de Jumonville," said the captain, reflecting solemnly as he coolly stated his brother's name.

"I didn't do it. It was the Half King," I blurted in defense. "Colonel Washington had nothing to do with it!"

Captain Jumonville ignored my own personal denial. "Nothing?" he asked. "Was he not in command? Was there someone else with authority over those soldiers and warriors when my brother was murdered?" He stared accusingly at me. "You perhaps?"

"Shit-for-brains is in charge of nothing," Van Braam said to defuse the situation. "Admitting responsibility, that particular term may pose a difficulty in the negotiations," he offered.

"Those are our terms," Captain Jumonville said firmly. "Unless you'd rather we resumed our barrage in the morning."

"We could withstand a siege from a thousand of you Frog-turds," I boasted.

Jumonville grinned. "That is the saddest fort I have ever seen. It is a deathtrap. It is a shame you survived this long."

Fort Necessity was, by consensus and in practice, a deathtrap. "You might be a bigger asshole than your brother," I muttered. In truth, at the time, I did not believe it. The elder Jumonville was carrying out his duties as a French officer with exemplary precision.

The captain smiled again before returning his attention to Van Braam. "Your colonel is young. One thing he should learn to do is send someone more diplomatic to these types of meetings if intends to continue losing."

Van Braam saw the flash of anger in my eyes. He stood quickly, rolling the capitulation papers and placing them in his coat pocket. "I'll be sure to give him your advice, captain. And I'll pass this document on to the colonel, but I cannot guarantee full agreement."

"For the sake of those men wading in your moat, I hope young Washington is able to see reason. Otherwise, tomorrow will be a bloody day in your valley. Good evening, gentlemen."

And just like that, we were dismissed. The young lieutenant returned and led us back through the field of slaughter to our poor fort. The entire way, I looked over my shoulder, expecting Jumonville to strike at me in some way in retribution for his brother's murder. But I was left alone. Apparently not everyone in the world was short-sighted like me and motivated by revenge. Jumonville was one of those rare breeds of men who could separate his personal feelings from his duty.

Only he was not one of those rare men. As we would soon discover, he was more diabolical than his ham-fisted brother. He was certainly craftier than I. His method of revenge was refined, subtle, and, I'm sure, entirely more satisfying for him.

CHAPTER FORTY-SIX

It took Van Braam only five minutes to get Washington and Mackay to sign the articles of capitulation. Given our miserable conditions, the terms seemed generous indeed. One quarter of our men were ill with dysentery. A quarter of our fighting force had been killed or wounded. Another quarter lay passed out in the mud, drunk. That left only one more quarter left in fighting condition. And those of us in that category were hungry and had no usable powder to speak of.

"The Frog-swallowers are out of powder, too," I warned, thinking of the nearly empty gunpowder wagon. "That's why they've given us terms so quickly. They don't know we are out."

"You dare not suggest we continue to fight," Washington asked. "Shall we use rocks and clubs?"

"Of course not," I said. "But it does us no good to accept their terms too quickly. Take all the time they'll give us."

"Quite so," said the colonel. And he directed that the papers not be delivered for several hours.

"I talked with Shingas in the French camp, sir," I added.

"Who?" he asked.

"The Delaware chief," I said. "He says he's not happy with his current arrangement with the French. It sounds like he's willing to switch sides."

"And I'm to trust him like I did your bosom friend, Tanaghrisson?" Washington asked, rightly suspicious.

"No," I said. "I'm just telling you that if you can ever come back to the Forks, the right overtures to the Delaware may provide you with a few hundred other warriors."

The colonel nodded. "Thank you, Mr. Weber. However, I have to extricate us from this situation before I can begin contemplating some type of return. Besides, Governor Dinwiddie may see fit to relieve me of command when he discovers what occurred out here. There may be no coming back for me."

"One would hope not," Mackay said.

Too exhausted to argue or protest the turd, our meeting adjourned without so much as another word. The provincial officers went off to finalize plans for our departure. Mackay went to rummage through the rum stores for any that might have been overlooked by the mob. He'd be disappointed.

I went off to a soggy nook, sat my bottom into the mud, and fell asleep against the wall. There was no dreaming, pleasant or nightmarish. I slept like I used to sleep as a child. My eyes closed and I instantly became dead to the world. In what felt like a heartbeat later, I was awakened by calls from officers. I'd been asleep for five hours.

Washington and Van Braam stood over me. It was just before daybreak and the colonel shook his translator's hand. "We shall see you released very soon, Mr. Van Braam," he said stiffly.

"It will give me a chance to improve my language skills," Van Braam said with good-natured fortitude. He hiked a pack onto his shoulders as he and a Captain Stobo walked out through the gate of Fort Necessity. They joined the French lieutenant who had been waiting. This time the young man appeared confident, gloating almost. He bowed formally before leading the pair on the hike into the forest.

"You let your friend become a captive?" I asked the colonel from my place in the muck.

"He volunteered, Mr. Weber," was Washington's reply just as the eastern sky became streaked with morning light. "Mr. Van Braam did his part. His conscious is clear. I am certain he will be treated fairly."

"And Captain Stobo?" I asked.

"Good day, Mr. Weber," Washington said, stepping away.

I was left in that filth, soaked to the bone, but so dead tired I did not care. As others began scurrying about – even the former drunkards from last night – I watched the sun rise majestically over the ridge. Mother Nature obviously knew that the battle had come to an end, for July 4, 1754 dawned beautifully. The clouds had vanished. Overhead, a blue sky stretched from one mountain to another like an arching canopy. My feeling of relief was profound. Until another event that called for wild celebration took precedence some years later, I marked all my future July fourths with reflection and thankfulness.

At ten o'clock, while under the watchful eyes of our foes, we dragged ourselves out of Fort Necessity. Between two lines of white-bedecked French soldiers, our colors flapped, snapping in the fresh morning breeze. Drums and fifes played as if we marched away from a glorious victory. Five men had assembled a makeshift cart that carried our one piece of artillery. Even though throughout the entirety of the battle, none of our swivel guns had been fired, the lone gun we were allowed to take would prove to those officers back home that our capitulation had been honorable. However, with all of our pack animals killed, these same five, poor men would have to manually tow the gun over mountainous terrain.

Our wounded, ill, and hung-over outnumbered our healthy soldiers. Our pace was so slow that, should any decide to offer contest, we could have been passed by a bale of confused, three-legged turtles. Despite the fact that many of us wore ragged clothes and others were nearly naked, we held our heads high. And it was right for us to do so, for by luck or Providence we had survived Washington's deathtrap. The same could not be said for the Half King, whose body lay right where I'd left it.

As we reached the end of the twin columns of French, we approached our baggage train. Most of the train had been abandoned outside the fort's walls before we had retreated inside. Shingas and his band of loyal Delaware stood between us and our broken-down wagons that carried a small amount of supplies. Nonetheless, these were provisions which would prove useful during our long and slow march to Wills Creek. During and after the fight, the French had left the train unmolested. Shingas, despite his indications of support the previous night, would not.

Shingas stared at me as he raised his war hatchet and gave a whoop. At first, we gasped and clumped together for protection from the attack we suddenly feared. But then all we could do was watch as the victorious warriors turned on their heels and began looting the train. They tried on our clothing.

They feasted on what little food we had left. They stole our axes, saws, and other carpentry tools. His warriors stole our tents and the few wagons that remained in working condition. An optimist could have thought that we were thankfully left unburdened by excess luggage. I remember thinking that we would now be even more undersupplied for the march home.

"This is the man you think will ally with us?" Washington asked as he dropped back to where I walked. The colonel had his journal and important papers tucked under one arm.

"He may loot the train as a show for the French," I said. "He still has to live with them at the Forks. Maybe he figures he ought to give his French fathers what they expect to see from their savage children."

"Move along, Colonel Washington," Captain Jumonville called from atop his horse. He'd ridden to us. "I am unwilling to guarantee your safety from those savages for too long."

Washington gave me a satisfied nod and again marched to the front.

And so it was, while on foot, Lieutenant Colonel Washington led his tired army back toward Wills Creek on the primitive road it had recently cut out of the virgin forest. Groups of Delaware warriors harried us for many miles, not with musket fire or arrows. Instead they harassed us with hoots and hollers, mocking our destitute state. Five days later, diseased and half-starved, we wobbled into the settlement. Within hours of our arrival, desertions ramped up. The depleted army thinned further so that the only men who remained were the truly ill and indigent.

Should either Captain Jumonville or Captain Legardeur change their minds, we could do nothing to prevent them from marching their entire army to the heart of Virginia.

EPILOGUE

Three days after our ignoble arrival in Wills Creek a lone Indian trader, with a single pack mule and a pile of pelts he had purchased from Shawnee hunters along the Ohio, meandered into town. He had passed through Great Meadows just as the French were leaving.

"My English kind aren't welcome there any longer," the trader said. "Frenchies told me to keep going east and not come back."

"For now," Washington declared, putting on a confident, but false, face for the general public.

"Your little fort is burned, colonel," the trader added.

"I expected as much," Washington answered soberly.

"Then the stinking French and those Delaware headed back to Fort Duquesne at the Forks," added the trader. "That place is a monster! Saw it staked out with my own eyes."

Washington glanced out through the window of the trading post at what remained of his ragtag army. He could no longer contain his emotions. He sighed mightily. It sounded like relief that the French hadn't decided to press their advantage and drive all the way to Williamsburg, torching everything that reeked of English in their path. He had already sent word ahead to Dinwiddie detailing our defeat and retreat. He had further asked that the governor release the French prisoners who had been in his possession for just over a month. At length, the colonel again considered the trader. He asked, "Do you have anything else to add, sir?"

"No, colonel," the man said before, in fact, nervously adding something else. "Well, one thing. If you don't mind me saying so, you sure don't seem like one of those rash fellas. I don't rightly know you all that well. We've only just met. But I mean you aren't the murdering kind. Are you?"

"I beg your pardon," Washington asked, offended.

"He's probably heard about Ensign Jumonville," I explained to the colonel. "Even though it is mostly bare on the frontier, rumors spread fast, colonel. There's not much else to talk about."

"Oh, yes, that," Washington said, wishing the entire incident would disappear. "I was in command," he admitted to the trader. "Even though it was an Indian ally who attacked the soldier, it was my responsibility. The burden of command."

"Attacked a soldier, you say?" the trader asked, frowning.

"Yes, Ensign Jumonville," I said.

"Strange," said the trader, scratching his head. He studied his nails when he was done.

"What's strange?" the colonel asked.

"Well, the surrender papers you signed say something different."

"You saw the articles of capitulation?" Washington asked.

"Huh!" the trader exclaimed. "The whole frontier will see them soon enough. Ha! The whole world will see them! It's not every day that an English officer admits to assassinating an unarmed French diplomat, an envoy of peace."

"I did no such thing!" Washington said, rising to his feet. "Can you even read?"

"None of my native language I'm afraid," the trader admitted. "But I can read a bit of the Frenchies' tongue. It's how business gets done deep in the frontier. And that's what those surrender papers are written in."

Washington lengthened his neck in anger. "I merely admitted that Ensign Jumonville was killed during an engagement by men under my command. He died, yes. I assure you, shots were fired by both sides. No one was unarmed." As you know, it was never clear to me if a single Frenchman had any real chance to fire. Jumonville had discharged his pistol at me, but no one else was even able to gather a weapon. Washington did not, and never would, know all the facts.

"No, colonel. I'm afraid that is not what it says. The French are gladly showing anyone who passes by. Heck, they'll even show a beaver if they think it will do them any good. I can read a bit of French, as I said, and it clearly says that you admit to being directly responsible for this Jumonville's blatant *assassination*. It says he was a peace envoy, no more. By the way, you also admitted that you were trespassing on lands of His Most Christian King, whoever that is."

"The French king," I answered.

Washington had slumped into his chair. His face was buried in his hands. "Van Braam said he understood the terms."

Then I remembered the calm, cool, collected Captain Jumonville during our negotiations. "Van Braam asked about that clause. Jumonville merely said that as the officer in charge, you were responsible for his younger brother's death in the engagement. He said nothing about you being guilty of assassination." Captain Jumonville now had his revenge on those he believed murdered his brother. He hadn't exacted it in the physical sense. He'd attacked Washington's reputation. And reputation, as any man knew, was something much more precious, more difficult to build than ordinary physical health.

"God save us," Washington mumbled. "Heaven help me." It was the first time I had heard him beg God's assistance in a selfish manner.

Usually so confident, seeing him thus was a pitiful sight. "By signing those papers, colonel, you saved the rest of the men in your command. The sick, the ill, even the drunkards who didn't deserve it," I said trying to encourage him. "You saved a lot of lives."

He faced the table when he spoke. "It would have been better had I perished in that meadow."

I didn't think so. I still don't. Neither do a few million Americans.

"Mr. Weber, you must understand something. I am an officer, serving at the behest of the governor of Virginia. He, in turn, serves the crown. By admitting in writing that I assassinated an envoy who simply carried a summons for discussion and not a weapon, I alone committed the first official act of war against a sovereign power. And to make matters worse, I have now affixed my signature to a document that will be spread far and wide. In it, I have publicly stated that the Forks of Ohio belong to, not my king, but to that of France."

"But you thought you were signing something else!" I said. "We can explain that."

When Washington peered up at me, he had aged ten years. "If I signed it knowingly, I am an assassin. If I signed it unknowingly, I am a buffoon. In either case, I have disgraced my brother, my family, my colony, my governor, my people, my mother country, and my sovereign, King George."

The trader twiddled his thumbs nervously. "Sounds like a pickle," he said.

"Get the hell out of here!" I screamed at him. He needed no further encouragement. "And don't come back!"

I was left alone with Washington. He sat there, thinking, staring at his desk. I could tell he did the same things all men did. His failures loomed large in his mind. They must have. He wished and wished there was a way to undo much of what had taken place over the previous weeks. In the end, he discovered that he had the same limitations as the rest of us. Time went in but one direction and he was just as subject to its vagaries.

He straightened in his chair and studied me. Slowly, I saw the self-pity that was so unlike him, flee. Erased was any equivocation about the future, his future and mine. In its place settled the firm determination for which he has become famous. "Go and gather Mr. Croghan, will you?"

It seemed a strange time to discuss provisions and commerce or the Ohio Company or Croghan's suddenly and incredibly shrunken trading network. The colonel saw the puzzled look cross my face. "I think it is time that he fully releases you from his employ."

"To do what?" I asked.

"For the second time in my short lifetime, we will soon be at war with France," he said. "Only this time, much of the fighting will be done in the North American frontier, not just on the continent in Europe. We will need good young men who can fight, who know their way around Indian villages and towns."

"You've learned a lot, sir," I answered. "More than I ever will. You'll do fine without me."

"I've benefitted from your advice on more than one occasion," he answered. He had, of course. He never mentioned that I had also saved his life – twice!

"I'm no soldier," I said to deflect him off the subject.

"A blind man can see that, Mr. Weber," he said with only the slightest smile. "I envision you serving in some capacity, probably unofficial, but nonetheless necessary."

A gopher in the provincial army didn't sound like the most lucrative form of employment. I had always seen myself as a trader, a rich trader. How would I be allowed to marry Bess if I was a penniless ranger or scout? Unlike Washington, I had no land or plantation on which to fall back.

Washington saw my concern. "You'll be paid – somehow," he added.

Still not a ringing endorsement of the position. But Washington's face was one that was difficult to disobey or in any way disagree. Despite being headstrong and something of a novice, he was earnest, upright, and strong. I hoped his experience and decisions might one day grow into his confidence. The fool I was, I nodded. "On one condition."

"I've had just about enough of terms and conditions," he said. "As you know from my surrender at Fort Necessity, they have not been kind to me of late."

I marshalled on with my condition. "I'll only leave Croghan's employ if you do a better job finding an interpreter next time. One who is actually literate in French."

Washington grinned just a little more. I could tell he wanted to permit himself to enjoy the joke, but he had just lost many good men, a small fort, and the entirety of the Forks of Ohio to England's oldest and vilest enemy. There was more sadness behind his eyes than revelry. "Mr. Van Braam, I think, is paying for his mistakes with his own freedom."

I gave him a broad grin. "Yes, sir, he is."

"Now run along so that we can set you free from your current commitments," he said with a wave of his hand. The colonel began digging into his papers, quite eagerly. "And hurry. If, in a year's time, I hope to retake the Forks, I have planning and you have some work to do."

THE END
(Dear Reader-See Historical Remarks to separate fact from fiction)

HISTORICAL REMARKS

The attack on Pickawillany by French, Chippewa, and Ottawa warriors is barely a footnote in frontier history. Yet, it can be considered a fairly common – and brutal – example of the clash of multiple civilizations that played out in North America over the course of the long Eighteenth Century.

The assault is not necessarily *THE* inciting event of the Seven Years' War (called the French and Indian War in the United States). However, it does demonstrate just how much pressure France and its own Indian allies felt from the further encroachment by traders like George Croghan and Indians like Chief Memeskia who were affiliated with the British and her colonies. Pickawillany (modern day Piqua, Ohio) was attacked in more or less the method described while most of the men were away on a days-long hunt. Eye witnesses reported that a wounded trader was killed and his heart eaten. Memeskia was boiled and eaten by the victors. It is possible that he was still alive while the boiling started. My version spares the reader such horrors.

I have replaced the actual French-Canadian ensign who led the destruction of Pickawillany with Ensign Joseph Coulon de Villiers de Jumonville, who is most famous for what comes later in the tale.

For continuity sake, I have switched the order of events modestly. The Iroquois conference at Logstown actually happened just a few weeks before the raid on Pickawillany. However, the pressures demonstrated by the attack were already being felt by the Logstown participants. And those concerns are what prompted the Half King and his subordinates to acquiesce to the construction of a fort by the Ohio Company at the Forks of Ohio (modern day Pittsburgh, Pennsylvania). At the conference, Chief Shingas forced the Iroquois, and their local representative, the Half King, to recognize him as a de facto King of the Western Delaware tribe. This is significant in that it no longer meant that the council at Onondaga had direct control of treaty negotiation and alliances.

In our rapid-paced world of modernity, it may seem strange that over a year after the Logstown Conference no plans for or work on the proposed fort had begun. However difficult it is to imagine, we must recall that the travel, funding, meetings, and much more required of such an undertaking would have taken many months under the swiftest of conditions. The Ohio Company initially believed they had ample time to proceed. The French were not yet in the Ohio Valley.

But by the fall of 1753, rumors began spreading in the English colonies that the new governor-general of Canada, Duquesne, had authorized the construction of a string of forts in the Ohio Country. A very young, inexperienced George Washington was sent on something of a fool's errand by Lieutenant Governor Dinwiddie (I named him as governor for simplicity). Major Washington was still grieving over the loss of his brother Lawrence, who had previously held the position. The passing of Lawrence had a profound impact on the eager young Washington because his elder brother had long been a father figure after George's own father had died. Lawrence had also bequeathed to George shares in the Ohio Company.

Washington left Williamsburg on All-Hallows'-Eve. Along the way, he picked up his fencing friend and inexperienced interpreter, Jacob Van Braam. In Wills Creek, they added Christopher Gist and a few others to their party. After fairly miserable travel they met John Fraser, who hosted them for one night in his cabin. The group then made it to the Forks where Washington selected the site for the fort and sketched what has become a famous rendering of the rivers' confluence.

When Washington and the others arrived at Logstown, the misunderstandings between supposed allies began. The Half King was more worried about his own position of power within the Iroquois Confederation as well as the dwindling power of Onondaga among the tribes and whites. Washington was concerned with the encroachment by the French on lands claimed by his king and (hopefully) to be granted to his Ohio Company. Young Washington treated the Half King, not with contempt, but as a subordinate. He even sent for Tanaghrisson while he was away hunting and instructed him to return home. This endeared the major, who was called Conotocarius by the tribes, to neither the Iroquois nor the Delaware.

Nonetheless, with the Half King and just a couple Mingo warriors added to their band, they traveled north. Eventually, they made it to Fort LeBoeuf and Captain Legardeur. For several days, they exchanged pleasantries that you might expect of Eighteenth Century officers. During that time, since Washington was free to roam about, he took note of the vast amount of canoes and other boats that were bobbing on the nearby creek. The French were planning on moving in the spring.

By the way, Washington, with his pitiful number of representatives, told Legardeur to leave. Old Legardeur told Washington, no.

The two near death incidents on Washington's return trip to Williamsburg are well-known. In both cases, it was reported that Gist is the one who saved the young major. However, since Gist disappears from history shortly thereafter, I felt it within my writer's license to kill him off. Gist getting the credit was just one more way to anger dear Ephraim's sense of fairness.

In what can only be considered near heroic speed given the travelling constraints of the day, a crew of workers led by recently commissioned frontiersmen (most of whom were relatives of Croghan) began work on the Ohio Company fort in February 1754. Relieved beyond measure that he had backed the correct horse over the French, the Half King laid the first log and proclaimed it a fort for the English and a fort for the Indian.

In hindsight that was to be the high-point of English and Indian relations for years to come. It was also to be the high-water mark for frontier progress by the Anglo-Americans.

The workers had descended on the Forks so quickly that they came only modestly provisioned. Shingas and his Delaware hunters, now feeling they were out from under the Iroquois, refused to provide any sustenance even when offered fair pay. Therefore, Captain Trent was forced to make the long, arduous trip back east to procure staples. As soon as Trent was gone, Fraser returned home, leaving Ensign Ward in charge.

The day the gate was hung a thousand French, Canadian, and Indian allies landed at the Forks. Despite Ward's bold letter to the contrary, he was forced to surrender promptly. The actual officer in charge of the French at this point was a Captain Contrecoeur, not Legardeur. But you can only have so many French officers in your book. There was no bloodshed, no loss of life. So, it can be fairly said that the coming war could yet be averted.

Long delayed, Washington and his initial pathetic army had made it to Wills Creek when the courier came with the news of the fort's fall. Oodles of ink has been spilled trying to decipher just why such a young provincial officer suddenly thought it was a good idea to charge ahead against such overwhelming odds. I tried to lay out a rational case. Washington had received bits of encouraging correspondence all along. He'd been made to think that in an unheard-of move at the time that most of the colonies were coordinating to send aid his way.

He began cutting a crude road through the wilderness. After many weeks, he paused at Great Meadows, a pastoral spot. While there, Christopher Gist (John Fraser in my tale) rode in completely flustered from an attack on his outpost by a small band of French. This concerned Washington. He dispatched a large force to reconnaissance the area. Meanwhile, he led a body of men in a rainstorm overnight to the Half King's new camp.

After gathering up the Half King's warriors they moved on to the French force that had attacked Gist (Fraser). As Ephraim shared with the reader, to this day there are several versions of the events at Jumonville's Glen. Given the motivations and proclivities of the participants, I selected the one I thought most likely. In this version when the hostilities were clearly at a halt, the Half King supposedly stated his famous, "Thou art not yet dead, my father." He promptly buried his hatchet into the unarmed French ensign's head and grotesquely dug with his hands in the splattered remains.

The massacre of Jumonville was the spark that ignited the Seven Years' War.

Washington returned to Great Meadows with prisoners. They were shuffled back east. In *Quaker's War*, I have him loitering in the valley a little longer. In truth, once the South Carolina regulars showed up, Washington thought he saw another positive sign of support. He took his army with its new Virginians and began cutting more road toward the Forks. Mackay, unwilling to obey a provincial, stayed behind at the newly built Fort Necessity.

The next month of road construction played havoc with the army's equipment and provisions. With no adequate train of resupply, broken items remained broken. Clothes remained frayed. Soldiers remained hungry. When news came of a large contingent of French descending on them from the Forks, Washington wisely chose to retreat in haste.

The French, under the command of Captain Jumonville (the murdered ensign's real-life older brother, who had volunteered to go and seek revenge) pursued vigorously, closing the gap. Unable to continue on, Washington stopped at Fort Necessity and dug in. The sudden onset of continual rain, flooded the valley in the manner I've described. The Anglo-American army was already quite miserable and defeated before the French fired a single shot.

But shoot they did. For the entire day on July 3rd, their musket fire and the rain pelted Washington's troops. The casualty rate was very high. The French had negligible losses. The Half King did not perish at Necessity as my tale shows, however. He died at one of Croghan's outposts a couple months later.

All hope seemed to ebb completely by the time night fell at Great Meadows. Things got worse when a large group of the survivors mutinied and broke into the last stores of rum. Fortunately, the French were running out of gunpowder and would be unable to continue the siege. They offered what seemed generous terms.

However, Van Braam's inexperience as a translator came to a head. It would burst months later when the true nature of their capitulation became known. As in *Quaker's War*, Washington and Mackay had unwittingly admitted to trespassing on the French king's land and assassinating Ensign Jumonville. This would prove to be a magnificent propaganda coup for Duquesne and his Frenchmen as they could now claim that it was the murderous Englishmen who had thrown the world into what would truly become the first world war, one hundred fifty years before the Great War.

I relied on many terrific works to guide the history of my tale. The most important of those, follow. *Crucible of War*, by Fred Anderson has become the modern-day classic on the French and Indian War. Also by Fred Anderson is *The War that made America*, which is a shortened version, but includes a few interesting details not mentioned in his longer tome. Ron Chernow's *Washington: A Life* was instrumental in fleshing out details of the young major's first journey westward. Finally, *The Brown Bess* by Erik Goldstein and Stuart Mowbray was a magnificent reference on the ubiquitous musket. Any errors you spot in the yarn are my own.

If Providence be on my side, many more tales of Ephraim Weber's adventures are to come. He has battles to fight – both winning and losing. I know he still desires to return to Williamsburg to seek after the comely Bess. I hope you are willing and able to join him, perhaps even cheer him on as he navigates down the long fuse of liberty.

ABOUT THE AUTHOR

Jason Born is a popular historical novelist. *The Long Fuse* is a chain of novels that thrillingly captures the violent period of America's rise from ragtag colonies to independence. He is the author of *Lions & Devils,* a series which vividly describes the heroes and villains of the monstrous Islamic assault of Western Europe during the Eighth Century. Other works include *The Norseman Chronicles*, a multi-volume set detailing the gritty adventures of the faithful Viking, Halldorr, who desired only peace, but found only war in the Old and New Worlds. *The Wald Chronicles* set of historical novels centers on the rugged conflict and improbable outcome in Germania during the wars between the Roman legionaries and their tribal adversaries over 2,000 years ago. *League of the Lost Fountain* is his first work for kids of all ages. Jason lives in the Midwest with his wife and three children. If you enjoyed this work and would like to see more, Jason asks you to consider doing the following:

1. Please encourage your friends to buy a copy – and read it!

2. Go to his author page (Jason Born – Author) on Facebook and click "Like" so that you may follow GIVEAWAYS or information on his next book.

3. If you think the book deserves praise, please post a five-star review on Amazon and/or a five-star review on Goodreads.com.

4. Follow him on Twitter - @authorjasonborn

5. Visit his website, www.authorjasonborn.com.